MISTRESS AND SLAVE

Banneker stepped out of his trousers, flung off his shirt. His was the most perfect male body I had ever seen, as though Michelangelo had cast his most magnificent sculpture in black marble. "Take off your clothes, Miss Victoria," he said.

When I hesitated, he reached out and unbuttoned my shirtwaist with surprisingly gentle fingers. My breasts seemed milk-white against the brown-black of his caressing hands. He yanked my head back and swallowed my mouth with his, as though he was going to eat me alive, like a cannibal, from the lips down. In spite of myself, I felt a tremendous excitement as his powerful organ struck at the leather of my riding pants again and again . . .

Legally, Victoria Parkchester was mistress of Fir Crest. But now only the law of the jungle ruled this vast plantation where she was slave to this man's iron strength—and her own melting weakness. . . .

THIS PASSIONATE LAND

Big Bestsellers from SIGNET

* Price slightly higher in Canada

If you wish to order these titles,
please see the coupon in
the back of this book.

THIS PASSIONATE LAND

by

Harriet Janeway

Ⅺ

A SIGNET BOOK

NEW AMERICAN LIBRARY

TIMES MIRROR

NAL BOOKS ARE ALSO AVAILABLE AT DISCOUNTS IN BULK
QUANTITY FOR INDUSTRIAL OR SALES-PROMOTIONAL USE.
FOR DETAILS, WRITE TO PREMIUM MARKETING DIVISION,
NEW AMERICAN LIBRARY, INC., 1301 AVENUE OF THE
AMERICAS, NEW YORK, NEW YORK 10019.

SIGNET TRADEMARK REG. U.S. PAT. OFF. AND FOREIGN COUNTRIES
REGISTERED TRADEMARK—MARCA REGISTRADA
HECHO EN CHICAGO, U.S.A.

SIGNET, SIGNET CLASSICS, MENTOR, PLUME AND MERIDIAN BOOKS
are published by The New American Library, Inc.,
1301 Avenue of the Americas, New York, New York 10019

FIRST SIGNET PRINTING, JANUARY, 1979

1 2 3 4 5 6 7 8 9

PRINTED IN THE UNITED STATES OF AMERICA

For Ernest D. Bartee,
and the empires he will build

THIS
PASSIONATE
LAND

"But why?"

Because Grandmother said ... who has ... I am your son ... he all day ... to ... Mother myself. Same ... to Mother, that we are ... to pardon and ... to me. I in him, that ... and you are the ... any of this ... But Mother ... has ...

PROLOGUE

It is difficult to describe our true feelings about the War Between the States, or the tensions that preceded it. In her own headstrong way, my sister, Charlotte, seemed determined to ignore it. Mother was unusually reticent about the subject. Grandmother Parkchester loved any good fight; and one suspected that if she had still been a New Yorker when the nation divided, she would have been as sturdily dedicated to their side as she now was to ours in Virginia. In that respect, she seemed a kind of flaming-haired mercenary, a slave herself to the politics of geography, as, indeed, we all were. Although Father went to fight as soon as Virginia seceded from the Union on April 17, 1861, it was clear that he did so from a sense of duty rather than of dedication.

At Fir Crest, we were in what was known as a "privileged perimeter"—privileged in that we were carefully hidden in an area of hills, woods, and farmlands outside of Charlottesville that was neither far enough west to be defended by the South nor close enough to the eastern battle sector for the North to attack us. Indeed, our major disasters were inside the family, as though we had been marked by demon gods for tragedies commensurate with the agonies of the nation. Then the war ended and Father came home. Defeated, in his politics, he seemed to lose all interest in perpetuating the power and prosperity of Fir Crest, which had been ceded to our family by royal decree in 1625, eighteen years after the first of the Parkchester line had landed in Jamestown.

Fir Crest encompassed some five thousand acres of rolling hills, flatland, wooded areas, ponds and streams, and smiling valleys, all topped by a prominence of firs lining the tallest ridge of hazy blue hills that jutted toward the sky like the hump of a bull's back. We were in Albemarle

1

County, Virginia, some few miles outside of Mr. Jefferson's university. It was beautiful country, rich in tradition, proud of heritage, full of color and a certain delicious hint of scandal and intrigue that hung in the air like woodsmoke.

Father was less in favor of slavery than he was opposed to the federal government's intrusion into state affairs. "I'll roll up my sleeves and sweat and work with any man, black or white," he frequently said. And he was as good as his word, often working side by side with the woolly-haired field hands, joshing with them, drinking cool water from the same dipper. They loved and respected him for it. But Grandmother Parkchester admonished him that such a thing looked "bad." A convert from the peasantry herself, she was, like all converts, more devoted to style than to substance. "You ought to act more like a gentleman," she told Father one evening at supper. To which he replied, "Mother, I'd rather be a man than a gentleman. I'd rather be right than wrong."

It was his attitude that fortified mine. First with a tutor out of Washington, then with Mother gently correcting and guiding me through her great store of books, I read every word I could. Mother was dedicated to the cause of social justice, and she spoke earnestly on that subject. "All men *are* created equal," she said. "It is circumstance that makes the difference. Except for circumstance, we might easily be Negroes, and they us."

As I wandered through the long, airless corridors of Fir Crest, gown sweeping behind me, bowed to by liveried servants at every turn, I felt like a decadent princess prowling a musty palace. The mansion was filled with light and shadows, precious and semiprecious metals, polished furniture, stuffed divans, brocaded draperies; highboys, lowboys, carved hutches, chandeliers, a curling staircase, cabinets aglitter with crystal; silk sheets, brass beds, linen tablecloths, a spinet; and all manner of balusters, balustrades, balconies, pillars, porches, patios, fireplaces, chimneys, weathervanes, large iron bells, little silver bells—some domestic, some brought up the James River on ships from Europe, then to Charlottesville by train, and ultimately to Fir Crest on wagons drawn by mules.

With all this, and much, much more, either outside the mansion—where five hundred slaves could be summoned at a moment's notice—or stuffed into its fifteen spacious rooms, we certainly owned all the comforts and luxuries one could hope for. Yet, the essential element of freedom was denied us in our choice of being other than we were. And Grandmother Parkchester was the chief agent in this continued contamination of simple, democratic-minded American farmers with the same despotism that was even then toppling Europe's corrupt royalties.

Father's distaste for slavery, and for the central government as well, were both clear when seen in that light. While the two opinions appeared to contradict each other, he was, in both instances, expressing his *American* need for freedom and his *American* hatred of oppression. The tragedy of the South in those days was that it had to subjugate one of its parts in order to keep the other equally subjugated. So Mother had retired to the elegant cell of her sitting room; Father, Grandmother Parkchester, Charlotte, and I—even our slaves—were prisoners of a ritual involving foreign-bred ideas and deeds over which we had little or no control.

The true American southerner was he who worked his own land, cared for his own needs as other Americans did. We in the South called this kind of southerner "poor white trash." We lived in mansions, bought and sold and bred slaves, surrounded ourselves with opulence, and grew lazy and arrogant to prove that, white though we were, we were neither poor nor "trash."

To further buttress this image, we gave frequent balls and other social occasions in the great columned mansions. But those elegant balls, the intoxicating strains of music lifting over mansions ablaze with lights, even the questionable benefits of the hunt—all these were partly suspended during the war. So the Negroes became our chief source of entertainment, with their flashing white teeth, their camp meetings, minstrel shows, and all the thousand and one things that Benign gossiped about as she served our meals and kept us in stitches while we did our best to eat.

We took our first meal of the day in a large room off the kitchen when the seasons were not right for breakfasting in the golden rays of the young sun on either of two patios in the east garden. Dinner and supper were usually served in the oak-paneled dining room; but in good weather, these meals were had in the single patio to the west. From there we had a fine view of the waning sun as it consumed the haze over the craggy ridge that gave our land and home their name, making the firs there stand out in rich green relief.

After the war began, our only formal social intercourse occurred for reasons of an occasional funeral, some patriotic event, or a get-together of ladies to plan some dour benefit for the Confederacy. Our able-bodied men had gone away and left those who were too old to hunt or waltz—or even to protect us, if the situation came to that—left them to care for us while the others marched away to give the stamp of legitimacy to our society, or to die in the effort. Viewed in that respect, the sound of music was less to be yearned for than not to be wanted at all.

Mother and Grandmother Parkchester often argued bitterly at Fir Crest, each maneuvering unsuccessfully to dominate the other. But when the funerals and benefits, the patriotic teas, fell upon us like awful beggars with clawing hands, the two women declared a tacit truce, put on their very best, and piled into our most elegant carriage to attend. Charlotte and I went as well, along with a few servants. But I always found it refreshing to return to the erratic serenity of Fir Crest after the awesome hypocrisy of careworn ladies and creaky old gentlemen attending the certain death of our sad society as though they were celebrating its rebirth.

As for the Negroes, they seemed to maintain their outward demeanor; but it was easy to detect an inner tension that one had never felt before the war. Perhaps it had always been lurking in them, and we had been too busily dancing and curtsying to see or feel their turmoil. After the guns thundered at Sumter, our Negroes seemed to turn inside themselves, as frightened children do when they have provoked a quarrel between their elders. Yet, only Benign—possibly because of her lofty position as chief stewardess at Fir Crest—only she ventured to make a comment to me about the war. "Do you think we's worth fighting a war over, Miss Victoria?" she asked me one day. Her wise old eyes impaled me with a bland stare that gave no clue as to what answer she expected. "War is a terrible thing, Benign, whatever its reasons."

"Indeed it is," she said dryly, her large black hands pummeling a pile of biscuit dough. "Indeed it is." I left her as quickly as I could, full of confusion about matters that were then beyond my comprehension, but which cast a pall over everything. Only Grandmother Parkchester—she a transplanted northerner—seemed absolutely certain of our just cause, and readily bent her brawny shoulder to the task of supporting it.

In retrospect, however, several glaring ironies emerge from the example of the war. One was that accidents of climate and geography had made it possible for the North to practice democracy, however haphazardly, while the South could only preach it. And for the North to partake of Europe's excellence while the South imported Europe's worst excesses, along with Africans to be its slaves.

It was also ironic that the state of Virginia—cradle and bulwark of democracy in America, begetter of its greatest statesmen—should at one and the same time be in open rebellion against a democratic federal government. But perhaps the greatest irony of the war—indeed, of the entire antebellum South, as though a piece of Europe had indeed washed away and made America the less—was that our servants were freer than any one of us, for even in their bondage they could be as natural as God made them, while we had become mannered caricatures of what we ought to have been.

We would find out later, many of us with a sigh of deep satisfaction, that Mr. Lincoln had done more than to free the Negroes from slavery and reunite the country. He had reaffirmed democracy as the highest law of the land, and, in the doing, he had freed the South from an even deeper servitude to a ritual of artificialities that tortured and enslaved us all. It would also not be clear until later, after a series of puzzling and bizarre events, that a killer was actively at work at Fir Crest. And that I, mistress of Fir Crest at age twenty-three, was principal intended victim.

ONE

————◆————

It was Amos, the Negro stable hand, who came riding hard to tell us that Father was dead in the crest of firs that gives our land its name. It was the middle of May in Virginia, the year 1865, the War Between the States recently over, Mr. Lincoln more recently assassinated. Lance Harcourt, Charlotte, and I were in the spacious sitting room at Fir Crest, relaxing after a sumptuous dinner party, eating chinquapins which a pickaninny threw into the hot ashes of the fireplace and then fetched for us.

Father had gone riding with Amos after the dinner party over to Judge Gilliam's to discuss important business matters. There was a riding path that led from our land up the steep rise to the crest of firs, then down a sloping descent to Judge Gilliam's land where it joined ours on the other side near a creek in the low ground. Father and Judge Gilliam both had been home from the war for only a short while. And now Amos had come riding in panic and tears to say that Father was dead in the crest of firs, en route to the Judge's. "He fell off the stallion on the climb to Fir Crest," Amos said. He addressed me, since I was a year older than my sister, Charlotte, who was twenty-two. But even in that tragic moment, I suppose we were all aware that now I was indisputably mistress of Fir Crest.

It seemed almost impossible to believe that Father was dead, that he would never sit with us again at the table and encourage Benign into the most outlandish tales about what went on in our Negro quarters; that I would never see his flashing smile, or the sun raise flecks of gold in his red hair; that we would never go riding again together across the placid valleys, jumping creeks, chasing foxes to

7

the baying of hounds; dancing stately waltzes to chamber
orchestras summoned to Fir Crest from such places as
New York, Philadelphia, and Richmond. . . .

"I left him there, Miss Victoria," Amos said. "I didn't
want to bring Massa Parkchester home draped over a
horse. So I come for the wagon to bring him home decent."

"That was thoughtful of you, Amos," I managed to say.
"You go now and have your supper. We'll get some of the
other men to help."

"I couldn't eat a mouthful right now," Amos said. Tears
were streaming down his black cheeks. "It won't nobody's
fault, Miss Victoria. Massa Parkchester, he just fell off and
hit his head on them slate rocks. It won't nobody's fault."

"I'm sure it wasn't, Amos. You may go now."

"Yas'm." He waved the pickaninny away from the fireplace, and the youngster disappeared with him into the
kitchen, where Benign was finishing the dinner dishes. The
three of us stood in silence in the sitting room until we
heard a loud, anguished wail come from the kitchen, followed by Benign's shrieking and crying.

That seemed to break the trance that held Charlotte,
Lance, and me. I remember that Charlotte slumped
against the tall, muscular frame of Lance Harcourt, and
that he held her gently, manfully, murmuring condolences
into her ear. Lance and Charlotte were engaged, and their
marriage was scheduled for late June. Of course, that
would have to be postponed now. Charlotte had turned
very pale, and she was tragically beautiful in the light and
shadows cast by the fireplace and by the chandelier ablaze
overhead with crystal globes shrouding dozens of candles
made by our servants.

Charlotte was wearing a gown of pale green with white
lace ruffles at the collar and sleeves. She had Father's
same red hair, which she wore parted in the middle and
cascading down to her delicate shoulders. Her eyes were a
deeper green than Father's, and now they were darkened
with grief as she rested her lovely head on Lance's shoulder. He held an arm around her tiny waist; one of her
hands rested on his broad shoulder like an ivory bird
wounded in flight.

"What will we do?" Charlotte sobbed. She took a handkerchief from her bosom and wept into it.

I, too, felt like weeping. But there were things to be done now; weeping could come later, as Father used to say. "We must take the carriage and go for Father's body," I said. I pulled the sash cord near the fireplace; and when Amos himself reappeared in answer to its summons, I gave him orders to go for the carriage, a driver, and two strong servants on horses. He nodded and left.

"Of course, I shall go, too," Lance Harcourt said.

"Of course," I said. "It is good of you to offer, Lance."

He bowed slightly. Charlotte had curled on the settee and seemed inconsolable. It was common knowledge that, between the two of us, she had been Father's favorite. But that fact in no way lessened the sense of shock and unreality that I was feeling then. Father's proud boast was that Charlotte had his good looks, his impetuous nature, and a kind of pretty imp dancing in her empty head. But it was I, he used to say, who was decidedly my mother's sensible child. In that moment of heavy grief, while we waited for the carriage and the riders, I turned to the mirror over the fireplace and inspected my features in its sharp reflection.

It was as though my dead mother stared back at me. The eyes were large and blue, as though in a state of constant surprise. Under other circumstances, they would be filled with a quiet, almost mocking laughter. The coal-black hair, parted in the middle, as Charlotte's was, held a heavy sheen from the flickering lights of the chandelier. The face was almost oval-shaped, whereas Charlotte's was round. She had, my father used to say, the features of his English peasant ancestors, refined by time and breeding. "But you, my dear," he would say to me, "you are a true aristocrat." When he told me that, it had seemed that he was dooming me to an exile far removed from the bawdy, mirthful relationship that he and Charlotte had enjoyed along with Grandmother Parkchester.

But as I gazed in the mirror, I could not help but sense that there was an aristocratic tilt to my fine nostrils, as my mother's had been. And some delicate, yet undefinable strength in the cast of the jaw and the full red lips that threw their reflection back at me. I was wearing a plain velvet gown of powder blue, with a strand of my grandmother's turquoise around my neck, which was rather longish and pink-tinted in the light from the fireplace.

I felt a hand on my arm. It was Benign with our cloaks.

She had calmed herself somewhat, but she was still crying in great sobs. "I so sorry, Miss Charlotte, Miss Victoria." I nodded, and touched her black bulk gently as she wrapped the cloak about my shoulders. But as she went to attend to Charlotte, my sister flung herself in Benign's arms, and the two of them wept together copiously. "Perhaps we should go to the porch," Lance Harcourt said gently. With his hand on my elbow, we went outdoors to wait for the riders, leaving Charlotte and Benign to console each other.

I remember that the night air smelled of apple blossoms, the perfumed odor coming from the nearby orchard where the trees were heavy with fruit. But, above all, the air was alive and heady with the pungent presence of Fir Crest itself, an aroma which it wore like a signature, as certain women can be identified by their cologne. I breathed deeply, and the air was like a draft of strong, delicious drink as it filled my breast, making me light-headed with pleasure. Perhaps it will seem irreverent that I could have felt that way, knowing that Father lay dead in the crest of firs. But he would have it no differently, neither from myself nor from Charlotte. He would expect tears from her, strength from me. To this point, it appeared that neither of us had disappointed his prediction about how we would act in such a circumstance. It was well after seven o'clock, and a decided chill was fast moving in, bringing with it a resumption of a light, misting rain that had been falling sporadically all evening. I shuddered slightly as the damp air hit me, and pulled my cloak closer.

"I can't tell you, Victoria, how very sorry I am about this," Lance Harcourt said. "I'm absolutely stunned. It seems impossible that we were laughing and talking with your father only an hour ago."

Lance Harcourt and I were not the very best of friends. Although he was sandy-haired, handsome, well-built, and heir to one of the best names in Virginia, I felt there was something inherently weak about him. "Thank you, Lance," I said. "I know how important Father was to you."

He said nothing, but took a step toward me, then away. The four lanterns hanging at each corner of the porch made his face seem almost greenish-yellow. "I suppose this means the wedding will have to be postponed until a more appropriate time?"

"Of course," I said.

He heaved a long sigh, as though he had been holding his breath, waiting for my answer. But, less than one of passion thwarted and postponed, it seemed to be a sigh of relief. Or perhaps of decision. And I wondered, as I had done frequently even before the Parkchesters and the Harcourts had arranged what appeared to be the most brilliant marriage in years—I found myself wondering again whether Lance Harcourt was genuinely in love with my sister, Charlotte.

For her part, Charlotte seemed to positively dote on her intended husband. Although she was twenty-two, in many respects she seemed to be a naive child of twelve. With her high good looks, she had always managed to have her way with Father. And while the courtship between her and Lance had followed every existing rule of etiquette, there was a certain freedom about their manner which seemed healthy and good for Charlotte. Sometimes they sat together for hours before the fireplace, holding hands like the most contented of lovers. Charlotte talked up a storm when it came to plans about her wedding. She was Father's favorite, but she was my favorite as well. And what I was feeling on the porch that night was as much a sense of loss for Father as it was concern about Charlotte, her future as well as the frustration that would soon set in once the impact of Father's death fully hit her.

"I must say you're taking this very calmly," Lance said. He was dressed after the fashion of the day, but the tall hat with the curving brim and the plum-colored cape somehow ill-became him and made him seem especially vulnerable.

"Appearances can be very deceiving," I said. "Actually, I feel as though I'm falling to pieces inside."

He planted his somber eyes on me. Sometimes they reminded me of the limpid eyes of a hound that has failed to tree its prey. But even in the half-light I could see a kind of passion in his eyes—clearly, unmistakably. Passion for whom? Certainly not for me, not at such an awful moment in our lives and our destinies.

For a moment I despised him. It was a very real failing with me, Father used to say: that I was too difficult to please when it came to men. Perhaps. The available supply of men of honor in the county was pretty slim. So I had

acceded not only to being mistress of Fir Crest at the age
of twenty-three; I had also become the state's most desirable "old maid."

But how could that explain the fire I had seen in Lance
Harcourt's eyes? Certainly there was no need for him to
pay court to me when he was already engaged to Charlotte. It had long been my father's burning desire to link
our name to one as prestigious as that of the Harcourts.
"There were Harcourts in attendance at Windsor Castle
while the Parkchesters were still living in trees," Father
used to say with a rueful laugh. Name was as important as
fortune in those days, and Father had managed to outdis-
tance all the other families bidding for the Harcourt name.
When the marriage was arranged, Charlotte had been ecstatic. She truly seemed to love Lance Harcourt. But
now, Lance Harcourt was looking at *me* with feverish
eyes, even as we prepared to go for the corpse of my father. Or perhaps it was only sympathy I read. I did not
have an opportunity to ponder further, for the riders came
rolling up with the carriage; and Charlotte left the sitting
room and mounted with us. Someone, certainly Amos, had
had the forethought to order extra hands and to have a
buckboard accompany us. For Father's body. We left Fir
Crest in a gloomy caravan on a grotesque mission.

To get from the main house to the crest of firs, it is
necessary to travel almost a circular route; and we
rumbled up the gravel-filled road between the orchard and
the ripe fields where corn, tobacco, wheat, and other crops
were growing. Farther along, the road became smooth,
laid level by heavy logs dragged by teams of mules. Now
the rain had stopped again, and the moon rose suddenly
and unexpectedly, filling the star-studded sky with its soft
light, covering the fields and everything around with a
sheen like the yellow spinning of spiders.

Charlotte and Lance sat across from me in the carriage,
while I sat with my back to the driver. And as we mounted a low rise in the road, before entering the vast woods, I
looked and saw Fir Crest, the alabaster mansion, gleaming
in the moonlight. Charlotte was still crying softly; Lance
Harcourt was patting her hand, one arm around her shoulder. But even in the dark carriage, I could feel his eyes
upon me, like the shadow cast by a voyage of clouds ob-
scuring the sun. I *knew* that he was staring at me, even as

the woods closed in around us and the sound of crickets began whirring as though we had entered captivity with them inside a dark green jar. I felt very uncomfortable, not to mention the numbness that dragged at all my limbs as I thought of the reason for our grisly mission. But I was determined to remain calm. And I let my mind wander to the days before tragedy seemed to have come, like an unwelcome guest, and taken up residence in Fir Crest.

When the War Between the States broke out in 1861, I was nineteen and Charlotte was eighteen. Until then, we had been tutored privately by a nasal-voiced matron from Washington, who did her utmost to rid us of giggles, acne, and freckles even as she tried to stuff our silly heads with the subtleties of Socrates, Plato, and Aristotle, along with the social sciences, the social graces, and the South's peculiar social system, which would soon lead it to embark upon a course of war.

Once the first shot was fired at Sumter, our tutor returned to Washington, and Virginia went over to the side of the Confederacy, with the capital soon moved to Richmond from Alabama. All of us heard, from travelers and the like, how President Lincoln was mobilizing his forces to move against the South. "We can do no less than mobilize ours," my father said, although it was possible to detect a certain sadness in his voice. Like many more of his friends and neighbors, he was not going to war to protect the institution of slavery, which he abhorred and used only with great reluctance and care, as one must make use of a bad medicine to cure an even worse ill.

Only the most ignorant southerner did not know that our lives, our fortunes, our sacred honor—to quote Mr. Jefferson, himself an unwilling slaveholder—rested upon the backs of Negro men and women held in unpardonable servitude. But it was a system that men like my father, and Thomas Jefferson before him, could neither destroy nor ameliorate. "It is an evil, sickening thing," Father used to say. "But there is no other recourse. We need the Negroes for labor. And if it is an evil—and it *is* an evil—it is one that we have inherited rather than originated." Torn by a sense of decency toward all men, but burdened by the need to maintain the station to which we were born, he tried to steer the middle course between barbarism and abolition.

As I remember, his was the common attitude of Virginia gentlemen. There was not one who came to Fir Crest and did not say, over wine and cigars and out of hearing of the servants, that slavery was a "damned disturbance"—my father's expression; but he, like all others in the South, black and white alike, was caught like a pebble in the great tide of history. And when Virginia reluctantly joined her sister states in open rebellion against the North, it was more with a sense of burning sorrow that the underlying motives were not clearly understood. "It is not slavery we would preserve," they cried. "It is the sovereignty of the state against the federal government that has made us leave the Union."

But these sentiments were to come to light only later, once men had died, and passions had subsided, when historians sifted the ruins of a destroyed society and found that, indeed, there were good men fighting for causes which they truly thought were just. It would be untrue to say that the slaves at Fir Crest were forever laughing and jolly. But none of them were ever mistreated in my presence, nor did I hear of mistreatment. And once they had come to Fir Crest, they were never sold to other masters. That Negroes like Benign, her husband, Juniper, Amos with the solemn eyes, and a number of others remained at Fir Crest to work when they were free to go elsewhere seems to be the finest testimony to my father's ability to bridge the gap between servant and master, and to achieve a kind of understanding and affection between the two.

At any rate, when the guns began to thunder, my father and Judge Gilliam rode away to join the Confederate Army in Richmond. Father was made a captain; Judge Gilliam, because of his experience in the law, was offered a generalship and a desk job, but he chose to be a captain in the field, to remain on a level with my father, his friend. Until January of 1863, we had a full contingent of Negroes at Fir Crest; and things continued pretty much as before, except that Father's absence was like an ever-enlarging hole in the torn fabric of our lives. It fell to my mother, and to Grandmother Parkchester, a strong-willed matriarch, to keep the wheels of Fir Crest rolling.

As there was conflict and confusion between the states, it was best symbolized at Fir Crest by quiet but intense skirmishes between our mother and Grandmother Parkchester, who clearly looked upon our own mother as an unworthy intruder into the affairs and fortunes of Fir Crest, and all but banished Mother to her private sitting room.

Our mother, Patricia, had been a Devereaux out of New Orleans whom my father met and married on a business trip there. As one story goes—for there are many—when Father brought his new wife home to Fir Crest, the senior Mr. Parkchester—he who had brought *his* bride home from New York City—fell into an apoplectic fit and died, because Father had not observed the time-honored rituals of meetings between the parents, an examination of each other's manner and attire to determine whether one was marrying name, or fortune, or, most happily, a combination of the two.

"Old" money was far more acceptable than "new," but money in any form was sufficient to make "eccentrics" out of vulgarians, provided that they bought a proper piece of land, gave it a romantic-sounding name, and fabricated a history that made up in exaggeration what it lacked in authenticity. At the top of the heap were land granted by royalty and money handed down through generations until its existence was taken as a matter of fact and was rarely, if ever, spoken of.

This last category included those of us at Fir Crest and the plantations around. Grandmother Parkchester, Father's mother, was the head of our clan. A former New York schoolteacher to the children of immigrants, she had inherited Fir Crest from her apoplectic husband, and had managed to fall into the pattern of an eccentric southern *grande dame* by the simple process of being as outrageous as she possibly could.

She was the only woman of breeding I have ever seen smoke a cigar. She insisted on taking her sherry with the men, who seemed to enjoy her presence while the other women huddled together in shocked groups in another room—rolling their eyes to heaven, fanning to keep from fainting—and listened to her rich, throaty laugher coupling with that of the men.

She was tall, handsome, large-boned, broad of hip and

jaw, with those famous green eyes and the characteristic red hair of that side of the Parkchesters. In retrospect, I suppose that Father's rueful references to being a descendant of peasants were true. For Grandmother Parkchester, for all her refined airs when the mood was upon her, had about her a certain earthiness that seemed less indicative of "new" money than it did of "old" money in the wrong hands.

She was not vulgar in the common sense; in fact, her manner of speech and dress were singularly regal in most cases. Yet, it was she who taught my sister, Charlotte, the lyrics to tavern songs when Charlotte was a child, and then—with the help of Father—encouraged Charlotte to lisp the words to guests whose sense of *noblesse oblige* put a damper on their certain sense of outrage at such a spectacle. Grandmother Parkchester and Father, both in looks and manner, were so much alike that they might have been the products of Europe's peasant royalties, where decadence, intermarriage, and earthiness reduced monarchies to the level of Negro field hands at a minstrel show.

But if Father and his mother were creatures of the field, passing along their bawdiness to Charlotte—which she seemed to have transformed into a kind of pert and genteel enchantment—then it was our mother, Patricia Devereaux Parkchester, who kept herself and me aloof from the others as though we two were forest sprites in danger of contamination. And it was Mother who struggled to maintain the dignity of "our" side of the Parkchesters—we of the dark hair, the blue eyes, the full-bosomed and small-waisted bodies of Europe's most disciplined courts.

"There are only the two of us," Mother used to say. "Our obligation is to the art of refinement." When she was untroubled, her eyes held secret smiles, as though her best defense against absurdity was to be quietly amused by it. We would embroider, or read from her great shelves of books lining the walls. She was a voracious reader, and one side of her spacious sitting room was completely lined with books. Another corner was stacked, somewhat untidily, with newspapers and magazines that came to Fir Crest from all parts of the country before the war. Now, with the North cut off from us, she received periodicals from Atlanta, Biloxi, New Orleans, and even from Canada and England. Yet, as she labored over her sewing, shoulders and torso regally straight, slim legs crossed underneath the covering dress, it seemed impossible that a woman so fragile and beautiful in appearance, so elegant in her being and bearing, carried in her lovely head the knowledge of all man's foibles, and of those brief moments of majesty that occur when angels rush into human affairs and chase the true devils out. Meanwhile, Charlotte would be out riding with Father, or doing some other thing which Grandmother Parkchester thought was ladylike, Father thought was "cute," and Mother very clearly looked upon as being gross.

When I did learn to ride, it was over Mother's objections, because it was a clear indication that I had begun to draw away from her to the other side, pulled by a sense of camaraderie that seemed to keep them always laughing together. Mother seemed to smile only with her eyes, and rarely with her mouth. Certainly never, to my knowledge, with her mouth wide open, tongue hanging out, head thrown back, laughing to the high heavens as though life were worth laughing about. Before I had completed my full defection, however, the war broke out. And Father went away, leaving us all subject to Grandmother Parkchester, whose authority over us was enhanced not only by the absence of Father's more temperate nature but also by her own obsession about the war.

As I have said, Charlotte was eighteen then, and I was nineteen. In many respects, however, our ages and personalities might have been reversed. For Charlotte was much more knowledgeable than I about life and events, thanks to her carousing with Father and Grandmother Parkchester, while I had been locked in a greenhouse with our dear, lovely mother.

It was Charlotte who told me, the second year of the war, that the North was losing.

"How do you know?" I said.

"Grandmother says so."

Charlotte had long since discarded the hoop skirts and fancy crinolines of our prewar days, and wore overalls with as much confidence as any man. "How does Grandmother know?" I said. The first visible sign of my defection from Mother had been to don a pair of overalls, which I still wore with a certain sense of unease as Charlotte and I went down through the hayfield toward the cabins where

the Negroes lived. Some of them were working in the tobacco field, for it was spring planting time. Others moved
about slowly, occupied with hoeing, raking, sewing. Even
then, inside the barns and stables, pruning in the orchards,
cutting in the forest, tending stock in the pasturelands,
some five hundred Negroes still worked at Fir Crest.
"How does Grandmother know?" I said again, catching up
with Charlotte, who was taking me on some secret mission.

"Grandmother knows everything," Charlotte said. I
remember that white clouds hung like mares' tails in the
perfectly blue sky. Larks and mockingbirds tossed shrill
notes at each other. It was a fine spring day, full of the
freshness of reawakening. We were going in the direction
of the creek, and it seemed to whistle in its bed with a
lazy, gurgling sound.

"Where are we going?" I said.

"To the cabins."

"What for?"

"I want to show you something."

I was very excited, although I did not want Charlotte to
know it. I had never been to the Negro cabins, although I
had always wanted to see what they were like. But Mother
had forbidden it, and I had not thought to disobey her until now.

"Do you know what rape is?" Charlotte asked.

"It's a kind of plant, like turnip greens. The Negroes eat
it."

Charlotte laughed. She seemed so pretty and innocent
with her hair pulled back in a ponytail. She was wearing a
red-and-white-plaid shirt with the sleeves rolled up. At
eighteen, she stood almost as tall as I. Her breasts were
well developed, and she might easily have been my own
age.

"I'm not talking about that kind of rape," she said.

I felt my cheeks burn, but I said nothing. I suppose she
took my silence as an indication that I indeed knew about
the other kind of rape. But I did not want to mention the
word.

"Grandmother says that Union soldiers, white men, are
raping white women just like common nigras," Charlotte
said.

"Mother says 'nigra' is a bad word," I said hotly. " 'Negro' is the proper term."

"Grandmother says 'nigra,' " Charlotte said.

I dared not oppose the wisdom of Grandmother, since I was making every effort to join her camp. "Where are the Union soldiers doing this?" I asked. In my own ears, my voice sounded overly sharp, like Mother's sometimes did.

"Everywhere they go. Everywhere they find white women."

"Don't they rape Negro women?"

Again Charlotte laughed, but softly this time, for we were approaching the rear of the cabins. "Negro women enjoy doing it," she said. "It's not rape when there's enjoyment. Grandmother says she'd die if it ever happened to her."

The sun seemed to burn my arms, my back, it seemed such an awful act to contemplate. I was wearing a white cotton blouse with my overalls, and I felt heated all over. Yet the sun was not strong enough to cause such intense heat. I was about to ask Charlotte another question when she turned with her finger to her lips. We had come to the back of a cabin that was in fairly good repair, except for two or three gray, weatherbeaten slats that hung at crazy angles, as though they had been pried from their proper position.

Still with finger to lips, Charlotte beckoned me urgently with her long white arm. She had dropped to her knees and was carefully raising the loose end of a slat to reveal a small, dark hole in the shape of a triangle. Smiling, she placed one eye at the hole, looked quickly, and then pulled back. "Look," she whispered into my ear. Her breath left a damp film against my cheek. I nudged her aside, and looked.

A young black man named Banneker was making love to a Negro woman whose face I could not see. Banneker's eyes were closed and his head was very near the hole through which I was peeping, so that I looked down the length of his body, which was moving this way and that like a slowly impassioned snake. The woman had her glistening arms wrapped tightly around his broad shoulders. Her body was moving, too. It seemed that I heard a low humming coming from the two of them, as though they were singing softly to each other as they were making love.

All of this came to me in a flash, for I looked quickly, and drew away. Charlotte was smiling. I was about to scream at her for showing me such a sight; but she clamped her hand over my mouth and warned me with vicious green eyes to remain silent. "He'd *kill* us," she whispered, "if he knew we were out here. You know how Banneker is."

My body felt flushed with fear and excitement. Indeed I knew Banneker. He was the son of an old Negro woman named Yetta, and he had been born at Fir Crest. His father was also black, one of the men kept for breeding purposes, no doubt, for my father and the few white men who worked at Fir Crest as overseers were often heard to say that they did not believe in making love to Negro women, as some other white men did. In fact, such a thing was expressly forbidden by Father, and his orders apparently had their effect, for there were almost no mulattoes among our servants. Except for Banneker, and two or three more, our Negroes were as black as God intended them to be—which was Benign's way of describing her own satin-textured color when she was in that kind of mood.

As for Banneker, he was nineteen or twenty then, all hard muscle and bone, as though he had been hewn from a piece of ebony. But he was also our local agitator—which is what Father used to call him—although I was not certain then of what it was he agitated for, and no one ever went deeply into the matter, except to say that he was an agitator. Sometimes he was called "uppity" as well. But anything said about Banneker—whether by my grandmother, Father, or any of the overseers—was said with unmistakable affection and also a certain pride, as though Banneker was exactly the kind of Negro who could thrive at Fir Crest. It was clearly a sign of our own enlightenment that we could tolerate an "uppity" and dissident Negro while still maintaining full control over him and his people.

Again, these thoughts slashed through my mind with the rapidity of lightning as Charlotte held her eye glued to the obscene triangle. As I watched her, the color seemed to drain from her cheeks, while the sun set her hair afire. And she presented a peculiar study in contrasts, as though

all the blood had leaped from her face to her hair. I
wanted to run to the house, but I dared not do it alone,
for I was afraid of being seen. Also, I was torn by indeci-
sion. I certainly did not want to look through the hole
again. Yet, I did. Why wasn't Banneker working with the
other men, anyway? I felt very indignant. But if I reported
him, I would also have to report why I knew he wasn't
working. At the same time, I was absorbed with curiosity
about the woman. Who was she? There was little to recognize about her kinky plaited hair, those sinuous arms that
held Banneker's back like sculptured leeches. . . .

Charlotte grabbed me quickly. "Look now!" she hissed.
I planted my eye at the hole with a haste that disgusted
me. And saw Banneker with his head down now, nestling
in the curve of the woman's right shoulder. They were on
a creaking cot that sang under the combined threshing of
their bodies. For they were moving in a frenzy now, the
woman's body rising and falling to the cadence of Banneker's.

The muscles in his arms, legs, and buttocks were tight,
as though he were squeezing the woman to death. And
even above the singing of the cot springs, and the hefty
slap of their bodies together, I could still hear a kind of
humming through their gasping and moaning. Their heads
were less than six inches away from my eye. If I had
wanted to, I could have touched them with a long broom-
straw.

I felt a strong urge to touch them, and I was filled with
deeper disgust. But just as I was preparing to pull away,
their bodies suddenly went rigid, and the muscles in Banneker's arms tightened around the woman as her slender
arms tightened around his shoulders, his slim waist. Then
they were still. I could see the thick vein in Banneker's
neck throbbing. The moaning and humming continued.
And Banneker lifted his head, looked directly into my eye,
and smiled.

I fell back, as though he'd struck me. "He knows we're
here!" I cried. I certainly forgot to whisper. And I took off
through the field with Charlotte running behind, calling
me. But I ran until I got to the east garden, where I collapsed, completely out of breath, on one of the white
wrought-iron benches that Grandmother had ordered from
Italy.

Charlotte soon flopped beside me. And she sprawled there until our breathing subsided.

"Why did you run?" Charlotte said.

"He *saw* me! I told you!"

Charlotte laughed, and slapped her thigh. "I know he saw you. He saw me, too. He always sees me."

My head was spinning. "But you warned me to be quiet. You said he would kill us if he knew."

She shrugged, and made a disdainful sound with her strawberry lips. "That was to make it more exciting," she said. She grabbed my arm and stared me in the eye. "You are excited, aren't you?" There was gloating and accusation in her voice.

I didn't know what to say. It seemed incredible that she would watch two Negroes making love, knowing that they knew she was there. Or that she would want to watch them in the first place. I felt filled with a mild nausea, and with disturbing sensations that I had never felt before. Watching Banneker and the woman was the first time I had ever seen a man and a woman together that way. Was that why I felt so strange? I did not know. But I did not want to be with Charlotte then. I left her sprawling like a tomboy on the Italian bench, smiling to herself as though she enjoyed a dark, delicious secret.

I went to Mother's sitting room on the second floor. Opening the door quietly, I looked in. Mother had fallen asleep on the settee, still holding her embroidery. In her sewing, she made elaborate designs of leaping stallions and gazelles, deer and fowl in flight. But the pieces we did were never used; she starched and ironed them herself, and folded them away in a small cedar trunk.

I went to my own room down the hall and rang for water to bathe. While Benign filled the tub, I stripped off the overalls and other clothing and stood naked before the full-length mirror, which was shaped in the form of a triptych. My body seemed on fire. "What's the matter with you, child?" Benign said. She had often seen me naked, so her question must have referred to some new thing that she saw in me now.

"What do you mean, Benign? Do I look any different?" I felt different, but I did not think that Benign could see feelings as she cocked an inquisitive eye at me.

She was very fat and very black, with white hair that

she wore pulled back to her neck in a bun. Her breasts were enormous, and in her blue uniform and white bibbed apron, they seemed set against her chest like a solid ledge. She cocked first one eye, then the other. "Turn around," she said. I did as she ordered. The other two mirrors gave me a three-dimensional view of my body. It was slender, curved, and dimpled here and there. The breasts were hard cones with delicate pink nipples. The belly, flat as any boy's, had an almost subtle roundness.

"You's become a woman," Benign said plainly. "You been out there fooling around with some no-account man?"

"Benign!" I was truly shocked. But it was also true that I had suddenly felt the onset of womanhood, as though the thing Banneker was doing to the Negro woman, he was also doing to me.

"I just want to make sure," Benign said. She stooped in front of my legs, parted them, and examined me. Her probing fingers felt hot, disturbing. Abruptly I pulled away. "I don't want you ever to do that again," I said. And I drew a dressing gown about me.

"Yas'm," Benign said with heavy sarcasm. "But I sure would like to know who that man was excited you so. You still a virgin, child, but you a very excited virgin." She left the room, chuckling in that almost singsong way that old Negroes do. Angrily I flung a slipper at the door. Then I bathed, luxuriating in the warm water for a long time. I combed and brushed my hair until it shone. Then I put on my very prettiest dress, complete with hoops and petticoats. I never wanted to wear overalls again.

When I went in to see my mother, she was awake, working at her embroidering. She held out both hands and grasped mine warmly. "How lovely you are," she said. "Have you given up those awful overalls for good?"

"For good, Mother."

"I'm glad," she said. I took up my embroidering—my designs were of flowers, of country maidens with staffs, herding sheep—and plunged the needle through the fine linen captured in the twin circles of the hoop. I was working on a rose, and the thread was the color of blood.

"Mother," I said suddenly, "what does it feel like to make love?"

Her delicate shoulders moved in a slight shudder. She

was wearing a dress of blue-and-white paisley that covered her from neck to toe. "It's part of a woman's duty," she said, "but it is not at all pleasant. Why do you ask?"

"I'm nineteen, Mother. Aren't I old enough to know?"

She shook her head deliberately, fondly. "There's not very much to know, my dear. When you are married, you will find out quickly enough. Pray God that you marry a man of delicate sensibilities. That is all you need to know."

Marry? Certainly I had thought about it very much recently, for I was of that age. And Benign had warned me in the kitchen: "Soon's the war is over, every young white boy in the county will be swarming around here like flies." If lovemaking was so unpleasant, why would they bother? Why should I bother? Most of what I knew about the subject had come from Benign. As soon as possible, I would go to the kitchen and ask her. My mother, exiled to her sitting room, had very little contact with the real life of Fir Crest. I found myself wondering for the first time if her advice was reliable. Banneker and the woman had clearly been enjoying what they were doing. . . .

I stayed with Mother long enough for her to tell me that a letter had arrived that very day from Father. "He says that the South is winning," she said. "And that he and Judge Gilliam are both well. When I write him tonight, I shall send him your love. And, of course, Charlotte's as well." Whenever she mentioned Charlotte, there seemed to be a drop in her voice, as though she stumbled over the name. She almost never mentioned Grandmother Parkchester, and I was surprised then when she did.

"Mrs. Parkchester also got a letter. Of course, I do not know what was in it, although I was courteous enough to send her down mine."

"Maybe it was something very personal," I said.

My mother's fingers flew over the leaping stallions, who were taking form in fine brown thread. "Too personal for his wife to also know? Some men indeed are animals," she said bitterly.

That angered me, but I said nothing. Father an animal? Why had she married him, then? And why was he an animal? Because he had written to his mother from the battlefield? It was impossible to concentrate on my sewing. I kissed Mother, telling her that I would see her at supper.

But she said, "I shall take my supper here." She was quite angry, but it simmered in a very genteel way underneath her pale white skin.

"Then I shall see you before you retire, Mother." That seemed to mollify her some, for she pressed her face against my lips, and even patted my arm gently, which was not her custom.

Freed, I went to the kitchen, where Benign was stirring in pots on the stove. "Is you in a better disposition, missy?"

"I'm sorry I spoke harshly to you, Benign. Will you forgive me?"

She chuckled. "Sure, child. I just got finished making some dried-apple tarts. Here. You have one."

The tart was still warm. I took a small bite, for I had no real appetite.

Benign looked at me with deep concern. "What's troubling you, child?"

I have often thought it uncanny how Negroes like Benign seemed to know more about my shifting moods than either Mother or Grandmother. I sat at the table, toying with the sweet, while she waited with heavy authority for me to answer. It was never my habit to lie to Benign, for she was not above "taking a switch" to me, as she would say. Again I was struck by the fact that it had always been Benign who punished Charlotte or me, when punishment was needed, rather than our parents.

"I sneaked down to the Negro cabins with Charlotte. We peeped through a hole and saw Banneker making love to some woman. I don't know who she was."

Benign sighed heavily, and sat at the table with me. "You just forget about dogs like Banneker," she said. "He nothing but a pure dog." Then she laughed unexpectedly. "Although he sure is a good-looking one." Immediately she turned sober again. "Is that what's troubling you, missy?"

Without meaning to, without even knowing why, I began to cry. Benign jumped from her chair and folded her large arms around my shoulders, pulling my head to her ample breasts. "Did that Banneker say something out of the way to you, child?" She smelled clean and scrubbed, like brown soap. "Did he do something . . . *nasty?*"

I managed to shake my head in the prison of her arms.

"He didn't even speak to us," I blubbered. "He just looked at me and grinned."

"I'm going to speak to Yetta about him," Benign said firmly. "He's getting out of his place when he makes my pretty missy cry."

"I'm not crying because of him, Benign."

She stepped away, and cupped my chin in her hand. "Then why you crying, missy?"

"I don't know."

"Did Charlotte cry?"

"No. She was laughing. She seemed to think it funny, what we saw."

Benign shook her head very sadly. "Ain't nothing funny about making love, child. You'll find out when it happens to you."

My heart seemed to miss a beat. "Tell me about it, Benign."

"About what, honey?"

"About making love."

She plucked at a string hanging from the tablecloth. The kitchen smelled of roasting pork, apple tarts, and cinnamon. Sun poured through the window and landed on the hardwood floor in warm yellow puddles. "If you see Banneker," Benign said slowly, as though carefully picking her words, "you see nothing but lust. You didn't see no love. Banneker, he so hurt inside hisself, he don't know the meaning of love. What he do with them sluts of his ain't got nothing to do with love."

She rolled the string into a tiny ball and pulled it from the cloth. I was afraid to say anything, for fear that she would chase me from the kitchen. I had the feeling that I was on the verge of important revelations, and I scarcely dared to breathe. The kitchen was so quiet that I could hear the ticking of the clock coming like sharp, tiny footsteps all the way from the sitting room.

"Love," Benign said, "is something that happens to all folks sooner or later. It don't matter whether you white folks or black folks, except that you all love one way and we love another. That's the only difference."

I was compelled to speak. "Tell me about the difference, Benign."

She swelled her great breasts. She seemed to be on safer ground now. "White folks, they make puny love, honey.

Colored folks, they go deep down into the dirt, the same way rainwater seeps into the ground. White folks too busy worrying about everything to make real love. Colored folks ain't got nothing to worry about. They make love until it feels good."

"Does it ever not feel good, Benign?"

"Just in the beginning, sugar. You'll find out. There's a lot of blood in the beginning, just like I told you before. There's a lot of pleasure, too."

"Mother says it's not pleasant."

She seemed angry, her large forehead creasing in wrinkles. Perhaps to stifle words that might be used against her, she picked up the tart and took a large bite. Chewing, she said, "This here is *Benign* talking to you, sugar. I ain't saying your mammy ain't right. But I *am* saying that Benign here is done a whole lot more lovemaking than your mother has. So I ought to know what I'm talking about. It's pleasure, sugar. Especially if you got yourself the right man. It ain't nothing but pleasure. Even the pain is pleasure."

My whole insides seemed to relax. Of course Benign knew more than my mother, more than any other woman I'd ever met. More than even Grandmother Parkchester, who made me feel uncomfortable with her large, glowing eyes. I would never talk to her the same way I talked to Benign.

"There, now," Benign said. She reached across the table with a dazzling white handkerchief and dried my tears. "The trouble with you, honey, is that you got the sap rising in you. And that's perfectly all right. It's that time of the year, you that time in your life. All old Benign is going to tell you is not to go out there and do the thing with somebody you don't love and respect. Ain't no pleasure in that, not a speck of pleasure. You hear me, child?"

I felt very much better. "I hear you, Benign." We stood, and I hugged her tightly. "Thank you," I whispered. "Thank you very much, Benign."

She laughed, a deep rumble like the onset of thunder. "For what, child? 'Cause your juice is rising? You thank the good Lord for that. It means you a woman at last. Now, you run along, honey. Benign's got a lot of work to do."

Charlotte was still in the east garden. When she saw me

in the dress, she was openly disdainful. She might not have understood the reasons for my discarding the overalls—I was not even sure of them myself—but she rightly discerned that it had something to do with Banneker and the Negro woman we'd seen. Also, the overalls had made Charlotte and me allies with Grandmother Parkchester; the dress meant that I had returned to Mother's side.

"I certainly wouldn't want you fighting a war with me," Charlotte said. "I bet you'd run at the first sign of the enemy."

"I wouldn't want to fight a war with you, Charlotte. In fact, I don't want to even talk to you today. Or tomorrow either."

Charlotte turned slightly pale. She hated it when I imposed the silent treatment on her. "What did I do now?" she cried. I said nothing. In truth, I could find nothing wrong with what she had done, except to show me a sight I had never seen, and to arouse my curiosity more than it had ever been. But once the silence was imposed, it was never my policy to break it.

Still, Charlotte persisted. "Grandmother Parkchester got a letter from Father. He says he's been wounded. He's in the hospital. He doesn't want Mother to know."

Wounded? That was indeed disturbing news. And I bit my tongue to keep from asking questions. How badly was Father hurt? Had he lost a leg, an arm? Charlotte's face seemed filled with greed and gloating as she tried to make me talk to her. But I was determined not to. At times like this, I felt that I was dealing with a person far older than myself, rather than with my younger sister. She nearly crouched in front of me, like a wild animal about to pounce. It was not the first time that I had thought her inhuman. But even in her anxiety, her face was smooth and beautiful, her hair aglow with the afternoon sun.

Suddenly her face broke into smiles as she changed the direction of her attack. "Are you angry with me because I showed you Banneker? I didn't mean to make you angry, Victoria." Her voice held a wheedling quality that I had come to know only too well.

Suddenly a shadow fell over us. "What is this about Banneker?" It was Grandmother Parkchester, wearing overalls and a straw hat over a bandanna tied around her hair. She carried a basket and shears, and while she waited for our answer, she went to a rosebush and began beheading the flowers with the shears.

"There's nothing about Banneker, really, Grandmother." Charlotte had run to her and was holding to those awful overalls. From the very beginning of the war, Grandmother had rolled up her sleeves and gone to work like a common field hand. Perhaps it was my natural dislike of her that made me mistrust her motives in that respect. We were in the second year of the war, but it had not affected us in any tangible way, except for the absence of Father. Certainly with so many servants at Fir Crest, there was no burning need for Grandmother Parkchester to clump about in overalls and heavy boots. But she did so with a special delight, talking of patriotism and states' rights, a transplanted New Yorker who was more rebel than old Jeff Davis himself in Richmond.

Watching her as she cut the roses, I felt that it was all one large game to her—an excuse more than a cause, an opportunity to justify her outlandishness and enlarge upon it. As for Charlotte, she practically wrapped herself like a large puppy around the old woman—wheedling, cajoling, whispering into her red ear—until the two of them were convulsed in barroom laughter. It was disgusting. I rose to leave—I had thought about taking a walk in the orchard, where the apple and cherry blossoms were especially fragrant this year. But my grandmother stopped me with a sharp command. "Sit where you are," she said. Her eyes had narrowed like a vicious cat's. She had never spoken to me so sharply before, and I was stunned. "I was going to the orchard," I said.

She seemed to find that especially amusing. "For what? To daydream, as your mother does over her sewing?"

I felt an unaccustomed anger. "Mother likes to sew. She harms no one. If she likes to daydream as well, I would think it her affair and no one else's."

She actually seemed pleased. With Charlotte's arm around her waist, she took a step closer to me. I'd thought that she would slap me, and I had already decided that if she did so, I would slap her back. I was amazed at the audacity of the thought; and perhaps Charlotte detected something of my intended reaction, for I saw panic in her green eyes. But somewhere that morning—and perhaps it had happened as I'd peered through the hole at Banneker and his slut—I'd taken the first important step into womanhood.

But my grandmother did not slap me. What she did was to reach into a slender pocket on the bib of her overalls, take out a fat cigar, and strike a match on the seat of her overalls. She eyed me over the feeble flame. "You don't care very much for me, do you?"

"No."

She nodded once or twice slowly before she bit the head from the cigar and lighted it. "I don't care too much for you either, my dear. You're far too much like your mother. Sugar water, we'd call it in New York."

I had nothing to say to that, having never been to New York, so I stared at her brazenly. And she stared back, sending up great puffs of stinking smoke that were happily dispelled by the wind. "I am most pleased," she finally said, "to find that you do have some spirit after all. Your father and I had thought you were a lost cause. However, I would advise you to direct your arrogance at servants, where it might be better received."

"Servants?" I said, raking with disdainful eyes her and Charlotte in their peasant's attire. "It's difficult these days to tell the servants from the mistress. And now," I said, audaciously gathering my skirts, "I am going to the orchard. Perhaps to daydream. Perhaps not."

Turning my back on them both, setting my head at a deliberate angle, I swept from the garden with pounding heart and an undeniable sense of triumph. And the latter feeling was only enhanced when I heard Charlotte screeching after me. "Victoria! Wait for me! I'm going to the orchard too!" I did not wait for her; but I did slow my step almost imperceptibly so that she could catch up with me.

"Victoria, what is *wrong* with you?" Charlotte whispered, as though we could be overheard by the wind. "Grandmother's absolutely livid! She stormed from the garden as soon as you left. Dear Victoria, don't provoke her. She can cause real trouble if she wants to."

"Real trouble?" We were going past the stables, and the air smelled of horse manure and urine-wet hay. "She has been nothing but trouble since I can remember. And she has been worse since Father has gone." It was perhaps an unfair accusation, but certainly close enough to the truth for Charlotte to remain quiet, and for me to consider the fact that I had broken my vow of two days' silence against her.

She stopped suddenly in the middle of the road, and stood there with her hands hanging helplessly at her sides. Now she seemed a lost and bewildered little girl; and I wondered, with a sharp intake of breath, whether Grandmother Parkchester's hold on her had reached the breaking point. "What is it, Charlotte? Why do you look so strange?"

For she *did* look strange, as though the day's revelations were not to be mine alone. Behind her stood the imposing bulk of Fir Crest, with its glistening windows; the garden where roses grew like stains of blood, broken here and there by the pale yellow of forsythia and the erectness of hollyhocks. And Fir Crest itself, towering in two tall stories, stately and imposing in the afternoon sun. "What *is* it, Charlotte?"

In answer, she ran and flung her arms around me. "I feel so strange, Victoria. So very strange. When you talked to Grandmother like that, it was as though a spell was broken." She leaned back, inspecting me with her lovely eyes. "Is it true that you dislike her?"

"It is true," I said evenly. "Not only for what she has done to Father and Mother, but especially for what she has done to you." Now I thrust her away from me. "Look at you! If you were not my own sister, I'd think you were a boy!"

That seemed to hurt her deeply. And I was sorry that I had said it. But it was too late to take back the words.

"I like wearing overalls," she said. "I hate dresses."

"Perhaps so. Yet, it is a fact that men wear overalls, and young ladies of your category wear dresses and ribbons and do their utmost to look pretty. It may be a burden, but it is also an obligation. Look at Mother. Have you ever seen a lovelier woman?"

"Mother doesn't like me," she said meekly.

"Mother loves you, Charlotte! It pains her that you don't come to see her more often."

"Why does she hide in that room?" She was squinting now, for all the world like a little girl with the sun in her eyes.

"She doesn't hide. She simply stays out of Grandmother's way as much as possible in order to avoid conflict."

"But *why?*"

"Because Grandmother doesn't like her." I had gone too far to stop now. "Grandmother is crass and vulgar. Mother is refined. Rather than fight Grandmother, she prefers to withdraw and remain by herself. I'm afraid, dear sister, that you are the chief casualty of this conflict. But Mother truly loves you. She would never try to make you into a boy."

She shoved me away almost angrily. I was surprised at how strong she was. "I don't believe you!" she cried. "Grandmother loves me! Mother hates me! Grandmother says so!"

"You see?" I felt a certain pleasure in closing the trap she had unwittingly stepped into. "*Grandmother* says so. Have you ever asked Mother? Have you?"

She shook her head disconsolately. "I was afraid to."

Now I hugged her. "Charlotte . . . never be afraid. Go and talk to Mother. When you are finished, I'll be waiting for you in the orchard. Will you go?"

She hesitated, frowning. "Suppose she doesn't want to see me?"

"She wants to see you. She is always asking about you." The last part was quite untrue, but saying it did not seem to hurt.

"I hate embroidering," Charlotte said.

It was such an illogical thing for her to say that I was forced to laugh. "I'll tell you a deep secret, Charlotte. So do I. Perhaps if I thought about it enough, I'd hate being a woman as well. But it is the best we can do, considering that God made us as we are."

Already she seemed in a better mood. "Women, yes. But He did not impose the curse of embroidering as well. Victoria, I'm all thumbs when it comes to that!"

I kissed her happily. She never ceased to amaze me, how she could swing from one mood and one age to another as easily as skaters gliding over ice. She was very much the young woman now. "Go talk to Mother. I'll wait for you."

"I will," she said. Turning, she walked with resolute step toward Fir Crest just as Benign came from the kitchen and began hanging tea towels on the clothesline.

It is impossible to adequately describe what I felt as I continued to the orchard. Certainly today marked an important changing point in my life, and perhaps Charlotte's as well. Perhaps in Mother's, too. As for Grandmother Parkchester, if she had stormed from the garden, it had only been a temporary retreat. She would be in full sail at the supper table tonight, elegantly attired as usual, but imposing upon us every crudity that resided in her twisted mind.

I had come to the orchard, and I cleared a spot underneath an apple tree and sat down. Blossoms showered over me like snow, and I held my hand out to them, perhaps to sweeten the bitterness of my thoughts. Was it possible, I wondered, that Grandmother Parkchester was mad?

The very thought sent panic racing through my veins. I was certainly no expert on the subject. All of us had heard of insanity in other families. It was never openly discussed, but there were whispers about this family and that, grotesque stories about people who had lost their minds and were locked away in cellars and attics to prevent the horrible truth from being known.

After Father left, Benign had told me one of those stories and cautioned me, with a roll of her white eyes, never to mention what she said to anyone. "Some of them crazy folks, they act just as normal as you please. But they as batty as bedbugs. Don't you go telling nobody what I said, you hear?" I do not recall what it was that had led us into the discussion of madness—indeed, if anything, for Benign chose her topics as she saw fit, for reasons known primarily to herself—but I do remember that her voice had held a definite edge, as though she was trying to warn me of something.

Before I could probe further, Grandmother Parkchester had stormed into the kitchen and began upbraiding Benign and me for taking up each other's time. "With the war on," she'd said, "we all must do our share. There's hardly time for foolish chatter." Completely cowed, Benign had slunk back to her duties. And I had gone to Mother's sitting room to sew, for there was really less for us to do then than before.

It is true that we had heard stories of how other white women were left to fend for themselves after their servants had deserted as soon as the master's back was turned. But none of that was true at Fir Crest. Our Negroes remained loyal, and were working double, and sometimes triple, shifts, to raise stock and crops for the Confederacy, which were carried away to the trains in great caravans of wagons.

Of five white overseers, four had gone off to war. The fifth, a lovable old Irishman named Mr. McAdoo, had tried unsuccessfully to take on the duties of the missing four; but his age and a penchant for Dublin whiskey had made him unequal to the task. So Grandmother Parkchester had stepped in to help. I suppose that overalls were much more practical than chenille dresses, when one was overseeing the labor of field hands. Still, I remembered Benign's comments for weeks afterward, without really knowing why they had wedged in my mind. Once, in a light moment, I had wondered if Benign had been trying to tell me, in her discreet way, that *I* was mad!

But now, in the orchard, I wondered if she had been referring to Grandmother Parkchester. Negro servants knew every detail about the affairs of their masters and mistresses. Indeed, they were better informed than any newspaper, forming a veritable network of wagging tongues from Fir Crest to the Confederate line, and even beyond.

With conflicting reports about how the South was faring in the war, Benign or some other Negro probably had the most accurate accounts about how the war was really going. But it was considered in the worst possible taste to engage in gossip with one's servants. They talked, sometimes interminably, while one listened with something akin to bated breath, trying to sift fact from fantasy, to consider which comments referred to whom, without lowering oneself to the point of actually coming out and asking a Negro.

Within the entire institution of slavery, at least from a woman's point of view, this circumlocution was probably the most exasperating feature. For, regardless of how dearly I wanted to know, I could never run to the kitchen and ask bluntly, "Benign, is Grandmother Parkchester crazy?" First of all, Benign would never answer me directly. And by the time I had tried to figure out the routes she was using to carry me away from what she knew, I'd be crazy myself.

Secondly, young ladies of good breeding never asked such personal and inflammatory questions of one's servants, *although they knew*. There was, however, some consolation in remembering that Benign had said that some insane people acted perfectly normal. That either excluded Grandmother Parkchester, or doomed her to a madhouse. For, to use Benign's expression, Grandmother Parkchester indeed did act as batty as a bedbug. Using Benign's logic further, then that meant that Grandmother was as sound as a gold piece. . . .

So much thinking, and the delicate perfume of the orchard, had made me slightly drowsy. Apple blossoms were still showering on me, as though the tree overhead had a case of the palsy. I looked up, and saw Banneker silently shaking the flowering limbs with his big arms. My first impulse was to run; but he smiled so serenely that he hardly seemed the same man I had peered at through the hole in the Negro cabin.

"Afternoon, Miss Victoria," he said most respectfully. If he was willing to treat me as though I was not a Peeping Tom, then good breeding required that I treat him as though I had not spied him in his lustful act. "Good afternoon, Banneker. The blossoms are beautiful, aren't they?"

"Yas'm, Miss Victoria. I broke some and put them in the dining room. Benign told me to."

"Thank you, Banneker." I stood and brushed off my dress. "Now I must go." A distinct look of disappointment flashed across his handsome face. He was barefoot and bare-chested, wearing only a pair of thin gray pants. As he straddled two branches, he seemed like a half-naked colossus over my head. I remembered how his body had moved atop the Negro woman's in the cabin, and I felt my cheeks flush. I was curious beyond all reason to know who she was. But I would never ask him.

But he was a shrewd, grinning devil. "Can I have your permission, Miss Victoria, to take some of these blossoms to my woman?"

"Your woman, Banneker?" It offended me that he would carry his slut the same blossoms he had put in the luxurious dining room at Fir Crest.

"Yas'm. I got me a new woman. Name of Emerald."

I knew her. For a Negro woman, she was particularly beautiful. Very young, very black, with a slender, strong body. And those sculptured arms I had seen around Banneker's back.

"I suggest you take her blossoms from the cherry tree, Banneker. I'm sure she'd appreciate them more than these."

It was a definite refusal of his request. In all probability, if he was really keen on giving his slut the apple blossoms, he would simply wait until I was gone and then take them. But his grin widened, and he clambered to the ground like a large monkey. "That's a good idea, Miss Victoria. She'd like cherry blossoms, Emerald would." He struck his forehead with the flat of his hand. "Me an old dumb nigger. Now why didn't I think of that?"

"Good afternoon, Banneker."

"Good afternoon, missy."

As I walked to Fir Crest, I could feel his grin following my every step. But I did not look back until I got to the east garden. And when I did, he was gone.

I went to my room and napped until Benign called me to supper. I had forgotten that, in order to avoid Grandmother Parkchester, I had decided to take the evening meal with Mother. But, not having arranged with Benign to do so, I decided to brave Grandmother's wrath. I washed and changed rapidly, and went downstairs.

There were only two places set, one at each end of the long dining table. "You sit at the head of the table tonight," Benign said with something resembling a twinkle in her eye. "Miss Parkchester, she having supper in her room." She was referring to Grandmother; she and all the other servants called my mother Miss Patricia. "Miss Charlotte will be down in a minute. Least, that's what she said fifteen minutes ago." Her body was churning with silent laughter. Through whatever weird communications system, she knew all about the run-in I'd had with Grandmother Parkchester. Certainly Charlotte would never tell her.

"You look awfully pretty tonight, Miss Victoria."

"Thank you, Benign." I took a sip of water to keep from laughing. I felt exuberant, triumphant. I, a mere girl, had banished crusty old Grandmother Parkchester to *her* sitting room, if only temporarily.

Just then Charlotte came into the room. I couldn't believe my eyes. She was absolutely beautiful in a long white

dress of sheer silk embroidered with small roses and but-
terflies. Her flowing hair sparkled like raw gold in lights
from the bronze chandelier. And her smile was radiant.
She seemed like some fair princess from a storybook.
Benign, that sly old rascal, beamed proudly at Charlotte as
Juniper pulled out the high-backed chair to seat her.

"Good evening, Victoria," she said demurely. "How do
I look?"

"You're beautiful, Charlotte! You're absolutely beautiful!" I felt like running around the long table to hug and
kiss her. But Benign was already placing the soup before
me. I sat quietly until she had served Charlotte, and then
she left the room with Juniper.

"Did you talk to Mother?" I asked Charlotte.

Her smile broadened. "We talked all afternoon. You
were right, Victoria. She does love me. And she says I
need not embroider. She is so beautiful. I love her very
much."

"I'm so glad, Charlotte." I was almost too full to eat.
But the two of us did a good job on the roast loin of pork,
tender turnip greens, mashed potatoes, and warm apple
tarts with cold buttermilk for dessert. It was a perfect supper, a perfect evening. We used our best china, and the tablecloth was of the finest linen damask. The centerpiece
was an arrangement of low-cut apple blossoms that perfumed the room. Neither Charlotte nor I mentioned
Grandmother Parkchester. With Benign taking away and
serving dishes, and Charlotte so beautifully got up, acting
the perfect lady, I felt that a new day had indeed begun at
Fir Crest.

It is certainly the happiest memory of my life so far
as Charlotte is concerned, because we not only got to
know each other that day, but became fast friends as well.
While Grandmother Parkchester would make repeated attempts to reestablish control over my sister, Charlotte
would grow into radiant and independent beauty, free of
the old woman's vulgar influence. And from that day
forth, Charlotte, Mother, and I would form a strong and
formidable family unit that Grandmother Parkchester
would finally grow weary of assaulting, and go about her
own affairs, leaving us to ours.

However, another encounter awaited us before that
night of enchantment and reconciliation would end.

Robert Gilliam, the Judge's twenty-year-old son, arrived from the front with news of the war as Charlotte and I lounged before the fireplace in the huge sitting room and chattered like magpies. Benign herself brought him to us, for he had posted his horse behind the kitchen, and we had not heard him ride up.

"Robert!" Charlotte cried. Forgetting all her newly found airs, she dashed to him and nearly smothered him with kisses. I wanted to do the same; instead, I bombarded him with questions once he had laughingly fought Charlotte off. "When did you get home, Robert? How long will you be here? How are you? How is Father? How is *your* father?"

Laughing, he held his hands up. "Whoa! Whoa! Never was man so warmly welcomed," he said in that rough and cheerful way of his. "First, Benign tries to feed me to death in the kitchen, *forces* me to eat, mind you . . ."

"As if that was ever called for, Mistuh Robert," she said, holding her apron to her face, dissolving in giggles.

". . . and then I'm nearly squeezed to death by this lovely Charlotte." He gave her a final squeeze. Being much of the same age, he and I shook hands formally. But I could not restrain from brushing my lips against his dark, square jaw. "It is good to see you, Robert. And if Charlotte and I attacked you, it is because we have had a very special day. Seeing you has made it very special indeed."

He was disturbingly handsome, even in the funereal gray of the Confederate uniform. Tall, lanky, broad-chested, he seemed every inch the man now, certainly not the gangling son of Judge Gilliam we had grown up with. We had not seen him for some three years, for he had been studying at the military academy in Staunton. When the war began, the academy had sent its most distin-guished pupils into the heat of battle, where they proved that youth was no deterrent to valor. Some had died, and the South had publicly mourned them by proclamation from Jefferson Davis himself, as though any argument in the world justified the murder of children gotten up in uniforms and swords. So far, Robert Gilliam—Sergeant Gilliam, for he had three chevrons on his sleeve—had sur-vived, but not without damage. His determined restless-ness, a hidden pain in his deep blue eyes, and a sometimes resolute tightness to his broad mouth, ill-became a boy of nineteen, for all his show of manliness.

He and Charlotte were engaged in their usual banter as the sobering thoughts flashed through my mind. Once Benign, all smiles, had released him from captivity in the kitchen and brought him to us, she had disappeared. Now she returned with apple tarts and buttermilk for him, but it seemed almost ludicrous to serve Robert Gilliam the same dessert we had eaten. "Sergeant Gilliam will have some sherry, Benign," I told her. "Afterward, please tell Mother and Grandmother Parkchester that he is here. I am sure they will be anxious to see him."

"Yas'm, Miss Victoria." She seemed swollen with joy, for she had practically raised Robert along with Charlotte and me after he persisted in sneaking over from Judge Gilliam's to be at Fir Crest. As the only child of a taciturn and sometimes stern widower, Robert Gilliam had long ago adopted Fir Crest as his home and us as his family. With the possible exception of Grandmother Parkchester—who encouraged spiritedness in others, but had always resented Robert's—we all loved him dearly.

But certainly none loved him more than Benign. Only time would tell how long she had detained him in the kitchen before she released him to us. Ever jealous of her prerogatives, she now eyed the milk and tart with something like disdain on her black face. And laughed roundly. "Mistuh Robert, he done become a man, Miss Victoria."

I felt tremors of delight pass through my body. "He has, indeed, Benign." Charlotte, Robert, and I maintained an almost reverent silence as Benign left us. For the implications of her remark were very clear: if Robert was now a man, certainly Charlotte and I were breathlessly close to becoming women, following Robert Gilliam even into the sacred realm of adulthood as we had trailed behind him to the swimming hole, to pick hazel nuts or chinquapins, to a thousand places in our childhood where he led us like an older, wiser brother, rambling all over Fir Crest with us to escape the loneliness of being the only white child at Judge Gilliam's.

Benign came back with a bottle of sherry and three glasses. "This is a very special celebration," she said. She seemed full of sherry herself; undoubtedly, she and Juniper as well were hitting the bottle in the kitchen. Neither Charlotte nor I was a stranger to wine, for we'd always been allowed to sip from some adult's glass on special occasions. But now, for the very first time, Benign was serving us wine along with Robert, which seemed to put a cap on her pronouncement about our growth. She watched us with approving eyes as we took our glasses from the silver tray and toasted the Confederacy. "And to all her fallen sons," Robert Gilliam said quietly. "Amen to that," Benign said, with the unmistakable sound of tears breaking in her voice. And she went back to the kitchen.

Robert downed his wine in one drink; Charlotte and I sipped ours. "It is good to be home," he said, and I knew he was referring to Fir Crest. "Charlotte, Victoria, both of you *have* grown! Whatever happened to the fat little girls who screamed when I dropped caterpillars down their backs?"

We laughed together. The wine had caused his cheeks to flush, and he seemed more handsome than ever. His azure eyes were deep-set and brooding, even when he was in a happy mood. His hair was shaggy black and always seemed in need of combing. His lips were broadly shaped and quite red, as though he had just finished a handful of stolen cherries. He was tanned, perhaps from the elements; but he had always been olive-colored, for his mother had been of Spanish blood. Standing ramrod straight, he wore the gray uniform as though it were a second skin. The sword holster was empty, since it was customary to leave one's weapons away from the sight of ladies. His cap was jammed into the back pocket of his breeches, the stiff peak hanging out like a desolate orphan.

"Robert, do tell us about Father! Have you seen him? How is he?"

"He is wounded, Charlotte. But it is not serious. I saw him in the Alexandria hospital three days ago. He asked me to give the two of you a hug and a kiss for him." His dark eyes settled on me, dancing with their devilish merriment. "I will be happy to tell him that has been attended to," he said.

"Well, *I* haven't kissed you for Father," Charlotte said. And she promptly did, pecking at his lips like a chicken.

"Thank you, Charlotte." He was smiling broadly.

"You're welcome, Robert. Or should I call you Sergeant Gilliam?"

"Just call me Robert," he said quietly. And the smile disappeared from his face.

Suddenly Charlotte began twirling in her diaphanous dress, flinging her arms upward as though trying to touch the high ceiling, the chandelier, perhaps heaven itself. "Isn't it marvelous, the three of us together again? I'm so happy, I could positively dance."

A quick shadow fell like a warning across Robert's face. I touched Charlotte's shoulder to stop her. "I'm afraid Robert has come to tell us important news, Charlotte."

"About the war?" she cried. "I am sick of hearing of the war. It is all Grandmother talks about. Tell us about Richmond, Robert. And Washington . . . you've been there, haven't you? And the ladies there . . . how do they dress? Are they as pretty as Victoria and I?"

Benign had left the bottle of sherry on the tray, and Robert poured another drink and quickly swallowed it before he answered. "They are pretty, some of them. But none as lovely as you, Charlotte. Nor Victoria." His voice grew tight, and the muscles in his jaw tensed. "And certainly none quite as silly."

"Robert!" Charlotte sounded truly wounded, but I felt remarkably calm. I had already assessed the new Robert Gilliam and found him anguished and bitter underneath his cool exterior. As usual, Charlotte had been too wrapped in her own excitement to determine that a boy had gone to war, and a scarred veteran had come home. "You think us silly, Robert?" Her color had turned high, as though she would burst into tears.

"Excessively so," Robert said coldly. He bowed slightly, including us both in the angry incline of his body. "And now I must go. My regards to your mother, and to Mrs. Parkchester."

"Robert." I laid my hand on his arm. "If we have offended you, please forgive us. And please do not go. At least, not this way. Charlotte meant no harm. She has been under a terrible strain."

His eyes searched mine. They seemed to bore into my very soul. "I've been under something of a strain myself," he said. It seemed as though a cold wind passed over me as his eyes held mine, for his were the eyes of a man who has killed other men. It was the swiftest of impressions, and then it was gone as he wrapped his big hand around

mine and squeezed it warmly. And life and light seemed
to return to his eyes. A small smile played at the corners
of his rosy lips. Then he stepped to Charlotte and wrapped
his long arms around her. "Forgive me, Charlotte. Frequently I'm quite silly myself." He kissed her quickly on
the cheek, then held her away from him. "Do you forgive
me, Charlotte?"

"Oh, yes, Robert! And I am the silly one. Not you, certainly not Victoria. Please forgive me."

Again he hugged her. "Hush," he said, smoothing her
flaming hair. He kissed her now on the lips, quickly. "Let
us all have another sherry, and talk about pleasant things."

I poured, and then Charlotte and I sat on the settee
while he stood near the fireplace, resting an elbow on the
mantel. "How are things at Fir Crest?" he said. The fire
burned low, touching his strong legs with a warm glow.

"We live almost isolated from the real world," I said.
"That is why it is so difficult for us to understand about
the war, Robert. It has touched us, I am sure of that. Yet,
things are pretty much as before. Except, of course, for
Father. We miss him terribly. Was he badly wounded?"

He shook his head. "Not badly. He was shot in the leg.
But it was a clean wound. The shot went straight through
his calf. I talked to the doctors. They say he will be as
good as new in a few weeks."

"Poor Father," Charlotte murmured absently.

"And how is dear Judge Gilliam?" I asked.

"As pompous as ever," Robert said, laughing. Suddenly
he stiffened and grew somber. I turned in the direction he
was looking. Mother was coming down the winding staircase from the second floor.

She might have been a queen descending into the rich
splendor of the sitting room. She wore a high-waisted
gown that left her lovely shoulders bare, giving only a hint
to the swell of her pink breasts. The gown was smoke blue
in color, aglitter with sequins, and with a short train that
whispered softly as it glided from step to step. Her black
hair was piled in shiny coils, which gave way to a long
strand that lay across her left shoulder. How long had it
been since I'd seen her so absolutely radiant, smiling now
as she paused at the bottom of the stairs? Robert Gilliam
awaited her there like a young gallant. And he bent over

the beauty of her hand. "Mrs. Parkchester, ma'am. Indeed it is a pleasure to see you."

"And you too, Robert," Mother said. "You have grown. And you are terribly handsome." She inspected his face carefully. Whatever she saw there caused her to link her arm in his and guide him to where we were standing now near the settee. "Girls, have you been troubling Robert? He has been through a lot, you know. Do sit, Robert. Victoria, I shall have a sherry. And, of course, another for our young soldier." She and Robert took chairs facing each other as I poured Mother a sherry. It was impossible not to feel the strength of her towering presence, her impeccable sureness as she gauged Robert's mood and deftly handled it. Glancing back, I saw Charlotte sitting rigidly now in a third chair. If she had been silly before, she was serious now, as though the fact of Mother's presence had given a higher reality to Robert's own. As for Robert, he seemed to drink in her beauty. For she was inescapably beautiful; and yet, she wore her radiance almost casually, as though it were more bother than worth. Her breasts peered demurely over the top of her bodice like the swelling of small curious moons inspecting the universe, perhaps for the first time.

And for the first time in my life—at least, the first time that I could isolate and describe the condition—I felt a twinge of jealousy. For Robert's eyes held the deep, worshipful gaze of a man who desires a woman he is watching. Certainly not in the lustful way of Banneker and his woman—had it been only that morning that we had seen the lust of Negroes?—but with a keen refinement, a desire that was more of the spirit than of the flesh, and by far the more brutal and powerful for all that: the need to restrain one's hold on the physical and, at the same time, to whip the nebulousness of clouds into full gallop. I had always loved Robert Gilliam as a brother. Serving sherry to Mother, then to him, I felt my initial sense of jealousy melt into a puddle of confusion as his eyes brushed mine. And I saw a deeper desire there, like a light at the bottom of a dark and disturbing pool. My cheeks burned as I seated myself on the settee, forgoing sherry for the moment, because my head was swimming with exciting thoughts about the deep-voiced, handsome man who had shared my childhood with me.

Seated, Mother lifted her glass in a toast. "To the Confederacy, and all our brave men," she said.

"To the Confederacy," Robert echoed. They both sipped. Charlotte settled back in her chair. Her eyes were dancing, as though she were watching queen and prince speak their lines from the pages of a storybook.

"We are losing the war," Robert said flatly.

"I know," Mother said. "Whenever there is conflict, there must be victors. And those who are not victorious. Perhaps things will change. But I have heard and read that Mr. Lincoln is planning to issue a proclamation freeing all slaves." She finished her sherry and handed me her glass, somewhat imperiously. Her color seemed to have paled. "What do you hear of that, Robert?"

He nodded. "It is true. There is talk everywhere. Mr. Lincoln intends to free slaves in the South. That way, he will add more than three million fighters to the cause of the Union. The slaves themselves can effectively fight the South from within, as guerrillas. It is a devilish decision!" He slammed a fist into the palm of his hand. "There will be rape, slaughter, pillage!"

Mother lifted a soothing hand. "You will frighten the girls, Robert."

"But it is true, Mrs. Parkchester!" His eyes were darkly intense.

"Not necessarily," Mother said calmly. She seemed very composed; yet, it appeared that her color had grown paler still. And she finished her sherry with unaccustomed speed, and asked me for another. "If logic is applied to the matter," she went on, "then it does not follow that a proclamation of any sort will inspire slaves to do what they might as easily do without a proclamation."

"Logic?" There was a wildness in Robert's voice, his eyes. "It's late to be talking about logic, isn't it?" He leaped to his feet and walked around the three of us in an angry stride. I had poured myself a sherry, and I sipped it even as my heart filled with fear. At the same time, my head buzzed with questions.

Would Benign, and Juniper, and Johnny Cake, freed by some political announcement from Washington, be more of a threat to our personal safety than they were now? Any one of the three—any one of five hundred slaves, twenty-five of whom roamed the house at will—could have easily killed us in our beds, or poisoned us as we praised the excellence of their cooking, or burned the house down on our heads. I had never thought of Negroes as being a menace to my safety, even though we occasionally had heard of slave uprisings throughout the South. But they had seemed so remote from our own tranquillity. Now I wasn't so sure, and it was this lack of sureness that caused fear and confusion.

"Victoria!" Mother's voice was unusually sharp. "I asked you for another sherry. Please pay attention!"

"I'm sorry, Mother." I glanced at Charlotte as I stepped past. She, too, seemed worried and afraid. Certainly she was thinking about Banneker freed by proclamation, raised to a position equaling hers. How, then, would he react to the fact that the daughter of the master of the manor was also a Peeping Tom? If she was not thinking such thoughts, then I certainly was. And I ventured a question as I served Mother. "Are we in danger, Mother?"

She seemed calmer, but her tone was still sharper than I cared for. "Don't be foolish, Victoria. The hardest thing in the world is to remain sensible. Robert will have another sherry. Won't you, Robert?"

His tension also seemed to have lessened. And he bowed slightly. "I'd be happy to, Mrs. Parkchester. I'll serve myself, with your permission."

"Let Victoria do it," Mother said. "I'll have another one, too, dear." And she handed me her glass. Her cheeks were flushed now; mine were burning. Was she deliberately trying to humiliate me in front of Robert Gilliam? Or had a veil been taken away from my eyes so that I was seeing my mother clearly for the first time? Whichever the case, I was fuming. But another part of me was icy calm now. And even when Charlotte asked for wine, I smiled, poured, and served. It was a rare experience, being nigra to Mother, Charlotte, and Robert Gilliam.

But underneath it all was a sobering and burning question: If I reacted this way to requests for sherry, how did Negroes really feel when they washed, ironed, cooked, cut wood, hauled logs, bent over *our* crops . . . did a thousand and one things under orders from people who owned them, as though they were so much baggage? How did *they* feel? And, further, if my resentment could be so fierce in the sitting room at Fir Crest, what manner of devilment were slaves like Banneker and his kind brewing in their evil-looking cabins?

"It is a historical fact," Mother was saying somewhat pedantically, "that slaves launched into freedom make a mess of their bewilderment. If such a proclamation is issued, things will continue in the South largely as before."

She sounded arch, almost gloating. I felt compelled to speak. "It is also a fact of history, Mother, or so you have taught me, that the first shall be last, and the last shall be first."

She waved her hand somewhat dreamily. "That's in the Bible, dear. And while it may be Holy Writ, it is not generally accepted as history." Her eyes seemed brighter than I had ever seen them; her color was high, as though she had just come in from the snow.

"Mother, what is this all about?" Charlotte cried. "Will the slaves be freed? Will we then be in danger?"

But Robert answered before Mother could. "I foresee great danger. Your father does, too. It was he who asked me to come and tell you."

Mother handed me her glass. As hard as it was for me to believe, she was getting drunk. "You've seen my husband?" she said. "How is he? When will he be home?"

"He's fine," Robert said. Apparently he too did not want Mother to know that Father was wounded. "As for when he'll be home, I suppose when the war is over."

"The war," Charlotte said bitterly. "I am sick of the war!"

"We all are, dear," Mother said. "Victoria, my wine?"

Perhaps my response to her had been years in the making. Perhaps it was a result of the day itself, unique in my life, where values one had come to believe in and depend upon had suddenly seemed to turn topsy-turvy. I did not answer her, nor did I serve the wine. Instead, I went to the velvet cord and pulled it violently. Benign appeared at once. Most likely, she had been listening at the door.

"Yas'm, Miss Victoria?"

"Summon the house servants, Benign. And be quick about it."

"All of them, Miss Victoria?"

"All of them, Benign."

Mother stood, somewhat shakily. "I think I shall retire to my rooms," she said. But it was clear that she wanted to see what I was about. Charlotte's face was flushed with excitement. Robert Gilliam regarded me with a bemused smile, rubbing the dark slant of his chin.

In groups of twos and threes, the house servants came piling in. There were a good two dozen of them, who attended to every aspect of life in the mansion. Usually invisible, they were subject to the will and ways of Benign, who had taken it upon herself, her son Johnny Cake, and Juniper, to care for our most intimate needs, certainly at a great sacrifice to the three of them, in order to enhance her power and position at Fir Crest.

Nobody spoke until the servants were assembled. "They's here, Miss Victoria." I looked at their faces— black, tan, *café au lait;* their uniforms; the humble droop to their lips; the slack in their backs. And suddenly I was immensely ashamed. But I was also furious at Mother, and it seemed proper to show her so, since my own meager weapons were no match for her stunning wit and beauty. "I simply wanted Mother to know," I said in a loud, clear voice, "who the servants are at Fir Crest. Benign, my mother would like more sherry. Please serve her. And you may dismiss the others."

"Yas'm, Miss Victoria." Her broad features were perplexed; but it was not difficult to see that she was also pleased. "Y'all go on back about your business," she ordered the others. And they shuffled out. Benign served sherry. "As for me," I said, "I feel the need for fresh air. I think I shall go to the porch. Will you join me, Robert?"

"I'd be happy to, Victoria." He bowed to Mother. "A genuine pleasure, Mrs. Parkchester. I shall tell your husband that I saw you, and that all is well."

"Indeed," Mother said bitterly. She whirled away in a flurry of sequins and blue-smoke, and glided with the utmost grace to the staircase. "Charlotte, I would like to talk with you," she said pointedly. "Victoria, I shall talk to you later. Robert, may God go with you and keep you safe. I have no message for my husband that he does not already know about." With Charlotte behind her, she ascended the stairs. Every line of her body was rigid with anger. For a moment I felt sorry for her, even sorrier for Charlotte.

Benign brought my light cloak and wrapped it around me. "Hussy!" she said in a sharp, pleased whisper, followed by that dark molasses chuckle of hers. *I* a hussy? It pleased me that Benign thought so. Certainly she'd been listening outside the door to Mother ordering me about. As a matter of fact, after seeing the servants assembled, I was concerned now that they were so numerous, and they were everywhere in the large house. But silently so, like little forest people from fairy tales. Almost completely invisible, yet capable of taking off your head at a single stroke.

And now, Benign—titular head of the "little" black people—was chuckling about my being a "hussy." Certainly her description was overly enthusiastic, although I had managed to sink two *grandes dames* in full sail on the same day. First of all, I considered myself too young, at nineteen, to be a full-fledged hussy. Second, I was too timid to try. Although I did feel somewhat pert and saucy after the way I'd treated Mother. Or was it because of her treatment of me? Watching Benign as she served Robert Gilliam another sherry, I was far more concerned about the safety of us all. For the first time, I saw the possibility of our servants as being a real and deadly threat. At Fir Crest, there were some five hundred Negros to five white people. How many times had I seen the youngest Negro dismember a tobacco plant with the sharp, curved knife at cutting time, and then split it down the middle? From now on, I was resolved to pay far closer attention to them.

"Did you tell Grandmother that Robert was here?" I asked Benign.

"Yas'm. She sends her regrets. She's got a headache, she says." Her voice was as dry as toast. Smiling, Robert took my arm, and we went to the porch.

The night air was perfumed with all the sweet scents of May. "It's a very pleasant night," Robert said in his lazy drawl. He sounded very amused.

"It's an awful night," I said. "I made a perfect fool of myself. Robert, will you forgive me?"

We were standing near the long table, at opposite ends. "You have nothing to apologize to me for. It is the servants whose forgiveness you should ask."

"The *servants*, Robert? What on earth for?"

"For making them look like a bunch of damned fools. For involving them in a stupid quarrel between you and your mother. I've never known you to be cruel before, Victoria."

I felt on the verge of tears. Now he was belittling me. No matter how improperly I had acted, chastising was the last thing in the world I needed from him.

"Robert . . . ?" I was going to tell him how jealous I'd felt watching him and Mother together, he so intense, she so casually sophisticated that I had felt like a gawking country girl in plaid gingham. Possibly I was going to tell Robert Gilliam that I loved him. Possibly he might have said that he loved me, too.

But before I could do more than call his name, I was startled by the abject figure of a Negro male sitting in the shadows away from the light. "Who is it?" I said sharply, for the powerful outline of the bent shoulder, the bowed head, frightened me. Robert Gilliam straightened, ready to do battle if necessary, for he had turned and was also looking at the man.

"Just me, Miss Victoria." The man rose. "Banneker. I heard Mistuh Robert was home. I come to see him."

Suddenly laughing, Robert bounded across the porch. "Banneker, you devil! How are you?" Standing in the half-light, the two of them embraced like brothers. And I recalled that in those days when we had been children winding our way down green paths, splashing in silver streams, sitting for hours to catch a mess of catfish, it had been Banneker who attended us in every way.

"I'se fine, Mistuh Robert. You got right stout."

Robert laughed. "You got right stout yourself, Banneker. It *is* good to see you!" He slapped Banneker strongly on the shoulder. "Listen, Banneker, you come to the house tomorrow, you hear? We'll talk about old times. We'll get drunk and raise hell, just like before."

"Yassir, Mistuh Robert," Banneker said. But it was clear, from a certain evasiveness in his voice, that the "old times" held less charm for him than they did for Robert and me. And I was certain that he would not go to see Robert tomorrow.

"Is we free yet, Mistuh Robert?"

"Free, Banneker?"

"Yassir. There's been talk. You know how niggers talk. Everybody say Mistuh Lincoln done freed the slaves."

"There has been talk that he will do so, Banneker. But the South does not recognize Mr. Lincoln's authority. Only

Mr. Parkchester can free you. Or, in his absence, his wife or mother."

"Yassir, Mistuh Robert." In his simple gray shirt and pants, barefoot, he seemed utterly defeated. Yet, he managed to flash me a wry grin. "Emerald say thank you very much for the cherry blossoms, Miss Victoria."

"She's welcome, I'm sure, Banneker."

Without another word, he disappeared into the darkness like a silent black cat.

"Damn!" Robert said through his teeth. He went to the table and gulped down his sherry, and mine as well. "Damn! And double damn! All this talk of freedom is very dangerous. It gives the Negroes ideas they have never had before. Which is clearly Mr. Lincoln's motive. He would free the slaves; then he would have them murder us all." He strode the length of the porch, hands jammed into his back pockets, forehead furrowed in thought.

It seemed a rare time to defend Mr. Lincoln's motives, but I made bold to do so. "From what I hear of the president, he is a kind and thoughtful man. Would he really perpetrate mass slaughter in the name of justice?"

Robert stopped pacing. "I don't know. I really don't know. War makes men do strange things. . . . I've done strange things myself." When he gazed at me, his eyes were full of naked desire. "It is you I am worried about, Victoria. If anything ever were to happen to you, I think I'd die. . . ."

Suddenly we were in each other's arms, mouths hungrily searching each other's. His strong arms crushed me against the solid hardness of his body. My heart leaped up like a bird startled from a long nesting, and seemed to take rapid wing in my breast. "I love you, Victoria," he said. "I've always loved you, even when we were children. I've only been waiting impatiently for you to grow." He rained kisses on my face, my neck, the tip of my nose. "Do you love me, Victoria?"

"Yes, Robert! Yes!"

"Thank God," he whispered. "You are so beautiful. I pray I shall be worthy of your love."

"And I of yours, Robert." With his arms around me, I felt more secure than ever before.

"We will be married as soon as the war is over," Robert said.

"May it end tomorrow, Robert. And may it end with justice for all men."

"You are so wonderful. Even when I had to bait your hook for catfish, despising it as I do, even then I loved you."

I felt that I might swoon. Benign had called me hussy; and it was in response to boiling, brazen hussy's blood that I sought his lips, the cherry-red warmth, the delicate yet manly sweetness; and the two of us seemed to blend into one.

"I must go now," he said. "I shall see you tomorrow?"

"Tomorrow you're seeing Banneker," I said with a smile.

Robert shook his head. "You know damned well he is not coming. Will you come to our place, so that we can be alone?" He smiled. "It is the perfect place to be alone. There are only a few slaves, a few overseers. How I hated it as a child!" Again he pressed himself hard against me. "Will you come tomorrow, Victoria?"

"I shall come, Robert. After the noon meal."

We kissed again, this time with less passion. But the newly lighted fires were still burning in me. And my heart was singing like the song of a thousand thrushes. Robert Gilliam loved me! I could not believe, yet I could never doubt. My love for him threatened to overwhelm me, urging my heart on to higher and higher cadences in the same way that a master puts whip to the mare.

I walked with Robert to the kitchen yard, where he had tied his mount. It was a beautiful chestnut stallion, certainly one of Judge Gilliam's own. Robert and I embraced briefly, and then he hooked a boot in the stirrup and settled his lean body into the saddle. The night was alive with sweetness and moonlight, as though perfumed ghosts walked. Robert bent and kissed me again. My lips were hungry, pleading for his. Could I not mount up with him and ride away forever? But first, there was the war to have done with. Now, like Charlotte, I also hated the war.

"Tomorrow, Victoria."

"Tomorrow, Robert."

He caught the reins and urged the stallion from the grassy yard into the moonstruck road, where it took off at a gallop. Once Robert lifted his arm and waved in the moonlight. I waved back. The light was on in the kitchen, but I did not want to confront Benign's knowing eyes. I went around the house and entered from the front porch. The sitting room was empty. Charlotte had gone upstairs with Mother. And Mother had said that she would "talk to me," certainly about my impertinence. In my present mood, she had chosen a delicate subject to condemn me for. With the heat and flavor of Robert Gilliam's lips still on mine, I was feeling most impertinent indeed.

But when I got to the second floor, Charlotte was waiting for me outside of Mother's sitting room. "Victoria!" her whisper was like the sharp hiss of a snake. She put a finger to her lips, warning me to be silent. I was of a mind to sing, to laugh and dance, to storm the corridors of Fir Crest in a delirium of love. But I allowed myself to be guided by Charlotte's caution. "What is wrong?" I said.

"It is Mother. I cannot awaken her." She was whispering because Grandmother Parkchester's rooms were down the hall.

Suddenly, all my ecstasy disappeared. "Is she ill?" I opened the door to the sitting room, and saw Mother sprawled loosely on the fine brocaded quilt of her four-poster bed. "Quick! Run for Benign! Hurry, Charlotte!" Heels clattering, she rushed down the hallway.

I went to Mother's bed. As soon as I looked at her, I knew that she was not dead. She was drunk. It was possible to smell the alcohol from five feet away.

My first reaction was one of shock and disbelief. Mother a drunkard. This was the kind of thing people whispered about on other plantations. When some gentleman apologized too frequently to his guests, that "I'm afraid my wife is not feeling well today," it became apparent that another southern woman had fallen victim to isolation, boredom, frustration with a system that placed women on pedestals, like so many lovely tombstones lined in a row, and left them stranded upon the pure foundations, to die with a wan smile and a breath polluted with liquor.

Or wine, as was my mother's case. Perhaps I had been too fascinated with her, too blinded by her charms, ever to have suspected that she was shot through with the corruption of drink. But certainly others knew—Father, Grandmother Parkchester. And Benign. Always Benign, her tremendous bulk housing secrets like the finest library, every pore of her black body filled with the making of yet another book. . . .

I heard footsteps in the hallway, and I flew to the door and bolted it. Certainly there was no need for Charlotte's image of Mother, discovered only that very day, to be destroyed. I took an atomizer from an assortment of bottles and sprayed the room with lavender. Mother was completely unconscious, breathing profoundly. Yet, even in her present condition, she seemed absolutely beautiful. And as Benign's authoritative knock rattled the door, I wondered how many times Mother had been drunk like this before without my ever knowing it.

"Miss Victoria, you open this door! What ails Miss Patricia?"

I stood very close to the door. "She has an upset stomach, Benign. Nothing more. She doesn't want to be disturbed."

There was a heavy silence. *Of course she knows.* "All right, Miss Victoria. But if you want to give her something for her stomach, look in the high closet over the canopy of the bed."

It was a closet I had noticed before but had never explored. Not that Mother had forbidden it. Such a small space, it hardly seemed worth the effort. "Thank you, Benign. You may go now."

"Victoria." It was Charlotte. "Are you sure Mother is all right?"

"She's fine, Charlotte. She's sleeping now. And she'll be perfect tomorrow morning. You go to bed now. I'll sit with Mother."

"All right, Victoria. Good night."

"Good night." I waited until their footsteps disappeared. Then I pulled a cushioned chair to the small closet over the canopy and opened it. There were at least two dozen sherry bottles, perhaps half unopened, the other half empty. Mother was indeed a drunkard. As I climbed down, I had the sensation one receives when, biting into an apple, a wormhole is discovered in what had appeared to be perfection.

While my awareness of drinking women was by no means complete, Mother seemed to be effectively *hors de combat* for the night. I took off her slippers and covered her with a thin blanket. Then I left the room. The clock in the hallway was softly striking eleven. Such a long day. Yet, with events piling up as they had been doing, one could expect anything to happen in the hour that remained. I decided to go to the kitchen, where Benign was certain to be waiting.

She said nothing when I entered. But she set a cup of sweetened strong coffee in front of me. And as I sipped from the silver spoon, she stood over me, waiting for the inevitable question.

"How long has Mother been ill, Benign?"

"Ever since she come here."

"Does Father know?"

She did not answer, which meant that he did.

"And Grandmother Parkchester?"

Benign laughed unpleasantly. "Your grandmother a whole lot sicker than your mother, honey. I'm the one that carries their medicine bottles away."

Grandmother as well? It seemed unbelievable. I sat in stunned silence, stirring my coffee. How could I have been so unseeing, so unaware?

"We must make sure Charlotte never finds out, Benign."

"Yas'm. I figger a person's sickness is her own business."

We were talking about drinking, but to refer to it openly would have been gossip of the worst sort. As long as we maintained the facade of talking about "ailments," the code of conduct between oneself and one's servants would remain intact.

"We shall have to send for the doctor tomorrow, Benign."

"Yas'm. Except I expects your mammy'll feel a whole lot better by then."

I shoved away the coffee and rose to leave. "Is Grandmother ailing tonight too? Is that why she didn't come to see Mr. Robert?"

"I suspect so, Miss Victoria. Why don't you go to bed, honey? Don't worry your pretty head. Your mammy, Miss Parkchester too, they going to be fine."

"Thank you, Benign. Good night." She knew everything. I wondered if she knew that Robert Gilliam and I had declared our love for each other tonight. "I'm riding over to Mr. Gilliam's tomorrow, Benign. Will you fix a basket?

And have Amos saddle my horse? I'll leave before breakfast."

"Before breakfast, missy?"

"Yes, Benign." Although I had told Robert that I would be there later, I could not contemplate seeing Mother and Grandmother Parkchester fighting to control their hangovers, being elegant and genteel as their every nerve end was screaming for a drink of "medicine."

"That Mistuh Robert, he sure grow into a fine man. He sure would make some young woman a fine husband."

"He would indeed, Benign. Good night."

"Good night, missy." Her throaty chuckle was especially annoying. Was there nothing that went on that she didn't know?

I thought longingly about Robert before I dropped off to sleep. And I dreamed that he was making tender love to me in a field of green, with buttercups pressed to my breasts. There was the delirious sound of robins in the air. The sun was overwarm, frighteningly so. And Robert's face, as it ground into mine, seemed the dark face of a devil. . . . I struck out deliberately, frantically. . . .

"Missy, you done nearly knocked your coffee off the tray."

Benign set the tray down and bustled over to draw the draperies. The room immediately exploded with sunshine. "How you feeling this morning, missy?" It was comforting to see Benign with her broad smile. She served me a buttered biscuit and the cup of hot coffee. I sat up while she plumped the pillows behind my back. "Have you seen Mother this morning?" I asked. Benign nodded. "I seen her. She's fine, eating a big breakfast. Miss Charlotte, she still sleeping."

Yesterday had undoubtedly been the longest day of my life. And the most exciting. I practically wolfed down the light nourishment, for I knew that Robert Gilliam was waiting for me at his place. And that he would want to make love to me. And I would let him. It seemed a brazen, pleasant thought. But with two secret drunks in the family, was there not room for an open slut?

"Benign?"

"Yas'm."

"Would you dislike me if I let Robert Gilliam make love to me?"

She looked at me shrewdly, almost sorrowfully. "Would you dislike yourself, missy?"

"I would not."

"Then I wouldn't dislike you either, missy."

"Is the basket ready, Benign?"

She looked somewhat displeased. "Yas'm. The horse is ready, too. You the only one not ready."

Under her supervision, the pickaninnies were already filling the porcelain tub with hot and cold water. While I bathed, Benign laid out my riding outfit. And I sat before the mirror in a pale blue chemise while she combed and brushed my hair.

"Benign?"

"Yes, missy?"

"There is talk of Mr. Lincoln freeing the slaves. Although such a thing would clearly be illegal. But . . . suppose it were legal? Would you leave us?"

"No, missy."

She rested her hand on my shoulder, and I kissed it gratefully. "Thank you, Benign. I've been so afraid since last night."

"I seen that Banneker sneaking around. He talked to Mistuh Robert. I'm definitely going to talk to Yetta about him."

But I was too excited now to get involved in a lengthy discussion about freedom, or slaves, or Banneker in particular. Robert Gilliam was waiting for me. And it would be my first time leaving Fir Crest alone. But what if Benign had arranged an escort? And suppose Grandmother Parkchester saw me, and forbade me to go alone?

"Benign, where is Grandmother?"

Again that dark, knowing chuckle. "She ailing this morning. She in her room. She sent instructions to Mr. McAdoo." The chuckle came deeper this time. "I'm afraid he ailing, too."

"Benign, I am going to meet Robert Gilliam. I want to go alone."

"Just the way I figgered, Miss Victoria. I had Juniper and some of the men ride the trail this morning. There ain't a thing to be worried about, missy."

I jumped up and kissed her. "Thank you, Benign! Thank you!"

"Just don't get in no trouble, you hear? Your grandmammy would skin me alive if anything happened to you."

There had been talk of marauders—deserters and roustabouts from both sides—roaming the South to rob, rape, and sometimes murder. But the armies of Grant could not have kept me from Robert that morning. Besides, if Robert had thought there was danger, would he have asked me to come?

I dressed quickly, pulling on a yellow blouse, a cream-colored riding skirt, and soft brown boots. Benign tied a yellow ribbon around my hair, letting it hang down my back. "You mighty pretty this morning, missy." I twirled in front of the mirror. "Do you think so, Benign? Will Robert think so?"

She jammed a riding hat on my head. "If he don't, I'll take a switch to him."

I fairly crept past Charlotte's and Mother's rooms, downstairs, through the sitting room to the kitchen, where Sally, my chestnut mare, was tugging at grass in the yard. Juniper was holding her. "Morning, Miss Victoria," he said with a broad grin. Amos, the stable hand, was with him, and he helped me to mount. There was a wicker basket strapped behind the sidesaddle. Benign stood on the back porch, smiling. "You take care of yourself, child. You hear?"

"Yes, Benign. Thank you, Juniper, Amos." I dug the spurs lightly into Sally, and she took off at a grand gallop. I felt free as the wind, leaving Fir Crest for the first time alone, nineteen years old, going to meet Robert Gilliam.

Slaves in the fields stood and waved at me as I rode past. I made out Mr. McAdoo, who had apparently recovered. And the unmistakable figure of Banneker, who did not wave. The corn was tall and green; the wheat seemed like a field of burnished gold. Everywhere, Negroes bent to their tasks. I could not imagine Fir Crest being the same without them. Riding past the orchard, I was struck again by the sweet blending of blossom perfume. And the hayfields were alive with golden splotches of daisies, the delicacy of lady's slippers, the tall orange smiles of sunflowers moving gently from side to side in a gentle breeze.

In no time at all I had entered the woods, following the winding path between columns of maples and oaks, quiet as any cathedral except for the chatter of birds, the humming of bees. Occasionally a squirrel or an opossum scurried across my path, darting to refuge up a tree. And then the woods ended, and in front of me was pastureland where hundreds of cattle grazed lazily. Beyond them was the rise known as Fir Crest; and Sally began the climb with a steady gait. The path narrows as you near the top of the hill. First, there is an abutment of slate rocks, some of them as sharp as razors studded at crazy angles into the red earth. Then the firs set in, lining the road in unalterable dignity, perfuming the air with pine, following the road's rise and then its fall to Judge Gilliam's land on the other side.

At the topmost point, I reined Sally to a halt, for she was breathing hard. Behind me, through the tunnel of firs, I could see the sprawling splendor of Fir Crest, its stables, barns, storage houses, the patchwork of fields and crops, the neat order of its trees and lanes. Even the long gray slave cabins seemed appealing. The mansion stood in the middle of all this, gleaming like a white vision in the early sunlight.

Ahead lay the Gilliam farm. It was more modest than ours in every respect. The main house was a tall brick structure with white wood trimmings. And the creek that ran through their meadowland was a continuation of the one that flowed through ours. Still, there was the same neat order that was visible at Fir Crest. The Gilliams had less land and fewer slaves, but Judge Gilliam was a staunch believer in comfort and profit. From the promontory of Fir Crest, the Gilliam place looked both comfortable and profitable. Sally's breathing had quieted. I gave her the spurs gently. She began the descent on careful, delicate feet.

As we neared the bottom, I saw a rider approaching, and my heartbeat quickened. For it was Robert Gilliam, coming at full gallop. I reined Sally to a halt and waited for him. My entire body was heated. And when he pulled up on his prancing stallion, I thought he was the most handsome man I had ever seen. "Good morning," he said, grinning. "When the outriders came this morning, I figured you'd be coming earlier. So I've been waiting." He maneuvered his horse close to mine so that we could kiss. His hands held my shoulders in a solid grip. "I've got some wine cooling in the creek," he said.

"And Benign has fixed a basket for us," I said.

He smiled broadly. "Shall we go, then?"

"We shall."

He led the way. We skirted the edge of a watermelon patch, following a narrow trail until the land sloped past honeysuckle, with its cloying odor, until we heard the roaring of the creek in its shallow bed. Once there, we rode the left bank until we were in woods again. Great oaks and maples stood with solemn dignity, gray and somber on one side, bright yellow on the other, where the sun painted them. We came to a place where grass and moss blended in a perfect blanket by the water's edge. Robert dismounted and helped me down. As he tethered the horses, I wandered to the creek's edge, where I saw two bottles of wine standing side by side in the cold water. Suddenly Robert was behind me, his hands on my shoulders, turning me to face him. "You're lovely," he said. As he kissed me, his lips turned hard, almost brutal, against mine. Then they regained their tender sweetness.

When we were children, we had come to this spot to frolic in the creek, to chase each other shrieking around and around the great trees. In summer such as this, it was a cool, quiet sanctuary from the rigorous sun. In fall, it was like a place where large piles of flaming-colored leaves fell to die; and we would wrap our arms about each other and roll back and forth through them, or fling armfuls at each other. Or isolate a pile and set them carefully afire, getting red-eyed and slightly drunk in their pungent smoke. In winter, we had come here on sleighs pulled by horses with bells tied to their harnesses. And in spring it had been here that that we'd watched, with the intensity of young scientists, how the buds turned to leaves, the old trees seeming to grumble back to life as sun and sap warmed them, turning their bark and branches green, and brown, and a kind of antique gray.

As Robert and I held hands now in the towering woods, I knew that he was remembering, too. He was wearing black riding breeches, a red-and-white-plaid shirt, and black boots. "Wherever I was in the war," he said quietly, "I prayed God that I would survive to be here with you like this one day." Then his mood changed like lightning, and he was laughing, pulling me to the creek.

"Robert, don't you dare throw me in!" I cried. But I

was much relieved when, at the edge of the mossy bank, he freed my hand, knelt, and came up with a dripping bottle of white wine.

"I'm thirsty, and I'm starving," he said. "Let's see what Benign sent."

There was a picnic cloth in the basket, which we spread under our favorite oak, where the moss was thick and spongy underfoot. Benign had packed chicken, ham, biscuits, apples, and a quart jar of her own very special elderberry wine. While Robert went to put that in the creek, I prepared sandwiches. He came back and dived into the food. "How do you feel?" he said, his mouth full of ham and biscuits.

"I feel wonderful," I said. There were three crystal wine glasses in the basket—Benign always sent along a spare— and he poured each of them full of the sparkling white wine. "Whoever finishes first gets the third one," he said. And he downed his in one gulp before I'd had a chance to even taste mine. "Well, that's settled," he said, crossing his long legs like a Buddha. "Now, to more serious matters. How do you think I feel?"

"Hungry," I said, laughing.

He slapped his lean belly. "Famished." I watched him fondly as he put away most of the ham and chicken, eating vigorously, washing it down with wine. I had a sandwich and a piece of fruit. My appetite was nowhere near as robust as his. Indeed, watching him as he ate was enough to fill me with pleasure.

The woods were calm, beautiful. Occasionally, skirting through the treetops went a flash of red or blue as a cardinal or a jay flew overhead. And the sun seemed to smile on·us, falling in yellow patches like large polka dots on the green-covered earth. When Robert was finished eating, he went again to the creek. Stretching flat on his belly, he dipped his head to the water and drank. It was an action I had seen him do dozens of times. But as I watched him then, I felt a powerful excitement take possession of me. And when he stood, facing me, and said softly, "Let's get naked. Let's go in the creek," it was as though time had fallen away, and we were children again about to play in the cold, gurgling water.

He had already pulled off his boots and socks. Then he took off his shirt, pants, and underwear, standing completely nude. He had a fine, lean body, nearly the color of bronze, as though he spent all his time naked in the sun. "You're still dressed," he said to me, which was not exactly true, since I was without hat or ribbon. I fought with a sense of shame until it was replaced by wanton desire. He strode to help me. His chest was broad and flat, his waist trim. The hair in his groin was curly black. His manhood swung massively as he walked toward me.

With his help, I was soon undressed. I felt pure, free. Standing belly to belly, we kissed lingeringly. His hands stroked my shoulders, my back. His body seemed on fire. The great swell of his manhood probed against me like an inquisitive hammer. Gently he carried me backward to the moss, which felt like an inviting cushion. "Robert . . . Robert . . . Robert . . ." It was all I could whisper. His hands, mouth, eyes, intoxicated me. I was his to do with as he pleased.

His hands seemed to crush my breasts. Our teeth clashed like tiny swords as we kissed, giving way to sudden tenderness and a sweetness heated by passion. Then his lips were everywhere—on my neck, breasts, navel. And even lower. I experienced pleasure as never before.

As though moving in a dream, I fondled the silk hardness of his organ. It was enormous. I wondered if I would be able to bear it. And then, even that thought was gone, like a leaf taken up by a violent wind. For my body was racked by spasms almost unbearably sweet. I heard myself moaning. My thighs were churning. . . .

Then he was on top of me, the sensation of his weight almost impossible to support. His mouth covered mine; and, at the same time, I felt his muscles tense, like the meshing of a perfect machine. My arms went around his shoulders. Straining, I managed to lift my hips slightly from the ground. He lunged powerfully, and entered me. I felt a searing sensation of pain; and, if I screamed, he took it with his mouth and mingled my cry with his.

Now his body was moving in slow gyrations, his thick arms around me, crushing my breasts to his chest, holding me in a tight vise. Automatically, my body moved with his. Our bellies slapped together like pleasant applause. It seemed that the world spun inside my head. My body was being carried higher, higher, as though to the greatest height. And then, in a moment of unimaginable ecstasy, it came sliding down again, like a sled careening down a path of fiery ice. Again his mouth drank my cries, my moans. My nails dug into his back. His body turned unbelievably rigid, and then became flesh again.

We lay quietly awhile. He had relieved me of his weight by resting on his elbows. His organ was still draining inside me. Then he said, "Let's go to the creek." But I was too exhausted to move. Laughing, he picked me up. Lips locked to mine, he walked to the creek and into the water. Like a mother bathing her child, he eased me by degrees into the cold water. Almost immediately, what pain there was disappeared. Now his manhood was wrinkled and withdrawn, like a piece of shriveled tubing. We bathed quickly, and then dashed, shivering, to a place in the sun, where we lay side by side to dry.

He held my hand, gazing deeply into my eyes. "Are you sorry?" he said. "Nice girls don't do things like that before marriage."

"Perhaps nice girls should. Perhaps I am not a nice girl. At any rate, I don't feel sorry. Do you?"

He laughed. "Hell no. I feel wonderful."

"So do I."

"I love you, Victoria. God help me, I love you."

And there in the sun, we made love again. And again to the creek. Then to another spot where the roving sun could dry us. It was early afternoon when we finally drank some of Benign's elderberry wine. Then we dressed. "Ride with me to Fir Crest," I said. "Have supper with us."

"It will be a pleasure," he said.

We mounted up and rode from the woods. I felt . . . liberated. It is the only word I can think to use. Robert had spoken of "nice" girls. I cared not a fig about whether I was nice or not. Benign had called me, playfully, a hussy. Perhaps I was that, too. But as I rode behind Robert Gilliam, watching the sway of his back, the lean tightness of his buttocks in the saddle, I felt preeminently woman.

As I had known, he would carry me into that world as he had led me through the caverns of childhood. I could still feel the surging power of his manhood inside me, and that made me feel more completely woman than all else. We had enjoyed each other's bodies. Come what may, we were one, undeniably united. The ceremony of marriage, when it happened, would be only another ritual in a life of rituals that were primarily meaningless. . . .

Suddenly Robert pulled his stallion to a halt. And I rode to him and stopped. We were near the watermelon patch again, and the crisp green odor of the melons, those dark green lumps secretly ripening, spotting the field, smelled like the cutting of new grass. "Somebody's coming yonder," Robert said, shading his eyes.

I looked, too, and saw a Negro riding a white mare hard. "It's Banneker," I said, for I could never mistake him in the saddle. "After all," I said with a smile, "you did invite him over."

Robert grinned. "I did indeed. Let's go meet him." We spurred our horses and met him at the end of the watermelon field. But I knew at once, looking at his sweat-stained face, that something dreadful had happened at Fir Crest. "What is it, Banneker? What has happened?"

He was practically out of breath. "Them raiders, Miss Victoria. About thirty of them. They doing terrible things to Miss Patricia, to Miss Parkchester."

Robert took control at once. "What of Charlotte?" he said crisply. Already he had reached into his saddlebag and taken out a pistol.

"Ain't nobody seen Miss Charlotte," he said. "They burned down the fields, too. I managed to sneak away. But they everywhere."

"Go to the house, Banneker. To my house. Ask for Mr. Clarence. Tell him what has happened. Tell him to come to Fir Crest with thirty armed men."

"Yassuh, Mistuh Robert!"

He wheeled his horse about and took off. At first, I was too numb to feel anything. And then, shock and guilt hit me so hard that I nearly fell to the ground. Robert reached out and steadied me. "Easy now. Easy. We've got to get to Fir Crest. Can you make it?"

I nodded, although my whole body felt weak, and I was fighting down a bitter taste in my mouth. "Do you think Charlotte is all right?"

"I can't say. We have to go." He dug his spurs viciously into the stallion. I did the same to my mare. And the two horses whinnied and flew to the bottom of the craggy rise. Even then, we gave them no rest. Spurring, lashing, we finally got them to the top of the crest. And far below us, we could see Fir Crest enveloped in an ominous cloud of dark smoke, punctuated here and there by lusty red flames. "It seems they're burning everything," Robert said through his teeth.

We sped down the hill and into the woods. Then the horses took their head; and in a short while we had left the woods and emerged into the farm area of Fir Crest. There were flames and smoke everywhere. The raiders, whoever they were, had put the torch to the crops. And the vicious odor of kerosene was almost unbearable. We paused only long enough to test the air. It was blowing in a northerly direction, away from us, but bringing the smoke and fumes with it. "Cover your face with your scarf," Robert yelled. I did so. He had already covered his with a red bandanna. We galloped on.

As we neared the mansion, it was possible to see that only certain crops and quite a number of utility buildings had been set afire. But not one slave cabin had been touched. It was impossible to see any pattern to the destruction, as though some angry child with matches and kerosene had capriciously set fire to whatever happened to be in his way. The smoke was bearing down on us in great billows as we made our way to the house.

Despite Robert's pistol, his strength, and his undeniable resolve, I expected at any moment to be set upon by the raiders. But as the smoke parted before us, everything was strangely calm. And there was no one to be seen anywhere. As we passed the orchard, I noticed that two or three trees had been set afire, and were burning with sharp, crackling noises.

My heart leaped with joy when I saw that Fir Crest had been spared. The tall, stately house seemed somewhat soiled and strangely out of place in the dark destruction around it. We clattered into the front yard, and dismounting, dashed to the porch. Before entering the house, I looked around quickly. In the surrounding fields, under covering clouds of smoke, I could see Negroes frantically hacking with broad-bladed knives, throwing buckets of water, fighting the fire. Apparently the raiders had come, had done their dirty work, and had gone.

The sitting room downstairs was empty, but a great commotion from upstairs reached us even as Robert and I crossed the sitting room and bounded up the steps. There was a curious crowd of Negroes at the door to Grandmother Parkchester's room, and we went there first.

Benign was attending Grandmother Parkchester, who was propped in her bed on pillows. Her hair was undone and streamed down her shoulders and into her face like slender red serpents, giving her the singular aspect of a madwoman. From time to time she brushed the strands away, and her large green eyes, wide and unblinking, seemed filled with unforgettable horror. She was muttering something that I could not understand. "Benign, what has happened to Grandmother?"

"She been raped," Benign said bluntly. She was applying cold compresses to Grandmother's face. "I already sent for the doctor. Ain't no more nobody can do for her now." She seemed angry, intent on murder herself. I had never seen her so full of fury, like a heavy black cloud about to burst and bury everything under its violence.

"And Mother? Where's Mother? What happened to her?"

"She probably raped too. Ain't nobody seen her yet. We going there now." Suddenly she planted both hands on her hips and bellowed at the staring servants. "What you niggers looking at now? Get on back to work before I take a stick to every one of you!" They scattered like frightened sheep.

I was frightened of her myself, and I held to Robert's arm for dear life. Even he seemed unsettled. His usual olive-colored face had turned decidedly pale. Certainly both of us were blaming ourselves, perhaps irrationally, for the destruction that had taken place here while we were making love at the Gilliam creek.

Inexplicably, Mother's room was locked from the inside. "Miss Patricia, you all right?" Benign said, banging with a heavy fist. The three of us listened carefully. But not a sound came from the room. Benign stepped aside. "Break it down," she said to Robert. He lunged at the French door, and it gave way with a shattering of wood and glass. He kicked it once, and it swung open completely.

The sitting room was a wreck. It seemed as though a tornado had spent itself inside the four walls. Books, papers, and wine bottles were everywhere. Chairs were overturned. And, on the canopied bed, Mother was lying naked. And perfectly still. Her face was twisted and ugly, eyes staring with almost obscene hatred. Blood had dried on the inside of her thighs. She had, it appeared, been raped to death.

"Lawd! Lawd! Lawd!" Benign wailed, covering her eyes with her apron. Except for Robert's arm supporting me, I certainly would have fainted. "Where's Charlotte?" I cried. But Benign was wailing so loudly, I doubt that she heard. I pulled her hands from her face and slapped her soundly. "Where's Charlotte, do you hear? *Where's Charlotte?*"

"Missy . . . missy . . . I don't know where that child is. All I know is that one minute I'm peeling potatoes for dinner. And the next, some man's pointing a gun in my face, asking for money, food. I ain't seen Miss Charlotte since then." Large tears welled in her eyes and fell to her apron bib, like drops of rain.

While Benign had been talking, Robert had gone to the bed and covered Mother. She was undoubtedly dead, but he felt her pulse before pulling the spread around her.

"We must find Charlotte!" I cried. I was terrified that the raiders might have taken her with them. "Those men, who were they?"

"Just plain trash, Miss Victoria. Neither North or South. Some white, some black. Just trash, out looking to make trouble. They come in here with your mother and your grandmother. They laughing and drinking. They just want to make trouble and have their fun. They only looking for white ladies, they didn't touch one nigger woman. Not one."

And then, in the moment of silence that followed, I heard Charlotte's quivering voice clearly calling me. I spun, looking for the sound. "Charlotte, where are you?"

The underblanket on Mother's bed fell around three sides in a long fringe. As we watched, one side of the fringe moved. And Charlotte crawled out.

"Thank God," Robert whispered fervently.

But all of us were too stunned to move. Charlotte crawled toward us, one arm out in a pleading gesture. Whimpering like a wounded animal, she seemed in a state of the most terrible shock. She wore a green chemise. Her face was pasty white, and her green eyes were wide with fear and revulsion.

I dropped to my knees and wrapped my arms around

her. "Charlotte, dear Charlotte! Did those men do anything to you?"

She shook her head. "No. . . . Only to Mother. Dozens of them, it seemed. We heard them ride up, their laughing and talking. I was with Mother when they came. I wanted to go downstairs, but she made me hide under the bed. I was there all the time. All the time. There were dozens of them, Victoria. *Dozens.* . . ." She had been talking rapidly, hysterically. Now she stopped and threw her hand to her mouth. "Mother's dead, isn't she?" She sounded wistful, on the verge of bitter tears.

"Yes, Charlotte. Mother is dead."

"Those men . . . those men did it. I saw their boots. One after the other. I was underneath the bed all the time. I dared not breathe. . . ."

Benign sailed in to take over. "Give me that poor child, Miss Victoria. I perfectly all right now." She took Charlotte from me as though she were a wounded child. "There, there, honey. Don't you worry about a thing, sugar. Old Benign's back to her senses now. She ain't going to let a thing happen to you."

We left Mother's sitting room. Benign went with Charlotte to her room. I went downstairs with Robert. He helped me to the settee and poured me a glass of sherry, which I drank gratefully. "Are you all right?" he asked with deep concern.

"I'm afraid not, Robert. Somehow, all of this seems quite unreal. I fear that when the full impact hits me, I shall be uncontrollable."

"Benign will take care of you," he said. "I want to get my men and go after those murdering bastards. They can't be too far away."

I jerked up from the settee as though propelled by springs. Irrationally, I began beating him on the chest. "Do that, Robert! Do that! Kill them! *Kill them!*"

He embraced me as tears spurted from my eyes, blinding me in a fit of rage. "My darling," he murmured. "My sweet, sweet darling. This has been a terrible thing." He held me close as I wept bitter tears. And I was full of hatred for whoever it was who had killed my mother in such a vicious and indecent way. But Robert sobered my thoughts of revenge when he said, "We shall catch them and bring them to justice."

"There are more than thirty, Robert. Benign said so. Are such men so easily caught? They are sure to resist."

"Then we shall kill them," Robert said coldly.

So the war, the bloody side of the war, had touched us after all. And two lives were gone senselessly in a single afternoon, one forever, the other locked in the dark shroud of madness. When Robert rode to meet his own men, he went with two-dozen armed Negroes from Fir Crest led by Juniper. It was an eerie sight, watching from the porch as they rode out under the smoke and stench of destruction. It seemed that almost all our crops had been set to the torch, and it was too late to plant again this year. The outbuildings could be reconstructed. And the orchard could be brought to its former state by transplantation.

But what of Mother, so cruelly and grotesquely murdered? And Grandmother Parkchester—would she ever be well again? Tears blinded me as I went back into the house. I did not have the energy to go upstairs and look in on Grandmother, so I remained in the quiet sitting room and marveled again that the mansion had been spared by the murderers.

A door opened, and Benign came in. "Is you all right, missy?"

"Yes, Benign. How is Charlotte?"

"I give her something to make her sleep. And I done sent for the doctor. Miss Charlotte, she young and strong. She going to be just fine."

"How did it happen, Benign?"

"Like I told you, missy, I was in the kitchen when this white man come in. He took me outdoors. There was this other white man, he had a patch over his eye. He wasn't North, he wasn't South. He just trash. Your grandmammy, she's talking to him. She tell him to take anything he want, but not to harm anybody please. He laugh when she say that. His men laugh too. He say, 'Ma'am, we want you. Is you the only white woman around here?' When Miss Parkchester told him she was, that's when he sent some men inside. They find Miss Patricia upstairs. I suppose that's when Miss Patricia make your sister hide under the bed." Her face grew dark, ugly. "They had their fun. They drag your grandmammy upstairs. They leave us outdoors, telling us we ain't got no argument with dumb niggers.

They say they hate white people for what they doing to the country. All them got guns. Some of them go out and start burning everything. Then they come back and have their fun. Every one of them have their fun except for the one on the horse. He say they want white women. White men too. He just ride back and forth in front of us, looking at us with that one eye. His hair was dirty and yellow, like cornsilk with the blight. One after one, them men go in the house and come out again. Them niggers too, there was about four or five of them. Some of them go in two or three times. I was praying for your mother and your grandmother, missy. I reckon God don't hear no prayers from old nigger women. They take all the whiskey and money and jewels they find. They take candlesticks and silverware. Then one of them say, 'We going to burn the house, Cap'n?' And he laugh and say no. 'Where would they live?' he say. 'With the niggers?' Then they ride away, still laughing."

She had been weeping as she talked. I gave her time to collect herself before I asked, "How is Grandmother?"

"I ain't no doctor, missy. But she act to me like she done completely lost her mind."

A deep and dreadful silence descended on us. Mother dead. Father away fighting a feckless war. Grandmother insane. What was to happen to us? "Have you seen Mr. McAdoo, Benign?" He was our remaining white overseer. "Is he well?"

She shook her head sadly. "He dead, Miss Victoria. They do terrible things to him in the barn. Then they nail him to the wall and set the barn on fire."

"Benign!" It was a cry of the deepest despair. "What will become of us? Robert has to go back to the war! What will happen to us?"

I wanted to rush into the familiar comfort of her arms, but she folded them deliberately across her great breasts. "We going to keep on," she said. "I don't expect that kind of attitude from you, Miss Victoria. You old enough to sass your mother, you old enough to have a beau, you old enough to manage Fir Crest."

It was as though she'd slapped me in the face. I had never seen such strength in a woman before. And to think that only last night I had doubted her loyalty! *We* going to keep on. Indeed we would.

"Thank you, Benign. I suppose I've been suffering from shock."

"We all suffering from shock. What you think we feel about all this?"

It was an odd question, harshly put. "I hadn't thought, Benign."

She grunted heavily. "That's what wrong with white folks. They ain't never learned to think." She left me, carrying her massiveness with extreme dignity. I felt a terrible sense of shame. The servants shall become the masters, so the Bible says. With her enormous strength, her sense of duty, Benign was clearly better equipped than I to handle the affairs of Fir Crest. But such an idea was unthinkable, certainly more from her side than mine. I sat in a comfortable chair, trying not to think about the corpse of my mother—when *would* the doctor come to remove it?—and forced my thoughts into a semblance of order.

First of all, my earlier sense of guilt at being with Robert Gilliam when the raid took place was replaced by a consuming anger. Nothing could change the feeling I'd had with Robert by the creek. Certainly my being here would have only given the raiders another white woman to violate, possibly even to kill. I was worried now about Charlotte, and Fir Crest, and myself. And, of course, about Grandmother. As Benign said, we had to keep going. At least until Father came home to take control. Somehow, we would. . . .

I looked up. Benign was handing me a cup of thin, clear broth. "Drink this. When you get finished, you ought to ride out before sunset and see what damage is done. The niggers is waiting to see if any white people worthwhile is left alive here."

"You're right, Benign. Thank you."

Grunting, she went back to the kitchen. She seemed full of grunts that day.

I finished the broth, and then I rang for her. "Please send for my horse, Benign. I would like Amos to accompany me."

"Amos is waiting outside the kitchen with Sally. He been there twenty minutes by the clock." Her eyes were narrowed with clear contempt.

I drew myself up as Mother used to do. "Benign, your attitude displeases me. If you are unhappy in your present position, it can be arranged for you to go to the field. I'm sure there's another cook somewhere in the cabins who might consider insolence a vice rather than a virture."

Her face broke into a broad smile. "Yas'm, Miss Victoria. I likes my position. I likes it fine."

She was a sly black creature. Sometimes I wondered if she were a witch, the way she manipulated me. "We shall try, insofar as possible, to continue as before. When I return, I should like to see your accounts."

"Yas'm. But I know what's there. We got over ten thousand dollars down in the sugar sack."

The sum staggered me. But I tried not to show it. I swept past her, through the kitchen, and out to Amos and the roan.

Amos' face was sorrowful as he helped me mount Sally. But I felt a keen sense of satisfaction seeing that he had brought a rifle with him. There was a well-equipped armory at Fir Crest. But who had the key? I made a mental note to ask Benign.

As Amos and I rode from Fir Crest, we met Dr. William Seymour. A small, sour-faced man, he was also our local undertaker, and drove a hearse drawn by four prancing black horses, in case his patient should conveniently die. In his somber outfit, he resembled a mournful penguin. "Afternoon, Miss Victoria." He tipped his tall hat, peering over the tops of his spectacles. "I understand there's been a terrible tragedy."

"There has indeed, Dr. Seymour. Mother is dead. And Grandmother is quite distracted, or so it appears. We were attacked by raiders."

He made sad, cooing sounds, pursing his thin lips until they almost completely disappeared. "These are tragic times. But I shall take care of everything, Miss Victoria. Don't worry about a thing." He seemed full of quiet joy, which perhaps was quite normal, considering his dual role as doctor and undertaker, keeping all profits to himself by burying those he could not cure. "A terrible pity," he said, looking around.

My eyes were smarting, for there were still a few fires burning, and the air was filled with smoke. "I am going now to see what further damage has been done. Benign will help you at the house. Charlotte also needs attention."

"It will be a pleasure to help in any way I can," he said. "The poor child must be completely overwrought."

"At last report," I said dryly, "she was sleeping comfortably. Good afternoon, doctor."

He touched his hat. "Good afternoon, Miss Victoria." He rippled the reins along the back of his horse and moved out. Amos and I continued up the road.

"Is the damage severe, Amos?"

"It's pretty bad, Miss Victoria. They burned down three stables and four barns. We were lucky, though. All the stock was out grazing. They slaughtered three cows for food. And they took about three dozen chickens. The biggest loss is in the crops. They burned all the tobacco, all the wheat, all the corn. But they didn't touch the gardens. We got plenty to eat."

"Well, that's a blessing, Amos." I was impressed by the agility of his mind, how it encompassed the entire tragedy and fed it to me in manageable form. "I should like you to tell all the servants that we must begin clearing and rebuilding. But it cannot be done without their help. Do you understand, Amos?"

"Yas'm." He was grinning. "Amos sure do understand."

We rode the length and breadth of Fir Crest. And I found that the damage done was substantially as Amos had reported. As the afternoon wore on, we went from one area to another. What impressed me most was the Negroes themselves, how they responded to me. As Benign had said, they were waiting to make sure that one white person remained in authority over them. They greeted me with smiles and singing. Some of them told me how sorry they were about what had happened, making the tragedy very much a part of themselves. Remembering the example of Father, I got down from the horse, talked with them, inspected their cabins, their babies, drank with them from the same dipper. "We must all work together to make Fir Crest as it was before today," I told them. They were all pleased; but some of them, however polite, seemed surprised to find that I had enough gumption to even talk, much less to talk of rebuilding. Whenever in doubt about some action, I glanced at Amos. And he would nod, or shake his head surreptitiously. "You doing just fine, Miss Victoria," he told me once. "You doing just fine."

"Thank you, Amos." I deliberately kept my voice aloof. Benign had taught me that servants neither like nor respect weak mistresses.

By the time I returned to Fir Crest, I was tired, but excited and almost happy. How was it possible that I had ever thought that our servants might betray us? They were as much a part of Fir Crest as we were. It was their home as much as ours. That is what Benign had been trying to tell me.

Benign met me on the porch with a glass of sherry. It was stimulating, although I still felt quite fatigued. The sun was hanging now over the western hills like a malevolent eye. And still Robert and the men had not returned.

"The doctor come and took your mother's body," Benign said. "He say to keep your grandmother locked in her room. I took out everything she could hurt herself with."

It would not do to cry, although I felt like it. "Where is my sister?"

"Still in her room. She sleeping again. He looked at her, too. He say she all right."

"Thank you, Benign. I shall not have supper until Mr. Robert returns." It was too much to bear alone, the fears and doubts I harbored. "Do you think he's all right, Benign? Do you think they're all safe?"

"They's safe. I got Juniper and two sons riding with him. If anything happened to them, I don't care what it was, I'd know. They's all right."

The sun had dropped behind the hills, and twilight fell over Fir Crest like a thin gray veil. I went to my room. The tub was already filled with steaming water. A black gown was laid out for me. Its message was very clear: *This is a time for action, not for sleeping.* But my whole body cried out for sleep. Still, I felt better after I bathed. Benign brushed my hair and helped me dress. Then I went to see Charlotte.

She was awake, although still in bed. She looked pale and ill. Her eyes were swollen from crying. "Victoria," she said, holding out her arms to me. But I recalled Benign's earlier sternness. "We must be strong, Charlotte," I said, standing where I was. "Until Father comes home, there are only you and me. And, most importantly, the servants." But I did not want Charlotte to feel that she had any crutches to lean on, except her own strength. "The servants will look to you for guidance. They do not respect weakness."

Nodding, she fought back tears. "I just can't believe that Mother is dead. And that I saw all those horrible men, their boots. . . ."

I was neither as black nor as strong as Benign. And something in me yielded then. I sat on the bed and wrapped my arms around her. "You must not think about it, Charlotte. You must do your best to go on living. Mother would have wanted that. Grandmother would, too."

Her slight body trembled. "Is . . . is Grandmother insane?"

"I'm afraid so. But she is not dangerous. It is something we must all bear."

"How can you be so strong?" she whispered.

I nearly smiled as I stroked her hair. Strong? With Benign breathing down my neck, I dared be nothing else. Also, it was as though Robert Gilliam had given me a part of his strength that morning. . . .

"I hear horses coming," Charlotte said, tensing. "Lots of them."

"It is probably Robert coming back with the men," I said. But I was less certain than I sounded. It could also be the raiders returning. "You stay here. And lock the door after me."

She did as I instructed. Yet, hearing the lock click, and even in my haste and alarm, I was struck by a series of burning questions: Why had Charlotte locked Mother's sitting-room door—for only she could have done it—and then crawled back underneath the bed after the raiders left? Surely she had heard their departure if she had heard their arrival. Why, then, had she locked herself in a room with a woman who was obviously dead? Was it because of shock, horror, fear? Did she think the raiders would return? In that event, might she not have been safer hidden away with Benign or some of the other Negroes, rather than with the dead?

The questions were confusing, and perhaps of no importance; but they whined in my brain like annoying summer gnats as I rushed downstairs to the sitting room. And saw Robert Gilliam standing by a small blaze in the fireplace.

He looked very tired, and there was blood on his clothes. "Robert! Are you injured?"

"No," he said quietly. "The blood is theirs. We caught them and killed them all. I wanted you to know before I went home."

"The men, ours and yours—are they safe?"

He nodded. "Several injured. But all alive. Banneker fought like a devil, right at my side. He didn't get a scratch."

Vaguely, he passed a hand over his eyes. "Could you spare a poor man a drink of sherry?"

"Of course! How stupid of me!" I poured a drink for him. He sat, sipping it thoughtfully as I rang for Benign. She came almost immediately. "Benign, see to it that the men who went with Mr. Robert are fed. And instruct Juniper to find places for them to stay the night. They are far too exhausted to ride."

"Yas'm. Will you and Mr. Robert be having supper now?"

"In a short while, Benign. First, Mr. Robert will want to bathe. And to rest. Have a fire built in Father's room. And the tub prepared."

"Yas'm."

Robert drank another sherry before he spoke. "You seem to have got hold of yourself. And even in mourning, you look lovely." His face grew sad. "Did the doctor come?"

I told him what had transpired with the doctor. And about the unfortunate death of Mr. McAdoo.

His face turned ashen. "It's small consolation, I'm sure. But those bastards paid dearly. We caught up with them outside Lexington. We buried them in the deepest part of the woods."

"Don't talk about it, Robert." I kissed him on the forehead. "First you must bathe and nourish yourself. Come. I will take you to Father's room."

When we got upstairs, the fire in Father's room was giving off a cheerful warmth, dispelling the chill. It was a grand old room, with heavy draperies, a writing desk, a few books, and a large four-poster bed. One of the male servants was there to attend Robert. I waited until he had filled the tub. Then I sent him away, and helped Robert undress. As I looked at his naked body, my own seemed beset by prickly heat. He looked at me with heavy desire; but it was clear to both of us that we were in a house marked by tragedy, and that now was not the proper time to make love.

While he was bathing, I sent his clothes for Benign to clean and repair. When he stepped steaming from the tub, I wrapped towels around his body and dried him. "Here is Father's robe," I said. "It will be too large for you." But he held the robe a moment, draped over one arm. His body smelled warm and excessively male. And his eyes bored into mine like intense blue bits. "Nice ladies don't bathe gentlemen," he said softly. "At least, not privately. What will the servants say?"

The proprieties of the situation had not occurred to me until then. "The servants probably are already saying that I'm a lost woman. I'm also a very famished one. Are you ready for supper? Or would you like to rest first?"

"Supper," he said, wrapping the robe about him. "As soon as Benign sends my clothes." He sat on the bed with his long arms hanging between his legs. His black hair was tousled, and I restrained an impulse to oil and comb it. "Remarkable," he said absently, "how killing gives a man an appetite."

"Please don't think about the raiders, Robert. It was something that had to be done. Were I a man, I would have fought with you proudly."

"I want to make love to you," he said abruptly. "Killing does that to a man, too. It whets his appetite in every direction."

There were three lamps in the room that cast a soft yellow glow over everything. On the hearth, the fire burned like a large ruby, disintegrating slowly. "I want you to make love to me, Robert. But we must do so with our eyes, our hands, our words. To do otherwise tonight would make me more shameless than I already seem to be."

He nodded with deep understanding. "It was a declaration, not a proposition."

"I understand how you feel. My feelings are the same." I sat beside him on the bed. "When do you return to your post?"

"Tomorrow," he said softly.

I was too stunned to speak. Tomorrow! So this would

be our last night together, certainly for a long time, possibly forever.

"May I kiss you?" he said.

In answer, I kissed him, savoring the sweetness of his lips, but restraining my emotions at the same time. "Come back safely, Robert," I whispered. "I would not know how to go on living without you."

"Nor I you," he said, holding my head to his chest. "You are a lovely, remarkable woman."

"If that is true, it is because you showed me the joy of childhood and the excitement of being a woman."

He laughed shortly. "Those were good days, weren't they? All of this seems like a nightmare without end. I came to warn you of one potential threat. And you have been dreadfully harmed by another."

"The servants at Fir Crest are loyal, Robert. I have no doubts about any of them."

"I pray that you are right," he said. "Those who went with me today behaved as men. Banneker was the bravest." Now he cupped my chin, gazing deeply into my eyes. "Yet, if there is to be trouble, Banneker will be the one to start it. He is like a double-edged sword, both sides energetic in separate but opposite ways. He is a good friend; he could be a deadly enemy. Be careful of him."

"Yes, Robert. I have felt the same about him."

There was a knock at the door. When I responded, Juniper came in with Robert's clothes. Robert stood and laughed. "Juniper fought well today, too. We showed those devils, didn't we, Juniper? Not a single one got away."

Juniper grinned, but he also seemed perplexed. "It was a good fight, Mistuh Robert. But we didn't kill them all."

"What do you mean?" Robert had pulled on his breeches; he paused with a boot in the air.

"The leader got away, Mistuh Robert. I saw him riding away while you was fighting."

"Damn! Are you sure, Juniper?"

"I sure, Mistuh Robert. He that man with the yellow hair, the patch on his eye. He riding a white mare with a black star on her left rump. He got away, all right."

Now Robert's face was full of anger. "Damn it, Juniper! Why didn't you tell me before?"

"There was just so much confusion, Mistuh Robert. I thought you knowed. Everybody else knowed."

Robert sat on the bed, staring angrily into the fire. "It's all right, Juniper. I'm just disappointed, that's all."

"Yassir, Mistuh Robert." He left, shoulders drooping sadly.

"What is the problem, Robert? Is the leader a threat even without his gang?"

"Definitely! He can assemble another gang. He can go on raiding and killing. He might come back here." Grabbing my hands, he pulled me beside him to the bed. "Listen, Victoria. You're in charge of Fir Crest now. Arm three dozen men. Have them on constant patrol, three shifts around the clock. I shall tell Mr. Clarence at my place to do the same. If trouble does come, you will have the large bell in the yard rung. It can be heard damned near to hell. Mr. Clarence and our men will be listening for it day and night. Is that clear?" When I nodded, he pulled my head to his shoulder and stroked my hair. "You're trembling, my darling. Are you afraid?"

"Terribly afraid, Robert. Now I know the true meaning of war. Now I know what you must feel in battle."

He kissed me tenderly, gently. "You are very brave. If anybody can protect Fir Crest, you will."

His confidence gave me renewed energy. "My strength comes from you, Robert. We shall listen for the bell at your place, as your men will be listening for ours."

"Strange," he mused, "how we are in a position where we must trust the slaves, like it or not. There is no alternative. They were brave and loyal today. But who knows how they will be tomorrow? Or when Lincoln issues his damned proclamation?"

"They will remain loyal, Robert. You will see." I felt very firm about that. "Now, let us go to supper. Benign is probably having a fit."

We went down to the dining room. Charlotte was not present. "I sent her up a tray," Benign said. "She eating all right. Miss Parkchester even took a little soup herself."

Our main course was roast lamb. Robert and I, seated at opposite ends of the table, ate shamelessly. And we chatted about silly things, to relieve our minds of the day's tensions, and the fact that tomorrow he would be gone. The meal was delicious. Then we went to the sitting room, where Benign served coffee and sherry. But, all too soon, it was eleven o'clock, and Robert stood, smothering a yawn. "I must sleep," he said. "I must leave before dawn to be at camp on time."

"Of course, Robert." I sounded calm, but my insides had shattered, as though his words were a hammer striking at crystal.

"I shall not see you before I go," he said, offering me his hand.

"Go with God, Robert. And please give our love to Father, and to Judge Gilliam."

We embraced desperately. He kissed me hungrily on my neck, hair, and lips. "I love you, Victoria."

"I love you too, Robert." I fought to keep back the tears, and I succeeded.

He went upstairs. At the first landing, he turned and smiled. I smiled back. Then he continued up the stairs, holding himself very tall.

I sat before the dwindling fire for perhaps twenty minutes. Then I rang for Benign and told her that I was retiring. "Good night, Miss Victoria," she said. She took away the coffee cups and sherry glasses. But before she left the room, she said, "That man of yours going to war. He might never come back if he don't carry with him all the strength you can give him. And you going to be a mess here at Fir Crest if you don't get some strength from somewhere besides me."

"Benign!" My voice was sharp, certainly because of guilt. "What on earth are you suggesting, especially after all that's happened today?"

"Child, you knows what I'm suggesting. The dead bury the dead. The living keep on living." Just then, the clock struck the half-hour. "Besides, today's just about over."

Deliberately I turned my back on her. "Good night, Benign," I said coldly.

"Good night, missy."

I went to my room and undressed. I put on my blue nightgown and climbed into bed. But my head was spinning with a thousand unaccustomed thoughts. Down the hall, in Father's great bedroom, Robert Gilliam was sleeping. But I knew that no sleep would come to me that night.

Again my mind returned to Charlotte hiding under Mother's bed. Tomorrow I would ask her why she had acted so irrationally. And then it seemed that I had answered my own question: she had been afraid; it was natural for her to act as she did. Perhaps I would have responded differently, perhaps not. No, I would not question her. My duty was to help her forget.

 here was Mother's funeral to be arranged. And Grandmother Parkchester to be taken care of. Plus the monumental task of managing Fir Crest, to rebuild even as we protected it against another possible attack. As I tormented my brain, driving it from one area to another, I heard the hallway clock strike the midnight hour.

I felt weak and almost overwhelmed by so many problems. Was it possible that only two days ago I had been a carefree girl sneaking to the slave cabins to spy on Banneker making love? Now, with Mr. McAdoo so dreadfully destroyed, I would have to lean heavily on Banneker, for he was young, strong, and intelligent. To this point, he had proven himself to be supremely loyal. As Robert had said, we had to depend on the slaves for our own survival, like it or not. There was an irony in the thought that could not be overlooked: we had always depended on the slaves for our survival; now the question was whether they wanted to continue surviving with us, or to take up arms against us. . . .

I tossed and turned on the soft mattress. The thin gown seemed to scorch my body everywhere it touched. I left the bed and put on my slippers. Then I went to the door and opened it quietly. The hallway was empty. Yet, it could have been filled with a thousand disapproving eyes. I would have braved their stares—blinded them with hot lead, if need be—to get to Father's room.

Once there, I tried the knob, and it turned easily. Excitement rose in my throat, threatening to choke me. Opening the door carefully, I stepped into the room and locked the door behind me.

The room was pitch dark. I could hear Robert's breathing as I neared the bed. Lifting my gown, I pulled it over my head and stepped from my slippers. My heart thrilled as I heard the soft whisper of a sheet being flung back. Then Robert's hands, hot and tender, reached out and pulled me to him. His body seemed on fire. His mouth sought mine in the darkness; whimpering, I gave a small, anguished cry and melted against him. . . .

When I awakened next morning, he was gone. I was of

course disappointed, but I was calm. I put my gown back on and returned to my room. And when Benign came to serve me coffee, I was ready to bathe and dress, and to take charge of the tasks at hand.

"Mistuh Robert say to tell you goodbye," Benign said. Her stolid face told me nothing.

"Thank you, Benign. Did he have a good breakfast?"

She laughed roundly. "He sure did. He act like he starved to death." Her eyes flicked over mine like the tip of a gentle switch. "I got the same thing fixed for you."

"I shall have breakfast in the garden, Benign. Is Miss Charlotte up?"

She shook her head morosely. "No, ma'am. I going to give her one more day. If she ain't up by then, I going to take a switch to her behind. Ain't no room for weak people at Fir Crest. We got to be strong the best we know how."

"Indeed we must, Benign." And I went downstairs to the east garden, into the gentle sun, the gracious blue morning, the fragrance of dew-sweetened flowers. Already I could see Negroes at work clearing away debris, piling and hauling, wagons coming and going. Some of the Negroes were singing.

I felt supremely strong. And as the days and months progressed, I turned twenty; and my strength seemed to increase, as though I were an embryo growing and receiving nourishment inside the great womb of life itself.

Considering the circumstances of Mother's death, and the fact that she was not entirely popular in our community, her funeral was very well attended. She was buried in our family plot alongside other generations of Parkchesters, underneath ancient oaks and elms with intertwining boughs. Normally, such a funeral would have been preceded by a week-long wake, with the body lying in state in one of the great rooms at Fir Crest, and friends and relatives coming from near and far to gawk for a few moments, and then to take part in a kind of muted festivity wherein everybody praised the dead, even though some might have thoroughly despised her.

I had instructed Dr. Seymour to forgo this part of the ritual, a decision that he reluctantly accepted, in that certain ladies could always be depended upon to become quite ill at wakes. On rare occasions, the shock of seeing death even induced some of them to die. Ever hungry for profits, however dubiously gotten, Dr. Seymour was clearly disturbed by a shortening of his opportunity to seek further clients, whether among the living or the dead. But I was firm in my decision. Mother's body was on view for two days. Mourners came and went. During that time, a contingent of well-gotten-up Confederate soldiers came to investigate the circumstances of the raid. I told them all that we knew; they rummaged about Fir Crest for a few hours, and then rode away. Three days after her death, Mother was buried with little ceremony, but with sufficient eulogy from our local minister to make up for the slack. One or two ladies fainted, which made the affair an unqualified success, since no funeral worth the name is complete without a few fainting ladies.

Father was still hospitalized in Alexandria, and was therefore unable to come to the funeral. But he wrote us tender, sorrowful letters. At times they were filled with the loftiest observations. And at others, with the deepest despair. "You are correct in being contemptuous of the rituals concerning death," he write. "Your mother would have decried such a public display of something which ought to be a private matter. As you know, your grandmother and I have had deep disagreements on the subject. That our society sees fit to put our hollow shells on exhibition, to drape them with flowers and grief, is perhaps the strongest condemnation of our weaknesses."

Further along, he returned again to Grandmother Parkchester: "I regret that I am not able to be at Fir Crest to help care for her. Our relationship was close and loving, despite our differences on many matters. As I think of her locked away inside the twilight of madness, my body is racked with chills. I know that you, Charlotte, and Benign will do everything necessary to keep her comfortable. The devilish question that irks me about insanity is whether the victim retains any concept of comfort. I have done some reading on the subject, and have discussed it with Judge Gilliam (he is now Major); and we are in agreement that the motives and reactions of the mad quite frequently become the opposite of what we might expect from them if they were normal. It is those paradoxes that you must pay careful attention to in Mother. Lest one is perpetually alert to the fact that she is tragically mad, the danger exists that she may do harm to herself and to others, out of the mistaken notion that she is actually doing good. . . ."

Thus warned, I placed a constant guard at her door, and refrained from locking it. She seemed neither to notice nor to care. Her main activity was involved in lying in bed, muttering to herself, staring into space. On rare occasions, she managed to dress and powder and rouge herself. Then, supported by cane and servant, she went downstairs to take the air. Benign cared for her diligently, bathing her, fixing her hair; but she always managed to look disheveled, and quite mad. Yet, the aspect of strength had not diminished, although she moved somewhat feebly.

Sometimes, when I went to visit her, it seemed that a very active mind was still at work behind her staring green eyes. At times, they grew liquid as pools; and I wondered what memories she retained. She neither drank nor smoked, although she regained her appetite and ate quite heartily, which Benign took as a sign that she would eventually regain her sanity. "Good food cures everything," Benign said, with such assuredness that I found myself awaiting Grandmother's return to her former condition, as though she had only gone off on a short trip and soon would come home.

But, for the moment, there was heavy work to be done at Fir Crest. As Robert Gilliam had advised, I mounted patrols of thirty-six men in three shifts around the clock. Banneker became overseer at Fir Crest, accepting the position humbly, but acquitting himself with pride. Under his supervision, as the summer turned to fall, the destroyed buildings were restored. Several apple trees were hauled from the woods to replace those destroyed in the orchard. When fall came, there was nothing to harvest in the way of tobacco, wheat, and corn, for the raiders had set fire to those fields. They had, however, left the vegetable crops intact. So the Negroes were kept busy picking and canning supplies for the coming winter. They were loyal and cheerful, bending readily to whatever task. Banneker was an absolute blessing, with the natural leader's sure touch of how to handle those under him. His relationship with me was close, yet respectful. As for Benign, she was a solid source of strength when strength was needed. And by the time the first snow fell, shortly before Thanksgiving, Fir Crest had been restored to its former splendor. The burned fields had been harrowed and seeded with winter corn and wheat; the others would be ready for tobacco and other crops when spring came.

Father had spoken of paradoxes in his letters; and as I rode about Fir Crest escorted by Juniper or Amos in turn, I could not help but ponder several contradictions that had puzzled me since the attack by the raiders.

Why had they left the slave cabins, the stock, the forests, and the vegetable crops intact? And the mansion itself, if they really were bent on destruction? They had destroyed a life, a mind, and several acres of tobacco, wheat, and corn. But it should have been obvious to any marauder that the best way to deplete the resources of Fir Crest was to destroy its Negroes, its trees, its stock, its food supply. Yet, none of these had been touched. It was as though some distorted mind had embarked on a program of token destruction—but for what sane or earthly reason?—without causing any damage to Fir Crest itself that would be irreparable. Mother had been our main casualty. Was she the intended victim all the time, along with Grandmother Parkchester? Had the appointed caretakers of Fir Crest deliberately been annihilated or reduced to madness so that its affairs would fall into my inexperienced hands? If so, who was behind such a diabolical plot? And, further, what did they expect to accomplish from its execution? I thought thus, and came to no conclusions. Perhaps, I thought, my imagination was playing dreadful tricks on me. Then again, perhaps not.

During this time, Charlotte conducted herself extremely well. Under Benign's heavy prodding, she had come from her room and was beginning to pick up the flung threads of her life. It was at Mother's funeral that she met Lance Harcourt for the first time. He was visiting mutual friends in Charlottesville, and came with them, he said, out of respect for our "awesome tragedy."

While such an occasion hardly seemed the place for love to plant its first seeds, I was nevertheless happy to invite him to Fir Crest after the burial, as Charlotte had requested. "He's so *handsome!*" she'd whispered to me. "And charming, too!" At twenty-three, he was five years her senior. An unidentified leg wound had kept him out of the army, although it did not impair his ability to prance, preen, walk, or waltz. It was said that he had studied acting, a proper enough profession for a young man who was rich, remarkably free of vigor or vitality, and somewhat slack and dull.

But he seemed harmless enough. And quite pleasant in his physical appearance, if one cared for men with the watery blue eyes of basset hounds, pearls for teeth, a thin blond mustache; and thick, wavy hair the color of sandstone—clearly dyed, if one paid careful attention to what appeared to be its pale yellow roots. My initial impression of weakness, as he murmured utter nonsense over my hand on our first meeting, remained with me on every occasion that I saw him thereafter. But I was grateful to him for helping to ease Charlotte back into her normal happy and carefree state. And in those months after the attack by the raiders, he was invaluable in his advice and assistance to me. If I did dislike him, I was certainly prime victim of my own distaste, for I treated him in such a way that neither he nor Charlotte seemed to notice. That they would one day be engaged never entered my mind, for love seemed far removed from the pretty little flirtations, the batting of eyes, and the bleating of sighs that they did around each other, as though in competition to see who could best imitate the silliest sheep.

"He's a *Harcourt!*" Charlotte would squeal to me privately. Which of course was one of the most famous names in the South. Their estate—Harcourt Manor, three times ours in size, rich in tobacco and cane, tended by a thousand slaves—was a showplace in neighboring Buckingham County, far enough away for Lance not to be a complete pest, yet close enough for him to pass a weekend with us from time to time, giving me extraordinarily sound advice about the management of Fir Crest, and charming Charlotte nearly out of her wits with his elegant airs. Most of their contact took place by letters, which left Fir Crest in pink perfumed piles, the same number being returned with the imposing Harcourt seal stamped in red wax on the flap of the envelope.

I heard from Robert Gilliam at intervals that were all too long. His letters carried somber news of the war, and advice as well, sometimes in answer to questions that I put to him. The mails left much to be desired, but we endured without complaining because of the war. I cherished

Robert's letters, reading them several times over. In one of them, dated January of 1863, he told me that President Lincoln had issued the long-discussed proclamation emancipating all slaves in the South.

"I urge you to be calm," Robert wrote. "I have enclosed the text of the Proclamation, which was officially issued January 1, 1863. If the slaves have shown loyalty thus far, it is because they have trusted in yours. It would be extremely unwise to alter your treatment of them. I advise you to assemble them, read the proclamation, and explain its meaning in the simplest terms. Once you have done that, you will be able to gauge the true measure of their devotion by the number who stay. Since Fir Crest, and other large plantations, are almost totally dependent on the labor of Negroes, this is a devastating blow to the South, especially if the North is ultimately victorious and able to fully impose Mr. Lincoln's mandate. Your father has told me that his considerable fortune has been greatly enhanced by the war, so that any changeover from slave to cheap hired labor would not affect some as much as others. It appears that your father, and mine as well, have maintained large investments in the North, even as they have taken up arms against it. A more cynical observation would be that our fathers have helped finance the war against the South, and both have emerged the richer for it. Small wonder that we are heading toward defeat, our cause betrayed before it began. It is only a matter of time before the Confederacy collapses, regardless of bloody and hard-won victories that appear to mean the contrary. In truth, we are outnumbered, outfought, and desperately outfinanced. The event is in the hand of One far greater than generals or presidents. I send you my deepest love, my darling. May God help you."

I was in the study on the first floor of Fir Crest. After reading Robert's letter, I went to the large window overlooking the east garden and tried to collect my thoughts. Since September 17 of the previous year, with the great Union victory in the battle of Antietam, a creek in western Maryland, the question of emancipation had hung in the air like an arrow aimed at the heart of slavery. However little the South might ignore the legitimacy of such a proclamation issued by Mr. Lincoln, its real effects would be to brand the southern states as rebellious territories rather than a confederation that such countries as England and France could support against the North without incurring the wrath of the federal Congress with its vast treasury and its war-making powers. In that respect alone, Mr. Lincoln's proclamation was a master stroke, for it established the legitimacy of the federal government by undermining the moral posture of slaveholders, and, at the same time, compelled potential European allies to abandon all plans to aid the South.

Now the issue had finally and dramatically been joined by Mr. Lincoln's proclamation. It was a terse and moving document; and however much it might throw all of us at Fir Crest into the vengeful hands of our personal slaves, and millions of other freedmen, it was impossible not to see that its moral tone was lofty and proper. And, whatever its political impact, it was an exercise in justice and compassion.

I remember that the east garden, indeed, all of Fir Crest, was filled with snow. It was early in February of 1863, and the weather was bitter cold. A pleasant fire was crackling on the study hearth, and I went to it to warm my hands, which had grown quite chill. There was a mirror over the fireplace, and I inspected my features, perhaps to remember forever what I looked like before I summoned the slaves and announced to them that they were free. Robert's advice was not only well given; it was an unavoidable act. For if we wanted to keep any one man at Fir Crest to help us survive, it was essential to advise them all of the proclamation, to which they themselves could otherwise give legitimacy by deserting en masse as soon as they learned of its existence. That they were still with us was certainly due, in part, to the fact that winter had hampered their own private system of communications. Out there in the snow, in those gray cabins from which great billows of smoke curled upward in thick white ropes, some five hundred Negroes had come to the end of a long and arduous journey toward freedom, without their even knowing it. I gazed in the mirror and saw the face of a frightened young woman.

The face still carried a fresh youthfulness, but it was a bit fuller, perhaps more cynical, less roundly childish. My hair was parted in the middle, and gathered in a bun at the nape of my neck. My lips were full and undeniably sensuous. And my eyes were now a deeper blue, darkened by resolve as I pulled my shawl closer around my shoulders. I was wearing a blue velvet gown with white piping around the tall collar. I appeared to be a woman of courage and responsibility. The past months had been a fine training ground, and by all accounts, I had acquitted myself well.

While Fir Crest was now hibernating underneath a blanket of snow, somewhere under that smooth white covering next spring's corn and wheat were germinating in their deep, dark wombs. We had bought winter feed from other plantations around. The pantry and storage houses were packed to filling with canned foods of all varieties, preserved in glass jars after cooking. Wood was laid up in great piles to keep the fires going during the cold season. All in all, Fir Crest seemed more prosperous than it had ever been. I had transferred spending money from Benign's sugar sack to the study safe. There were some twenty thousand dollars there in Confederate money. Practically speaking, I was happy that Father had seen fit to guarantee our financial stability by having investments in both North and South. While I shared Robert Gilliam's horror at such obvious cynicism, I was still sensible enough to applaud the strength that such a decision must have required.

Having reviewed our many successes and our few failures since the attack of the raiders, I rang for Benign. When she came, I asked her to tell my sister that I wanted to speak to her. "Meanwhile, please tell Juniper to have all the servants assemble in the sitting room within the hour. You may open the doors to the dining room, the parlor, and the sun porches so that there may be room for all. I have an important announcement to make."

"Is we free, Miss Victoria?"

"Yes." I could not bear to look at her. Instead, I took the poker and stirred the fire. *Is we free?* What quiet joy her voice held! I was almost envious of her for a moment, that she could, if she chose, have a far greater freedom than I could ever experience. She could leave Fir Crest with her husband and children. For the time being, barring any unforeseen tragedy, I would have to remain here without her or any of her kind to help me. "Yes, Benign," I said quietly, "you are free. That is the announcement I want to make."

"Why you want to tell them other niggers that?" she said heatedly.

I was surprised at the passion in her voice. Clearly, she wanted to protect me. At the same time, she was panting to be free. I could not understand the contradiction, and told her so. "Would you be free, Benign, and have others remain in servitude?"

She pondered that. Her great black face seemed deeply troubled. She wore voluminous purple skirts, a heavy blue blouse, the eternal apron and headrag. It seemed impossible, after so many years, that we were on the verge of a parting of the ways. I felt sad for her, sad for myself. Yet, the matter must be settled once and for all. If a nation divided against itself could not stand, certainly a mere plantation so divided was destined to fall. My only option was to inform the slaves and wait for their decision as to whether or not they would remain.

"I wants everybody to be free," Benign said petulantly. "It's just that some know how to be free, and some don't."

It struck me as an extraordinary observation, coming as it did from a woman who had been a slave all her life. She was stating a clear warning.

"I have considered that, Benign. It is a chance one must take. Also, I release you from your promise to remain in the event that such a proclamation were issued. Now, please tell Miss Charlotte and Juniper what I have asked. Naturally, your decision as to whether or not to stay will be your own. Others will be free to make their choice."

"Yas'm, Miss Victoria." She left the study on feet that seemed made of stone.

When Charlotte came, I told her substantially what the situation was. She had turned twenty only a few weeks before, and she seemed to be at the height of her beauty. She wore a simple dress of green velvet. A ring given to her by Lance Harcourt, a small emerald, was lovely in a gold band on her finger. Her red hair was loose and flowing. A white woolen shawl was around her shoulders. When I finished explaining, she looked at me with eyes that were calm and sober. "This means, then, that we must make do without the slaves?"

"I'm afraid so. We would not be able to keep them now against their will."

"Have we ever kept them against their will?" she cried suddenly. "There are no bars around Fir Crest! It is not a prison! I do not understand, Victoria."

"Calm yourself, Charlotte." I fought to remain calm myself. What she said was indeed true—no man, woman, or child wore shackles at Fir Crest. The urge for freedom, then, was certainly less physical than it was emotional. "It is the difference," I said, "between whether we own them or whether they own themselves. In the first instance, they belong to us as surely as though they were mules or cattle. We have bought and paid for them, have bred some of them as though they were animals. We have taken care of their every need, even as they have taken care of ours. With freedom, they will be at liberty to decide whether they wish to continue here as servants. And those who might want to continue must receive wages for their work. That is the difference."

"Why tell them?" Charlotte whispered bitterly.

"Because not to tell them would be dangerous. It is to our advantage to tell them, for it puts them at a greater disadvantage. Where would they go? The weather is miserable; the ground is filled with snow. Now is the best time to tell them."

Her eyes suddenly glittered with pleasure. "You've changed," she said. "I've never heard you talk like this before."

"I've never had to talk like this before," I said. "Suddenly, there are five hundred freed slaves on our hands. It does not matter that we might prefer them not to be free. They have the authority of numbers on their side, so it is they who can impose the truth of the proclamation upon us."

"And Banneker?" Charlotte said. "What will Banneker do?"

"That remains to be seen. He has been extremely loyal. Soon, however, we will know what all of them will do." For, as I talked, I could see them through the window, converging on the mansion in large numbers, huddled against the cold in rags. I could hear them stomping their feet on the porch before they entered the house. It would be the first time for most of them to enter the great sitting room, or even to set foot inside the mansion itself. Suddenly I felt another chill course through my body, and I wondered if I might not be coming down with the grippe. "Let us have a sherry, Charlotte. Then I shall make the announcement. Will you come with me?"

"Of course," she said stoutly. We drank a sherry before the fireplace. Then Benign came to tell us that the Negroes were assembled. I thanked her, and she left.

"Give me your hand, dear Charlotte. I need your support just now."

"And I need yours," Charlotte said. "Do you think they will harm us?"

"I do not think so. But if so, they must harm us together."

She kissed me quickly on the cheek. Then, holding hands like frightened children about to face the uncertainty of wrathful parents, we went into the sitting room.

There were Negroes everywhere. Even the staircase was filled, some of them standing three and four abreast. Mothers held their pickaninnies. The men wore jackets or blankets around their shoulders; the women, shawls, which they eventually discarded as the cold left them. I looked, and saw Banneker, which gave me a certain sense of comfort. There were Amos, Juniper, Benign; Johnny Cake, now a strapping thirteen; the girl Emerald, who had enjoyed our cherry blossoms. And hundreds more crowding together in the sitting room and the surrounding chambers. The room smelled somewhat evil, all those black bodies, certainly most of them unwashed. That they were all standing was not unexpected; still, it frightened me, as though they were prepared to attack us at the first opportunity. "You niggers keep quiet," Benign said authoritatively. "Miss Victoria got something to say."

I dropped Charlotte's hand, and left her standing among a group of Negroes. I saw that Banneker moved quickly to stand somewhat near her. That was a heartening sign. I stood on the first steps of the staircase, where the Negroes made a place for me. They were squeezed in around me on all sides. I held the text of the Emancipation Proclamation in my left hand. As Robert had suggested, this event, too, was now in the hand of God. I read in a loud, clear voice:

BY THE PRESIDENT OF THE UNITED STATES OF AMERICA:
A PROCLAMATION

I, Abraham Lincoln, President of the United States, by virtue of the power in me vested as Commander-in-Chief of the Army and Navy of the United States in time of actual armed rebellion against the authority and government of the United States, and as a fit and necessary war measure for repressing said rebellion, do, on this first day of January, in the year of our Lord one thousand eight hundred sixty-three, do order and designate as the States and parts of States wherein the people thereof, respectively, are this day in rebellion against the United States, the following, to wit:

Arkansas, Texas, Louisiana (except the parishes of St. Bernard, Plaquemines, Jefferson, St. John, St. Charles, St. James, Ascension, Assumption, Terrebonne, Lafourche, St. Mary, St. Martin, and Orleans, including the city of New Orleans), Mississippi, Alabama, Florida, Georgia, South Carolina, North Carolina, and Virginia (except the forty-eight counties designated as West Virginia, and also the counties of Berkeley, Accomac, Northampton, Elizabeth City, York, Princess Anne, and Norfolk, including the cities of Norfolk and Portsmouth), and which excepted parts are for the present left precisely as if this proclamation were not issued.

And by virtue of the power and for the purpose aforesaid, I do order and declare that all persons held as slaves within said designated States and parts of States are, and henceforward shall be, free; and that the executive government of the United States, including the military and naval authorities thereof, will recognize and maintain the freedom of said persons.

And I hereby enjoin upon the people so declared to be free to abstain from all violence, unless in necessary self-defense; and I recommend to them that, in all cases when allowed, they labor faithfully for reasonable wages.

And I further declare and make known that such persons of suitable condition will be received into the armed service of the United States to garrison forts, positions, stations, and other places, and to man vessels of all sorts in said service.

And upon this act, sincerely believed to be an act of justice, warranted by the Constitution upon military necessity, I invoke the considerate judgment of mankind and the gracious favor of Almighty God.

In witness whereof, I have hereunto set my hand, and caused the seal of the United States to be affixed.

Done at the city of Washington, this first day of January, in the year of our Lord one thousand eight hundred sixty-three, and of the independence of the United States of America the eighty-seventh.
By the President:

ABRAHAM LINCOLN
WILLIAM H. SEWARD, Secretary of State.

When I finished reading, there was a deep hush to everything. The ticking of the clock and the fire crackling on the hearth seemed to suspend all else in an eternity of silence.

Then Banneker spoke. "That mean we free, Miss Victoria?"

"Yes, Banneker. You're all free to go where you please, to do as you please, insofar as it is lawful."

They turned to each other, muttering, whispering. I did not see one smile, one grin, one slap on the back. But my nostrils were invaded by the heavy stench of fear. And that truly surprised me. Also, their faces, some of them, seemed surly, almost indignant.

"Where we supposed to go?" Benign said gruffly. "No food, no money. What we supposed to do?"

"I shall give fifty dollars and supplies to each man and his family who wishes to leave," I said.

Several of them grunted disdainfully. "We supposed to walk?" one said.

I looked to Banneker for aid; but his face, too, wore a mask of puzzlement. I was quite bewildered. Charlotte looked alarmed. And Benign was clearly angry, perhaps because I had not listened to her advice. But it had not occurred to me that freeing someone could be so involved. It struck me forcibly that freedom and slavery both had their roots in economics. And I suddenly understood why the slaves had not left Fir Crest before now. Not because of law, or love, or loyalty. They had not left because they could not afford to.

"No one is required to leave," I said. "No one is being evicted." Rapidly, my mind formulated a new approach. "Henceforth, however, there will be wages for all who work. It is something that must be cleared with Father before I can tell you what the wages will be. Obviously, there are too many of you for all to be paid, however. Those who cannot be paid may elect to farm individual plots, receiving a share of what they plant, giving a share of the yield. . . ." I paused, for the enormity of the thing almost overwhelmed me. At the same time, I was grateful that Mother had educated me to the extent that I could propose an alternative to freedom to slaves too poor to be other than slaves. "Does anyone have anything to say?" I went on. For they were ominously silent. I looked to Benign, but she still appeared furious. There was only Banneker to turn to. "Banneker, you have been overseer. What do you say?"

He ducked his head, shuffled his feet. He looked at his woman, Emerald, that beautiful black creature with flashing eyes and brilliant white teeth. Then he grinned. "If I'se free, Miss Victoria, then I guess I'll stay. I certainly ain't got no appointments nowhere else."

Now there were nods, a stirring of feet. A growing of voices tinged with hope. I felt exuberant. And I looked at Charlotte, who was smiling.

"I am happy you have decided to stay, Banneker. Please talk to the others individually. Let me know how many wish to remain. Then we shall discuss wages and farming arrangements. We are fortunate that the winter is ahead of us, which gives us sufficient time to plan." I pulled my shawl around my shoulders. "I thank you all for coming. Those who stay will be welcome. Those who go will do so with our heartfelt thanks, and our blessings."

Then, holding my head high, I went to Charlotte. We left the room together and went back to the study.

Charlotte was ecstatic. "You were marvelous, Victoria! Simply marvelous!"

"I was scared to death," I said tightly. I poured a sherry and drank it down. Charlotte had one, too. "We're becoming drunks." She giggled. In answer, I poured another. My body had been trembling, but now I felt more confident. "It has been done," I said. "Thank God it's over."

"Wasn't Banneker wonderful?" Charlotte said.

"He was helpful. Now, Charlotte, I have much work to do." We kissed and embraced. "I shall see you at supper. For the moment, it appears that Fir Crest still stands."

"It will stand," Charlotte said confidently. And she left.

I was not quite so sure as she. I had made grand statements to the Negroes. Now it was necessary to find money and land to fulfill those promises. For one thing was exceedingly clear to me: the slaves wanted their freedom, but they did not want to leave Fir Crest. Which raised a delicate question: could Fir Crest afford to keep them as free people? At the same time, who here had sufficient power to impose Mr. Lincoln's freedom on them by driving them away? I waited for Benign to come to see what her reaction had been. But she did not come to the study the rest of that afternoon, nor did I call her.

Only when supper was ready did I hear a timid knock at the door. And when I answered, it was her son, Johnny Cake, who told me, in what can only be called an insolent tone, "Mama say to come and eat supper."

Freedom indeed had come to Fir Crest. The problem was how to handle it so that the servants, in truth, would not become the masters. Insolence was the first sign of rebellion; capitulation, the first step toward final defeat. "Tell your mother," I said crossly, "that I am not having supper. Nor will Charlotte, nor Grandmother Parkchester. Also tell your mother that she is to quit the kitchen at once until further arrangements can be made." I reached out and tweaked his ear. "As for you, young man, if you ever dare use that tone of voice with me again, I shall slap your stupid face. Then I shall have you whipped. Is that clear?"

He looked absolutely terrified. "Yas'm, Miss Victoria!" And he skedaddled.

I had worked the afternoon on accounts and other papers. Now I sat behind the massive desk and began a letter to Father to tell him what I had done, and to ask his advice on how to proceed further. But before I was barely past the salutation—"Dear Father: Today there have been momentous decisions made at Fir Crest . . ."—there was Benign's unmistakable thumping on the study door. "Come

in, Benign," I said, without looking up. I heard her bustle
in, but I kept her waiting until I had finished the sentence:
". . . and I am somewhat uncertain as to the justness of
the decisions, or of the eventual benefit of their outcome. I
have read the Emancipation Proclamation to all the slaves,
and find, initially, that they appear to want freedom, and
to continue at Fir Crest as well."

As I wrote, I heard Benign shuffling from foot to foot.
Then she went to throw wood on the fire, stoking it with
the poker. When she turned from the fireplace, I had laid
down the pen and was looking at her coldly. "Yes,
Benign? What is it?"

She actually curtsied, a thing I hadn't seen among the
servants in Fir Crest for years. "Supper is served, ma'am."

"Thank you, Benign. Would you be so good as to advise
Miss Charlotte?"

"Yas'm, Miss Victoria. I already sent somebody to feed
Miss Parkchester."

"Very good, Benign. You may go."

"Yas'm, Miss Victoria."

She had another try at curtsying, and pulled it off fairly
well this time. If I had not been so incensed, and even a
bit terrified of the reality of the situation, I probably
would have smiled. But as it was, I eyed her with near-
contempt. Sending her insolent pickaninny with his insolent message—"Mama say to come and eat supper"—she
had deliberately tried to test my authority on perhaps the
most crucial day of my life. And to test was to undermine.
I had to show that I was still in charge of Fir Crest, and
that I would brook no nonsense from anyone. Benign had
stepped out of line, and had as quickly fallen back into
place. But what of the others? Benign was the key; as she
went, so would go the others.

For the moment, she was running respectful and afraid.
The thought of returning to those cabins as a field hand
was certainly unappealing to her. "Is everything all right,
missy?" she said, grinning, bobbing her head.

"Everything is fine, Benign. You may go."

"Yas'm, missy."

She scurried out, moving her great bulk with surprising
speed. When she was gone, I opened the top drawer of Father's desk and took out his derringer. There was a small

box of shot in the drawer. I loaded the pistol. Father had taught both Charlotte and me to use it expertly. In the event it was ever needed, he'd said. Well, the event seemed to have occurred.

Charlotte was already seated when I entered the dining room with the derringer underneath my shawl. The room still held the strong, unpleasant odor of the Negroes who had crowded even here as I read the proclamation. The snow and mud from their shoes were still on the floor, but Juniper was judiciously mopping. When I entered, he took one last swipe, bowed more or less in my direction, and ran.

"Good evening, Charlotte," I said. Benign was standing like a statue near the serving table.

"Good evening, Victoria."

I waited until Juniper returned, dusting his hands, to seat me. As he did so, I drew the pistol from underneath my shawl and laid it on the table. "We shall be served now, Benign."

Her eyes bulged, as though I had brought a live cobra to supper with me. "That pistol . . . is it loaded, Miss Victoria?"

"It is loaded indeed, Benign."

Supper went extremely well. Charlotte regarded me over the top of her water glass with a sly smile. I was hungry, and ate the baked ham, garden peas, and whipped potatoes with a hearty appetite, refusing all wines. Charlotte had two small glasses. We chatted about things of no consequence, maintaining a rigid demeanor. Benign came and went with dishes; Juniper or Johnny Cake remained in respectful attendance, taking away empty plates to make room for others that Benign brought. The derringer stayed on the table all through the meal.

When we were finished, Charlotte and I went into the sitting room, as was our custom. It was spotless and clean-smelling, as though an army of elves had been working hard to dispel the odor of Negroes, their mud and stain, while we had been at supper. Benign served coffee and sherry. Again, I had the pistol on the table at my side. Again Charlotte and I made chitchat, until the name of Lance Harcourt came up. He was due to spend the coming weekend at Fir Crest.

"He is bringing out his sleigh, so that he and I can go riding. You must come with us, Victoria."

"Thank you, Charlotte. But I think not. Why is he bringing a sleigh when we already have several?"

Charlotte laughed. "He says his is so much prettier. Won't you please come, Victoria?"

"I'll think about it, Charlotte." At my side, I heard Benign grunt quite clearly. She had no liking for Lance Harcourt, although she had never told me so. By grunting now, she was indicating her continued disapproval of his foppishness.

"Benign?"

"Yas'm, Miss Victoria."

"You may take the pistol away and put it where it belongs."

She grinned from ear to ear. The siege, thank God, was over. "Yas'm, Miss Victoria." She picked the pistol up delicately and walked as though it might explode in her hands.

Only when Benign was gone did Charlotte hit me with a barrage of questions. "What has happened? Why did you bring Father's derringer to the table? Why have you treated the servants so icily?"

Briefly, I told her. When I finished, she grinned mischievously. "It appears that the Negroes have gone down in defeat."

"Perhaps," I said. "Or so it seems for the moment."

Charlotte stayed a bit longer; then she went to her room to write to Lance Harcourt. I looked in on Grandmother Parkchester.

Grandmother seemed fair, her condition having reached a point where it had leveled off into a routine of eating, sleeping, and relieving herself. She seemed harmless enough, and I had even taken the guard from her door. The room was comfortably warm. I had learned that it was useless to talk to her, so I fussed over her collar, her hair. She seemed enormously strong as she sat imperiously in her straight-backed chair near the bed. An empress gone mad. I wondered briefly how she would have handled today's attempted insurrection. Probably with a cannon. Kissing her damp forehead before I left, I mused that my approach had apparently worked as well, without any damage thus far from cannon shot. . . .

Two days passed before Banneker came to me with the decision of the Negroes. I received him in the sitting room, and even had Benign serve him a whiskey. He was smartly gotten up in a hand-sewn suit of thick gray flannel. He wore black boots that seemed to pinch his feet, and suspiciously resembled a pair I had seen on the late Mr. McAdoo. His hair was neatly cut and nicely brushed. He wore a collar and a purple tie, which I also suspected had been Mr. McAdoo's.

If Benign's approach to freedom had been a momentary insolence, Banneker's seemed one of thoughtful respectability. He sat comfortably, quietly, in the armchair before the fireplace, which gave me an opportunity to examine his new aspect. In winter, his color was like that of cinnamon, perhaps a shade lighter. His hair was a kind of reddish-brown—a sure sign that some unknown white man's blood did, after all, flow in his veins—and his eyes were the color of hazel. He was extraordinarily handsome, with fine mulatto features. When he laughed or smiled, which he frequently did, his teeth glistened like crystals of snow.

He smiled now. "Benign say you been toting a pistol, Miss Victoria."

"It seemed necessary at the time."

He shook his head. "It won't necessary. Don't nobody here mean you no harm."

"I'm happy to hear that, Banneker. What is it, then, that they mean to do?"

He wrinkled his brow, figuring. "Two hundred and seventy-five want to stay here and get paid. One hundred and ten want to farm. Fifty-eight want fifty dollars so they can go North. Fourteen ain't made up their minds yet. Three I can't find . . . I think they just took off."

I had been making written notes as he talked. "That takes care of four hundred and sixty. What about the other forty?"

Now he squirmed uncomfortably in his chair. "I'm afraid there's a problem with them, Miss Victoria." His eyes shifted from mine to the fireplace.

"A problem, Banneker?" My heart seemed to surge with

fear. I had been expecting problems, so I held myself under tight control. "What is the problem, Banneker?"

Now his handsome face turned surprisingly ugly. "Them forty niggers just won't go. They won't work and they won't go. They took over the front cabins. They say Fir Crest owe them."

My body was trembling, and I stood, hoping to still it. My first impulse was to order a party of Negroes to dislodge the dissidents. At the same time, I was aware that our present position was too uncertain to effectively cause such a step. I began pacing the sitting-room floor, careful to maintain my proper carriage and dignity. From time to time I cast a glance at Banneker, who was now standing near the mantel. But there was a slant to his shoulders that told me he felt as hopeless, helpless, and ridiculous as I did.

Counting myself, Charlotte, and Grandmother Parkchester, we were two reasonably sane, young white persons and one mad old woman suddenly caught up in the tides created by Mr. Lincoln's damnable Emancipation Proclamation. Which way would the tides eventually shift? How far in either direction would they go? And even as I asked myself these questions, I spied the enormous bulk of Benign where she unsuccessfully tried to hide and eavesdrop in the hallway leading to the kitchen. Seeing her lurking there, I felt an unaccustomed anger. But if there were rebellion in me, now was certainly not the time to think about it. "Perhaps we should give them more time, Banneker. It is possible they will change their minds."

Banneker grunted loudly. "Them dumb niggers, they ain't got no minds to change. They going to stay right there until you run them off."

I shook my head. "It is best to leave them alone for now, Banneker. There is no need at this point to take on more trouble than we already have."

Banneker nodded somewhat reluctantly. "Yas'm, Miss Victoria." He shuffled his feet and fumbled with his cap. "Now that I'm free, Miss Victoria, can I say anything I want to?"

"Of course, Banneker. You have always been free to speak your mind."

A slight smile hardened his lips, as though he were appreciating a special irony. "About them niggers," he said quite firmly, "I'd starve them out. If you don't give them nothing to eat, no candles to burn, no wood for their stoves, they got nothing to stay for."

The ghostly bulk of Benign seemed to stiffen in the hall shadows. "That might be a solution, Banneker. But it is my decision that we should wait awhile longer."

"Yas'm."

"Is there anything else, Banneker?"

"Yas'm."

"What is it?"

I saw that he was now decidedly ill at ease. And, further, that Benign had disappeared from the hall. That, more than Banneker's apparent unease, filled me with a sense of deeper apprehension.

"It's about Miss Charlotte," he said in a near-whisper that sounded full of despair. "She been messing with me. I sure would appreciate it if you told her to stop."

His eyes settled on me like twin beacons, and I felt my face flush. Certainly he was talking about Charlotte's trips to spy on him in the cabin with his woman. But had he known that I was also there with her? It seemed incredible to me that in the middle of winter, especially with all that was happening now, he could still be resentful about a girl's prank. If he had known that I was with Charlotte, then common sense made him leave me out of the accusation. It seemed unwise to probe further than his own comment. "I shall speak to her, Banneker. Is there anything else?"

"No, ma'am. There ain't nothing else." With a slight bow he made his exit. I wandered around the sitting room for several minutes before I poured a glass of sherry and sipped it standing at the window. Although it was only a few minutes past two o'clock in the afternoon, the sky was overcast with cumbersome gray clouds that kept a silent vigil over Fir Crest, as though they were bloated with snow and waiting for the appropriate moment to drop it. For as far as I could see, the plantation seemed asleep under deep white mounds from an earlier storm.

There was so much to do, so much to think about. I stood at the window awhile longer, thinking of merrier days when we had been young, and carefree, and laughing in snow to the sound of sleigh bells, filled with a sense of the finest well-being. I was standing at the south window—the cabins of the dissident slaves were to the north of the house—and the magnificent sweep of Fir Crest, the long, snow-filled plain that stretched in front of me until it dipped to meet the low ground, filled me with a sense of pride. This was our land, and it was well worth the fighting for. I took a last sip of sherry and turned to go into the study, where I could sit quietly and make plans for the future. But I met Benign as I was on my way from the sitting room.

"Miss Charlotte just pulled into the yard in some kind of contraption with that Mr. Lance Harcourt," she said dryly. She seemed perfectly recovered from our encounter of a few days ago, and I was pleased to see that the old familiarity had returned. However much I might have mistrusted it then, I was filled with excitement and curiosity about the arrival of Lance and Charlotte in their "contraption." So I slipped into the cloak Benign held for me and went out onto the porch.

The sleigh was parked in a clearing near the east garden. Lance and Charlotte, their arms around each other, laughing gaily, were trudging down the path to the house. Locked together that way, they seemed a perfect couple. And for the first time since I had met Lance, I found myself almost liking him. But it was the sleigh beyond them that held my rapt attention.

It was a contraption, indeed, but certainly a marvelous one. Drawn by four prancing white horses with a liveried Negro occupying an elevated driver's seat, it was certainly the largest and most elaborate sleigh I had ever seen. Except for the curling silver runners, it might have been a blue-and-white wedding cake being drawn about the countryside for all to admire. There were bundles of what appeared to be fox furs on the seat; and I could imagine, certainly not without a twinge of jealousy, Lance and my lovely sister fleeting along through the wintry afternoon, bundled in those furs, warmed further by their sense of companionship.

Lance was smiling somewhat theatrically as he greeted me. "Dear Victoria, what a pleasure to see you again." As always, he bowed and kissed my hand, which must have left an unpleasant sensation on his rosy lips, for it was somewhat withered and dry from the cold. And whatever sense of acceptance I might have had for him was quickly replaced by the same old distaste for his mannerisms. "A pleasure to see you, Lance. You're always welcome at Fir Crest." I retrieved my hand from his, for it seemed that he held it overlong; and then I turned to Charlotte. "You are radiant, Charlotte. I can tell you had a wonderful time."

"Most wonderful!" she cried, slapping her gloved hands. Then she hugged me and whispered quickly, "Oh, thank you for letting him come, Victoria!" And I realized that Lance Harcourt had come for the entire weekend, even as his smiling servant appeared carrying a lavishly brocaded bag that must have contained his belongings, and especially his overly sweet cologne. "Do let's go indoors," I said, leading the way. But I suddenly went on an impulse to the other end of the porch and stared at the squat gray cabins fronting the line of buildings in the slave quarters. Those were the cabins of the dissidents. However much I may have wanted to forget them, such a thing was impossible in light of their arrogance and insubordination. "What is it?" Lance Harcourt said. "You look troubled, my dear."

He had been such a help with advice before, that I was on the verge of telling him about the problem with the Negroes. But he hardly seemed the kind of man to deal with insurrection. "It's nothing, Lance. I suppose I'm only a bit tired."

"What a pity," Lance murmured. "Charlotte and I had so hoped that you would go sleighing with us."

"I'm afraid not, Lance." I took a last look at the cabins, and then we went into the sitting room.

They were going sleighing after supper, so we passed the time until supper in the sitting room, laughing, talking, and being taught a new version of vingt-et-un by Lance. Benign served a delicious white chilled wine that Lance had brought with him. And, as the afternoon passed in this most pleasant way, I finally felt relaxed enough to tell them about the Negroes who refused to leave Fir Crest.

"So that is why you were troubled," Lance said, fingering his bottom lip. His color was high, probably from the wine and the overheated sitting room. I myself felt extremely gay, which was certainly due to the wine. As for Charlotte, she was staring into the fire with a bemused smile on her full lips. In a purple velvet gown, with a cameo pinned at the neck, she was lovelier than I had ever seen her. However much I may have felt that Lance Harcourt was conceited and foppish, he had been a tonic for Charlotte, bringing her from the depths of despair that had seized her after the raid and Mother's death. For that service to Charlotte, I would always be grateful to him. At the same time, I knew that I could never like the man.

He stood, lean and tall, and strode deliberately back and forth in front of the fireplace. He still held his bottom lip between two fingers, and I half-expected him to recite from *Hamlet* on the spot. But all he did was stride, like a general contemplating momentous decisions. Everything about him seemed excellent and in good taste—the dark blue satin trousers that held his slim hips and slender buttocks as tightly as a corset; the white silk shirt, every ruffle in place from his constant arrangements of them; and the wine-colored coat, pinched at the waist, flaring slightly in the tail. Yet, I felt a sense of deep misgiving about him. He impressed me as being a pretty jackanapes, hardly fit for more than card-playing and compliments, the latter which he received as though they were his due, and which he gave out in a constant flow, so that all of us would have been floating out to England had they carried the weight of water.

My examination of him was interrupted by Charlotte's somewhat wistful voice. "What is this about the Negroes, Victoria? I'm afraid I was daydreaming."

"Banneker has brought me a list of those who want to stay, either for wages or to sharecrop. But there are forty more who refuse to leave. They also refuse to work."

"Such arrogance!" Charlotte cried. But almost at once she seemed taken away again into her own private reverie. At the same time, Benign came with more of the white wine. I refused to have more, but Lance and Charlotte both took the glasses eagerly.

"If I do say so myself," Lance said, passing the wineglass under his aquiline nose, "it has an excellent aroma. It's from France, you know. I've brought a dozen bottles to keep us all in a gay mood for the weekend."

"Thank you, Lance." I had told him about entrenched Negroes, possibly expecting some solid advice from him, and he served up talk of wine instead. As a prancing peacock, he fulfilled my every expectation. I was therefore surprised when he returned to the subject of the Negroes.

"We have had such demonstrations by slaves at Harcourt Manor. We have always dealt with them summarily. To do otherwise is to lose one's grip on the helm of power."

I nodded. "Banneker has suggested that we starve them out. While it may be the remedy required, the idea is distasteful to me."

"And rightly so," Lance said. "They would become objects of pity. Then the danger exists that they would be joined by other blacks." He stiffened suddenly. "Those black devils!" he said, with a kind of bitter admiration. "They are indeed clever!" He threw his head back and downed his wine in a single draft. He was more energetic than I had ever seen him, pacing back and forth like an excessively elegant and overly perfumed peacock.

"We have one thousand of them at Harcourt Manor," he went on. "I have stood for hours on end watching them. Have you done so? Have you seen how they merely give the appearance of being busy even as they are idling? God, what actors *they* are!"

I found myself in the ridiculous position of defending the Negroes at Fir Crest. "It is not the same here, Lance. Our servants have always given us an honest day's labor. Perhaps it's because Father has always treated them honestly. Many a time he has worked with them himself. I am certain that we have no slackers here."

He laughed. "Only rebels and dissidents," he said with light sarcasm. And then his mood grew serious again as he twirled the stem of the crystal wineglass between long, slender fingers. "Charlotte told me that you read them the Emancipation Proclamation. You can see now what an error that was. I have made no mention of it at our place. The proclamation has absolutely no legitimacy."

"Perhaps not," I said somewhat defensively. "But it has tremendous moral authority. As for how you and your father manage your affairs at Harcourt Manor, I am sure you do what you think is right. We try to do the same here at Fir Crest."

He bowed slightly, stiffly. "And you do very well indeed. I did not intend to imply otherwise. My main concern is for you. And, of course," he added after an embarrassed second, "for Charlotte as well. She is my chief concern."

As though the mention of her name had called her

from her reverie, Charlotte drew the hassock where she was sitting away from the fire. Her color was very high, and her green eyes seemed murky and somehow withdrawn. Although the wine was light and delicate, it was very potent; Charlotte obviously had drunk too much of it. "I had the most extraordinary thought," she said. "It unfolded before me like yards of the most exquisite silk. Then, suddenly, the silk became an expanse of land, covered over with peach blossoms that fell all around like a gentle snowstorm. There were men and women dancing. . . ." She looked at Lance shyly. "You and I were dancing, Lance. It was so beautiful. . . ." Then fear clouded her face, and she turned to me. "It was so strange, Victoria. I could hear you and Lance talking about the Negroes, the Emancipation Proclamation. Yet, I was also held motionless, only my mind working, my feet dancing on the peach petals. . . . Am I all right, Victoria? It was a terrible sensation."

Lance and I laughed together. "It's the wine," I said, and I went to calm her, for she was truly disturbed. "I feel as though I'm dancing on peach petals myself."

Now Charlotte laughed. "You mean I'm drunk?" she cried most inelegantly.

"I'm afraid so, dear Charlotte," Lance said. "The French are famous for their ability to export revolutions. I must say I far prefer mine inside a bottle." He went to the wine container where Benign had left it in ice, and poured himself another glass. "Victoria and I were having an interesting conversation. I assured her that you are my chief concern at Fir Crest."

Charlotte beamed. "Oh, did you, Lance? Am I?"

"Of course you are, dear. Are you blind? Can you not feel? Don't you know that I'm absolutely insane about you?"

If it was a declaration of love, Charlotte took it as a joke. Which it seemed to be, whatever Lance's intentions might have been. Indeed, at the moment he seemed to be a costumed court jester, dedicated to the amusement of his betters. And even as I thought such a thing, I was ashamed. Charlotte was very fond of Lance. Despite my own misgivings, she seemed to be falling in love with him. Yet, at times, his blue eyes fell on me with a sort of mocking, amused gaze that also seemed to be mixed with desire.

And I wondered if he could be serious about anything. My impulse was to ask him once and for all what his intentions were toward my sister, for I did not want her hurt. Whatever his intentions were, whatever glimmer I might have of them, he and his inclinations both struck me as being dishonorable.

"I heard you talking about the Negroes who won't leave," Charlotte said to me. "What will we do?"

"We must either find a way to make them leave peacefully, or we must persuade them to stay productively. In no way would I condone their violent removal."

Lance Harcourt exhaled a pretty snort. "I'm afraid Victoria is not being realistic in this case, Charlotte. She does not know Negroes as well as I. They will never leave peacefully. They will remain to sow further dissension. Apparently one of her own Negroes has also recommended drastic action. But she is determined to follow a peaceful course." His eyes and smile were mocking now as he lifted his glass in a toast. "To you, lovely lady. May you never live to regret."

The man infuriated me, the way he dilly-dallied and set little traps for me to fall into. And he was expert at making even banality sound like an indecent proposition. "I can only do what I think is right," I said evenly. "Until Father returns, and with the deepest respect to yourself and to Charlotte, I shall continue to follow my own mind."

Charlotte caressed my cheek, smiling into my eyes. "Victoria, you always do what is best. And please don't think I'm criticizing. But perhaps Lance is right this time. After all, there are so many Negroes, and so few of us—"

Lance interrupted her eagerly. ". . . And their every endeavor is to destroy us! I have seen it a thousand times over! If they were fit to be other than slaves, would God have made them so? They *disgust* me! We have one thousand of them at Harcourt Manor, yet half that number of white men could do the same work in far less time and more efficiently as well. But it would take an equal number of white men a year, an *eternity*, to do the damage that they do in one day. I would gladly give them all their freedom, and a fine fare-thee-well, if it were possible to survive without them." He paused, checking his bitter flow of words. He had turned quite pale, and it struck me, incredibly, that the man was afraid of his servants. Not only a fool, but a coward as well.

There was a loud clearing of a throat behind us, inserting itself into the silence as effectively as a clanking of chains; and we all jerked around in surprise. It was Benign, her hamlike arms placidly folded underneath her breasts. "Supper's ready, Miss Victoria." I wondered how long she had been standing there, how much of Lance Harcourt's diatribe she had heard. Her impassive face told me nothing. But as I approached her, she took a deliberate step backward and attempted a curtsy. Certainly not for my benefit, but for Lance Harcourt's. Those downcast eyes, the impassive jaw, were eloquent indeed. If she had not heard everything that Lance said, she had heard enough. But he seemed quite oblivious of Benign, her obvious distaste for him, as he escorted Charlotte and me to the dining room. Once, as she served, I caught Benign looking at him with her large black lips drawn down in utter disdain. The two of us—my Negro servant and I—couldn't have been in greater harmony when it came to our opinions of Lance Harcourt.

Supper, as usual, was excellent. Benign had prepared braised venison, with corn, green peas, and small turnips from last year's crop. For dessert there was an excellent peach cobbler topped with whipped cream. Charlotte and Lance talked pretty nonsense as Juniper, Benign, and Johnny Cake served and took away dishes. Charlotte had regained her composure and was quite beautiful. The light from the chandelier, candles ablaze inside globes among the hanging crystals, sparkled in her red hair like a thousand bits of diamond. The arch of her long white neck, as she turned to make some comment to Lance, was lovely indeed. Her eyes glittered with excitement, certainly at the prospect of going sleigh-riding with Lance after supper; and she seemed quite happy.

Preoccupied as they were with each other, I had ample time to pay attention to my own thoughts. Robert Gilliam was very much a part of them. The contrast between him and Lance Harcourt was so striking that it seemed impossible that they were both part of the same South, patrons of the same cause. Thinking of Robert, I felt a warmth entwining me as strongly as the curvature of a vine; but, in truth, it was my recollection of Robert's incredible strength, and every place he had touched me now seemed a shrine to our love. If he were here now, I could not possibly feel incomplete, unsupported, or subject to the whims of however many Negroes.

While I could overlook Charlotte's excitement at the prospect of a night sleigh ride, there was something indecent about Lance Harcourt turning cartwheels in the snow while the South and all that it represented were being squeezed in the fist of the Union. The light struck his careful curls, the side of his jaw, and seemed to nestle in his long lashes, making him appear boyish and somehow diabolical at the same time. He displeased me enormously, and the idea of having him around for the entire weekend was suddenly not at all to my liking. Yet, there was nothing I could do, for the courtesies forthcoming to a guest at Fir Crest were his for better or for ill. At the same time, I was not required to be an audience of one to my sister's silliness and the preening of an overelegant popinjay. Assisted by Juniper, I shoved back my chair and stood. "Charlotte, Lance, will you forgive me? I have a slight headache and think that I shall lie down."

They were both deeply concerned, or so it appeared. Charlotte insisted on accompanying me to my room; but I insisted, successfully, that there were a dozen servants who could do the same thing and that she should remain with Lance. For his part, he seemed completely prepared to go back to Buckingham and take my headache with him. "We had both hoped you'd go sleighing with us," he said. He sounded disappointed and petulant, blue eyes turning as limpid as a hound's. Charlotte must have noticed that I was becoming irritated, for she rang for her cloak, leaving me to the ministrations of Benign. "I am perfectly fine, Benign. You may go back to the kitchen." As I went upstairs, I could hear Lance and Charlotte outdoors, laughing together. And then, the proud pull of the horses against the gaudy sleigh. The silver bells resounded like the chimes of miniature cathedrals until everything grew quiet in Fir Crest except for the ticking of numerous clocks.

I looked in on Grandmother Parkchester, and she was sleeping soundly. I left the door open, as was our custom. We had even taken the lock from the door, to prevent her locking herself in. Then I went to my own room, where the winter sun was a pale, dying glow in the west windows, from which I could see the crest of firs outlined as though touched by weak candles. A fire blazed on the hearth in my room, making it stuffy and unpleasant. I went to the windows facing the slave quarters, parted the draperies, and flung open the window. The cold air was sharp, invigorating. I enjoyed its freshness for several minutes while I stared at the cabins of the dissident blacks, where window after window in its turn grew yellow with candlelight against the encroaching darkness.

How helpless I felt at that moment! What was to be done? Lance Harcourt had been right in one respect: if such arrogance went untended too long, then the danger did exist that other Negroes would join the idle ones. And if that happened, no army would be able to move them, if one were available. Our supply of white men, as represented by Lance Harcourt and poor old Mr. Clarence, who oversaw the Gilliam place, was woefully lacking in verve and imagination. Sleighing, indeed!

As I closed the window and draperies and turned away, I thought again of Robert Gilliam, how he had possessed me by the creek, and how we had languished in each other's arms before he returned to the hated war. Even though the day had not been particularly trying, I felt exhausted, as though a malaise suddenly took hold of me. The room seemed to spin gently as I stumbled to the bed and lay face down on the brocaded quilt. Before I knew it, I was crying softly. And whispering the name of my beloved. "Robert . . . Robert . . . Robert . . . When will we be together again?" There were letters of his in my writing desk, most of them which I knew by heart. And I drew comfort and strength from remembering portions of a recent one:

While it is perhaps too early to predict which way the war will ultimately go, at this point I am so desperately lonely for you, my love, that I would willingly accept the mandate of even Mr. Lincoln himself if it meant that we could spend the rest of our days together. I am nearly moved to say, "Damn the South and all its causes!" And may I be hanged for treason, if indeed it be treasonable that I should love you more than I love land or law or even the liberation of men. I have learned well, my darling, the true meaning of selfishness. For you are now part of myself, and dearer to me than any other cause in the world. . . .

I must have slept, for I awakened suddenly to a great hue and cry that was audible from outside. But, for a moment, I was completely disoriented. I had the terrible sensation that I had somehow been transported to the very front lines of the war, for I could hear the stern drumming of horses' hooves, the screams of men and women, and a general confusion everywhere.

Then it became clear to me where I was. The fire on the hearth had burned low. My skin felt damp from a mild perspiration. The room was completely dark except for the blood-red coals. And then, my heart seemed to hesitate before it picked up its rapid beat; and I wondered if last summer's raiders had returned while I slept.

The thought was even more alarming as I heard the household come alive, Benign's voice riding the crest of chatter and excitement coming from the floors below. I dashed to the window, where I had refreshed myself, and tore the draperies apart. The scene that confronted me froze me with terror.

Some dozen white-hooded and -shrouded figures mounted on horses were attacking the dissident blacks. The Negroes were screaming, holding their heads, running everywhere, falling down, wallowing in the dirty snow. They were being beaten and whipped by the shrouded riders, who sat astride their mounts with the unmistakable authority of white men. Some of them wielded clubs; others set the air afire with the vicious cracking of bullwhips. They were concentrating on the front cabins where the dissident blacks had settled. Riding back and forth in front of the cabins, they bathed the screaming, fleeing blacks in red by torches held by some of them. I could see the other cabins, untouched by this mayhem, where crowds of curious Negroes piled in windows and doors, but did not venture from their own sanctuary.

All this I saw in a mere instant. And then I whirled and raced from the window down the hall to Grandmother Parkchester's room. I saw that she was safe, sleeping undisturbed. Then I raced for the staircase, and met Benign puffing up to get me even as I went down. Her face was sweaty but filled with bold determination. She carried two rifles cradled in her arms. "Miss Victoria, there's some folks in sheets out there beating up them niggers that won't leave!" Before I could say a word, she jammed a rifle into my hands. And I saw, with some alarm, that she was hastily checking out her own. "I come to get you, Miss Victoria, so you could give the order to fire."

I did not have time then to think how heaven had either blessed or cursed me with Benign, her solid loyalty, and how she had managed to make the right decision before I had even thought of one. Obviously, it was our duty to protect the dissidents if we were not to be victimized ourselves by these hooded riders. At the same time—and this thought did occur to me as I rushed outdoors with Benign, where we were joined by an excited gang of house servants, some women among them, all of them armed—it was not entirely unbeneficial that the hooded riders were attacking the dissident Negroes.

Then, I had no further time for speculation. Bareheaded, uncloaked, practically unshod, I was suddenly at the head of my own small army. Their presence behind me compelled me forward over the drifts of snow to drive away the riders. I was aware enough at that point to realize that the prevailing confusion might result in one of my own allies accidentally shooting me. So I shouted at the top of my lungs, "Do not shoot at anyone! Fire into the air! Is that clear?"

The snow pulled at my frozen feet like reluctant mud; and I wondered if anything were clear to anyone in the all-consuming darkness. But it was Benign again who saved the day. "Y'all niggers shoot them guns into the air!" she bellowed. "Don't act a fool and shoot yourself! And I don't want nobody shooting me!" Removed from this situation—the screaming and confusion, horses whinnying, the solid thud of clubs against flesh, the stench of pitch from the glowing torches, all that lay ahead of us—except for that, I might have fallen into hysterical laughter at Benign's broad interpretation of what she knew I had meant to say. And so, frozen to the bone, certainly all of us frightened to death, my Negroes and I went to meet the riders.

I was glad that Charlotte and Lance Harcourt were

probably miles from the house by now, on their sleigh ride. I knew the stuff that Charlotte was made of. But could Lance be counted on in a situation like this?

As we went slowly forth toward the noise, light, and smoke from the evil-smelling torches, Benign put her lips to my ear and said, "We's getting mighty close, Miss Victoria. Ain't it time you told them to fire?"

I jerked like a puppet pulled by hidden strings. "Fire!" I cried. And Benign repeated the order, her voice a firm baritone that seemed to resound down the corridors of time. There were immediate tremendous explosions behind me, like the bursting of thousands of firecrackers.

The effect was magical. Even as my own senses inspected me with the care of an examining physician to make sure that my Negroes indeed had not mistakenly shot me, I saw the riders freeze in a grotesque tableau, as though the armies of Joshua had descended upon them. In an instant, they formed a large knot, staring in our direction from dark hollows in the white hoods.

It occurred to me then that I had not fired my rifle. I aimed at the dark sky and squeezed the trigger. The single shot parted the air like an explosion of thunder. To my amazement, the riders wheeled their horses about and fled, flinging their torches into the dirty snow, where they died with a sizzling sound.

"You sure did show them a thing or two, Miss Victoria." It was Benign's voice, as dry as browned biscuits. Even then, I felt like laughing at the absurdity of it all. Insofar as I could see, none of the milling Negroes ahead of us had been mortally wounded. And certainly the riders had meant us no harm, or they would not have fled under such ragtag provocation. As for the dissident blacks, they were pouring now from their cabins, carrying bundles and babies, some of them with steaming pots of food which they held carefully, almost indignantly, as though they had been interrupted as they were preparing to dine.

"Y'all niggers can go on back to the house," Benign said, dismissing our army. "And put them guns back in the kitchen." I felt, more than saw, their departure, like a black wave receding from us until it formed a solid line of figures entering the lighted kitchen door. I felt that I would collapse any minute from the cold; but there was an even deeper sensation of fear, which kept me on my feet.

"Where did you get those guns, Benign?" I said through frozen lips. "There was no time for you to go to the armory."

It was too dark to see her face; but I felt the warm swell of her body as she seemed to inflate with invisible power. "I got the key to the armory, Miss Victoria. You know that." Her voice was gentle but sly.

"I do know that, Benign. Still, you did not have time to go to the armory. The rifles were hidden in the house all the time. Weren't they?"

She answered without hesitation. "Yas'm." Now her voice was full of pride.

"Why were the rifles hidden in the house, Benign?"

She made a little noise that sounded like perfect surprise. "In case we needed them for something like what just happened."

Or, I thought, in case they needed them against us.

I started for the house. My feet were like blocks of ice, and Benign held my elbow to support me. I felt chilled to the very marrow of my bones. My teeth were chattering, making a sound like the wind rousing empty pods in a cottonwood tree. "I want the key to the armory, Benign."

"Yas'm." We had reached the kitchen door. She practically lifted me up the three steps and deposited me gently in the kitchen.

As she had ordered, there were perhaps two dozen rifles stacked against the wall around the kitchen. "I want the key now, Benign."

"Yas'm."

She sat me at the table, and in an instant a scalding cup of sassafras tea was in my hands. "Poor little child," she said, crooning in that peculiar, hypnotic way that Negro women have. "You near froze to death. And white as a ghost. You set right there and Benign's going to run and fix your fire and make you a nice hot bath so you can go to bed." She herself seemed as robust and unruffled as though she had just come in from a summer stroll.

"The key, Benign." The rifles around the kitchen filled me with dread.

She went to a drawer and took out a large ring filled with keys of all shapes and sizes. Selecting one, she gave it to me. Did I see a message, a warning, in the dark glitter of her eyes? Or was it Negro laughter? For the moment, I was at her mercy, and she knew it. I dropped the key into my dress pocket; later, I was to find out that it was the key to the lower drawer of the French armoire in Mother's sitting room.

"Now, you drink your tea, honey. You done right well tonight. Them men in sheets chased them niggers off. And then you chased them men in sheets off. Now I'm going to personally fix your fire and your bath."

She patted my hair with a large but gentle hand, and left, humming one of her heathenish hymns. I sat at the table, cold, shivering, but somehow quite content. I was drowsy as well. But I was thinking clearly enough to realize that while Mr. Lincoln had emancipated the slaves, no one on God's green earth would be able to free me from Benign except Benign herself. Truthfully, for the first time in my life, it seemed that I, more so than any other, had in some strange, secret, and almost mystical way, become a true servant to servants.

Yet, when Benign came bustling back some twenty minutes later to get me, she was as obsequious as ever, as though the existence of the rifles and her control over them had not dramatically changed our positions almost to the point where she had become mistress of Fir Crest and I her most humble and obedient servant. "Come and get your bath, child. The water's nice and hot, and I done turned your bed down for you."

I had a keen sense of unreality as she escorted me from the kitchen and through the huge sitting room, dim and silent now in its baronial splendor, and up the polished staircase. I found myself stumbling along with her as though I were blind and she was my guide through all the dim corridors that life takes us down. How could I best her in a very real sense? I knew now that she had been no more afraid of my theatrics with the derringer than she had been afraid of the riders tonight. As for the rifles which she controlled, it was obvious that they had been hidden somewhere in the house since they were turned in by the Negroes we had marshaled against the prospect of the raiders' returning last summer. Every event at Fir Crest from that point on, every incident that counterpoised black against white, had been an enormous farce. For the hidden cache of guns had made all the difference in the world.

I was thinking this as Benign undressed me and helped me into the tub. The water was deliciously warm, and it seemed that I was involved in some kind of healing baptism as I soaked there. It was as though strength flowed to me from Benign's hands even as I mistrusted her, even as she bathed me, dried me, powdered me, and put me to bed. "You sleep now, you hear me, child?" Her face was stern but loving. "I hear you, Benign." It was as though the clock had turned back and I was a child again. She kissed me on the forehead and blew out the lamps. But there was sufficient light coming from the fireplace for me to make out her figure, her ambiguous face.

"Benign?"

"Yas'm." Her voice was quite gentle as she turned at the door with her hand on the knob.

"In the morning, Benign, I would like a complete report on the condition of the Negroes who were attacked."

"I already know, Miss Victoria. Nobody got killed, thank the Lord for that. None of the women and children were touched. Some of the men got a few lumps on their skulls, and some bruises. That raid didn't do them a bit of harm. They all gone by now."

I marveled at the excellence and speed of her intelligence system. "Thank you, Benign. Good night."

"Good night, missy." She closed the door softly behind her, and I listened to her footsteps until they disappeared down the hallway. Although I felt like a child, I was aware that Charlotte, Grandmother Parkchester, and I were victims of either the most superb loyalty or the crassest hypocrisy imaginable. Certainly the blacks could overrun us anytime they wanted to, by virtue of the sheer weight of numbers, with or without rifles, with their many bare hands. In a violent moment, Benign herself was capable of doing away with the three of us all by herself. Did the rifles, then, constitute loyalty or subversion? The answer seemed quite obvious: loyalty of the most inordinate kind; for one rifle or a hundred in the hands of our Negroes could neither add to nor detract from the superiority they enjoyed in numbers and force and potential brutality even without the weapons.

Now my mind turned to a series of unanswered questions about the riders who had come so opportunely. Who had sent them? How had they known of our plight? Their coming, their careful selection of targets, and their sudden disappearance, paralleled in almost every respect accounts I had heard of the raiders who had come last summer. It appeared that someone, or some group of individuals, had developed a benevolent but secretive interest in the affairs of Fir Crest. And grossly destructive as well, for it could not be denied that the first group had murdered Mother and driven Grandmother Parkchester out of her mind.

The second group—quite different from the first that Robert Gilliam and his men had pursued and destroyed, except for their leader—had come under the protection of hoods and shrouds. Obviously one or some or all of them wanted to keep their identities hidden. They had appeared to be white men, from the manner in which they sat in their saddles. But was it possible that they were Negroes? If so, whose Negroes? And why such a special interest in Fir Crest that they would brutalize, perhaps even murder, their own color, if not their kind? The questions were intricate and confusing. It was as though we were being prepared for a tragedy of Grecian proportions, wherein the gods were determined to first drive us mad with puzzlement before they then passionately destroyed us.

I was still wide-awake, thinking along these lines, when I heard Lance and Charlotte return. The sleigh bells, muffled now as though held in the black grip of night, were comforting. They settled to a slow tinkle, and then picked up again with increasing rapidity even as they diminished, which meant that the driver had dropped Lance and Charlotte off, and was going to store the sleigh in the carriage house, then to bed down with the other Negroes. I listened quite carefully as Lance and Charlotte came upstairs together. They whispered awhile in the hall, and then Lance went into Father's room, where he would stay during his weekend visit. Charlotte came to my room and tapped on the door.

"Victoria? Are you awake?"

"Yes, dear. Come in. I'll light the lamps."

"No, don't. I shan't stay but a moment. I wanted to see

if you were all right." The fire had died on the hearth, and the room was perfectly dark. But Charlotte knew her way well; she found the bed without difficulty, and sat on it, searching for my hand. She still had her gloves on, which struck me as being somehow odd. At the same time, my nostrils were filled with a faint but peculiar and familiar odor that I could not then place.

"I'm fine, Charlotte. Did you have a good time?"

"It was wonderful! And I have the most marvelous news to tell you!" Her voice slid from a high plateau of excitement into a delighted whisper. She squeezed my hand so hard that it hurt. "Lance took me to a place deep, deep in the woods. Then he sent the driver away. And then he made love to me, Victoria, on pine branches which we broke. Wonderful, marvelous, exquisite love. On a bed of pine boughs, in the pure white snow."

I did not know what to say, except perhaps that it sounded scratchy, messy, and certainly cold. I was amazed that Lance Harcourt had sufficient energy or imagination to make love anywhere to anybody.

"Then you are no longer a virgin?" I said.

"No." She sounded wistful. "I am a woman now." It seemed a sacred moment that only two women could truly understand. I sat up in bed, and we embraced.

"Are you angry with me, Victoria? Did I do wrong? I love him, and it seemed the right thing to do. I love him very much, Victoria. And he loves me, too."

"Then you did the right thing, Charlotte. Of course I'm not angry." I embraced her again. She felt so frail and delicate as her arms tightened around my neck and her cheek touched mine. The odor I had noticed when she came in was stronger now; and I wondered, somewhat distastefully, if it were the scent of her virgin blood that Lance Harcourt had somehow managed to spill on pine boughs in the snow. When she released me, I lay back. Against my will, I felt unclean.

"Lance asked me to marry him, Victoria. I told him that we should wait until the war is over, when Father comes home."

"That was a wise decision, Charlotte." My nostrils rankled from that abominable odor. It was as though Satan himself had come into the room, stinking of fire and brimstone. . . . And then I recognized it quite well. It was the odor of burning pitch from the torches that the hooded raiders had carried. I had not yet had the opportunity to tell Charlotte about them, but I was surprised that the stench of torches would linger for so long and with such intensity. Then I drew in a breath, as softly and carefully as the falling of a snowflake. I knew precisely where the odor was coming from. "Charlotte, light the lamp, please."

"Oh, no! Let's just sit in the dark awhile longer. Then I must go and bathe. And sleep." Her voice sounded drowsy and content, as though she were reliving her romantic encounter with Lance Harcourt.

"I would like the lamp lighted, Charlotte. I want to see your lovely face."

She laughed. "It's the same face I had when I left."

The stench of pitch rose up and almost overwhelmed me. I had resisted laying one fact of logic alongside the other. But now I felt almost nauseated with the need to know the truth. "Why do you smell of pitch, Charlotte?"

She moved slightly away from me. "Isn't it awful? The air is filled with it." Her voice had changed dramatically. Now it sounded as though she were drugged, or very close to sleep. It frightened me. I jumped out of bed and lighted the lamp on the dresser.

It took a few seconds to adjust my eyes to the yellow intrusion of light. But when I did, I saw that Charlotte was nearly slumped on the bed. Her hair was undone, and hung to her shoulders, hiding her face from me. But what held my horrified attention was the dirty white garment that was draped over her right arm.

I approached silently, for she seemed to be half-asleep. What devilish thing had Lance Harcourt done to her? For it was obvious that the garment on her arm was a white hooded shroud. Charlotte had been with the riders who routed the Negroes. But how? And why? And had Lance Harcourt summoned the energy to be with her?

Cautiously I brushed her hair back from her face. She straightened somewhat at my touch, and then fell back into what seemed a hypnotic trance. Her eyes were glazed, yet alive with merriment, staring into a reality that only she could see. Her lids and lips were puffy, as though filled with the nectar of some indescribable joy.

I touched her arm lightly, for her whole demeanor frightened me. "Charlotte?"

"Yes?"

"You were with the riders, weren't you?"

Again she answered without hesitation. "Yes."

"Was Lance with you and the other riders?"

"Yes."

I kept my voice at a soft pitch, for it seemed that any loud noise might cause her to shatter, like fine crystal. Yet, for all her fragile looks, she was an expert rider. And I for one knew that she could be as strong as a steel trap, when the mood was on her. "How did you meet the riders, Charlotte?"

"It was after Lance and I made love. They rode up while we were waiting for the sleigh to return. They were going to another plantation where some Negroes were causing trouble. Lance persuaded them to come here first. They had some extra cloaks. They lent them to us so we could ride with them."

She laughed, but without any humor. "I have never been so excited in my entire life, Victoria! It was certainly the sensation of someone drowning in wine. I saw you leading Benign and the other Negroes from the house. I even smiled under my hood, for I knew you'd never dream I was there. When the rifles fired, we left. But we had done what we'd come to do. The others went on to their former mission. They call themselves the Avengers. They organized only recently to protect decent whites from the fury of Negroes. Lance and I rode back to the sleigh. We hid our cloaks from the driver, and then came home. It was marvelous, Victoria! Absolutely marvelous!" As she talked, her color returned, and she became more animated.

"It was a dangerous thing to do, Charlotte." Even to my own ears, it sounded like the mildest possible reprimand.

She stood. She seemed her old self again. "Dangerous, perhaps. But entirely necessary. Fir Crest is as important to me as it is to you."

"Oh, Charlotte!" I burst into tears and flung myself into her arms. What a dreadful toll the war was exacting from us all!

TWO

———◆———

From then until the Christmas season of 1864, we were caught up in a kind of mad social whirl hosted by Lance Harcourt and his friends, who seemed determined to greet the destruction of our society with an almost hysterical gaiety. These were sad and strange times; and if all of us did unusual things, it was certainly due to the general confusion and growing fear. Even now, aroused by the scent of blood, unscrupulous men and women in all manner of disguise were converging on the South from other parts of the country, to profit from its death throes and, eventually, to steal pennies from the eyes of its battle-scarred corpse.

During this time, I turned twenty-two and then twenty-three with little ceremony attending either occasion. But there was plenty doing elsewhere, and, under constant prodding from Charlotte and Lance, I had finally fallen into the mood of false gaiety. We were like revelers who had gathered at a masked ball, perhaps thinking that the noise of our partying would confound the plague outside and drive it away. In that respect, we were like savages rattling bones to frighten sickness away from the ailing South. But our magic was less than the Union's might; and at the beginning of 1864, a large portion of Louisiana, Mississippi, Florida, and the Rio Grande frontier of Texas; all of Arkansas, Kentucky and Tennessee; and the entire length of the Mississippi River were under Union control.

In our own area of the country, Richmond had already been attacked and was mobilized against further onslaughts. There was fighting in the Shenandoah Valley. Union forces had established important bases on the James River. General Lee had boldly crossed the Potomac, but then was forced back into Virginia in the Battle of Antie-

121

tam. There was fighting at Fredericksburg and Chancellorsville. We mourned the death in the latter battle of General "Stonewall" Jackson, who had masterminded this costly victory for the South. Again General Lee crossed the Potomac, foraging this time as far north as Pennsylvania, where he retreated after the Battle of Gettysburg.

But the true magic of history rests in the logic of the players upon its stage. We spoke our lines with a certain brilliance, and our costumes were impeccable. But we were illogical, fragmented, frightened. I could excuse such lapses in Lance Harcourt, Charlotte, and the host of ne'er-do-wells who clustered together like a plague of flies on rotten fruit. But I could neither excuse nor overlook the pestilence that had overtaken me. During the twelve months ending in February of 1864, Fir Crest survived and even flourished under the careful supervision of Banneker and Benign. The task of administration—parceling land, paying wages, maintaining the careful checks and balances necessary to ensure the survival of Fir Crest as an estate of freedmen while, elsewhere, slaves were all around us—this was taken over by Lance Harcourt, who came several times a week and worked in Father's study. Ever since the attack on the dissidents, I had looked at Lance in a new light. He still displeased me with his gaudy airs, but he was eager, competent, and helpful. In the changeover from slavery to freedom, all of us were affected by the unusualness of the situation. Surprisingly, Lance Harcourt seemed the least affected of all.

In the unlikely event that the South did win the war, we could easily shift our resources back to the machinery of slavery. But if the Union won, then we would already be several steps ahead of others into the area of reconstruction that would follow the war. Lance handled the affairs of Fir Crest with his eye on both possibilities. If he did have an inbred distaste for Negroes, he did not show it when dealing with Benign and Banneker. He was active, alert, and as agile as a snake, being able to move among a mass of contradictions with almost liquid grace. He could be firm and flexible by turn, and underneath his foppishness, which seemed to be merely a mask he presented to the world, he wore a rather perfumed manliness which suited the purposes of Fir Crest admirably at the time.

I was like a constitutional monarch, entitled to the glitter and glory of office because of an accident of birth, but unworthy to accept its true responsibilities, which Lance discharged for me. Thus freed, I danced and sang and laughed as loudly as the rest. But it pleased me, in the middle of the charade, to believe that only I could hear the hollowness of the celebration. And deep in the background, the thunder of cannon lined along every southern front, aimed like an arrow that would eventually pierce the heart of Appomattox.

I of course heard from Father and Robert Gilliam with a certain regularity; but I had reached a point where I fully understood that all of us in the South were the objects of events rather than their initiators. We were the first American people ever to await defeat, without even the privilege of foreign armies to conquer us, or of being bested in a contest more honorable than a civil one, accompanied by a war of nerves. Mine had been scraped raw from having to grow too fast in too little time, with the same lack of comfort that a fat lady feels squeezed into an ill-fitting corset.

I drew small comfort from Robert's letters; and he apparently received less from mine, for his soon took on a truculent tone that nicely matched my own indifference and evasion. As for Father, he had become pessimistic to the extent that I feared for his life, as though, in the midst of despair, he might willingly give it away. I sent him my most optimistic, if most inaccurate, accounts. To which he replied with the sourness of an Old Testament prophet:

I am tired of having it said that these are hard times, for all times are so. What affects me now is a sense of doom as I see the end of empire, and no suitable substitution to take its place. It is inevitable that the South will emerge from this war with more than scars. It will be a despised stepchild to her sister states for so long as they see fit to hold her in isolation. Neither black nor white will flourish, and both races shall be imprisoned with one another as an almost eternal suffering, to remind us of our mutual sin. For if whites have erred in imposing slavery, blacks are no less guilty in their acceptance of it. . . .

Despite Father's pessimism, our audacious experiment—that of giving freedom to slaves even in the midst of slavery and war—showed every sign of working, partly because of our location in an isolated sector of Virginia, but largely due to the industry of the people involved. Wherever a disadvantage occurred, it was offset by an equal and opposite advantage. With the paying of wages, for example, our expenses had increased considerably. But, impelled by their new sense of freedom, the Negroes produced more, destroyed less, and earned every cent they worked for, leaving Fir Crest with a comfortable margin of profit as well.

Despite its success, the changeover caused a drastic dislocation in our own sense of reality, for we were overseeing the death of one society and the simultaneous birth of another. We were still treated with the utmost respect by the Negroes, but it was clear that in the giving of freedom to others, we had given it to ourselves as well. And we were ill-suited to handle it, for we had been more deeply enslaved than our lowliest field hand. While Banneker, Benign, and the others never demonstrated by word or deed their awareness that they were now equal to us— if not in the eyes of others, then by our own admission— there was about them a certain enlargement of spirit which seemed, at the same time, to diminish our estimation of ourselves.

Also, by our act of emancipation, we aroused considerable anger and indignation among our neighbors, whose own plantations were thought to be endangered by the liberal policy at ours. Fortunately, Fir Crest was large and powerful enough to keep wagging tongues still, at least in front of our faces. But it is certain that we were called "damn Yankees," "nigger lovers," and "traitors" behind our backs. But for the constant patrolling of Fir Crest by Banneker and his men in a magnificent display of strength, we might even have been attacked by night raiders.

However successful we were on the surface as a unique social experiment, there was tension brewing underneath the surface at Fir Crest. A neighbor woman put it most succinctly in conversation with Charlotte and me at a party. "My dears, you are an estate suffering from an excess of refinement." In reality, I felt only bitterness and resentment, my sole forms of rebelling against the holocaust that was soon to fall upon us, and against the asinine opinions of my neighbors. It was this sense of rebellion, certainly coupled with guilt and inexperience, that sent me brazenly down from Fir Crest to the most decadent festivities imaginable in and around Charlottesville. Except for some last sense of civilization which prevented such barbarisms, we might have seen huge Negroes rip white virgins apart while we sipped French wine and laughed at these parties. Or children spitted and roasted over open fires for entertainment purposes, as the Romans are said to have done in their last days of empire. We did not see these spectacles, but there were others almost as vile. I have sat in one of the most fashionable homes in Charlottesville, nearly sotted on wine, and watched in fascination and disgust while two fighting cocks maimed each other with metal spurs. My bet was on the one that died, which meant that Lance Harcourt received a kiss in payment. He sought my lips, but I gave him my cheek. If my neighbors wanted to see whether I had the nerve to come to these affairs, I had more than sufficient nerve to show that I did. Whatever their opinions may have been of us in private, they treated us most genteelly in public, and with a certain amount of pity, as though we had lain down with dogs and come up with fleas. Or, more precisely, as though we had lain down with Negroes and come up black.

The basic error of most revolutions is that they occur too violently and too suddenly to maintain their effectiveness over the long range. If slaves were captives and we their captors, a special relationship had grown between us which permitted them a certain amount of flexibility even inside of bondage, while we were held rigidly to the codes of southern aristocracy. Then, in one fell swoop, slaves went from being owned by and absolutely subject to us, to being our equals. One would have thought that the dislocation would have taken place in their heads; instead, it took place in ours. Possibly, it is because they were insulated by their number, while we were exposed and made all the more vulnerable by ours. After that, I often wondered how much of a fraud I seemed to be in the eyes of Negroes. For nearly 250 years they had been taught, in effect, that whites were sacred, as inviolable as the scrolls in the Ark of the Covenant. After the proclamation, they had been allowed to peep into the ark, and found that it was filled with turnips and fluff, rather than with Holy Writ. My only defense against this exposure was to join Lance, Charlotte, and the rest in a display of arrogance as false and as futile as trying to catch water in a sieve. It was only natural that things would come to their head when I least expected.

It was October 1864. Charlotte and I had been at yet another party with Lance the night before, and I awakened under the rough pummeling of Benign's hands. When I finally opened my eyes, she poked a hand mirror at me. "Just look at yourself! You a complete mess! And I'm tired of seeing you this way. Lord knows there's too much to do around here without having to put up with you and Miss Charlotte acting the fool. I could expect it from her, but I'm ashamed of you."

"How dare you!" I cried. And I pushed the mirror away, trying to shield my face at the same time.

"I dàre!" Benign cried in turn. Amazingly, she caught both my wrists in one large hand and held them captive. "Look at you!" But I closed my eyes and shook my head stubbornly . . . until I was jolted by a slap that nearly broke my neck. I was shocked almost beyond belief. This black beast of a woman had struck me!

Now I knew why secret bands of white men were organizing under such names as the Klan, the Hooded Avengers, and the like, to ensure the safety and protection of whites from the black population.

I had met some of those men; and I swore by God— even as I lifted my head and stared dry-eyed into the accusing mirror—I swore by God that I would find a way to punish Benign for this outrage.

But for the moment, I was at her mercy. She was raging mad, easily holding my wrists in her big hand. "We had two drunk women in this family already. Now we got two more in training to take their place. Just look at yourself!"

I looked. I looked hard and long. The right side of my face was red from the impact of her slap. But my eyes were puffy and glazed. And my face showed the price I was paying for those many nights of false gaiety. I flung the mirror from me, turned down on the cool sheets, and cried.

The bed sank in deeply as Benign sat beside me. "Don't

cry, missy. You don't look so bad we can't make you pretty again." She patted my shoulders, my hair. Her hand was cool and gentle.

"I look terrible, Benign! I look absolutely terrible!"

"You sure do, child. But don't you worry none. Benign's got her own special conjure. She'll have you looking all right again in no time. I'm going to fix something to put on your face. Now, you get up and dress." It was an unmistakable order, however couched in gentle terms. "I'm going to get Miss Charlotte up, feed you a good breakfast, and then send you out horseback riding. Both of you need some fresh air and sunshine."

Other servants prepared my bath and assisted me while Benign went to Charlotte. I wondered, with a certain amount of amusement, what Charlotte's reaction to Benign would be. Relaxing in the tub of perfumed water, I felt considerably better, although there was a throbbing pain in my jaw where Benign had walloped me. Certainly I had needed it to bring me to my senses. Nonetheless, I still felt resentment that Benign had chosen such a primitive way to do it. Could I ever forgive her? Perhaps, I thought, if she makes me pretty again. And perhaps never, even if she made me more beautiful than Helen of Troy. My own parents had never attacked me so brutally. Could a servant be allowed to do such a thing with impunity? The answer was clearly no, even if it was for my own great benefit, even if it was done by Benign. . . .

The fragrant water, and the soothing hands bathing me, made me drowsy. But I was brought back to sharp reality by the sound of Charlotte's voice raised in the hallway. I could hear her angry footsteps storming toward my door. And then she flung it open, looking for all the world like the wrath of God—red hair streaming down her shoulders, eyes blazing. Her taut, angry body was enveloped in a billowing nightgown of the most delicate black lace. Even without Benign standing solidly behind her, I knew what had happened by the angry red welt on her cheek.

"Benign *slapped* me!" she cried. "I want her whipped! I want her dismissed from Fir Crest at once!"

I stepped from the tub into large, soft towels held by two impassive Negro women who seemed to have lost the ability either to see or to hear. Yet I knew that their every sense was alert, that what transpired in this room today

would be talked about down to the smallest detail in the
Negro quarters tonight. "She slapped me too, Charlotte. I
needed it to bring me to my senses. I suspect that you
needed it, too."

Her lovely face was quite pale. "It is true what they say
of you!" she cried.

I raised my arms, and one of the Negro women
dropped a pale blue shift over my head. Another held soft
slippers, which I stepped into as I adjusted the gown. I
could feel their tension as they stood stiffly nearby.
Clearly, the circumstances seemed to suggest that I send
them from the room. But there were no secrets at Fir
Crest any longer. To send them away, or to pretend that
they were indeed deaf and dumb to Charlotte's flaming anger, would only have added another layer to the prevailing
hypocrisy. "And what is it that they say of me, dear Charlotte?" Benign stood in the doorway, arms folded underneath her breasts, eyes lidded like a wise old turtle's. I sat
at the vanity, and one of the women brushed my hair
while the other drained the tub. My face seemed less worn
than before, but I was still anxious for Benign to start her
treatments.

"They say that Fir Crest has been taken over completely
by Negroes!" Charlotte cried. She was flinging herself
around the room in a perfect rage. "They say that you
have become a Negro yourself!"

"I can think of many things worse," I said evenly,
watching her carefully from the mirror. Today's events
were even now being taken in and recorded by the Negroes; how I comported myself would be crucial to the
continued success of Fir Crest. "And as for Fir Crest
being taken over, it would seem that Lance Harcourt has
done a most effective job of that. He is due again today to
work on the books, is he not? I have been like someone
stumbling about in a deep sleep, and he has acquitted himself well during this time. But today I shall let him know
that Fir Crest is once again in my hands."

Charlotte seemed disconsolate. Flinging herself into a
chair, she asked meekly, "How can you speak thus of
Lance Harcourt? He has been most generous with his
time."

"Perhaps too generous, Charlotte." Even as I said so, it
appeared to be the height of ingratitude. Looked at impas-

sionately, however, it was true that Lance had encouraged my weaknesses rather than my strength. And had moved into a position of unwarranted importance at Fir Crest.

Even as I was thinking this, a kind of signal passed from Benign to the other two black women. One laid down the brush in mid-stroke, the other stopped her work with the tub. Both bowed simultaneously and joined Benign at the door. "Breakfast is ready, Miss Victoria, Miss Charlotte," Benign said. Her face was an impassive mask, revealing nothing. Before I could go through the formality of thanking her, she closed the door. I could hear no footsteps in the hallway: either they were listening at the door, which seemed unlikely, or they had floated away like wraiths, which seemed quite within their possibilities.

For several minutes the room was quiet except for an occasional agitated sigh from Charlotte. She had quit the chair and was pacing on the thick carpet. I picked up the brush and worked at my hair until it shone. Finally I said to Charlotte, "I think you should go and dress. Benign has the day planned for us. First breakfast, then horseback riding. Then, only the Lord knows."

"Why do you take orders from her?" Charlotte cried. "Why do you put up with so much from her?"

Looking at her petulant face, I was filled with a kind of fear, certainly with exasperation. There had been fighting very near us last May in the Wilderness campaign outside of Chancellorsville. Now, Confederates were being routed from the Shenandoah Valley. In the east, General Grant had set up a base on the James River and had Petersburg under siege. Charlotte, as everyone else in the South, was aware of these developments in the war. And now she was asking me why I put up with Benign, when it was clear that we were closer than ever to final defeat. "It's only a matter of time before Richmond falls," I said, far more calmly than I felt. "What would you have me do, Charlotte? Benign is absolutely right in this respect, because we have been frittering our lives away like frightened children. And because we have no alternative but to take orders from her, if she sees fit to give them. What would you have me do?"

She was still livid with anger. "I shall tell Lance. He will know what to do."

"And what will you tell Lance? That even as we are losing the war, Benign is concerned for our health and welfare? For the well-being of Fir Crest? Lance appears concerned, but his seems to be almost self-serving. Benign's seems genuine."

"You dare compare the two?" Charlotte cried. "Lance will be most happy to hear that!"

I had dressed while we were talking. "I do not care a fig about Lance Harcourt at this moment, Charlotte. I am concerned about getting things back on the right track again. We have gone terribly astray. I blame no one but myself for that. If it has taken a slap from Benign to make me see the light, then I am happy for the intent, if not for the act." I touched my jaw, trying humor to bring her from her dark mood. "She is heavy-handed indeed."

But Charlotte was too irate to be so easily seduced. "You make a joke of everything! The simple truth is that you are afraid of her! Well, I am not! And she will pay dearly for this! I promise!"

With that, she left, slamming the door so hard that it seemed close to falling from its hinges.

I had put on my riding outfit, having some difficulty with the boots, as I was accustomed to being helped by servants. Yanking and tugging, I finally got them on. Then, after a quick inspection in the mirror, I went downstairs.

Breakfast was served in the east garden by one of the other house servants, which meant that Benign was showing her displeasure, or was otherwise occupied. It had been a long time since either Charlotte or I had dined formally at Fir Crest, and it was delightful sitting among the late-blooming roses and other flowers sweetening the autumn air. The morning sun laid a warm hand across my shoulders, my cheek, like a gentle caress. And the sky was remarkably blue, not a cloud in sight. As far as I could see, trees were lavishly adorned in red and gold, yellow and brown. And there was the rich, masculine odor of woodsmoke and burning leaves, which reminded me of Robert Gilliam. Thinking of him, I felt almost consumed with guilt. Now that a certain order had been restored, I would write him this afternoon and make a clean breast of how we had spent the past months running around in desperate circles. Had I lost Robert's love during the panic? I prayed God I had not, but it was a question that only time could tell.

As I nibbled at a biscuit with honey, I saw Amos coming down the road leading Charlotte's mount and mine. At the same time, I saw Grandmother Parkchester being helped by Juniper and Benign to the candle house. Johnny Cake and a younger son of Benign's were parading after them. Like most of the utility buildings at Fir Crest, the candle house was a squat gray structure covered over with weatherboarding. All the candles used at Fir Crest were made there in several vats of boiling tallow into which cotton wicks were dipped. The candles were stored there as well, and the structure was secured by iron bars on the windows and a heavy oak door with padlock, to prevent pilfering by Negroes who used up their rations before the appointed time.

Grandmother Parkchester had been especially active in the making of candles before her illness, and had turned out quite artistic ones. Even now, it was Benign's habit to take the old woman there on candle-making day, prop her in a wooden chair, and let her gaze with those great, mad green eyes at the assortment of pickaninnies and women who worked over the candles in the smoky house. The shutters on the windows were flung open, allowing for a certain ventilation through the iron bars. But I had asked Benign if the smoke from several open fires might not be too harmful to Grandmother. "She enjoy it, Miss Victoria. She really do. Last time she was there, she made a little drawing on a candle." I had seen the candle, and there were several fingernail scratches on it, hardly anything that could be called a drawing. But it had pleased me, and I kept it on the dresser in my room. Perhaps Grandmother Parkchester would be restored to good health. But for now, like a crippled galleon being towed to port, she was being led by Juniper and Benign to the candle house. Red hair flaming, tall, elegantly attired, she was a tragic shell of her former self. Two pickaninnies pranced behind as though to catch her should she fall.

"Good morning, Victoria."

Called from my musing, I looked up to see Charlotte standing near me. She, too, was wearing riding clothes. And she was smiling. Presumably she had gotten over her pique, and had decided to follow the restored discipline at

Fir Crest. "I'm absolutely famished!" she said, taking her seat. "Isn't it a lovely day? Is that Grandmother Parkchester and Benign going to the candle house? And Juniper?"

I told her that it was. "With Johnny Cake and one of Benign's other sons." I did not know the younger boy's name, for he rarely came to the house. Benign and Juniper had five sons, at least two of them in their middle twenties. Along with their father, Juniper, the two eldest had ridden with Banneker and Robert Gilliam against the raiders. Before emancipation, Benign's children had been among a dozen or so Negroes who regularly made candles; now Benign and her sons had incorporated this task into their other duties, adding extra pennies to their wages. I made a mental note to find out and remember their names. But for the moment, I was watching Charlotte closely. She had helped herself to sausage, eggs, and biscuits and was eating with a hearty appetite. Her color was lovely, and she seemed her old self again. The ugly scene in the bedroom might not have happened at all. She did not mention it, and I was content to let the matter rest. The most important thing now seemed to be that we should take over the reins of a new Fir Crest, which we had relinquished, however unreluctantly, to Lance Harcourt. I was happy to be back inside the discipline we had abandoned. Watching Grandmother Parkchester and the others enter the candle house, I was pleased, though somewhat guilty, that the routine had continued apace, even to the smallest detail, without my participation.

After several moments of furious eating, Charlotte pushed her chair back and stood. "I feel wonderful!" she cried. She looked wonderful. And I would have hugged and kissed her if she had not run to the waiting horses, calling over her shoulder, "I'll race you to the chestnut tree. First one there gets an extra tart for supper." It was an old child's game, which made me smile. I rushed from the table to my own horse; but Charlotte was already in her saddle and heading at a vigorous pace up the road between the orchard and the cornfield. Amos was grinning as he helped me into my saddle. "You won't have no trouble catching her, Miss Victoria. Sally here is better than that gelding Miss Charlotte's riding."

"Thank you, Amos. Please tell Benign we'll be back for dinner."

I gave spurs to Sally, and she sped from the yard with a tremendous surge of power. Charlotte was far ahead of me, slowing down some to at least give me the semblance of an equal chance. She was waiting near the edge of the cornfield, smiling and waving, the gelding prancing impatiently, when I saw a figure dash from the cornfield and attack her.

At first I was too astonished to do more than watch. It was impossible to tell who the person was who had leaped at Charlotte. But whoever it was had snatched the reins and was pulling her with furious strength from the saddle. Charlotte was slashing wildly with her riding crop. Fighting the air with agitated feet, the gelding reared. And I saw my sister fall to the ground. The figure was on her in an instant, attacking with the violent grace of a panther. Now I dug spurs to Sally, and she took off like the wind. My heart was in my throat as we galloped up the road.

It was Emerald, Banneker's woman, fighting Charlotte down in the dirt. They were locked together like two incensed cats, rolling and wallowing on the pebble-studded ground. The woman Emerald had both hands full of Charlotte's hair, as though she wanted to yank her brains out. For her part, Charlotte was beating the black woman about her face and breasts with surprisingly solid fists. They were both screeching loudly enough to awake the dead, so that when I jumped down from Sally and ordered them to stop, it is probable they did not hear me. I tried to part them, but there was such a flurry of arms, hands, bare feet, and boots in my direction that I stepped cautiously back.

As I watched them, they settled down into a quiet but intense struggle. I suppose that I was struck by the oddness of my own sister fighting in the dirt with a black servant woman. What really impressed me, however, was the way they fought in a kind of furious slow motion, certainly with every intention to wound and maim each other, perhaps even to kill; but there was little blood that I could see, except for a stain under Charlotte's nostrils and a long streak above Emerald's breasts where Charlotte's fingernail had slashed like a keen, eager knife.

It suddenly occurred to me that I had to take drastic action to stop them, for they seemed prepared to struggle until one of them was dead. Yet, I was filled with a sense

of unreality, perhaps because it was the first time I had
seen women fight before. I was reminded of the cocks we
had seen bloodying the living room in Charlottesville in
their battle to the death. There was about Charlotte and
Emerald the same eager colliding of bodies, the withdrawal; a searching of hands and arms, legs and feet, for
the final advantage; and then the withdrawal again. Struggling in the warm October sun, they might have been involved in some primitive form of lovemaking. The black
woman's gray blouse was torn, and her full breasts moved
in a kind of lovely rhythm to her struggle. Charlotte's riding habit, being more substantial, was practically intact,
except for a tear here and there where Emerald's nails had
made their penetration.

Even as I tried to analyze the reason for their conflict,
and marveled at the violent beauty and rhythm of their
bodies in collision, I had taken my riding crop from the
saddle and set upon them viciously. I was filled with loathing and disgust, and I attacked them with telling blows.
They both seemed amazed at my reaction, and stopped
fighting at once. "Get up!" I cried. I thrashed them both
soundly, as though they were children. And it seemed that
I saw the same satisfaction on their faces that happens to
children when they are stopped in the middle of a tan-
trum.

Charlotte was the first up, trying to straighten her riding
breeches, her blouse. Her hat had come off in the struggle,
and her long red hair was undone. I had been careful not
to strike her on the face and arms and she seemed in fine
form, except for the blood that stained her nose. Then
Emerald came to her feet. Whatever her reasons for attacking Charlotte, she seemed to have gotten the worst of
the bargain. She wore an ill-fitting skirt that matched the
gray of her blouse. Her breasts were full, lovely, unin-
jured, insofar as I could see. She gathered the torn ends of
the blouse and tied them to hide her nakedness. Her frizzy
hair seemed to stand on every end, like fine black wire.
Her eyes were as dark and defiant as any thundercloud.

I was breathing more heavily than either of them.
"What is the meaning of this?" I cried.

"You tell this hussy to leave Banneker alone," Emerald
said. Although her breasts were heaving, her voice was
even, threatening, but somehow remote.

Charlotte laughed. "Banneker? What on earth am I doing to Banneker?"

"You know what you doing," Emerald said. "Everybody know what you doing. You nearly driving him out of his mind, that's what you doing. Every chance you get, you sneaking off with him somewhere."

"If that's the case," Charlotte said, "then why don't you talk to Banneker instead of attacking me? I have no argument with you."

And with that comment, I knew what it was that had puzzled me about the way they had struggled. They were two women fighting about a man they both desired. Whoever won stood the chance of losing the very man they were fighting about, so neither had really tried to win. However shocked I was by Emerald's accusation, Charlotte's defiant reaction proved that the woman was not lying. Moreover, they had made enough noise to raise an army of Negroes. Yet, not one had come. That was more telling than anything that Emerald could have said.

"I got a big argument with you," Emerald was saying to Charlotte. "You white. You pretty, if you go by what a nigger man likes. And you *easy*. All I want you to do is leave my man alone."

By this time Charlotte had repaired herself sufficiently to climb aboard her horse. "I tell you the same thing I said before: if what you say is true, then why don't you talk to Banneker?"

The black woman's eyes seemed to fill with a kind of sorrow. "Ain't no talking to him now. When a nigger get a taste of easy white meat, ain't nothing a nigger woman can say to him."

Charlotte wheeled her horse about. "Then perhaps you should change your color to white," she said viciously. "Until then, I warn you that henceforth I shall be armed. Think twice before you attack me again." Her eyes settled on mine. "That goes for you as well, dear sister." She kicked the gelding brutally and rode down the path to Fir Crest.

I stayed awhile longer with the black woman. "Is it true what you say?"

She met my gaze without flinching. "It's true. I seen them together three times. They been together a lot of times. Benign know. Everybody know. You don't believe me, you ask Benign." She stepped across the road into the cornfield. Reaching behind her back, she came out with a shining dagger from her waist. "And you tell Miss Charlotte that Emerald's armed, too. Emerald's always armed. The only reason I don't cut her throat is because Banneker'd cut mine. That how full of the white fever he is." Without another word, she disappeared into the brown stalks.

I rode slowly back to Fir Crest in a state of high agitation. Negroes were cutting corn of the far side of the field, and I could hear the harmony of their voices murmuring in a kind of subdued, mournful singing. The orchard, to my right, was heavy with apples and pears, hanging almost like a garden of forbidden fruit. October had fallen on us with the golden somnolence of a heavily perfumed veil, touching everything with an unaccustomed drowsiness. Still, my mind was unusually agitated, like the gyrations of a moth trapped inside a warm globe.

It was no longer possible to evade burning issues. Charlotte had been publicly accused of having a sordid affair with Banneker. He himself had privately warned me to tell Charlotte to "stop messing with him" when he had come with the report of how our Negroes had responded to the Emancipation Proclamation. I suppose that, deep within my consciousness, I had known even then what he had meant, but had avoided confronting it. The South had always abounded with tales of white women who had found Negroes more desirable than white men—presumably because there is more pleasure to be gotten from one's servants than from one's equals. It was common knowledge that white men frequently preferred black wenches, and they openly boasted about their clandestine trips to the slave cabins. There were even rumors that slave men and boys were often forced into sexual relationships with their masters.

If such stories were true—and reason demanded that not all of them be dismissed as false—then Charlotte was a prime candidate for the thing that Emerald had accused her of. Spoiled, strong-willed, temperamental, she had always set a goal and then forged toward it with the accuracy of a well-aimed bullet. If there was a perverse nature in her, it had been triggered by the bawdiness of Grandmother Parkchester, not to discount Father's own permissiveness. If she had made Banneker the target of her affection, she had fallen into a deeper decline than even I had thought possible. Not merely because he was a Negro, but because he was intelligent, and capable of extreme passion, loyalty, and contempt. If Charlotte had wanted to seduce a Negro man, she could not have made a poorer choice, for any other Negro would have been subject to her without question; Banneker would insist upon dominating her without giving any quarter.

All the available evidence was against her. She had taken me to the slave cabin to watch Banneker make love to Emerald. She had not denied Emerald's charges today. Perhaps I was improper in judging her without hearing her defense, but she was certainly in a defiant mood now, one that would make her affirm or deny according to that mood, rather than to the facts. It would be impossible to pin her down today, even if she were not guilty. And if she were, it would be more than impossbile to draw a confession from her.

All these thoughts were swarming in my head as I entered the side yard at the house and dismounted. There was no servant to tend my horse, so I looped the rein around the branch of a thorn bush and headed for the kitchen. Before I entered, I turned and took a quick look at the candle house, where smoke seeped from the barred windows like the pale breathing of monsters. At least Grandmother Parkchester, if she could comprehend at all, was removed from the possibility of a noisy, all-out argument between Charlotte and me.

Benign was busy at the kitchen stove when I entered. Too busy, for she neither turned nor greeted me, as she usually did. So she had heard about Charlotte and Emerald. And disapproved.

I was tired of the opinions of Negroes—at least, of this particular one. I took off my riding gloves and slapped them commandingly on the table. "Benign, I have something to say to you. I want you to turn around and listen carefully, for I shall say it only once."

She turned slowly, almost insolently. So that I was surprised at the expression on her face—one of the deepest sorrow imaginable. But I had learned not to be misled by the tricks she did with her mobile face.

"I would like you and all the other Negroes to know

that I am tired of being treated as though I were an idiot child. The facts seem to be pure and simple: you and the rest are here now of your own free will. Any one of you is able to leave whenever you wish . . . or whenever I so desire it. If you stay, at my pleasure . . . if you continue to eat my food, live in my quarters, accept my money in wages, enjoy all the comforts of this estate . . . then it must be understood once and for all that I shall no longer tolerate insolence or insubordination. If that is displeasing to anyone, I want to know it now. And I want them off the plantation within the hour. From this point on, I am mistress of Fir Crest in every solitary respect."

Her face still appeared sorrowful, but her eyes seemed slightly amused. "I'm glad you finally found that out, Miss Victoria. Mr. Lance Harcourt, he been acting like he mistress of Fir Crest. He come down the back road while you and Miss Charlotte was out riding. He in the study drinking sherry, prancing about with his hand on his hip. He call hisself working. Maybe you ought to tell him that, too."

"Perhaps I shall, Benign. At the same time, I am especially displeased by your continued insolence. As I have said, if you are unhappy here, you may go elsewhere."

She grunted. "Maybe I will. Right now, you better look in on your sister. She need that fire of yours more than I do."

She had pushed me beyond the brink. "I shall return in an hour, Benign. When I do, I expect either your sincere apology, or I shall chase you off the land myself. Is that clear?"

She seemed very amused. "Yas'm, Miss Victoria. That's clear." Deliberately she turned her broad back on me and stirred in some pots.

There was Lance to be dealt with, and Charlotte. I decided to attend to Charlotte first, for I would need her as an ally in any showdown with either Lance Harcourt or Benign. I went directly to her room.

It is a rare sensation to approach someone you have known all your life as though you were meeting a stranger. As I rapped at Charlotte's door, I was filled with a sense of great foreboding. At the same time, I felt almost invincible, certainly the sensation that sent Amazon women into victorious battle. Whatever awaited me beyond that door, I was prepared for it. I knocked once, and then again. And heard a voice respond with ineffable sweetness: "Come in."

The room seemed to have been painted in soft gold from the sun's rays that stretched long, slanting fingers over everything. Charlotte had changed from her riding outfit into a beautiful gown of pale green. She had fixed her hair, and a strand of emeralds glittered around her neck. The room had been decorated in soft shades of green, amber, and white. In those surroundings, Charlotte seemed pure and delicate. She held a tiny yellow hankerchief, which she dabbed under her nostrils from time to time, which I supposed was to stem blood from the wound that Emerald had inflicted there. Nonetheless, I had never seen her so radiantly beautiful. She smiled happily when she saw me, and we embraced. Again, it was as though the immediately preceding events had completely escaped her mind, while they preyed heavily upon me. I almost lost my resolve; but there was more at stake now than just the feelings or the follies of my sister. Fir Crest would either stand or fall this day; I was determined that it would stand now and for the thousand years to come. As Charlotte released me, I looked at her with dispassionate eyes. From long experience, I knew that she was capable of changing her mood to fit the moment, like an especially lovely chameleon. But I was on my guard as she led me to a chair near the fireplace, taking one herself near me.

"Is it true, Charlotte, what the woman Emerald says?"

She dabbed at her nose with the handkerchief; it seemed that she sniffed it for a moment, as ladies do with sachet. "It is true," she said.

I was somewhat taken aback. She could be as brutally honest as she could be cunning and circumspect. But I had come to mistrust her honesty, as though it were a rose with a deadly thorn hidden underneath its petals.

"Why have you chosen to dirty and dishonor yourself, to dishonor us?"

She shrugged her delicate shoulders. "I did not see it as being either dirty or dishonorable. Banneker is a man. I am a woman. Is race all that important?"

The question seemed extraordinary. At this very moment, men were killing and dying on not-too-distant battlefields to preserve the integrity of one race even as they made their best efforts to free or subjugate another. I looked very closely at Charlotte. Her eyes seemed glazed and sleepy. I wondered if she had been drinking, but I did not smell liquor, nor did I see a glass anywhere. I remembered Benign's comment that Charlotte and I were on our way to becoming drunks. On that score, I felt completely safe. But what of Charlotte? Was she to follow Mother and Grandmother Parkchester down the lonely road to drunkenness?

But another question interceded. "Then you were not a virgin with Lance Harcourt?"

"No." She shook her head dreamily.

I accepted that as fact. Certainly Lance Harcourt could be deceived into believing that Venus was a virgin.

"Have you been drinking today, Charlotte?"

She seemed quite surprised. "At this hour of the day? Heavens no!"

She sounded so genuine that I was disposed to take her word. I watched as she raised the handkerchief to her nostrils, dabbed and sniffed, and then rested her pale white hands in the lap of her gown.

"Tell me about Banneker," I said. "How long has it been going on?"

"Perhaps a year. Certainly not longer than a year."

"Did you consider the consequences of such a relationship?"

"No. I did not care. When he makes love to me, I care about nothing in this world. Besides, I did not think that anyone would find out. Although I did not care. We would meet once a week at the crest of firs."

Once a week! I was almost staggered by what she was saying; yet, she seemed supremely calm. Sex with Banneker once a week for nearly a year? The wonder was that she had not yet dropped a mulatto bastard in the sitting room downstairs.

"Have you considered pregnancy?" I whispered, as though the very walls had ears.

She smiled wanly. "I have been taking . . . something. It comes from his mother, Yetta. There is no danger of pregnancy."

I was too disturbed to sit any longer. I stood, and walked to the north window. There was a clear view of the candle house, still issuing smoke in pale clouds. "It must stop," I said firmly. "You are never to see Banneker again that way. Do you understand me, Charlotte?"

"I understand." Again the handkerchief was at her nose. There was no blood that I could see anywhere, and it annoyed me that she should continue to repeat such a senseless action while we were discussing vitally important matters. In a sudden angry moment, I snatched the handkerchief. "You have compromised all of us by your stupid acts!" I cried. It is possible that I was going to strike her, she appeared so smug, so remote from the very situation she had created. But she was in such a perfect daze that no amount of violence seemed capable of arousing her. I held the yellow handkerchief, not knowing what to do with it, when I was assailed by the faint but noxiously sweet odor of laudanum. And my very knees seemed to turn to water. For it was clear now that, along with everything else, my sister Charlotte was an opium user.

My first impulse was to become angry, but it was as though the act of holding the opium-drenched handkerchief had sent me into an unaccustomed euphoria. My pores seemed to open and drink from the opiate; and, for an instant, I was filled with indescribable joy, as though China's opium dens had suddenly been transported to the orderly sedateness of Fir Crest.

"Do you have more laudanum?" I said. My throat felt constricted, and my speech was thick, as though my tongue had suddenly bloated.

"There is more," Charlotte said. "There is a bottle in the top drawer of my vanity."

I moved in a half-daze to the vanity. I was still holding the handkerchief, and a part of my mind wondered whether I was under its spell, or simply in a state of shock that my sister had sought comfort in the soothing shadows of laudanum. If so, she would not be the first southern female who had done so. Again, the practice was a thing more gossiped about than documented. But if there were a basis in fact for even part of the rumors, at least half the ladies who kept to their rooms with vaguely described ailments were laudanum users. The other half were said to be drunks. Common sense dictated that every rumor not be treated seriously; it also required that they not be treated overlightly as well.

I found the laudanum in a corked bottle in the vanity.

As soon as I touched it, I jerked back to my senses. I was filled with disgust. First liquor, then illicit sex with Banneker, now laudanum—what other ills was my sister capable of? Sitting in her half-stupor, she might have been a drugged madonna waiting to be handed her child. More than anger, I felt a need to protect her, to remove her from the influences that had brought her to this point of depravity.

I kindled a small fire on the hearth and threw the handkerchief in. It disappeared in a slight gasp of smoke, as though swallowed by hungry imps. I dropped the bottle of laudanum into my dress pocket, where it sagged with surprising weight. Then I sat near Charlotte and held her hands. They felt cold, as though she had been playing in snow. "Can you hear me, Charlotte? Do you understand me?"

She nodded readily to both questions, and so I continued. "As you know, we have relations on Mother's side in Georgia. When I wrote to tell them of her death, they were most gracious. They even invited us down to overcome the horror of what had happened. I had thought of sending you then, but you seemed to have come from your depression quite nicely." As I talked, she kept her head to one side. There was an almost beatific smile on her lovely lips. "I intend to send you there now," I said softly. "You have come under devilish influences, thanks to Lance Harcourt. The best solution seems to remove you as far as possible from him."

Her eyes snapped green fire, and her whole body seemed to come awake. "Lance Harcourt? Georgia? What does one have to do with the other?"

I felt the deepest pity for her. "Was it not Lance who introduced you to laudanum?" I cried. "Do you think that he is a good influence on you?"

Snatching her cold hands away, she stood with a majesty that reminded me of Mother. "He is an excellent influence!" she cried. "The laudanum did not come from him. And, unless he has discovered for himself, he knows nothing of it from me. As for Mother's relations in Georgia, I absolutely refuse to go. You are my sister, that is true. But you are not my warden. I shall remain at Fir Crest as long as I please." With a swirl of her green gown, she turned her back on me in a gesture of dismissal, as though I were an offending servant. "Now, if you'll excuse me, I've had quite enough of this for one day. As for the laudanum, do not believe that by taking one bottle, you take all. Obviously, there is more where that came from."

I stepped around in front of her. Normally lovely and placid, her features were twisted with ugly confusion. "Charlotte, this is for your benefit! You know that laudanum is an evil habit! If not from Lance, then whom?"

Her eyes grew calculating. "That, dear sister, is for me to know and you to find out. But I swear to you that it was not Lance. I also swear to you that I shall never go to Georgia or any other place away from Fir Crest. I love Lance, and I want to be near him."

Suddenly she seemed to slump, holding her hands to her forehead as though she had been stunned by excruciating pain. But when I moved to help her, she shoved me away. "Please leave," she whispered. Her face was ghostly white. "Leave me!"

I had the strangest sensation that if I did leave then, we would lose each other forever. Daringly, I grabbed her arms with as much strength as I could muster. "If not Lance Harcourt, Charlotte, then who?"

She smiled most evilly. "Are you too stupid to figure that out for yourself?"

Banneker? I could not believe that he would do such a thing. Yet, it seemed strange that I could so easily place the blame on Lance Harcourt. He was waiting for me now in the study. I intended to get to the bottom of this however I could. Meanwhile, I had Charlotte's well-being to think about.

"I am having two guards placed on your door," I told her. "While you may be indisposed to go to the Devereaux in Georgia, you will go nowhere henceforth here at Fir Crest without my knowledge or permission. As for Lance Harcourt, he is waiting for me in the study. Today will be his last at Fir Crest. If you love him as you say, I trust that it will suffer a long separation."

I swept past her and went to the door. Somewhere beyond the barriers of her stupor, a dam had broken and she was crying. But there was still enough strength and venom in her to utter a sleepy-sounding threat: "You shall pay for this, Victoria, and dearly!" I left the room without another word. Had I been too harsh with her? Perhaps. And perhaps not. Drastic circumstances seem to require drastic solutions.

On my way to the study, I stopped in the sitting room and rang for Benign. She came immediately. "I want a twenty-four-hour guard placed on Miss Charlotte's door, beginning tomorrow," I said. With the laudanum Charlotte had sniffed while we were talking, I did not think she could cause further mischief today. "There should be two men night and day. You yourself are to accompany her whenever and wherever she goes upon leaving her room. Is that clear, Benign?"

"Yas'm." She seemed to have lost her earlier insolence. Indeed, she was quite her old self again. And, in a moment of the most inspired gentleness, she reached out and drew me to her large bosom. "Missy, I sorry I talk to you so rough. You got your problems, but I think you handle them right well. I'll have a guard on Miss Charlotte first thing tomorrow morning."

I was deeply touched. It was like the return of a cherished friend to a house that had been empty overlong. "Thank you, Benign. Now I shall see Mr. Harcourt in the study. Please bring me a coffee. I desperately feel the need for it."

Her face grew amused, almost sly. "I'm making some tarts in the kitchen. With cold buttermilk. All my children working in the candle house with Juniper, and I figured I'd give them some, too. They'll be ready by the time you get through with Mr. Harcourt."

"Very well, Benign." She, more than any other, knew my main weaknesses. "With tarts waiting in the kitchen, I shall make short shrift of Mr. Harcourt."

"You do that, honey. The children, they just dying to show you how much they done growed. You just do that."

She went back to the kitchen, and I into the study. In his shirtsleeves, Lance was, indeed, sipping sherry and prancing about, giving the appearance of being in deep thought. It was certainly no time to dilly-dally, so I retrieved the bottle of laudanum from my pocket and thrust it under his nose.

"What on earth is that?" he said. "It smells excessively cheap and heavy, the sort of thing a servant might use."

"It's laudanum," I said. I restrained myself from telling him that I had taken it from Charlotte's room, in case he really didn't know. "Are you so unenlightened that you don't know what laudanum is?"

"Of course I know, my dear," he said smoothly. "It's an opium derivative, widely used in medicine to ease suffering and pain."

"And by others to escape into a dream world," I said.

He pursed his pretty lips, then swallowed his sherry. "Am I being accused of something?" he said. His speech was slurred, as though he were quite close to being drunk. "If so, I should be allowed to dress like a gentleman." He slipped into his waistcoat and fastened his tie. How I detested the man, his prancing and preening! However much Charlotte denied it, however much he might feign ignorance about the landanum, I was positive that he had introduced her to the habit.

"I accuse you of nothing, Lance. But I do wish to give you my deepest gratitude for the work you have done at Fir Crest . . . and to advise you that your services are no longer needed."

He smiled infuriatingly. "Am I being dismissed, as one does a lowly Negro?"

"Dismissed? Yes. As one does a Negro, perhaps not. Under those circumstances, I would have you whipped back to Buckingham. As it is, with Charlotte professing her love for you, I am extending you the courtesy that her sentiment deserves, however misguided it may be."

He turned quite pale. "*Charlotte* loves me? Poor child! I swear to you, Victoria, I've done nothing to encourage her emotions!"

"Nothing?" My voice snapped like a whip. "You have taken a young, impressionable woman. You have made love to her. You have flattered and wined and dined her beyond all reason. You have even told her that you loved her, in my own presence—"

"But I was only joking," he interrupted weakly.

"Which makes it all the more despicable!" I cried. "You have played with her feelings as though she were a toy. And, in the process, you have nearly destroyed her. You have nearly destroyed me as well. I want you to leave Fir Crest at once!"

What followed then completely unsettled me. Lance's eyes brimmed with tears, and he dropped to his knees, clutching my hands, raining wet kisses on them. "Please do not send me away! It is you I love! Not Charlotte! Never Charlotte! I love you, Victoria! Will you marry me?"

I could not have been more shocked if the house had collapsed around my head. Lance Harcourt in love with me? The idea was laughable. And I would have laughed at his groveling except for the apparent genuineness of his tears. The man was completely overwrought. "Everything I have done has been for you," he sobbed. "If you do not love me, I can understand that. . . . I will give you time. . . . But please do not send me away. At least, not forever."

A sensation crept through me as though I had turned over a rock and seen all the damp things crawling there. I pulled my hands from his, but I did not step away, for I had the horrified notion that he might follow me on his knees. He stank of sherry and cologne, obviously drunk, or nearly so, on his own odors. It was a pathetic scene; he on his knees, like a supplicant at an altar; and I staring down at him in utter disdain. "I think you should get up, Lance. You might wrinkle the knees of your trousers."

Now a look that was part cunning passed over his face. Did he take my interest in whether his trousers were wrinkled as being a sign of growing love? "Yes, yes. You're right," he said. And he sprang to his feet like a grotesque jack-in-the-box. "May I have another sherry?"

I poured one for him, although it was obvious that he'd had more than sufficient. He gulped it down as though he were exceedingly thirsty. The blood returned to his cheeks, and he avoided looking directly at me. Which showed at least that he had the good sense to be embarrassed.

"You do not love me, Victoria?"

"I do not. I love Robert Gilliam, if he will still have me."

He nodded slowly, pulling at his bottom lip. "I'm afraid I've made a terrible ass of myself."

While I agreed with him, it would have been extremely impolite for me to say so. He wandered around the study, dusting from time to time at the knees of his gray flannel trousers.

"I received a letter from Robert," he said. He and Robert had met socially in Staunton on several occasions, when Lance had been a student in Washington and Robert had been at the Staunton academy. "He asked about your welfare. He also asked me to look at his father's place, which I did today." Now his eyes settled on me with a bleak seriousness. "I did not know about you and Robert," he said. "It would not have changed my love for you, but I would not have been foolish enough to mention it."

The interview was dragging on too long, and I left myself becoming irritated. "Please do not be offended, Lance. But I believe it would be in the best interests of all concerned if you were to leave Fir Crest now."

"And never return?" he whispered.

He looked so pale and stricken that I was forced to relent. "We all need time to think, to get ourselves back in order again. I shall write you and let you know when you may resume your visits."

He rushed at me as though to attack me in an amorous embrace. But I held him away with a rigid arm. I disliked the feel of his chest underneath the hollow satin shirt with matching ruffles. "Good-bye, Lance. I shall have Amos ride with you as far as the chestnut tree."

He smiled bitterly, scratching in his curly hair. "Yes . . . that would be helpful. I have drunk a bit too much, I'm afraid." Looking at me sharply, he asked, "Is that why you do not love me? Because I drink?"

It seemed to me the least of his visible vices. "I love Robert Gilliam," I said, "I shall always cherish you as a friend, if you will accept that."

He straightened considerably. "These things take time," he said confidently. "Perhaps, with time, you will come to love me."

I went straight to the bell cord and rang for Benign. She opened the study door immediately, without knocking. How long had she been listening in the hallway? "Benign, have Amos accompany Mr. Harcourt to the chestnut tree." I gave my hand to Lance, which he shook limply, as though I had handed him a dead fish.

"Good-bye, Lance. Thank you for everything. I shall write to you."

"*Au revoir,*" he said smoothly, smugly, with excessive confidence. "Perhaps we shall see each other sooner than you think." He bowed slightly, and left the study, with Benign striding purposefully behind.

My head was reeling. It was obvious that Lance was

somehow unbalanced. How could he have mistaken my contempt for love? Had I masked my true feelings for him so well that he had wrongly assumed that I loved him? Impossible. A man less involved with himself would have fathomed my distaste from the very beginning. I thought briefly of Charlotte. Of course I would not tell her of Lance's proposal to me. The important thing now was to get her back on her feet. But first, I had to write Robert Gilliam a note:

Dearest Robert:

I have acted so foolishly and irresponsibly in the face of the inevitable defeat that I am almost ashamed to tell you of it. For the moment, I want you to know only that I love you deeply and sincerely. Please forgive me for my weakness. And may God keep you. I shall write at greater length this very night.

I signed and addressed the note, and went to the kitchen, where Benign had returned to her station at the stove. The kitchen was rich with the odor of cooked apples and cinnamon. A large pile of tarts cooled in the window. Beyond them, I could see the candle house, still issuing smoke in faint clouds.

"Have you looked in on Miss Charlotte?"

"Yas'm. She act just fine. You want me to go get her?"

"Please. Perhaps a tart will improve her disposition. I believe she likes them even more than I."

Benign laughed roundly. "Don't nobody love my apple tarts better than you, Miss Victoria. Unless it's my children." She served me one with a silver fork on a blue china plate. After pouring a large glass of cold buttermilk, she went for Charlotte.

The tart was delicious. I felt guilty not waiting for Charlotte, but I was not even sure she would come. Sitting at the kitchen table, I felt calm and peaceful for the first time today. The fruit and spice odors might have been incense in a temple consecrated by years of Benign's cooking, her own substantial presence like an oracle who served tarts, advice, or remonstrations with equal ease.

In a few minutes she returned with Charlotte, who had changed into a plain cotton dress reminiscent of either sackcloth or prison garb. "Good afternoon, Charlotte." I said calmly. "You will love the tarts. As usual, Benign has outdone herself."

She seemed all right except for her eyes, which were slightly swollen from crying. But I could see that she was determined to follow my lead—if only until she could take the reins herself. "Benign makes excellent tarts," she said. She, too, looked through the window. "Are they still making candles?"

"Not very long, missy. Juniper, he took the oldest boy and the four young ones with him. They all out there making candles. There's Juniper and our five children. My sister, she there, too. Juniper's sister, too."

"And Grandmother Parkchester," I said, accepting another tart. "I do hope that the smoke does not affect her."

Benign laughed. "I expect it might clear her head."

Charlotte and I were seated across the table from each other. Impulsively she reached over and touched my hands. "Will you forgive me, Victoria?" she whispered. "I have been such a terrible fool. And I am so ashamed. Of course I shall go to Georgia if you still desire it."

My eyes filled with tears at her obvious sincerity. "I don't want to send you away, Charlotte!" It was hard to keep my voice to a whisper, which seemed useless anyway, since Benign heard whispers better than anything else. "I wouldn't know what to do without you."

"You all better eat your tarts before they get too cold," Benign said. And she peered out the window. "Sure is a lot of smoke coming from the candle house. They must be making enough for an army."

Whatever they were doing, the smoke was pouring now from the windows in long blue clouds that swirled through the bars almost hesitantly, caught in a cross draft that pulled and propelled it at the same time.

"Lance Harcourt has left Fir Crest," I told Charlotte. It seemed best to tell her now while she was in this pleasant mood. "I have told him that I shall write him when he may return."

Charlotte nodded. "I am sure you are right, Victoria. I have been acting the perfect fool. Benign, may I have another tart? They are so delicious!"

At that very moment the candle house seemed to explode in a cataclysm of blue smoke and red flames. It was so unexpected that I could only look in utter horror at the scene. Charlotte followed my gaze, and her face turned pale. But it was Benign who barreled into action. "Lawd!" she cried. She dropped plate, fork, tart. I remember that the fork hit the floor with a sound like the tinkling of a fine bell; the china shattered severely, as though reluctant to meet death.

Benign burst through the kitchen door and out into the golden sunlight. Suddenly alert, I grabbed Charlotte's hand and raced after her. For all her weight, Benign ran as smoothly and rapidly as an athlete. "My whole family in that house!" she cried, certainly to no one in particular. Charlotte and I were fast on her heels. I saw Amos coming at a fast gallop down the road, apparently returning from escorting Lance Harcourt to the chestnut tree where he would take the road to Charlottesville.

Other Negroes were running toward us from the fields. It seemed that once, when the smoke at the windows cleared, I could see terrified black faces briefly there, before the smoke closed in again. And all the time I was wondering: if the windows are barred, why don't they come through the door? I thought of Grandmother Parkchester among the fire and smoke. How was she reacting?

Even as these questions tormented me, we covered the three hundred or so yards to the candle house. But it was burning with such intensity that we could not get too close. There were wails, screams, confusion, the smell of tallow, and the noisy, greedy flames that bore down on what was left of the wooden house with oppressive weight. Banneker had come from somewhere and was wrestling with Benign to keep her from throwing herself into the holocaust. Everywhere there was screaming and shouting. But I heard Banneker plainly cry, "Ain't nothing you can do for them now! Ain't nothing nobody can do!" And Benign screamed, "My whole family in there! Every child I got! Juniper too!" And Banneker: "Ain't nothing nobody can do but the Lord!" Benign rolled her large white eyes back and dropped to the ground in a dead faint, like a giant oak suddenly felled in a forest. Even Benneker's large arms could not hold her.

I looked around anxiously for Charlotte. She was crouching near the flames, as though to make a desperate bid to rescue those inside the inferno. Even in my horrified state, I could see that such a plan was useless, as Banneker had said. With Grandmother Parkchester—poor, mad creature—Benign's husband, their five children, and the two Negro women, nine lives were even now being consumed in the candle house. As for Benign, several Negro men, Banneker among them, were lifting her and carrying her away from the disaster area.

I ran to Charlotte and grabbed her just as she made ready to go into the flames. Her face was covered with soot, and her hands seemed burned, as though she had already made one unsuccessful effort. "There is nothing you can do!" I cried, dragging her away. But she fought free and got to the flaming door before I could stop her. She was engulfed by smoke, and it seemed for a dreadful moment that the fire had caught her hair. But it was her dress that was on fire, and she was snatched by several Negro women and rolled unceremoniously in blankets.

But I had seen one thing that caused my blood to chill even in all that heat: the heavy oak door had been padlocked from the outside! With windows barred, and the door locked, the candle house with all its vats of tallow and open fires had become a veritable death trap. Deliberately.

Who had locked the door from the outside? Who had set the fire—for obviously it had been no accident—and had so callously snuffed out nine lives in almost as many minutes? And for what purpose? Charlotte, Benign, and I had been together in the kitchen when the fire broke out, so that certainly absolved us. Amos had been riding to and from the chestnut tree with Lance Harcourt, which seemed to absolve both of them. And while I could not account for Banneker's actions before the fire, he had certainly appeared concerned for Benign's safety. Would that have been true if he had destroyed her family?

Or had the true target of the murders been Grandmother Parkchester again? She had escaped her first encounter with death during the visit of the raiders, only to find herself mad and burned alive in the candle house with Negroes. Were we once again victims of selective mayhem by some mysterious person or persons?

Obviously these questions came to me later on, primarily when I put pen to paper and apprised Robert Gilliam of what was going on. But one thing was clearer then than ever before: a murderer stalked Fir Crest, a demented individual capable of the most bloodcurdling mischief. Without further evidence to support my theory, it also seemed clear that eventually I was to be among his victims.

Fir Crest, Virginia
December 31, 1864

My dearest Robert:

As the old year ends, and the new awaits outside like a somewhat unwelcome caller, I am sitting in Father's study reviewing events since last October when the candle house burned down. To go beyond that point to earlier tragedies requires more strength than I am presently able to come by. Furthermore, there is something almost uplifting and rewarding in the tragedy of Negroes which seems to intrude upon any other.

I have told you how Benign in her noble sorrow seemed to reign over the funeral and subsequent burial of all her family. Charlotte and I were there, and one or two other whites, in the gray shack with a brass cross above the pulpit where they hold their religious meetings.

I was tremendously impressed by Benign's noble demeanor; and it was impossible not to contrast that event with the funeral of Grandmother Parkchester, which had taken place only the day before. Perhaps because whites are thought to be an older and wiser civilization, or, more precisely, God's most recent handiwork—perhaps it is because of these attitudes that whites adorn themselves with all the entrapments of hypocrisy when death comes calling. This is possibly done to hide a horrible fear of the authoritative knock at the door. The putting away of Grandmother Parkchester aroused in me more anger for her mourners than pity for her bones—at least what we thought were her bones. There was the mood of a circus about the entire proceedings; and those who had liked her the least mourned her the most. It can be safely said that except for Charlotte, who passed the day in stricken silence, dry-eyed, and somehow deeply preoccupied—except for her, and hopefully myself, a good time was had by all. The pity was that no one seemed capable of standing and laughing in Death's face, banishing him once and for all to the attic where ghosts, hobgobblins, and the like hold dominion over cobwebs and dust.

Among the Negroes, there was a purity of emotion which could not be denied. Benign was dressed in a fabulous gown of black lace with white piping at the collar and sleeves. She occupied the front part of the church like two rather large pumpkins piled upon each other. But hers seemed the only sorrow among the blacks; and, what sorrow one discerned in her seemed not so much because her family was dead as because of the horrible way they had died. There were curious-looking drums, tambourines, rattles tied to wooden sticks, and a chorus that might have been sent from heaven as they sang and praised God for being "free at last."

It was an extraordinary sensation; and it is perhaps this attitude toward death that best distinguishes white from black. At Mother's funeral, Grandmother Parkchester's, and others that I have attended, the prevailing attitude has been that the loss of life is the loss of liberation. At the funeral for Benign's family, the exact opposite was true. She has lost eight members of her family, but it was clear that the general attitude seemed to be that they had gone out of earthly bondage into heavenly bliss. I know that such an attitude is thought by many to be pagan and simplistic. Yet, it is the true Christian teaching insofar as I am aware. Why, then, do whites draw long faces at death, and blacks greet it with a grin? Is it because we are so sure of our immortality that when the evidence proves our error, or even our arrogance, we are unable to cope with reality?

I do not intend to burden you overmuch this New Year's Eve with a recapitulation of tragedy or its aftermath, for I have kept you fully informed of events as they have occurred. But my mind is uneasy tonight, as it has been for the past two months. And I am compelled at this point to make you aware of one fact which I have withheld, perhaps to prevent causing you greater alarm, but only increasing my own in the process.

I have described to you the general horror and disorder that prevailed at Fir Crest even after the funerals were done with. It was, in fact, impossible to tell which body belonged to whom; and the bones that went into Grandmother Parkchester's grave might well have belonged to Juniper or to his sister. But they were said to be Grandmother's by Dr. Seymour, possibly because they were whiter than any other. At any rate, I have told no one other than yourself of my firm belief that what was said to have been a gruesome accident was in reality a heinous act of murder.

After struggling with Charlotte, I did see that the lock to the candle house was snapped shut. While preparations were being made for the funerals, Banneker and ten good men sifted the ashes that remained until they found the lock. And I have the word of Banneker and his men that the lock was open.

Two possibilities immediately come to mind: first, that I was mistaken in thinking that the door had been deliberately locked from the outside; second, that Banneker and ten other Negroes found the lock closed, opened it, and conspired to lie to me. I discount completely the second possibility only because I fully accept the truth of what I saw. *The door was locked.* If not, why didn't the victims escape? That they did not escape implies that the lock was indeed shut. Whoever set the fire in the first place took advantage of the confusion between the fire and the funerals to find the lock, open it, and replace it among the ruins. This I know despite a lack of evidence to corroborate it. How pleasant it would be to believe that I had taken leave of my senses rather than that a madman even now stalks Fir Crest! Who will be his next victim? What diabolical need motivates him? I have set these facts down, my darling, so that you may seek the answers in the event that I do not survive until you return. I have grown suspicious of everyone, even of myself. Only my death—clearly at the hands of the one we seek—should convince you that I myself am without guilt.

And now, to other matters. A certain order has returned to Fir Crest. Considering all that has happened to us, we have had a good harvest. Benign was in her quarters for one day—that of her family's funeral—and part of the next, when she came back to the kitchen and chased away her substitute. I had gone to Benign's cabin on several occasions and tried to console her; but what happened was that she wound up comforting me. Whatever strength I have that does not come from you certainly comes from her. She is a brave and remarkable woman. As for Charlotte, we have overcome our problems and are closer than ever. Indeed, she is so much the young gentlewoman that I have lifted the ban on Lance Harcourt and have sent today a special rider to Harcourt Manor to invite him to dine with us on New Year's Day.

While it pains me to turn now to matters of the war, it is necessary to do so. You have tried to spare me by speaking less and less of it; but poor Father is not faring well, and this seems only to sharpen his perception of all the horror and mayhem to the highest degree as he passes it along to me in his letters. I am deeply concerned for him, and I wish that you and he, along with your father, had continued together. But it is hardly appropriate to speak of my wishes at such a time. That I miss you goes without saying. Here at Fir Crest and the surrounding plantations, we are like watchers at the deathbed of the South—Petersburg under siege and sure to succumb; General Sherman regrouping his forces after his March to the Sea to unite with Grant in an assault on Richmond that will surely prove fatal to the Confederacy. Sherman has laid waste to Georgia and has given the city of Savannah to the Union for its Christmas tree. How fortunate for us all that Charlotte rebelled at my sending her there.

You have told me on many occasions that we have been fighting a lost cause. One wonders what it really was in the beginning, and if its true value has been worth the cost in blood. With Banneker accompanying us, Charlotte and I have ridden several times to your place. It is in good repair and all seems peaceful. Yet, it is impossible not to think of what will happen once the South has lost.

I love you, I hunger for you. And the future—whatever it may hold—does not cause me to turn away with horror, only because, God willing, it shall be spent at your side. Bless you, and may God keep you.

Victoria

There were of course many other things that I wanted to tell Robert but that I dared not trust to an erratic postal system. If I was suspicious of myself and everyone else at Fir Crest, there was an even greater air of mistrust throughout the entire South. For, as travelers came and went, and defeat became an accepted fact, awaiting only time to give the decisive blow, all manner of southerners suddenly found that they had been Yankee sympathizers since way before Fort Sumter. Even the neighbors who had decried our giving what amounted to a very real freedom to the Negroes at Fir Crest suddenly became red-faced with excitement about the positive way the experiment had worked out. It gave me almost sadistic pleasure to show them our bins swelling with corn, wheat, pumpkins, sweet potatoes, and a variety of other crops that far exceeded any previous yield from the land at Fir Crest. Not surprisingly, our visitors were full of murmurs and coos, as though we had achieved the most marvelous feat imaginable merely by anticipating what had been obvious from the very beginning—that slavery as an institution is destructive in and of itself. Even an ounce of freedom inspired Negro men and women to do marvelous things.

Yet, there was Banneker—handsome, brooding, suddenly morose and withdrawn, as though his very soul had gone into hibernation—who seemed a living contradiction to all that I might have written Robert Gilliam, but did not. After the candle house burned down, he wandered about for weeks like a man in a daze. There was no complaint I could make about his work, overseeing the other Negroes; but it was clear that he was suffering under a great burden. There was enough of the cynic in me to wonder whether he might not be acting for my benefit; but the man was so obviously distressed by more than the candle-house tragedy that I finally spoke to him about his changed personality.

"Is it only because of the fire, Banneker? Or is there some other problem you would like to discuss with me?" Neither he nor I had mentioned the vulgar encounter between his hussy, Emerald, and my sister, Charlotte. A guard was still maintained on Charlotte's door, at her insistence, which greatly surprised me, since I was unwilling to treat her as though she were a prisoner. When I told her so, she said serenely, "It is best that way. Furthermore, with all that's going on, I feel safer knowing that I am being guarded." I was surprised because her answer indicated that she, too, was aware, if only intuitively, of deep danger at Fir Crest. So I maintained the guard on her door, which meant that, even if she had been so inclined, she would be unable to continue her meetings with Banneker at the crest of firs.

Was it his loss of Charlotte that was troubling Banneker? When I thought of them together, I found that my breath caught in my throat at the picture of Charlotte's delicate white nakedness being possessed, perhaps even brutalized, by the muscularity of Banneker. "Is there some problem you would like to discuss with me, Banneker?"

"No, ma'am. I just brought you the weekly accounts."

It was late fall, and the fields and woods were aflame with the vibrant red and golden hues of Indian summer. Banneker's color had turned a deeper brown, and his huge chest swelled under the thin gray cotton of his shirt. His arms were bare, and beautifully muscled. The rest of him was clearly outlined in his white cotton pants, which suited him like a second skin. He seemed perfectly at ease while I glanced over the sheet of paper he'd handed me. When I'd finished, I looked up and said, "Won't you have a seat, Banneker?"

"No, ma'am. I want to look in on the men picking in the south orchard." I wondered how long it had been since I'd seen him smile.

"Perhaps a sherry, then?"

He allowed himself a slight smile, as though he'd read my earlier thought. "Nothing, thank you, ma'am. I'll be going now . . . unless there's something else you'd like."

He put such an odd emphasis on the last part of his sentence that I felt my cheeks burn. It was almost as though he had made a sexual proposition. But there was no evidence of it in his stance or the somewhat amused expression on his face. "There is nothing, Banneker. You are doing an excellent job. Father will be most pleased when he comes home."

"Thank you, ma'am." He turned and left the room, certainly a man pursued by demons far too private to be talked about.

It was perhaps a week later—Benign back to work, all funerals done with, the harvest being brought to the barns by laughing, singing Negroes—that I happened to look from my bedroom window and see Banneker standing barefoot and shirtless in the area where the candle house had stood. I was dressed and prepared to go downstairs for breakfast, but there was such an attitude of restrained tension about his body that I remained at the window watching him.

At first I thought that he was looking for something that might implicate him in the fire. But if he were, he had picked an odd time to do so—in broad daylight, with every eye at Fir Crest open to see. Furthermore, the ashes and burned wood had been removed, so that only the outline of the candle house foundation remained. But there was something that seemed to be puzzling Banneker. He walked several times around the clear outline of the rectangle, placing one foot carefully before the other like a boy balancing himself on a wooden fence. Then he slapped his forehead with a heavy hand, hitched up his pants, and plodded away with his head bowed. The muscles in his arms and back seemed greased with sweat.

Charlotte was already seated in the east garden when I went down. "I thought you'd overslept," she said. "You're very pretty this morning." I kissed her cheek and took my place. She was wearing a tan-colored cotton dress; her hair was pulled back and tied with a green velvet ribbon. "You are the pretty one," I said. Benign was serving melon, biscuits, honey, and iced milk. "Good morning, Benign."

"Good morning, missy. Did you rest well?"

"Very well, Benign. And you?"

"Well enough, missy. Now, eat your breakfast before the melon gets hot and the biscuits get cold."

We might have been surrounded by the restless ghosts of Johnny Cake and Juniper, who had served us so well until the fire. Certainly Charlotte and I made our best efforts to function as though the morning were not incomplete without them. Only a woman, a mother, of Benign's towering strength could have performed as though her dead husband and children were out on some errand rather than buried underneath the cedars in the Negro cemetery.

I took a spoonful of the melon, which was cold and delicious. We were near the middle of November, but enjoying an unaccustomed heat, one of those rare, glorious days with which nature seems to reward us before the onset of winter. Charlotte was eating slowly, thoughtfully. From time to time she sighed, as though fighting the onset of depression.

"Is something wrong, dear?"

She shook her head. "Not exactly wrong. I feel better than in months. But I also feel uneasy for some reason. Banneker has been out in the ruins of the candle house."

"I saw him." I inspected her closely. Had seeing him rekindled old desires? But she seemed calm enough on that score. "Perhaps it is the weather affecting us all," I said. "Or perhaps you would like to see Lance Harcourt. Shall we ride into Charlottesville and surprise him?"

She shook her head wanly. "I do not especially want to see him." Yet, her voice broke in what seemed a near-sob before she finished.

I laid down my spoon and touched her hand. "You do miss him, don't you, dear?"

Now her eyes were bright with tears. "Very much," she said. "I wait for a letter from him every day, and when none comes, I feel as though a part of me dies." Desperately she caught my hand. "I know that you do not approve of him, Victoria. But is it wrong that I should love him? I have done everything to forget him, but nothing seems to work."

As she talked, Banneker had returned to the ruins of the candle house with four other men bringing timber. He himself brought a saw, a hammer, and a bag of nails. From all appearances, he was going to rebuild the candle house.

"All of us need some diversion," I told Charlotte.

"These have been very trying weeks. Would you like to ride into Charlottesville with Benign and spend the night there?" I mentioned the name of a prominent lady friend in Charlottesville. "I am sure she would be glad to have you. And I shall send along an escort of twelve men, although I anticipate no trouble whatsoever on the way."

She leaped up happily. "Oh, may I, Victoria? May I?"

It was almost too much to bear. How she must have suffered being away from Lance! I was nearly too ashamed to speak. "Of course you may, Charlotte. And forgive me for treating you as I have. I had no idea you were so unhappy."

"Dear Victoria." She dropped to her knees and embraced me. "You are not to blame. I have been the foolish one. You have acted correctly and most responsibly. And you have been very patient with me. There is nothing to forgive."

I put my finger to her lips. "Hush, now. And go and prepare for the journey. I shall tell Benign. And do give my warmest regards to Lance."

She kissed me hurriedly and fled. For a moment I felt incredibly old, like a spinster locked inside of loneliness. How I longed to be with Robert Gilliam now! Still, I could not begrudge Charlotte her happiness. In the past several weeks, her conduct had been above reproach. She had been cheerful, lively, even jolly. And her response to tragedy had been heroic, however dignified and controlled. I felt no qualms whatsoever about sending her to Charlottesville for twenty-four hours. And I told Benign so when she returned with coffee.

"You want me to go, missy?"

"Yes, Benign. Of course, I could send one of the other women. But I'd feel ever so much better if you went along."

Benign grunted. "Them other niggers wouldn't do nothing but get on Miss Charlotte's nerves. But who's going to look after you while I'm gone?"

I couldn't help but smile at her concern. "I shall manage, Benign. Don't worry about me."

Again she grunted. "Somebody's got to worry about you. I'll have Yetta come up from the cabins, if it's all right with you. She Banneker's mother, but she the only nigger I halfway trust in my place."

Banneker's mother attending me? For some reason, I found Benign's plan unsettling. But I did not complain, for to do so would keep her and Charlotte at Fir Crest fussing over me forever. "Yetta will be fine, Benign. And, speaking of Banneker, what on earth is he doing out there?"

"He say he building him an office."

"An office? Would not another candle house be more appropriate?"

Benign laughed roundly, and it was good to hear her do so, for she had seen very somber days. "He build a candle house two or three days after the old one burn down. It's in the quarters."

"I didn't know," I said weakly. And I looked beyond her at Banneker as he raised a two-by-four and held it in place while another Negro hammered nails. "I suppose he should have an office," I said, "as long as he's overseer."

"That Banneker, he the devil," Benign said. "He got them books he study every night. He say he going to be a politician when the war is over."

When the war is over. So Banneker was already deep into his plans for that eventuality, studying to be a politician. It struck me for a moment that he was far too handsome, and certainly too honest, to be a good politician. "That will be all, Benign," I said. I was filled with confusion. Our own future seemed held inside a vise; we could only wait for the screw to be loosened or tightened according to events.

As I finished my breakfast, looking from time to time at the edifice that was taking shape with surprising speed, I found myself wondering if there were really such a thing as freedom for anyone. Or are we all handled, molded, perhaps even mangled, by the unfeeling hands of blind fate?

It was nearing noon when Charlotte left Fir Crest squeezed into a carriage with Benign, accompanied by an escort of twelve armed men. Banneker was still working, and as the carriage rumbled up the road, he straightened, shaded his eyes, and then went back to work again.

I waved until the carriage was out of sight; then I went to the kitchen to talk with Yetta. She was a very light-skinned Negro of indeterminate age, certainly Banneker's mother, for her features were as comely as his own were handsome. "Good afternoon, Yetta. I suppose Benign has instructed you as to your duties."

"Yas'm." It amused me to see that she had rearranged the chairs at the kitchen table, perhaps to place her mark on the area if even only for a short while.

"I shall be in the study if I'm needed," I said. I wanted to talk with her about Banneker, yet I did not have the faintest idea of what to say. I had known her all my life, but we had never had a conversation that went beyond the boundaries of servant and mistress. "It's extremely hot weather we're having for November, isn't it?" I said.

"Yas'm." In those few seconds, she seemed older, wiser, her brown eyes suddenly bright with greed. Would she steal something from the kitchen, the smokehouse? Certainly Benign had counted even down to the last fork, and would expect all to be as she had left it—including the kitchen chairs.

"Weather this hot in November," she said, "mean something bad supposed to happen."

"Well, I hope you're wrong there, Yetta. I shall be in the study if something does happen."

"Yas'm."

I was smiling as I sat down to work. There were many things to be done, and I spent the better part of the afternoon working there, forgoing dinner, then back to work until suppertime. Yetta had prepared baked pork chops with applesauce and mushrooms, a delicious dish, although I would have to tell Benign that it was mediocre in order to keep peace in the family. All too soon it was nine o'clock, and I went upstairs to my room. The heat had not broken with the coming of night, and I flung the windows wide to allow some air to enter. I was surprised to see that most of Banneker's office was almost completed. There was a light inside, and I could make out the form of Banneker hunched shirtless over a desk, presumably studying his politics.

Yetta helped me with my bath. While I was soaking, she applied a sticky black substance to my arms, neck, and face that Benign had been imposing on me for the past several weeks—to restore my beauty, as she said. From its odor, it was concocted of several unspeakable things, at least one of them from the cow pasture. But I had never gotten up the courage to ask Benign what it contained, nor had she summoned the courage to tell me. Whether as a matter of fact or because of my own imagination, my skin did seem softer, lovelier. So I lay back in the tub while Yetta laid on the appalling mixture with her fingers. There was no danger of the bedclothes being dirtied, for the mixture dried as hard as mud within a few moments. In the morning, it would readily yield to soap and water.

As I stepped from the tub into towels, Yetta laughed at the way I looked. "Anybody didn't know would sure say you was part nigger." I resented such familiarity from her, whereas I would have welcomed it from Benign. "That will be all, Yetta."

She cocked an inquisitive eye. "Don't you want me to brush your hair, missy? Benign say it have to get two hundred strokes."

"I shall brush it. Good night, Yetta."

"Good night, ma'am." For some reason, she seemed disappointed. Banneker's mother though she might be, I did not like the woman. She seemed capable of the most incredible duplicity, an idea which I dismissed at once as being totally unfair. On no account did I have reason to doubt her loyalty.

I dried with the soft towels, and managed to work my way into a thin blue shift. The unaccustomed heat had abated some, but the room was uncomfortably warm, as though we were at the peak of summer. It seemed impossible that Thanksgiving was only a few weeks away, and that hunters from Fir Crest were shooting wild turkeys and geese daily in the woods. Salted and smoked, they would be part of our annual festival.

My face was hot underneath the devilish pack, and my neck and arms were slightly stiff in their casing. I wondered what Charlotte was doing now. And Benign. They had left Fir Crest with five suitcases between them, as though they were going on a month's journey rather than overnight. Whatever Charlotte was doing, Benign was certain to keep a steady eye on her. Poor Charlotte, I thought, with a certain amount of amusement. Could Lance Harcourt say pretty things with Benign planted like a black stump between them?

As I was thinking thus, I heard the sound of something hit against the balcony. At first I thought it was a bat in the middle of some mishap, possibly thrown off course by the heat. But there it was again . . . and this time I recognized it. A pebble, thrown with great urgency. I climbed from the bed and went to the window. The moon was full, covering everything with an eerie light. Cautiously I went onto the terrace. It was like entering a world where everything was coated with silver . . . including Banneker, who stood stark naked in the yard beneath my balcony. His tremendous manhood was fully erect, perpendicular to his body. . . .

I stepped immediately back into the room. It was difficult for me to breathe. I was filled with panic as I closed the French windows. But another pebble hit them with a resounding ring. Fearfully I cracked the windows, certainly with no thought in mind other than to keep him from breaking them. It struck me that he was either drunk or mad, possibly both. As I crouched at the partly opened windows, his voice came to me from below in a hoarse whisper. "Miss Victoria, I know you there. Ain't no use trying to hide."

I could not have spoken had my very life depended on it. My throat and lips were dry, and my breasts heaved as though I had been chased by the devil. Most carefully I pulled aside the curtain and peered below. Banneker stood like a beautiful silver statue in the yard, head thrown back, staring at my window.

"I want you," he said. His voice was thick with passion. "I need me a white woman bad. You don't have to worry about Emerald . . . she ain't going to bother nobody no more." He shook his head, as though to collect his thoughts. "I know you want me, Miss Victoria. Every woman wants me, the way I make them sing. . . . You just stay right there. I'm going to climb the trellis up to your balcony. Nobody in the world ever need to know."

Surely he had gone mad. I closed the window quietly, sliding the latch into position. Then I ran to my dresser, where I had stored a pistol. It was fully loaded. I released the safety and cocked the trigger. In his present condition, mere French windows could never keep Banneker out. Even now I could hear the soft scrape of his body as he climbed the trellis. Then I heard the flat slap of his feet as they landed on the balcony, followed immediately by an obscene scraping on the window.

"Open up, missy. Banneker got something nice for you."

I stood at the window, hoping to hold it against his thrust. At the same time, his fist hit the glass a heavy blow. But he kept his voice to a whisper. "Open this damn window, or Banneker going to break it in."

With the French doors at least cracked, I would have a better chance of shooting him accurately. There was no doubt in my mind that I would shoot him if I had to. I released the latch and opened the windows a few inches, holding them in that position with my body.

"That's better," he said softly. "In a little while now, Banneker's going to come in. Banneker's going to love you like you never been loved before. . . ."

I could see his silver-black body through the opening; the turgid, threatening organ; and I turned my back against the windows, holding them, holding the pistol at the ready. My panic had, without my knowing it, turned to excitement. My breathing threatened to strangle me.

"I hear you breathing. That's all right, sugar. That's perfectly all right." His body was hard and heavy against the windows, pushing ever so slightly until they parted a few inches more. "Banneker, he like to do things slow."

I shuddered as his arm snaked through the opening, fingers spread, searching. They touched my hair, my cheek, burning me. He chuckled deep in his throat. "Benign don't need to put that conjure on you. You pretty enough already." Then his hand lifted and stroked the gun barrel, almost lovingly, as though its lethal hardness were blood kin to his own.

"You put that gun down," he said harshly. "Put it down now, before you make Banneker mad."

Incredibly, I leaned to a table near the window and laid the gun down. With only a part of my body holding the door, he had eased the perfect column of his leg through, and a portion of his shoulder. His hand went back to my hair, my face. Then it cupped my left breast and crushed it until I bit my lip to keep from screaming. At the same time, he pushed through the door and caught me in his arms, pulling me to him like a frenzied beast, smothering my lips with kisses that had a strange, hot taste. "Fir Crest belong to you and me," he whispered. "We don't need nobody but the two of us. Just Banneker and Miss Victoria."

Now the excitement turned to panic again. And it seemed that all the strength in the world came to me, for I shoved him hard in the chest, and he staggered backward to the balcony. In a flash, I retrieved the gun. Now I was furious that he should have taken such liberties with me. And even angrier that I had let him. I flung open the windows and placed the gun directly in the curly hair of his groin. "Get out!" I hissed. "Get out before I kill you!"

His eyes turned wide and white. Shaking his head, he blinked like a man awakening from a deep sleep. He looked at me and at the gun planted against his manhood. Then, in one huge leap, he twisted from the balcony. I looked in time to see him land in a perfect crouch, like a large silver cat. Almost immediately the kitchen door opened, piercing the moonglow with an even deeper light. And Yetta rushed out and half-dragged Banneker inside.

I was almost too overwrought to think. But it was impossible not to realize that Banneker had come here with Yetta's knowledge. But for what purpose, other than to violate me sexually? And what had he meant when he said that Fir Crest belonged to him and me?

I felt confused, and utterly filthy. Yet, some instinct told me that I should keep tonight's encounter to myself. So I poured cold water into the tub and bathed secretly in the dark. I washed off the noxious paste, never to use it again. And all the while I was thinking. What had inspired such a vile conspiracy between Yetta and her son? Surely his visit tonight had been motivated by greed, and was part of a desperate power play. For if Banneker was already presuming to be a politician, could he not—with his evil mother's urging—also presume to be master of Fir Crest once all obstacles had been removed? If freed slaves could become politicians once the war was over, they could also marry white women. And what better time to attempt to seduce me over into their camp than when both Benign and Charlotte were away?

I finally felt clean. Toweling myself dry, I remembered another of Banneker's strange comments: "You don't have to worry about Emerald . . . she ain't going to bother nobody no more." Had she left Fir Crest? What had he meant? I suddenly felt chilly, and the outdoors turned ominously dark. The weather had changed. There would be frost in the morning, if I could survive the night to see it.

I got up and double-checked the locks on the door and windows, although I was sure that Banneker would not return tonight. Then I lay across the bed with the gun at easy reach. I was determined not to sleep. But it seemed that only a few minutes had passed before the room was alive with pale sunlight, and Yetta came bustling into the room. "I knocked, but you didn't hear me," she said. "So I used my key." She had coffee on a tray, which I refused. If she saw the gun, she said nothing. But what she did say completely unsettled me.

"There's been another accident, Miss Victoria. You know that woman Emerald, used to mess around with Banneker? Well, they just found her, facedown in the creek, shot in the back of the head by one of them hunters. I knowed something like this was bound to happen with so much shooting going on." She grunted most eloquently. "Thanksgiving. What's there to be thankful for?"

I didn't even bother to answer her. Certainly I was sorry to hear about the unfortunate death of Emerald. But had it been accidental? *You don't have to worry about Emerald . . . she won't bother nobody no more. . . .* Indeed she wouldn't. "How do you know it was an accident, Yetta?"

"Amos say so. He found her. You not drinking your coffee this morning? The weather changed overnight. There's frost on the ground. You need something hot in you."

"Please take it away," I said. "And send Amos to me at once. I shall attend to my own dressing."

"Yas'm." She looked at me strangely. Did the woman think I was a fool? Banneker's actions last night had certainly been inspired by her tongue. And now, Emerald dead. And Banneker's throaty voice in my ear: *Fir Crest belong to you and me.* Mother, Grandmother Parkchester, and the woman Emerald conveniently out of the way. Banneker's inept attempt to make love to me, once he had been denied access to Charlotte. All the motives were not clear, but an insidious pattern was beginning to take shape. However much I recoiled at the idea, the madness at Fir Crest—those senseless, brutal killings, beginning with Mother; the selective mayhem that seemed designed to strike terror even as it preserved the wealth and usefulness of Fir Crest—all that, in some inexplicable way, seemed to have originated with our Negroes. With Banneker leading them, and Yetta, that shrewd old crone, whispering instructions into his gullible ear. Charlotte had claimed that Lance Harcourt was with the raiders who had routed the dissidents. But suppose that it was Banneker who had been her companion hidden under the white shroud?

I was fully dressed when Amos appeared. He at least seemed to be someone I could continue to trust. "I would like to know about Emerald, Amos. Was it an accident?"

He shifted from one foot to the other. "That's the way it seem, Miss Victoria. Like you know, the weather changed. So when I found her body, it was cold. But that could've been due to the frost. I can't say when she got killed. She used to go hunting with us for the sport of it. I found her facedown in the creek with a rifle shot that went in the back of her head. I kept telling them niggers to be careful. I'm surprised somebody ain't got killed out there hunting before this. It had to be an accident, Miss Victoria. Ain't nobody I know of would want to kill Emerald, pretty as she was."

"Was Banneker hunting this morning?"

"No, ma'am. He sleep when we left. I tried to wake him, but he just turn over and go on sleeping."

I believed Amos. But was it possible that Banneker had only been feigning sleep? That, once the hunters had gone, he crept down to the creek, murdered Emerald, and then returned to his cabin? At the same time, why would he feel the need to kill Emerald? Certainly he had sufficient control over her to rid himself of her without having to resort to murder.

My head was so full of unanswered questions that it was almost impossible to think. "It is a terrible tragedy, Amos. Please see that she is properly buried. And please tell Banneker that I wish to speak with him in the study in one hour."

"Yas'm." He left with a sorrowful step—honest, certainly; but perhaps a bit too naive to understand the complexities of why pretty women, even black ones, are frequently killed.

I prepared myself carefully for the interview with Banneker, for it is rare that a woman has an opportunity later on to confront her would-be assailant on a superior footing. Furthermore, if Banneker did find me desirable, perhaps I could use that desire to extract vital information from him. I donned a blue silk gown with high white ruffles around the collar, which opened in a discreet V, showing the swell of my breasts. The sleeves were long and tight, also with ruffles at the wrists. The dress showed off my tiny waist and the rest of me to excellent advantage. I also wore small diamond earrings, a long-ago present from Robert Gilliam, for I felt the need for some token from him to help me in the coming encounter. And I pinned my hair up to bolster my confidence further.

On my way to the study, I met Yetta working in the sitting room. "You sure do look pretty, missy. Dressed like that, you could turn any man's head." I detested her pointed, greedy face. Certainly she knew that I had sent for Banneker. "Yetta, you may return to your cabin. We shall make do until Benign returns in a few hours."

Insolent creature! She kept up her pretense of dusting. "I might as well stay here until Benign gets back," she said. I was not unaware that she was working her way gradually to the door opening onto the study, certainly to eavesdrop when I talked to Banneker. I felt as though a devil seized me. I rushed at her and grabbed the oily rag, hooking my fingers in her shoulder at the same time. "I do not like you," I said in a fierce whisper. "I do not want you around me. Now, leave this house at once, and never again presume to tell me what I might or might as well not do."

Her face turned gray. For a second I thought that she might burst into tears. Certainly the quickness of my attack had surprised and unsettled her. "I didn't mean no harm, ma'am."

"Leave this house!" I said. My voice was low but deadly. She grabbed her skirts and fled toward the kitchen. I followed her, and watched as she paused just long enough to remove a pot from the stove. Then she opened the door to the yard, bounded down the steps, and ran toward the Negro quarters. On the upper side of the office he was building, I saw Banneker on his way to the house. The structure between them hid mother from son. I watched until Yetta had disappeared down among the gray cabins. Then I watched Banneker approaching. He had on Mr. McAdoo's suit of thick gray flannel, the same black boots, collar, and a purple tie. And he was walking with a step less sprightly than usual. But what shocked and offended me was that he was bringing a small bouquet of flowers, holding them carefully lest they break, as though he were coming to see his best girl.

I was seated behind Father's desk when he tapped at the study door. "Come in," I said. The drawer holding the derringer was partly open, in case I had to defend myself again. But the man who entered was someone nearly broken, certainly beaten down by circumstances that perhaps he himself did not understand. "Good morning, Miss Victoria," he said. He attempted a smile, but his lips were rigid and gray.

"Good morning, Banneker. Please come in and shut the door. Lock it as well."

He did so. I did not wish to be interrupted by anyone, regardless of which way the conversation went. As he moved from the door toward me, I noticed that he walked with a slight limp, certainly the result of his leap from the balcony last night. "I brought you these, Miss Victoria." He handed me a small bouquet of bluebells, some of them withered. I took them gingerly, as though he had handed me a dead mouse, and dropped them in the wastebasket. That seemed as good a way as any to open the conversation.

"I would like you to account for your disgusting actions of last night, Banneker. The only reason that I do not discharge you on the spot is because you and your family have been among our most loyal servants for many years. Nonetheless, I am terribly upset by the entire incident. I was barely able to sleep last night for thinking about it. Except for my own restraint, they would be preparing you now for burial with Emerald."

Whatever was holding him up seemed to give way, and he slumped into a chair, pounding his head. "I don't know what got into me, Miss Victoria. Mama, she give me something to drink. I ain't a drinking man, and it made me act like a fool. I'm sorry, Miss Victoria. I swear before God I am. I'll leave Fir Crest right now if you want me to." He stood, somewhat shakily, as though to demonstrate the truth of his intent.

"We'll discuss that later," I said. I left him standing, although he was clearly in pain, perhaps in need of medical attention. "You know of course that Emerald is dead?" I watched his face carefully, but saw only deeper sorrow.

"Amos told me just before I come here. I just couldn't believe it. I told her she ought not to be traipsing around with men, calling herself hunting. I was mighty sorry to hear it, even though she wasn't my woman no more."

"Then you believe it was a hunting accident?"

There was no way he could fake the puzzlement on his face. "What else, Miss Victoria?"

"Perhaps," I said, "it was murder."

His eyes popped. "Who'd want to murder Emerald?"

Both he and I knew the answer to that. At one time, Charlotte had been angry enough to do so. Indeed, Charlotte had even threatened Emerald in my presence. I thanked God that she was safe now with Benign in Charlottesville. At least no cloud of suspicion could fall on her.

The interview was branching out in strange directions; I tried to aim it back toward my original intent. "Last night you said that Fir Crest belongs to you and me. What did you mean by that?"

He shook his head disconsolately. "I don't know what I mean by anything last night. I was drunk off something Mama give me. I'm real sorry, Miss Victoria. If I'd been in my right mind, I never would've done such a thing."

It was perhaps an excuse, but certainly not a compliment, however he may have meant it.

"I am still very upset, Banneker. You are a good worker, and I would hate to have to dismiss you. Yet, what you did last night was not only unforgivable, but extremely dangerous. When word gets around—as it certainly shall—then any buck with a drink in him and a yen for a white woman can be expected to come to my room."

"No, ma'am, Miss Victoria. Any nigger here even try to bother you, I'll kill them myself."

I felt somewhat better. His declaration was too full of fire and passion to be doubted. Yet, there was the problem of his mother. "What did Yetta give you to drink?"

He shook his head. "I don't know. Something she brew in her cabin. She drink that stuff, then she talk a whole lot of foolishness."

"What kind of foolishness, Banneker?"

He shrugged broadly. "She say Fir Crest belong to her. At least, partways."

To *Yetta?* The idea was astonishing. "Why does she say that?"

Now Banneker grinned. He knew that, questioning him as I was, I was not about to dismiss him. "Because she drunk. She smoke locoweed, too." He ducked his head, and aimed an amused eye at me. "I smoke some locoweed last night, too. That's probably why I didn't break both my legs. All I did was sprain one."

We were both startled by a loud knocking on the study door. I was determined to ignore it. "I do not like your mother, Banneker. She is sneaky, and I do not like sneaky people."

Now he grinned very broadly. It was impossible to dislike him for long, to forget that he, Charlotte, Robert, and I had grown up together. "I don't like her either, Miss Victoria. Benign always been more a mother to me than Yetta. Yetta real sneaky."

The knocking at the door increased. Then Amos was calling me. "Miss Victoria. A rider just come from Charlottesville. He got a letter for you."

Suddenly I felt very afraid. Had some other tragedy occurred? "Open the door, Banneker."

He hobbled to the door, opened it, and retrieved the letter from Amos. "Have him wait," I said, "in case there is an answer." I tore open the envelope, addressed to me in Charlotte's writing, and read:

Dear Victoria:

Please do not be angry with me, but Lance Harcourt has invited me to stay the full week—longer, if possible—and I have accepted. I shall of course be with Mrs. Pennington, and Benign guards me like a hawk. If you wish, however, that I return to Fir Crest, I shall do so immediately.

Your loving sister,
Charlotte

I took a pen and wrote a brief note, wondering all the while how Lance Harcourt could continue his relationship with Charlotte after having proposed to me:

Dear Charlotte:

Of course you may stay the week. I do, however,

expect you in time for Thanksgiving, ten days hence. Another unfortunate accident has happened—Emerald has been shot while hunting—so it is just as well that you and Benign are away until after her funeral. My fondest love to you, and my regards to Mrs. Pennington, And, of course, to Benign.

Your sister,
Victoria

I sealed the envelope and gave it to Banneker, who handed it to Amos. Before Amos left, I called him. "Benign will be away with Miss Charlotte for another week, Amos. I would like your wife, Charity, to take over the household duties during that time."

He grinned with pleasure. "Yas'm, Miss Victoria. She'd be happy to do it."

When he left, Banneker went to lock the door, but I stopped him. Very little had been accomplished during this meeting except that Banneker had convinced me that last night's doings were his mother's idea rather than his own. Which somewhat displeased me, for no woman wants to think that she is undesirable, even to a Negro man, unless he is half out of his mind.

"I shall not rest easily, Banneker, unless you are punished for last night's actions. That is the only way you may stay on as overseer at Fir Crest."

He actually seemed pleased. "You right, Miss Victoria. You absolutely right. Just name the punishment, and I'll do it."

His face was so eager, I looked away. Did he think I had in mind his washing windows for an afternoon? "I want you to receive twenty-five good lashes at the whipping tree. I want all the Negroes assembled to see your punishment."

I heard his sharp intake of breath. "You want *me* whipped? And them to see it? They won't pay no attention to what I say after that."

"That is your concern, Banneker. What you did last night was clearly improper, and most serious. I think I am being more than fair. If Father were here, he'd have you shot. Or at least given fifty lashings."

That seemed to sober him some, although his handsome

face was sullen. "I guess you right, Miss Victoria. When you want it done?"

"Right away, Banneker. I shall be watching from my balcony."

He turned to leave. Then he faced me again. "Can I take them bluebells from the basket? I stole them from the church on the way here. If you don't want them, I'd like to take them back."

When I said nothing, he knelt and retrieved the pitiful flowers from the wastebasket. Then he left, looking surprisingly strong and tall, despite his limp.

Within the hour, he was tied to the whipping tree near the apple orchard. All the Negroes of Fir Crest were gathered around like eager, curious blackbirds. Banneker wore only thin white cotton pants, which hung dangerously low on his lean hips. He embraced the whipping tree as though it were a woman, his hands tied together around it with a rope. A large, very black Negro administered the whipping, drawing blood with the first stroke. I watched from the balcony, as I had promised. Banneker had his neck twisted around, watching me. He did not flinch or cry out as the cruel lash rose and fell. Even from where I stood, the desire in his eyes pierced my heart like an arrow.

He had received a dozen lashings, and his body was covered with blood. Yet, he had not taken his eyes off me, as though the sight of me gave him strength. But I could bear no more. I left the balcony, closing the French windows and the draperies as well. When Amos' wife came to call me later on for supper, I refused. "What news is there of Banneker?" I whispered.

"He all right, missy. After they put salt in his wounds, he had to beat him up two niggers to show he still the boss."

"Will there be scars from the whipping?"

"No, ma'am. Yetta got some of her conjure healing him. He'll look as good as new the next time you see him."

The next time I saw Banneker was after Thanksgiving. He was laughing and jolly, as though I had not ordered him whipped. He brought the account books, took his drink of sherry, and went on his way. A few days after that, he completed work on the office he was building where the candle house had stood, and I saw him moving in his books and other belongings. For Christmas, he gave me the figure of a horse, whittled by himself from a piece of birch. I gave him a pair of woolen socks that Benign had knitted. Certainly I could not, and never would, tell Robert Gilliam about these encounters with Banneker. For if Robert would not understand them, I was not sure that I understood them myself.

Lance Harcourt did come out and dine with us New Year's Day, 1865. He seemed his usual self, and treated me amiably, although somewhat distantly. I was beginning to feel disturbed by the seemingly neutral effects that my banishments and punishments had on men. But it was only a droll thought, and I was pleased that neither Lance nor Banneker seemed to hold a grudge against me for what I had done to them.

Charlotte was absolutely radiant during the entire holiday season. I has long since removed the guards from her door, and she was free again to come and go as she pleased. Indeed, except for the war—which pervaded everything like a noxious odor—we might have been enjoying a normal holiday season at Fir Crest.

But following a winter that was sometimes mild, sometimes violent, but generally uneventful insofar as Fir Crest was concerned, Petersburg eventually sagged on April 2, 1865, after a siege of nearly a year. Richmond was captured the next day. On April 9, General Lee surrendered to Grant at Appomattox Court House. And with that event, the Confederacy collapsed. Soon thereafter, we received word that Father, Judge Gilliam, and Robert Gilliam were on their way home. The war had ended; now we were faced with establishing a new order in which we would be forced to stand face to face with unyielding reality for the first time since the guns thundered at Sumter.

THREE

———◆———

There was at Fir Crest a sense of joyous excitement mixed with stunned disbelief. For Father was coming home today; simultaneously, news had reached us that President Lincoln had died in Washington after being shot by a crazed actor. Would the violence never end? Whatever excitement I felt about Father's imminent arrival was held in check by a sense of apprehension that nothing could dispel. Certainly Robert Gilliam, along with his father, was even now on the way home. And Amos, with five armed men and a carriage, had ridden to Mount Rush, where Father had spent the night, to accompany him home.

Charlotte ran repeatedly from the sitting room to the porch, asking breathlessly, "Have they come yet?" To which I would reply gently and automatically, "No, dear Charlotte. Not yet." She was beautiful in a gown of deep gold taffeta. Her red hair was a mass of curls that framed her lovely face. I had also worn taffeta, in soft blue. The house servants were starched, pressed, scrubbed, some of them exuding the effects of purloined perfume and cologne. It was a Tuesday morning near the end of April 1865, and the day was absolutely perfect, like a salute to springtime. Everywhere around us birds were singing in the fields and trees like a welcoming orchestra. The house itself was spanking clean inside and out. Banneker had worked with a large contingent of men laying another coat of whitewash on the mansion, and it gleamed in the sparkling sun. Indoors, everything was in perfect order. Benign had been cooking for days, as though she were preparing for the arrival of an army rather than for an individual. And out in the barbecue area, quite close to Banneker's office, where the candle house had stood, Amos' wife, Charity, playfully supervised a group of pickaninnies who slowly roasted a suckling pig over an open fire.

Lance Harcourt was with us, elegantly dressed, nervous, abstaining from drink, for it would be his first meeting with Father. It amused me to watch his fidgeting, since he had, at different times, asked for both Charlotte's hand and mine in marriage. When the news of Lincoln's death arrived, he had been especially distraught. "I knew John Wilkes Booth very well," he said, speaking of the assassin. "I studied under him. He was a fine teacher, an excellent actor, but something of a fanatic. I understand from friends that he was part of a plot to kidnap Lincoln last year. What a terrible tragedy—for Lincoln, of course, but for Booth and the country as well."

I was struck by his compassion, for I had seen him display very little of it concerning other matters. While his dress was elegant, it was also tasteful; and it was clear that he wanted to make the best possible impression on Father when it came time to ask for Charlotte's hand, for I hoped I had made it quite clear that my affections lay with Robert Gilliam. And where was Robert now? Riding happily with his father toward the Gilliam place? Or perhaps directly to Fir Crest. My heart fluttered as I thought of him. Would he have changed much? Would he see very much change in me? It was indeed a day for excitement and apprehension. Yet, there was the music of meadowlarks and mockingbirds; and, in the fields, the rich, throaty chorale of Negroes about their work, which did more to lift my spirits than anything else.

April is one of the loveliest months in Virginia. There is almost a sense of forgiving and generosity, as though nature spreads her most glorious attire before us for the purpose of making us forget, however briefly, that we have suffered and been lashed by her winter temperament. Standing on the porch at Fir Crest, I felt a sense of enchantment looking out across the fields and forests, listening to the clear conversation of the creeks. The sky was perfectly blue, with a cloud here and there in the farthest distance, like a dab of white upon a painter's easel. Where the young corn grew, the fields were full of morning glories twining up the tender stalks. And out in the pasturelands, there were dandelions with golden heads, lilies with their yellow fragmented petals. And a breathtaking green everywhere, as though nature not only forgave but also played a flirtatious role equally well.

Benign came with a pitcher of cider, which Lance Harcourt dived into with the eagerness of a thirsty tadpole. The day was warm, but certainly not enough for him to be perspiring so. "I suppose I'm nervous," he said, smiling apologetically as he accepted a second glass from Benign. I nodded, without comment. For a man on the verge of bigamy—in the event that he asked for both Charlotte's hand and mine, and Father agreed—he had every right to be nervous. But for a man who was heir to one of the oldest fortunes and most prestigious names in the South, he conducted himself like a shy schoolboy about to recite before a meeting of adoring mothers.

"You have another glass, Miss Victoria?" Benign was perhaps the calmest of us all. She had the entire mansion smelling of cinnamon, sage, nutmeg, marjoram, and sherry for her sauces and her own private nips. She herself had supervised the cleaning of Father's room. And then, to be sure that it had been properly done, she cleaned it again herself.

"No, thank you, Benign. Where is Miss Charlotte now?"

Benign smiled. "Running up and down stairs like she crazy. I think she changed dresses twenty times. She got on a green one now."

But when Charlotte came again to ask if anyone had come, she had on the gold taffeta. But she had put her hair up, which made her look somewhat older and taller, but certainly no less lovely. I took her by the elbow, and called Lance, who was walking about in circles on the porch. "Let us all calm down," I said, "before we're nervous wrecks when Father gets here. Remember that he has been away for four years. Seeing us again is probably a greater ordeal for him than it is for us. Why don't we sit in the garden and play cards?"

"Oh, I couldn't possibly!" Charlotte cried. "I think I shall change my dress. Does this one become me, Victoria?"

"You look absolutely lovely, Charlotte. You'll wear yourself out, changing clothes every five minutes. As it is, when Father does come, he will find you completely nude."

She and Lance Harcourt both laughed, and seemed to relax. Lance's eyes were bright—Fir Crest cider is known to carry a decided kick—and he poured himself a third glass. "This is excellent," he said. "Are you sure it's cider?"

"Perhaps I shall have some, too," Charlotte said. "It's what Benign calls cider. Elsewhere, it's called apple wine. After several glasses, grown men have been known to go out and knock mules down with their fists."

She laughed prettily, enjoying Lance's look of alarm. "Wine?" he said, sounding like a perfect teetotaler. "I don't want to meet your Father with wine on my breath!" He rushed into the garden, where he grabbed a handful of mint to chew.

Which gave me the opportunity to ask Charlotte a question that had been bothering me. "Do you and Lance still plan to marry, now that Father will be home?"

"Oh, yes!" she cried. "Why do you think I'm so nervous? Lance will ask him sometime today."

"I'm sure Father will agree," I said. "Now, stop fretting so. Everything will work out fine. You'll see."

"I hope so," Charlotte said. And she downed her cider. Laughing, she went to chew mint with Lance, just as Amos came riding hard. He pulled his horse up to the fence and bounded down. "They coming now, Miss Victoria! They'll be here in five minutes!"

We all sprang into action. I rang for Benign, who came at once. When I told her the news, she disappeared into the house, and returned followed by every servant there. They made an impressive lot. One of the young boys carried a bouquet of early roses. All of them lined up behind Benign in the yard where the carriage would stop. Charlotte and I, flanking Lance, stood before the Negroes. And then we saw the carriage, surrounded by prancing horses, moving slowly, almost regally, down the road past the cornfield, the orchard, and into the yard at Fir Crest. Immediately the armed riders wheeled and rode away, as though their presence would detract from the serenity of our meeting, as it surely would have. The driver was somewhat dusty, and, it seemed, somewhat morose. Glancing quickly at Amos, I saw that he, too, appeared glum. But before I had a chance to divine the reason for their countenances, Father himself opened the carriage door.

Without meaning to, I sucked in my breath. Lance, standing next to me, seemed to stiffen. And Charlotte, to his right, gave a small cry that sounded like a subdued sob.

The man who had left Fir Crest four years ago had been tall, handsome, strong of jaw and bearing, with flaming red hair that seemed, by day, alive with light. His green eyes had been merry and devilish, as though ignited by imps. He had been firm of figure, exuding a sense of power and authority that seemed the perfect embodiment of what Fir Crest and its proud tradition symbolized. Grandmother Parkchester, for all her vitality, had been merely a pale reflection of her heavy-browed, lean-jawed son. When he rode away, he had seemed like a prince mounted on his stallion, sitting so firmly in the saddle that one seriously doubted whether even the armies of Lincoln could dislodge him.

But the man who stepped from the carriage, grumbling at Amos and the driver as they helped him, seemed a desperate, embittered ghost, as though he had somehow managed to escape his tomb and were being forced back to it. In his gray uniform, his body seemed slack and cadaverous. His eyes were hollow and angry; and the great bony forehead with the bushy eyebrows jutted over the angular narrowness of the rest of his face—the thin nose, waxen-colored jowls, and a brush of a mustache that matched his brows. There were thin traces of spittle at the corners of his lips, as though he had just finished a fit of coughing. When he had gained his two feet on the ground, he pulled peevishly at his uniform coat and growled with surprising venom: "Well, I'm home, damn it! What the hell is everybody staring at?"

At least the voice had held its own against the ravages of war, and it startled me into action. "Welcome home, Father," I said, even as I curtsied. And then I rushed to embrace him. His body was emaciated to the touch; and as his arms encircled me, I felt that all the joy had been drained from him, as one extracts syrup from a maple. Following my lead, Charlotte also welcomed him. Then we introduced Lance, who seemed absolutely terrified as Father extended a hand marked most noticeably by bones, which Lance shook with extremest delicacy. "Heard about you," Father said to Lance. "Expected to see a lot more man than you're showing me." His voice sounded deliberately rude. As for Lance, he seemed to shrink by several inches.

Then, moving slowly, Father went to greet the servants. Benign curtsied low and with great dignity; it was obvious that she had practiced long and well for this occasion. "I sure glad to see you home again, Major Parkchester. We done our best to keep things like they was before you went away." He nodded briefly at the rest of the servants, and then pointed at the new gray building that was Banneker's office. "What's that doing there?" he growled.

"It is where the candle house used to be," I said. "Banneker has built himself an office there where he studies and also works on the records. I did not have time to write you about it."

"And why is Banneker not here?"

For some reason, I found myself becoming angry. Certainly he had fought a war that had ravaged him. But the tone of his voice, every aspect of his bearing, seemed designed to offend. "I do not know why Banneker is not here. Perhaps because he was not invited. Perhaps because he is at work."

Those famous green eyes slid over me like long-standing water that suddenly decides to move. There seemed to be a glint of amusement in them. "You have grown, Victoria," he said. His tone was somewhat kinder. I had no answer for that; he seemed to expect none. Charlotte had been watching him in a kind of wonderment. Since she had always been his favorite, I expected that he would treat her kinder. But he reserved his most devastating remark for her: "And I see you've grown into a regular slut!"

"Father!" It was my shocked voice. To say such a thing under any circumstances was gross. But to say it now, when we had all gathered like foolish, eager children for him to spew his venom on—that was unforgivable.

Charlotte had turned very pale; and she said a surprising thing. "I am not only my father's daughter," she said clearly. "I am my mother's as well."

Now it was Father who paled. "I shall go to my room," he said. "I see that everything has continued as though no war were being fought. On my way here, I saw not a blade of grass out of place." It was impossible not to detect the jealousy in his voice. Would he have preferred that Fir Crest suffer as he had? I was on the verge of asking him, but he held up a gaunt hand to still me. "And is that pig roasting out yonder? So, you have planned a celebration. Well, I'm in no mood for celebrations or any other such foolishness. I shall go to my room, where I shall take my meals. I do not wish to be disturbed by anyone, except Judge Gilliam when he gets home. As you can all see, I am tired, bitter, and very nearly mad. There is nothing any of you can do other than to follow my instructions to the last letter." He turned to Lance Harcourt and looked him up and down with the greatest disdain. "Which of my daughters are you here to court, young man?" Fairly trembling, Lance told him that it was Charlotte, although I had written Father about their relationship. Father grunted offensively. "You would have done better with Victoria, except that she would have the good sense not to have you around."

That was too much for Charlotte. She burst into tears and ran into the house. Father actually seemed pleased. As for Lance, he had turned as white as a ghost. He pulled a handkerchief from somewhere and dabbed at his lips. "Perhaps I should be going to Charlottesville," he said. And Father rejoined, "Perhaps you should." But not even Lance Harcourt would allow himself to be dismissed in front of Negroes in such a vulgar fashion. Instead, he made a deeper error. "What is it that you dislike about me, sir?"

The look that Father aimed at him seemed to cause him to wilt. "You are too pretty," he said. "While good, brave men were dying in the cause of the South, you were waltzing your legs off. You are a Harcourt, to be sure, and that is a name to conjure with. But if you are any sample of the breed, then it is a dying one. Indeed you should go to Charlottesville. I bid you good day, sir!"

Then he turned abruptly and went into the house, possibly to console Charlotte. But she swept past him as he entered, head held dangerously high. There was something grand in seeing her that way, for she was a Parkchester to the core; and if she had been even a very small ship, the wake of her indignation would have drowned Father as he stepped aside to let her pass. She went directly to Lance Harcourt. "I shall go to Charlottesville with you," she said. "Since I am a slut, no servant need accompany me." Linking her arm in his, she seemed to give him a part of her strength. For he moved to his waiting carriage, helped her in, then turned to us all. Father still waited on the porch. Lance bowed to him stiffly. "I bid *you* good day, sir!" He swung up into the carriage beside Charlotte. And the driver pulled off with a great clatter of wheels and horses' hooves.

It was absolutely incredible that such a thing could happen within fifteen minutes of Father's coming home. Now I was furious. "Dismiss the servants, Benign!" I cried. And then I went to the porch, where Father stood like a manifestation of the greatest evil. "I shall try to understand that you have fought a war and lost," I said evenly. "I shall also try to understand that you are bitter and tired and mad, as you have said. But I shall neither understand nor tolerate your bad manners. It will be most beneficial to all of us if you do remain in your room until you have learned to live with civilized people again. Now it is I who bid you good day, sir!" And, so saying, I swept past him into the sitting room, where I poured a hefty drink of sherry and downed it.

I heard Father moving across the sitting room behind me. Deliberately I kept my back to him, stiffening my shoulders. Whatever it is that war does to good men, I found myself praying that it had not had the same offensive effect on Robert Gilliam. I listened for Father to make his way upstairs, but he had obviously stopped and was watching me.

"Standing that way," he said gently, "you remind me of your mother when she was young."

"Were you in the habit of insulting her publicly?" I asked coldly.

"I was different then," he said. His footsteps dragged closer to me. Slowly, pitifully. At the same time, I felt frightened, as though an impostor had donned a lusterless red wig and mask and had come home to imitate Father.

"Won't you light a fire?" he said. "I am chilly. I have not been well, you know."

I lighted the fire on the hearth and drew a chair close for him to sit. "We heard that you were wounded. Was there something else?" I asked. Now I was sorry that I had been angry with him.

He tapped his forehead, his temple, with a long finger.

"I fear that I am going mad," he said. "I have seen such horrible things done in the name of justice. I have seen good things done as well. But I am haunted by nightmares. And even when I am awake, I hear the screams of dying men. . . ."

"Father!" How could I dislike him? I felt so very ashamed that I fell to my knees at his chair and embraced him. Now I recognized his embrace from the old days. He even kissed me on the cheek. "You have grown into a lovely woman," he said softly. "And you have done an excellent job of keeping Fir Crest going. I was astonished, and a bit jealous, too, I must admit. I wondered if I really were needed here." He held me away from him, inspecting my eyes. His seemed perfectly rational; but with the fire adding color to them, they also seemed to hold a glint of madness.

"Envy, jealousy, is an evil thing," he went on. "It is possible that I shall even come to hate you, for you have shown me, by the job you have done here, that I am obsolete. I have been defeated by my country, my daughters, and my servants. Is there nothing left for me?" Laying his cheek against mine, he wept in great, racking sobs.

"Of course there is something for you, Father. We could not have survived without knowing that we were maintaining all of this for you to come back to. Certainly you have known greater tragedies than we have here at Fir Crest. But we have known tragedies, and we have overcome them, because we knew that one day you would be home to take over again."

He was shaking his head slowly. "No, never again. You are mistress of Fir Crest, and so you shall remain. I have no further interest in it. I have no interest in anything."

"You are tired," I said, helping him to his feet. "After sufficient time, you will feel differently. You made Fir Crest what it is. You will not so easily relinquish it."

He seemed to smile like his old self. "I have always said that you were the strongest. Perhaps you are right. But for now, I want only to be left alone. Do you understand, dear girl?"

"I shall try to, Father. The most important thing is that you are home again. Nothing else matters."

He kissed me on the forehead. "Robert Gilliam and the Judge will be here in three days. I wish to see the Judge as soon as he arrives. As for Charlotte, do go for her. Do not send anyone; go yourself, for I have done her a great wrong. Only you could explain the reason, if indeed there was a reason. She simply appeared to be a slut, and I said so. As for young Harcourt, he seems worthless, although I understand that they do have money."

"I shall go for Charlotte," I said. "Now, you should go and rest. I shall instruct Benign to attend you. She will have you feeling better in no time."

I helped him to his room, where two male servants were waiting to help him. The tub was filled with water, but he waved the servants away. "I want to rest," he said. He lay on the bed. "Go for Charlotte," he said. And then he closed his eyes.

After dismissing the servants, I closed the draperies, darkening the room. My father's breathing was loud, regular. I thought that he was already asleep. But he called me as I neared the door.

"Yes, Father?"

"Are we alone?"

I told him that we were.

"There are certain things you should know," he said, "but I shall tell you only this for now: Banneker should have been downstairs to greet me, because he is my son. A foolish indiscretion with Yetta many years ago. As for Charlotte, I have seen disturbing signs in her which remind me of your mother when I met her in New Orleans." It seemed that he laughed softly, bitterly. "Another foolish indiscretion of my youth. Your mother, Patricia Devereaux, was a whore, a well-known prostitute in New Orleans, when I met and married her. A high-class whore, but a whore nonetheless. I thought she was the most beautiful woman I had ever seen. I fell hopelessly in love with her. When you wrote me how she died, it seemed most appropriate, considering her life before she came to Fir Crest. . . ."

Now his voice had fallen to a nearly inaudible murmuring, as though he were very close to sleep. "It is to her great credit that she became 'respectable' once we were married. I thought that I could forget what she had been, but it stood between us like a wall. You and your sister are the results of our only married intimacy. Incredible? Certainly not, for converts are always the greatest fanatics.

So I sought relief in the cabins. Banneker is the result of that indiscretion." His voice had strengthened as he talked; now it turned hoarse. "I swear you to secrecy. Do you swear?"

It was almost impossible for me to speak. "I swear," I whispered.

"Then go," he said.

Was he simply a man driven mad by defeat, fabricating tales to justify his sense of personal failure? Or was he telling the horrible truth about Banneker and my mother? I would not have the chance to ask him then, for the room suddenly resounded with his snores.

I gathered sufficient strength to go into the hallway, where I slumped against the wall, holding my hands to my head. What manner of man was this who had come home from the war? More important, what manner of man was he who had gone to the war, who had harbored the most obscene secrets even as he had preached morality and justice? Before I knew it, I was weeping bitterly. I slumped to the floor, completely oblivious of the fact that servants might see me.

But would it matter now? If Banneker, indeed, were Father's son, surely the Negroes must have known all along. And laughed at us behind our backs. As for the dreadful things he had said about Mother, it seemed impossible that he would have demeaned her memory by falsifying the facts. It was clear that the war had been more than he could manage. We would find later on that many others like Father had returned to their homes like hollow, embittered ghosts, full of envy and venom because those they left behind had not failed while they had failed miserably.

I felt, more than heard, the approach of Benign. I struggled to my feet and was wiping my cheeks when she wrapped her huge arms around me. "You just go ahead and cry, missy. It's a pity what done happened to Major Parkchester. But he going to be all right. You just go ahead and cry now."

But I was finished with crying. If Banneker were really my half-brother, how many more bastards had my father sired in the cabins? And if Mother had indeed been a New Orleans slut, what did the future hold in store for us if the truth were ever found out about her past? At that moment, I wanted to put a torch to Fir Crest, to its glittering white facade of respectability. I found myself wishing that Father had died on some far-off battlefield, or that he had never come home at all. Anything to spare me the burden of what he had revealed to me. Crushed against Benign's awesome warmth, the comfortable strength of her body, I wondered how much she knew of what Father had said. I pulled away from her and inspected her face. It seemed that she had been crying, too, for her eyes were red and somewhat puffy. But had her tears been for the secrets of the past or the reality of the present? Did she know about Banneker? And Mother? Certainly there was someone who did. If Father's word could not be trusted, Yetta would be more than happy to tell me the truth.

"Father will be fine," I told Benign. "He has been through a terrible ordeal, which will take time for him to forget. We must continue as before, Benign. I know that I can count on you as I always have."

"You certainly can, missy."

"Good. Now, I want you to order a carriage for me. I am leaving for Charlottesville within the hour to bring Miss Charlotte home. Father is remorseful for the terrible things he said, and he has asked me to go for her. Please tell Amos that I would like him to drive, and I would like five armed men to accompany me."

"You want me to go with you, missy?"

"No, Benign. You stay here with Father. I shall be all right."

She nodded somewhat sadly and went down the hallway to the stairs. The slow sound of her receding footsteps indicated the sorrow that she felt.

I went to my room, where I quickly changed into something more appropriate for the forty-mile journey to Charlottesville. Then I went down through the sitting room and out the front doors of Fir Crest, moving almost furtively. I lingered awhile in the west garden, fingering a rose there as though I were deep in thought. At least, it would seem that way to anyone who might see me. And even as I stood among the plants and flowers, I thought how ironic it was that I persisted in trying to maintain a show of respectability when it was almost certain that Fir Crest and its inhabitants were shot through with corruption, however chaste and respectable our exteriors might appear to be.

Once it seemed safe, I walked slowly down the path to

the cabins, as though I were killing time until Amos readied the carriage. It would be the first time I had entered the Negro quarters on foot, and I wondered if I would be safe. But there were greater considerations than my own personal well-being. For one thing, if Banneker were indeed our half-brother, then another heir to Fir Crest had suddenly and dramatically appeared, and would have to be contended with. Even as I considered the reality, it seemed clear why Banneker had long enjoyed a special position on the plantation. And there was his own warning to me, the night of his naked visit, that he was more than a mere servant: *Fir Crest belong to you and me, Miss Victoria.* If such were the case, why had he eliminated Charlotte from the running? And what were the "crazy things" that Yetta talked about when she was drunk on her brews and crazed with locoweed? How, in a moment of the most incredible obscenity, she had wallowed in my father's arms while he planted the seed of their handsome bastard?

These questions buzzed in my head like bothersome flies as I approached the quarter. Yetta would tell me. I neither liked nor trusted the woman; yet, I firmly believed that she would tell me the truth, if only this one time. In her own distorted way, perhaps she had been trying to tell me the truth last fall, when she incited Banneker and sent him naked to my room. Had she also encouraged him in his relationship with Charlotte? However repugnant the idea of brother lying with sister, would there not be a special advantage in having Banneker lay claim to our hearts, and, ultimately, to the entire splendor of Fir Crest—especially if he himself were unaware of his rightful claim to at least a part of it? For Banneker's own arrogance would never allow himself to be a lowly servant if he knew that he was, in truth, the master's son.

Yetta's cabin, like the others, was squat and gray with weatherboarding. Someone, perhaps Banneker, had planted geraniums on either side of the plank steps leading to the door, for the cabin rested on a brick foundation that raised it perhaps three feet from the ground. I climbed the steps and knocked at the door. Immediately there was a heavy rustling inside, as though nervous mice had taken up residence there. Then Yetta herself opened the door.

"Come in, Miss Victoria," she said sweetly. "I been expecting you."

I went in. The cabin was spotless, with a cot, several chairs and a table, and a cookstove. I was glad to see that Banneker was not there, although I saw some of his shirts hanging from a hook on the wall. Yetta pulled two chairs together, motioning me to one. When I had sat, she took the other.

"Why have you been expecting me, Yetta?" The room was fragrant with a musty odor that seemed to come from an assortment of herbs piled on a long shelf against one wall.

"I figured you'd come see me after you'd talked to Mr. Parkchester," she said. Her deepset eyes seemed amused, and very shrewd.

"You figured correctly, Yetta. I have talked to Father. However, I fail to see what that has to do with you."

She grinned. "Then why you here? From what I see, even from a distance, that man been through hell. Hell makes men tell the truth."

There was no way around that, so I went directly to the point. "I was curious," I said. "There are certain questions I wanted to ask you."

Nodding, she pulled a corncob pipe from the pocket of her blue dress and sucked on the stem without lighting it. "These questions have to do with Banneker?"

"Perhaps."

"And with Mr. Parkchester?"

"Perhaps."

"And with Fir Crest?"

This time I only nodded. Which seemed to infuriate her. She slammed one wizened hand in the other and pulled her chair so close that I thought she might attack me. "You in no position to be acting coy, missy! You ain't talking to no slave woman no more! Before, you chase me from your house, acting all high and mighty! Well, now you in Yetta's house! If you come here to talk about something, you talk! I don't like nobody playing with me!"

I simply stared at her. Whatever questions I had to ask, whatever answers she might give, certainly would benefit her more than they ever could me—if Father's confession and my premises were correct. So the advantage lay on my side. And the finest proof of that was the way she reacted to my stare. All at once, she lost her fury and slumped back in her chair. I held myself straight and imperious, impaling her with my gaze. She was waiting for me to speak, but finally it was her own unease which caused her to break the silence.

"You here to find out about Banneker," she said, putting away her pipe. "He Mr. Parkchester's son, although Banneker don't know it." She looked around the neat cabin, as though to do so helped her collect her thoughts. "I never told Banneker, because he a born rebel. He wouldn't been no slave if he'd knowed he was Mr. Parkchester's son. I feared for him. I feared Mr. Parkchester might have him killed."

Again I impaled her with an unwavering gaze. She was certainly telling the truth, for my whole body responded with an unpleasant warmth, as though I were sitting too close to fire. My mind was working frantically even as I stared her down. Could she *prove* that she was telling the truth? In any contest between her and Father's credibility, Father's certainly would win out. Unless, of course, there were written documents.

"Can you prove these things you're saying?"

She shook her head sadly. "Mr. Parkchester know I'm telling the truth. Ain't no record of nothing, except in my heart . . . and his head."

She seemed particularly filthy and grotesque at that moment. "I have been told that you are spreading this vile rumor about my father," I said coldly. "I have come to tell you that you are to stop. It is degrading to me and my entire family that you should be saying such things . . . especially without proof." She seemed most surprised, and I stood, to press my advantage. "The true purpose of my visit indeed has to do with Father, and with Banneker. But certainly not to hear ugly rumors about one being the illegitimate son of the other. First of all, why did you encourage Banneker to come to my room as he did? There is no use denying it. He himself has told me that you provoked him. Furthermore, I understand that you drink, and smoke jimsonweed as well. Perhaps it is the weed which has created these obscene fantasies that you speak of."

She seemed completely undone. "You trying to tell me I crazy? You ain't fooling Yetta one bit. I drink when I please. I smoke locoweed when I please. You tell me one nigger don't smoke locoweed when they feel like it. But ain't nothing you can say going to make me change my mind. Your daddy is Banneker's daddy. Banneker is your half-brother. He Miss Charlotte's half-brother. He just as much heir to Fir Crest as either one of you. Maybe more, because he a man, he strong. He born before you or Charlotte. And he don't take no foolishness off nobody."

She had risen from her chair as she talked, as though yanked to her feet by the excitement of her greed. "He Massa Parkchester's son, all right. And that mean that he the rightful heir to Fir Crest. Furthermore, I ain't send Banneker nowhere that night. He his own man, he do as he please. He been laying with Miss Charlotte any time he want to. What make him think he can't lay with you as well?"

I slapped her as hard as I could. "You will guard your tongue when you speak to me!" I cried. "And you will stop telling lies about my father and yourself!" She was holding her jaw, staring at me now in abject fear. "In the event that you persist with these lies and rumors, I shall take you before Judge Gilliam and charge you with slander and defamation of character. You know what that means, don't you?"

"Yas'm."

"And what does it mean?"

"They put me in prison." She slumped to her chair.

"Stand up when you speak to me! You have offended me beyond all reason! How dare you suggest that Charlotte and Banneker have been having an affair? How dare you claim that my father has been intimate with you?" I felt more than a bit mad, but it was essential to protect Fir Crest from the greedy claims of this black woman and her son, however true they might be.

"I sorry, Miss Victoria. I terribly sorry."

"It is not enough to be sorry! I want your solemn word that you will never say such things again. You must understand that I have tremendous resources at my command. Judge Gilliam is only one of them. There are the night riders as well."

Now her eyes opened wide in horror. "You'd tell the night riders?"

"I most certainly shall . . . unless I have your word."

"You got my word," she said most sullenly.

There was a black leather-covered Bible on the shelf with the fragrant herbs. I snatched it down and held it before her. She recoiled as though I had handed her a snake. "Put your hand on it and swear!"

She shook her head. "I don't like fooling with God's business."

"Very well. Then I shall ride immediately to the courthouse and swear out charges against you. And Banneker as well. I shall tell them that he came to my room naked and drunk last fall. He tried to rape me. I did not complain against him because he has been a faithful servant. I was also thinking of your welfare. If you see fit to ignore mine, then I shall have you both jailed."

It was a terrible scene. Even as I held the Bible, it was as though another part of me had stepped aside and was watching me with a mixture of admiration and the worst possible distaste. But were Fir Crest, and the legitimate claims of Charlotte and myself, to be put in jeopardy by one old Negro woman? "Swear!" I cried.

She was terrified. Her face was a nasty gray; and her body jerked as though she, too, had been musing the consequences of this incredible encounter. I thrust the Bible at her. And her withered hand came up, touched the leather cover, the fingers spread like separate lizards. "I swear," she whispered. There were tears dampening her eyes. I put the Bible back on the shelf most rapidly, for it suddenly seemed to burn my fingers. If there were a God, hopefully He was white, a plantation owner, and fully aware of Virginia's law of primogeniture, which meant, in this newly liberated South, that Fir Crest would go to Banneker at Father's death, if Yetta's claim could be proven—leaving me and Charlotte subject to whatever whim of our black half-brother and former slave. It was a prospect so unpleasant and unbelievable as to justify any act on my part.

"You are not to say a word of this to Banneker, is that clear?"

"Yas'm."

My head was spinning with a sense of triumph. Fir Crest was safe. And Father would not be held up to ridicule on account of Banneker and Yetta. But, most important, Charlotte's legacy, and my own, was secure. At least, for the moment. I would have to be more alert than ever. For Yetta seemed a formidable foe.

"Now," I said quite calmly, "to the other purpose of my visit. Father has asked me to go to Charlottesville to bring my sister home. I would like you to accompany me, since Benign must care for Father. And I would like for Banneker to come with us, since he is strong and trustworthy."

"Yas'm." Her voice sounded dry, however defeated. It was clearly a bribe, having her accompany me to Charlottesville. All the Negroes loved to go into town to see the sights there. But, to my own mind, it was a way of keeping a sharp eye on Yetta and Banneker, at least for this most important day, when her viciousness, coupled with Banneker's possible indignation, could create the worst mischief imaginable.

"I shall be ready to leave within the hour," I said.

"Yas'm."

She opened the door for me. I turned once to look at the room. The leather-covered Bible seemed to regard me accusingly. "You have a very lovely cabin," I said.

"Thank you, ma'am."

Holding my skirts up, I went down the stairs and back to the mansion. My heart was beating so fast that it was almost impossible for me to breathe. In the encounter with Yetta, I had turned a most important corner in my life. Would I live to regret it? Only time and the unfolding of events would tell.

So, it was off to Charlottesville, with Banneker heading the armed escort and Yetta riding inside with me. She maintained complete silence all the way to town, and it was obvious that she had not only taken some of her brew, but some jimsonweed as well, after I had left her cabin. It was also obvious, from the depth of her brooding coupled with Banneker's high spirits, that she had thus far kept to her end of the bargain. But for how long? Negroes were very religious and excessively superstitious, so it was possible that Yetta's oath on the Bible might hold her tongue for a while. But certainly not forever. Even then, it seemed that I could see the wheels of her crone's mind at work behind her knitted brow. As the carriage maintained a sedate pace toward Charlottesville, the wheels of my mind were working as well.

Several things were now clear which had been hazy before. From the very beginning of our troubles—the raid on Fir Crest while I had been with Robert Gilliam at the creek at his place—the ultimate object of our unknown stalker had not been an individual, but an estate. Whoever was behind the tragedies that had befallen us was after Fir Crest itself. Certainly Grandmother Parkchester had been principal intended victim in the candle-house fire; the Negroes had been considered expendable, and were perhaps part of a smoke screen to keep us believing that the fire had been accidental rather than deliberate.

As for the initial raid, which had claimed Mother's life, her death at the hands of dozens of lustful men had been carefully orchestrated to give it the appearance of an accident as well. But it had been cold, calculated murder, executed in the most callous way possible. That Grandmother Parkchester had escaped actual death, and had been driven mad instead, could not have been foreseen by the killer. Nor could he be certain that she might not regain her good senses and interpose herself between the killer and his designs on Fir Crest.

In our immediate circle, Banneker, Charlotte, Lance Harcourt, and I—looked at objectively—were the most logical suspects. Could Yetta and Benign be overlooked? They might not have been part of the initial raid, but it was within the realm of possibility that they might have planned it. But where would any Negro, Banneker included, be able to command and direct the intentions of a band of predominantly white raiders? They had descended on Fir Crest, they had brutalized and murdered Mother and Mr. McAdoo. They had attempted to murder Grand-mother Parkchester as well. I clearly remembered Benign's comment about the raiders: *They only looking for white ladies, they didn't touch one nigger woman. Not one. . . . They had their fun. They drag your grandmammy upstairs. They leave us outdoors, telling us they ain't got no argument with dumb niggers. They say they hate white people for what they doing to the country. . . . Some of them go out and start burning everything. . . .*

A strange story, hardly believable. Yet, Benign had little reason to lie. Furthermore, her account of the raid had been corroborated dozens of times by other Negroes whom I had questioned. Except for small details, their accounts matched hers in every respect. *Some of them go out and start burning everything. . . .* But they had burned very little; and, if they indeed were against "white people," then why had they not burned the mansion, all the food, all the supplies, which really would have devastated us? We had lost a few crops, a few outbuildings. Had these really been men intent on destruction? Or had their coming been merely a prelude to other murders which would leave Fir Crest in the hands of one of them?

Among the possible suspects, Lance Harcourt was both least and most likely. If Fir Crest were really the object of his affection, he had made the stupid move of proposing to both me and Charlotte, which meant that if he did win one of us as his wife, he would make an enemy of the other. At the same time, he had demonstrated that he could be shrewd and efficient. During our period of decline, he had moved into the governing position with surprising energy. He had come with other raiders to chase away the dissident Negroes. But he certainly had not been with the raiders who had raped Mother to death, for Benign would have spotted him with her eagle's eye. And he was on his way to Charlottesville when the fire had happened in the candle house. Was it possible that he had a hidden army of agents at work at Fir Crest? If that were the case, they had done remarkably little damage. The horror of what had happened was that events occurred sporadically, yet, with unbelievable savagery, as though someone fully intended to bring us to our knees through a reign of terror, and then to take over Fir Crest once we had become unable to resist.

If it were Lance Harcourt engineering the horror, what rational purpose did he have in mind? Certainly his own estate was larger, wealthier, and far more worth the having than Fir Crest. There was no doubt that Lance himself was wealthy, somewhat lazy, certainly too sensitive to be a party to mayhem. By any standard, he was capable of donning a white hood and helping others to rout a band of Negroes. That had been a lark, probably done for Charlotte's benefit. Even though he was the most obvious suspect, at least in terms of being the only available logical one, I had to dismiss Lance Harcourt as being the author of our tragedies.

But what of Charlotte? As distasteful as it was to consider that my sister might be a murderess, objectivity demanded that I at least analyze her situation. Upon my death, she would become mistress of Fir Crest. But both of us had to await the death of Father. Then, once Father was gone, I would have to follow him almost immediately for Charlotte to benefit. It was a complicated procedure, for Father might well live for a very long time. If Charlotte were the murderess, then Father would be the next to die. And I the next. But Charlotte certainly had had no part in the work of the raiders who had killed Mother. She had been hiding, terrified, under Mother's bed. The terror I'd seen on her face, and the subsequent horror that kept her to her room, had not been artificial. As for the fire in the candle house, she had been sitting in the kitchen with Benign and me, which seemed to absolve all of us from guilt. For, certainly, whoever was responsible for the first event—the raid—was responsible for the second.

Looked at that way, then our tragedies seemed part of an exceedingly clever Negro plot, and Banneker immediately became the chief suspect. He was a natural leader of men. Was it not possible that he was hidden chief of the band who had first come to Fir Crest? And that he had sent one of his agents to burn down the candle house? But if the intended victim there had been Grandmother Parkchester, the whole fabric of my reasoning was shot to pieces. For Banneker was far too clever not to have gotten rid of Grandmother by some other means without having to resort to the fire. And what of Benign's family? Why would he want to kill them off if Fir Crest were the prize he was seeking? Another smoke screen to throw us off the track? However much I suspected, even Emerald's death did not make sense as an act of murder. For what possible motive? What might she have known that would cause someone to kill her? If her death were an act of revenge, then Charlotte was also clear on that point, for she had been visiting in Charlottesville when Emerald was killed.

Yetta was dozing now on the seat in front of me. With the lines in her face relaxed, she seemed a benevolent witch. Unable to realize secret and impossible dreams, could she really move Banneker to murder? I doubted so. Which left me right where I'd begun. If the tragedies at Fir Crest had been deliberate, I was unable to point my finger at any possible suspect with any certainty. If they were not deliberate—if, indeed, they were only a series of unrelated and shocking coincidences—then I was the victim of an overactive imagination. The only solid evidence I had—and I had been the only one to see that—was the charred lock from the candle-house door. It *had* been locked during the fire; afterward, Banneker had found it open. That was all I really had to go on. . . .

The road to Charlottesville is a lovely, winding highway that goes through some of the most beautiful country in Virginia. While other areas might have been scarred or devastated by the war, that around Charlottesville remained largely untouched. There were grand oaks, maples, and elms on either side of the road, with yellow and red flowers growing around their feet. But the roads were more heavily traveled today than usual. There were all manner of stragglers, hawkers, bawds, ne'er-do-wells, unkempt Union soldiers everywhere on foot, or arrogantly on their mounts. It was as though the South had died and rotted, and these carrion had come to pick her bones. We were stopped twice by Union officers who asked what our business was about. One of them poked under the carriage seats, patted a horse's rump, and then sent us on our way. I was most impressed at how they treated the Negroes with the utmost respect, reserving their restrained contempt for me, as though I had held millions of blacks in slavery single-handedly. Indeed, but for the Negroes, I might have been dragged from the carriage and violated there on the very road; for the soldiers' distaste for me, a lone southern white woman, was almost a palpable thing. It was as though I were a symbol of all they had hated and fought against. The recent death of President Lincoln at the hands of a southerner only made matters worse. Some of the soldiers spat on the carriage. One pulled out his organ and sprayed urine in our direction. There were black soldiers as well as white, but they all seemed united in their utter disregard for me. To that point, Banneker had ridden with two other men in front of the carriage, with three bringing up the rear. Now he set two in front, two behind, with himself and Amos on either side of the carriage. Once, he swung low from his mount and stuck his head into the carriage window. "Don't you be scared, Miss Victoria. These men ain't nothing but trash, don't matter whether they wearing uniforms or not."

I was glad that he had come with us, for he would be uncontrollable if anyone dared try to molest either me or his mother. She actually seemed to be enjoying the specta-cle, leaning from the window on Amos' side, grinning at the grossest displays of arrogance and hatred. I had often thought that with the war's end, a sense of friendship and brotherhood would prevail, as it had, however unevenly, before the attack on Sumter. But it was clear that dark days lay ahead of us. Three times I saw soldiers openly copulating with what appeared to be painted prostitutes in the lovely green fields. Drunks wandered up and down with bottles in their hands. Some of these were young southern men who, like my father, found the dregs of de-feat hard to swallow. They were harassed with insults and catcalls. I saw at least two of them knocked to the ground by Union soldiers who sped past on their horses and struck them in the head with their fists, as though they were playing a kind of human rugby. Before his death, Mr. Lincoln had called for malice toward none, with char-ity for all. But it was clear that the spirit he invoked had become narrow and mean in the very men he had com-manded. To make matters worse, a southerner named An-drew Johnson had become president of a still-divided United States upon the death of Lincoln.

Apart from my disgust at seeing grown men and women act like the very worst animals, I was quite apprehensive about Charlotte and Lance Harcourt. How had they fared with this rabble? It was useless to urge the driver to go faster, for the crowd grew larger and more disorderly as we neared Charlottesville. At times, it was possible to see in the distance some of the historic mansions for which Albemarle County is famous. We passed Monticello, Mr. Jefferson's home, which has been preserved. Ash Lawn, the home of President James Monroe, was also nearby. Both were being patrolled by heavy guard, for it seemed quite clear that the mob which made our passage almost impossible was intent on profit at any cost. Finally, we came to the true gem of Charlottesville—the University of Virginia, with its stately, graceful architecture. That was also being patrolled, but the crowd was sparser in its vicin-ity, as though they feared the possible contagion of good manners and education if they came too close. There were not a few notherners among them, outstanding not only by their dress and gait, but by a general sense of greed that they wore like a halo. Their eyes darted here and there as though they expected to find diamonds lying in the streets. Some carried their belongings in gaudy carpetbags, which would soon lend their names to one of the most nefarious periods in southern history. We clattered through these carpetbaggers and scalawags, past the university, then turned down a somewhat narrow street toward the imposing home of Mrs. Pennington, where Charlotte had been staying, and to which she had most likely returned after Father's offensive remarks.

Mrs. Pennington was a rather stout woman in her middle fifties who surrounded herself with young people, as she frequently said, to keep herself from feeling old. Her husband, a tobacco broker, had died long before the war and left her an elegant home and a sizable fortune, both of which she used to attract young people like Lance Harcourt and his hangers-on, who filled her with compliments while they gorged themselves from her cellar and larder. If she dreaded growing old, or appearing so, she had fought an unsuccessful battle. Aside from her stoutness, which she insisted upon stuffing into dresses that were plainly too small, thereby giving her the appearance of a very chic sausage about to part in the middle, she seemed to believe that people stay young if they wear bright colors. With dyed yellow hair, auburn eyes, orange lip paint, beige rouge, and a satin gown the color of her hair, she gave the impression of being a rather desperate rainbow. But a pleasing one, and of the highest reputation, despite her eccentric nature. Only her eyes revealed that her fetish for youth was really a fear of dying, for they peered at one from rouged folds of flesh like the frightened eyes of some small animal trapped by the hounds of heaven in a vast cave.

She greeted me cordially, the satin causing her to whisper like an overly perfumed breeze as she moved. Then I inquired about Lance and Charlotte.

"Yes, they were here," she said. "But only briefly. Charlotte seemed very upset. I suppose it is because of all the rabble in the streets." Rustling, she went to the French windows and peered out. "It is a disgusting display. And what a waste! So many young people, moving without direction, lost inside their confusion. So terrible!"

"Did Lance and Charlotte say where they were going?" I asked. "Perhaps they went to his place?"

"Perhaps," Mrs. Pennington said. "But won't you stay awhile for tea? Wherever they are, I am sure they are fine. Lance is an exemplary young man; certainly he would never let anything happen to Charlotte."

Of her last observation, I was not so sure as she. I declined her invitation, stressing the importance of my finding Charlotte at once, and gave myself up to her pudgy arms in a farewell embrace. Her short, tapering fingers were bright with red lacquer on the nails, as though she had been gouging in blood.

"Farewell, my dear," she murmured.

"Good-bye, Mrs. Pennington. Thanks for your courtesy."

I went back to the carriage and instructed the driver to continue to Independence Street, near the outskirts of town, where Lance Harcourt maintained a rented house for his frequent visits to Charlottesville.

Once again Banneker had deployed the guard so that one rode at each side of the carriage, with two in front and two bringing up the rear. Banneker guarded the side of the carriage nearest me. He rode without saddle, and his muscular leg curved the horse's girth like a thick stave. The crowds in town were heavier than any we had encountered. We moved slowly through a sea of insults, angry faces, threatening fists, until we arrived at the house on Independence Street.

Normally isolated, even here there were crowds, but of the lowest possible kind; for Lance Harcourt had rented his home near the worst section of town. Perhaps it had appealed to his sense of the bizarre to flaunt his wealth in this neighborhood. He'd had the house redone, and a fence of sturdy iron planted around it, like a perimeter of spears. Yet, as I climbed from the carriage, I saw that the gate was open, and Lance's carriage, unattended, was waiting in the drive. As I approached the gate, with Banneker firmly holding my elbow, three Union soldiers staggered past. "Now, there's a pretty one!" one of them cried. And another said, "Yes, but she's with her buck!" The three of them laughed together, and continued on their way, perhaps to one of the several taverns that flourished in this neighborhood, along with every other possible vice.

There was something ominously quiet about Lance's house, given the excitement and confusion that swept around. I had been here many times before. Except for its location, the refurbished mansion held its own with the very finest of Charlottesville in terms of furnishings and decor. It was here that I had seen the two gamecocks rip each other to shreds. As Banneker lifted the heavy knocker and let it fall, I felt a keen sense of evil. To make matters worse, a dark cloud suddenly obscured the sun, and the air turned moist, as though we were in for one of the storms that frequently lashed this section of Virginia.

Banneker knocked twice more, but when no answer was forthcoming, he said, "I think I'll go to the back. Somebody might be around there."

"Very Well, Banneker." Still he hesitated. "I shall be fine," I said. Amos and the other men, plus the carriage, were within leaping distance, if the situation came to that. Still, his concern pleased me. I almost felt guilty about the fact that I was studiously trying to rob him of his birthright and his inheritance, if such were indeed the case. At the same time, I wondered if he would have any compunction about robbing me of mine, if matters were reversed.

He stepped from the porch with the ease of a large panther. He was barefoot, wearing the thin gray shirt and pants that Negroes favor. He disappeared around the corner of the house almost secretly. I waited on the porch, fanning with my lace handkerchief, for an unpleasant humidity had sudden fallen on us.

Banneker was back in perhaps five minutes. "Is anyone there?" I asked.

His face held a peculiar look of disgust. "Mr. Harcourt, he there. I looked through a window."

"Is Charlotte with him?" I could not fathom his look of disgust; but obviously he had seen something that displeased him.

"I didn't see Miss Charlotte. I don't think she is in the house anywhere." He glided to the porch and knocked rudely, angrily, with both large fists.

It seemed an indelicate question, but I had to know. "Is Mr. Harcourt with another woman, then?"

He banged his fists again, then answered me with head down. "He ain't with no other woman," he said bitterly.

His whole body was seething with almost visible anger. What had he seen around the house? He lunged at the door with his fists, beating the panels as though to rid himself of violence.

Suddenly the door opened, and Lance Harcourt stood there. Booted, in gray flannel trousers and a ruffled white shirt, he seemed as urbane as ever. "Victoria! What a pleasant surprise!" he cried.

To my great consternation, it was Banneker who answered. "It sure is a surprise," he said, deep down in his throat. "We been out here knocking. Then I went around the house and peep in through the window."

Lance's face turned very pale. "I was occupied," he murmured.

"Yes, you was," Banneker said. At the same time, I saw the slight figure of a Negro youth slip down the drive, leap the sharp-pointed fence, and run away. "You certainly was." He, too, was watching the young man, and his fine lips curled in a further expression of disgust.

I turned in time to see Lance Harcourt's eyes as they followed the flight of the young Negro. They were narrowed, bemused. His teeth worried his bottom lip, as though he were in deep thought. Then he seemed to come from his reverie. "I suppose you have come for Charlotte?" he said. "She is not here. But do come in. How very rude of me! I do not know where she is. She went away against my wishes, for she was very upset. Perhaps if we put our heads together, we can figure out where she went."

He stepped aside. I was about to tell Banneker to wait for me in the carriage, but something about his demeanor, the determined thrust of his thick neck, told me that he would be with me. Good manners required that I ask Lance's permission for Banneker to enter. When I did so, Lance's eyes fell on Banneker; they seemed filled with the deepest amusement. "Of course, Victoria." But both he and I knew that his consent was only a matter of form. Wild horses couldn't have dragged Banneker from my side. Whatever he had seen that disgusted him had also made him bold. I was extremely grateful that I'd had the good sense to bring him along. His mother, in a gaudy purple bonnet, waited in the carriage surrounded by the guards like an impatient black empress. Banneker and I followed Lance Harcourt into his house. From the distant hills I heard the rumble of thunder, like an accumulation of demons preparing to spew forth their evil. And even as we entered the house, the first rain began to fall.

"Do be seated, Victoria," Lance said most graciously. "And, of course, you, too, Banneker."

The sitting room was more modest than ours at Fir Crest, but nevertheless imposing. Lance's tastes, or those of his decorator, tended toward the vulgar; and, at first blush, one might have thought that one had wandered into a rose-colored sunset where large pieces of furniture had been stored. However, the effect came from ceiling-to-floor damascene draperies that covered an entire wall, including several windows opening on the driveway. There were carpets in various shades of darkish pink on a polished hardwood floor. The free walls were covered with paintings of rather ample female nudes on lacquered canvases in large gilt frames. These ladies were kept from each other by splashy landscapes of streams, shepherds contemplating far-off mountains, while their flock wandered hither and yon, and forests where each tree stood like a seperate leaf-filled phallus. There were round, marble-topped mahogany stands with statues of languishing male nudes. And several velvet-covered divans and plush chairs, all in bright red or plum purple, with cushions that seemed to reach out and enfold one as Benign might do when she was being her most consoling. Lamps with decorated globes were everywhere, some of them lighted against the gloomy afternoon. And there was a heavy miasma of incense in the air, as though a procession of priests had recently passed to the dining room beyond, chanting hymns and swinging their censers. The dining room opened onto the rear yard through three French doors, and I could see the rain coming down in buckets, sometimes giving the appearance of a deluge of silverfish as lightning exploded in bright bursts, followed by the thunder's authoritative baritone. I heard footsteps throughout the house as servants closed and shuttered windows.

Lance summoned his personal servant, Ambrose—a white-haired man in formal attire who gave the impression that he would lie down and die as soon as he could find a spare moment—and ordered a fire lighted on the hearth. It took some time for the old Negro to do this, and even longer for him to negotiate the pouring of three glasses of sherry, the third which he served to Banneker with obvious

disapproval. As for Banneker, he was covertly examining
everything from under partly drawn lids. If he was
impressed, his impassive face showed nothing, and he
seemed completely at ease. While Ambrose was leaving us
with decrepit step, the storm increased with astonishing
fury. The room turned as dark as midnight, despite the
lamps. Lance himself lighted more. And he instructed his
servant to have our Negroes quartered temporarily with
his, a feat which I wondered if Ambrose would be able to
do without getting drowned in the process, or without finding Amos, Yetta, and the rest drowned by the time he got
to them.

"Let us drink," Lance Harcourt said, "to the conclusion
of the war." It was a generous toast, however ambiguous,
considering Banneker's presence, Lance's sentiments, and
the almost certain fact that the Harcourts, despite their
vaunted wealth, faced a period of the most depressing
transition at their plantation in Buckingham, where the
South's defeat had dramatically given all the prerogatives
of freedom to a thousand Negroes. "To the conclusion of
the war," I said. Banneker lifted his glass and said nothing; but he did drink.

"Now, as to Charlotte," Lance said. "If we wait until
the storm is over, there are several homes where she might
be found."

How long would the storm last? "If you will give us the
addresses, Lance, we shall go now. I am very worried
about her."

He raised an eyebrow, then shrugged. "As you wish," he
said. After putting on his jacket, he sat at a massive escritoire with carved base, and wrote several addresses on a
sheet of paper that carried the engraved crest of the Harcourts. "If she is at none of these," he said, "then I am at
a loss to her whereabouts. As I have said, she was most
distraught."

"All the more reason we should find her as quickly as
possible," I said. I read five addresses on the paper before
Banneker gently took it from me. "I'll go, Miss Victoria,"
he said. "It's raining too hard out there for you. I'll take
Mama with me."

It was raining very hard indeed. And the rain was
lashed by high winds, which slapped the house as though
punishing it. "Very well, Banneker." He would do a good

job of finding Charlotte, if she were to be found. Yetta's presence would lend the proper respectability—strange word and stranger sentiment, in a society suddenly gone topsy-turvy, where our former slaves were invited to take sherry even in Lance Harcourt's sitting room. "I shall wait here for you. But do be careful, Banneker. You have seen how the streets are."

He smiled. "This rain going to wash all the filth away," he said. His eyes seemed to settle on Lance Harcourt for a second. Then he was gone, opening and closing the door against the storm as though all its muscle, for him, were merely a spring shower.

"He's a strong, handsome devil," Lance Harcourt said, standing near the fire. "However, I find him somewhat forward, to be a servant."

"Banneker grew up with Charlotte and me. And Robert Gilliam. We have always considered him someone quite special."

That seemed to close that part of the conversation as Lance strode to the decanter and poured two more glasses of sherry. I accepted mine gratefully, for there was a decided chill in the air, despite the fire's best efforts. At the same time, I heard the carriage pull off from in front of the house, the roll of wheels and the clatter of hooves muffled as though moving underwater.

"You don't care very much for me, do you?" Lance Harcourt said, twirling the stem of his wineglass between delicate fingers.

In truth, I detested him—how could he have lost track of Charlotte in the present chaos, whatever her mood?—but now hardly seemed the time to make what could be a shrewd and powerful enemy. I laughed, feigning surprise. "Whatever gives you that idea, Lance? Because I refused your proposal of marriage?"

He was immediately defensive. "That was a foolish thing to do, especially since I had already proposed to Charlotte." He grinned sheepishly. "I'm afraid I'd had a bit too much to drink that day. You were absolutely proper in throwing me off the land."

"Dear Lance." I touched his pale hand. "I am your greatest champion and your most adoring friend. I am quite anxious for Father to approve the marriage between you and Charlotte as soon as possible. It is one of the reasons I am worried about her whereabouts. Father himself sent me for her."

Now Lance's whole demeanor changed. "You mean he would approve the marriage? From the dreadful things he said today, I could never imagine such a thing."

"Don't fret," I said, smiling with all the charm I could muster. "Father is terribly upset about the way he spoke to you and to Charlotte." For an instant there was a lightning flash at the French windows, and I could make out what appeared to be several pigeons blundering like overburdened peasants to the sanctuary of the stable eaves above them. "In fact, Lance, Father has asked me to have you and your father visit this Saturday coming. You may rest assured that the marriage will be discussed then." It was a bald lie, which he swallowed with the greatest enthusiasm. I only hoped that Father would be as receptive. "Damn!" Lance cried. "I never would have believed it!" He grabbed my shoulders with a grip that was surprisingly strong. "Surely it is you I must thank for this, Victoria! Sometimes I *am* a perfect dolt! How could I have imagined that you disliked me?"

How, indeed? Meanwhile, how much convincing would Father need before he approved such a liaison? "You are in love, Lance. When a man is in love, he is not responsible for his acts."

He flung himself to a low settee, supporting himself on his elbow, his head propped between thumb and forefinger. "That is true!" he cried. "Sometimes I find myself staring vacantly into space. Love is a tonic, but a toxic one at the same time." He ran nervous fingers through his hair.

My cheeks absolutely ached from smiling. But his energy and passion seemed genuine, and I was happy that he was not made entirely of sugar water, at least where Charlotte was concerned. He seemed for all the world like a man in love; still, I could not shake the uncomfortable feeling that a large part of his passion was aimed at himself. Charlotte would have many walls to tear down before she got to the real Lance Harcourt. My own opinion was that, once the excavation had been done, she would find very little there worth the effort. Smiling, nodding as he spoke of my sister in the most lyrical terms, I decided to have Judge Gilliam make discreet inquiry about the finan-

...i condition of the Harcourts. While it was inconceivable
...at Lance might be pursuing Charlotte for her money, it
...eemed prudent to lay the matter to rest once and for all.

Considerably bolstered by the lies I had fed him, Lance
was in full strut when Banneker returned some two hours
later. He wore a slicker, and dropped small puddles
around his now-booted feet. But Yetta was with him,
huddled and shivering inside her clothes like a drowned
rat. As I went to greet them, Ambrose, Lance's servant,
was in the process of closing the door against the wind
and rain, pushing with his frail old body as though he
fully intended to take a century to do so. Banneker
reached back and shoved the door shut with one hand.
"We know where Miss Charlotte is, ma'am. We thought
we'd better come get you to go with us."

He seemed so solemn, his wicked old mother so full of
woe, that I immediately grew alarmed. "Where is she? Is
something wrong? Why didn't she come with you?"

Then Lance was at my side, arrogantly asking questions.
In the middle of his tirade, it occurred to me that he
might have gone with Banneker to find Charlotte, if his
heart were genuinely where he claimed it was, rather than
send a Negro to do a fiancé's work. Possibly now that I
had assured him that Charlotte would indeed be his bride,
he felt more protective of her welfare than before. Whatever the reason, he berated Banneker so roundly that it
surprised me. "Where is she, indeed?" he cried. "Is she
hurt? Why is she not with you, then?"

Banneker looked him squarely in the eye. "Why do you
have in your stable," he said softly, "the horse rode by the
man who led the raiders on Fir Crest when they killed
Miss Parkchester?"

For a moment, all I could hear was the rain beating
against the house. It was as though time came to a stand-
still, stumbled awake, and then picked up again.

Lance laughed with little humor. "You black devil!
What an extraordinary question! I'm tempted to take a
whip to you myself!"

"You do that," Banneker said dryly. "That still don't
take away my question. What you doing with that man's
horse in your stable?"

Yetta, in her soggy bonnet, nudged Banneker almost

secretly. He was indeed on dangerous ground, for the implications of such a question were enormous.

"Are you certain it is the same horse, Banneker?" My voice sounded unusually calm, considering the confusion I felt.

"It's the same one, Miss Victoria. I ain't never going to forget that horse. Or the man that rode it. If I ever see the man, I'm going to kill him. The horse he rode is in Mr. Harcourt's stable. It's a white mare with a black star on her left rump. She's out there now eating oats in Mr. Harcourt's stable."

"Damn!" Lance slammed one fist into the other, making a rather puny sound. "It is a new mare I bought only the other day from Mr. Boswell on State Street. He is a dealer in horses. I will show you the bill of sale if you wish." His face was quite pale. "Is it possible, Victoria, that Boswell led the raiders? Or is connected with them in some way? My God, he's every bit of fifty-five! His reputation is above reproach. I believe he also has a very bad heart."

"At this point," I said thoughtfully, "anything is possible. I certainly do not doubt your word, Lance. But, for the moment, we should forget the mare and concentrate on Charlotte. Banneker, you might well be mistaken."

"I ain't mistaken, Miss Victoria. It's the same horse. And the leader was a young man. Strong, like me. I ain't never going to forget him." Again Yetta nudged him in warning.

"Let us speak of it later," I said firmly. "Now, take me to Miss Charlotte. I am extremely worried about her."

"I shall go too!" Lance cried.

Banneker shook his head. "Only Miss Victoria go."

"By God, you are an uppity devil!" Lance said. But his tone was subdued, which meant that he accepted Banneker's mandate, however reluctantly. He seemed quite shaken by the news of the mare in his stable. I believed his story, and was therefore anxious to clear up the mystery of Charlotte's whereabouts. "As soon as I have word, Lance, I shall let you know. Now, we must go."

Ambrose had finally arrived with my cloak. Yetta bestirred herself to help me put it on. Then the three of us went out into the darkness and rain, on our way to Charlotte, wherever she might be.

I took a last glimpse at Lance Harcourt's house before

we pulled off in the carriage, and saw him standing in the partly opened door, looking for all the world like a lost, bewildered boy. As a possible brother-in-law, I far preferred him to a strong-willed individual who might meddle in my management of Fir Crest. For it was clear to me now—possibly from Banneker's unmistakable attitude of freedom—that we at Fir Crest, and, indeed, the entire South, had entered a new era in which conflict would play the major part on all levels. Father never again could be permitted to become overly involved in the affairs of Fir Crest. Weak, disillusioned, embittered, he seemed an older version of Lance Harcourt.

Amos drove the carriage, and Banneker rode inside with Yetta and me. The rain was still coming down fiercely, flooding the streets, assailing the carriage in great sheets. "Now, where is Charlotte?" I said. "Why all the mystery?"

"She down the street at a tavern full of Union soldiers," Banneker said. "She drunk, and she going to be in trouble if somebody don't get her out of there."

There was no need to ask him how he knew this. Obviously, as he and Yetta had made their rounds, asking house servants about Charlotte, they had come up with this information. I could only appreciate the discretion Banneker had used in not revealing such a sordid story to Lance Harcourt. Although the possibility existed that Lance would hear it from his own servants, Charlotte would be able to better deny it if the knowledge were kept among those of us who were loyal to her. Of Banneker's devotion and Amos', I had no doubt. But Yetta was a different matter. She was squeezed next to Banneker, her large body giving to every roll of the carriage. We were enveloped in darkness, but I had the distinct impression that her crone's lips were curved in a smile.

"Thank you for finding her, Banneker. And thank you for being so discreet."

He grunted. "I don't have the time of day for that Mr. Harcourt. He sneaky, if you ask me."

Except for the hard facts of history, his frank appraisal of Lance Harcourt, however just, would have been extraordinary. But the truth was that history had given us the back of her hand even as she had loosened the bonds and tongues of Negroes. That Banneker and the other blacks at Fir Crest remained loyal to us seemed a signal compliment to Father's foresight, and to my own as well. "It ain't far from here," Banneker said, interrupting my thoughts. I settled back in my seat and tried to appraise what had happened to me, to my own personality, over the last several weeks.

Certainly I was different. The cruel encounter with Yetta had convinced me of that. But I felt no remorse about intimidating her into silence. With Father's reappearance, it was obvious that strength and cunning were more necessary than ever, if we at Fir Crest were not to go down the drain with the rest of the Confederacy. As I did not relish the idea of being subject to Banneker in a new order sanctioned and supported by the armed might of the United States government—bloated now with victory, certainly intent upon punishing whites until we shrieked for mercy, while giving every advantage to blacks—neither could I entertain the idea of giving up Fir Crest and all the privileges that it implied. Word had already reached us that other white women, their land devastated by the war, their wills broken by vicious circumstances, had already taken to farming and other menial chores. If the Parkchesters had begun as peasants, we never would finish up as peasants. That was my solemn vow as the carriage swung around a corner and came to a halt before a thoroughly disreputable-looking place which announced itself pompously on a broken piece of wood as being the Jefferson Inn.

Surprisingly, a church bell struck nearby, sounding murky, as though it, too, were underwater. The rain beat down relentlessly. At the same time, Yetta began a low moaning in the dark carriage, the sound of an animal in pain. "Mama, shut up!" Banneker said sharply. But she kept on moaning. Twisting, he opened the carriage door and stepped down. "You better come with me, Miss Victoria." I gave him my hand, and he helped me out. The church bell was still tolling, as though a funeral were in progress. Yetta's moaning, for whatever reason, only heightened the unpleasant sensation that we were somewhere in the vicinity of death.

"What's wrong with your mother?" I asked Banneker as he angrily slammed the carriage door.

"She probably got the colic," he said. There were both apprehension and amusement in his voice. "But I think she really worried about this." He lifted the slicker, and I saw a long-barreled pistol jammed into the waistband of his pants.

"Do you think we'll need that?"

"We might. Now, we better get out of this rain before we drown to death." He turned and called Amos. "Get on in the carriage, Amos, and wait for us. Ain't you got enough sense to get in the carriage?"

"Not unless I'm told," Amos said. It was a delightful exchange. I, too, was aware that I was taking orders instead of giving them, and asking questions of servants that protocol alone would have made impossible before the war. Later on, I would understand that the freedom brought to Negroes had also been given to me as well. And certainly to Charlotte, if she really were inside the Jefferson Inn. I felt a perfect fool standing in the driving rain; but I felt as though, for the first time in my life, I was a free spirit as well. Before the war, no Negro would have dared keep me waiting in the rain, even if it meant constructing a canopy over me on the spot. Indeed, their earlier attitude seemed to be that I might have melted in rain, as though white people were made of cheap sugar. Now, I watched Amos. He was a black, sodden bundle; but, moving with the agility of a monkey, he swung from the driver's seat into the carriage in one fluid motion. Satisfied, Banneker propelled me by the elbow to the door of the tavern, opened it, and walked in.

It was like entering a tomb that has been sealed for many years. Although the single room was fairly large and well-lighted, there was a general sense of noise and hilarity which rose up and hit me like dank air, as though we had entered a festival of cold, wet ghosts. There was a tarnished brass lamp hanging from the ceiling, with perhaps a dozen candles shrouded in dirty globes, which cast a sickly yellow light over everything. The patrons—if they could be called that, for it was doubtful that they had a penny among them—were largely Union soldiers, some country stragglers, and a whole array of painted sluts who seemed to use the same hairdresser and clothes designer as poor old Mrs. Pennington. There was a heavy stench of whiskey, wine, perfume, and sweat. Several soldiers stood around a ramshackle piano where one played doubtfully while the others caterwauled "The Battle Hymn of the Republic," that most pietistic and self-serving of all songs. The tavern-keeper seemed thoroughly intimidated, and very down in the mouth, for it was clear that he was being drunk out of house and home, and not receiving a penny in return. Even as my eyes searched the smoke and almost tangible stench of the place, a sudden silence fell as Banneker's presence and mine were noticed. And, in the hush, which surrounded us like the soft stuff of nests, I saw Charlotte at a table with three Union soldiers. One of them was kissing her passionately, as they clung to each other half out of their respective chairs. The other two were smiling impatiently, obviously waiting their turn. All the men seemed to have whiskers sufficient to stuff an oversized mattress.

"Ah . . . look at the lovely lady!" It was a drunken soldier, staggering toward me, holding himself up with his thumbs hitched in his broad black belt. At once Banneker was in front of me, diverting the soldier's path with a gentle blow that sent him spinning halfway across the room, upsetting chairs and one or two people as he went. "Let's all get the nigger!" someone yelled. But they were all too drunk to move with much energy.

By this time, Charlotte was through kissing the soldier and had spotted us. The expression on her face changed from alarm to arrogant amusement as she rose from the table, disdaining the soldiers' pleading hands. Even as her eyes locked with mine across the sordid room, Banneker stooped, raised his slicker, and brought out the pistol. "Everybody stay right where they is," he said with quiet authority. I expected them to fall upon us like dogs upon a bone, but, amazingly, everyone froze except Charlotte.

She threaded her way through the tables toward us. It was obvious that she was drunk—certainly not without reason, after Father's stinging insult—as though she were determined to free the slut in her that Father had invoked. Surprisingly, she seemed lovely even in the environs of the Jefferson Inn. Her hair was carefully combed, every strand in place, as though she had sternly forbidden the soldiers to touch her there, even as they were pawing every other part of her. She wore a wine-colored gown that seemed strikingly modest in this place. The other women, those painted sluts, looked at her in complete envy.

"Come on, Miss Charlotte," Banneker said encouragingly. "We going to take you home now."

Perhaps it was the gentleness of his tone. Or perhaps some innate sense of her own worth, certainly superior to that of all the others around her. Or perhaps it was only shame. At any rate, Charlotte's face turned red, and she began to cry. At the same time, I stepped forward to steady her, for she seemed on the verge of fainting. "Victoria! Help me!" she cried. And I reached out and enfolded her in my arms.

I felt a hot disturbance of air near me, dangerously close to my head; and then I heard the shattering of a viciously thrown bottle. I hastened to get Charlotte to the door, but she reached backward for Banneker, who was slowly retreating with us. "Am I a slut, Banneker? Do you think I'm a slut?" she asked through copious amounts of tears.

His eyes were darting from left to right, sweeping every face, every corner of the room. "You a perfect lady, Miss Charlotte. Now, you go on out and get in the carriage. Don't worry about me. You just go ahead with Miss Victoria."

We were near the door when a giant of a soldier suddenly stiffened from his chair and dived for us. Banneker caught him in midair with his left fist, holding the pistol all the time in his steady right hand. The solder hit the floor like a heavy log. "Let's go!" Banneker hissed. "Don't you ladies know how to *run*?" And so we did, he and I practically dragging poor Charlotte out into the rain by an arm each.

Amos had opportunely resumed his position in the driver's seat. Yetta opened the carriage door, and Banneker leaped in. Then he reached down and dragged first Charlotte, then me, into the carriage even as it went thundering down the street. Looking back, I saw that a crowd was pouring from the Jefferson Inn, shaking their fists, shouting curses. In the excitement, I had lost one of my best shoes. But it seemed a small enough price to pay to save my sister's honor, if not her reputation. She was still crying in great sobs with her head on my shoulder. I felt most uncomfortable, soaked to the skin, shoeless on one foot, trying to escape the instrusion of Yetta's bony knees as they punctured mine in the close quarters of the carriage. My main reaction to the vulgar scene we had just escaped had to do with what Yetta would think. Whatever Banneker's sentiments, I had the feeling that Charlotte would always be a lady for him, even when she was at her worst. I wondered if he would judge me so liberally under like circumstances.

"Where to, Miss Victoria?" Amos yelled down from the driver's seat. The horses were going like sixty through the empty streets of Charlottesville. There were places where the cobblestones dipped and water had accumulated to a depth of two or more feet. The driving rain plagued us, dripping into the carriage, sliding back and forth across the floor. It would have been simpler to spend the night at Lance Harcourt's, repair ourselves, and then proceed to Fir Crest in the morning. But I did not want Lance to see Charlotte this way; nor did I want him to see me semi-shoeless, which I suppose had to do with my own vanity. But it was really Charlotte's welfare that I was worried about. Come Saturday, when Lance arrived at Fir Crest, probably with his father, as was the custom when marriages of our category were to be discussed, I would throw my full weight behind marriage for Charlotte to Lance as soon as possible, before her temperament and reputation doomed her to remain single forever. Furthermore, with her safely married and removed to Harcourt Manor in Buckingham, mine would be the sole power at Fir Crest.

"We shall stop briefly by Mr. Harcourt's to pick up the other men," I told Banneker, which he transmitted to Amos. "Then we shall proceed to Fir Crest."

Yetta began that damnable moaning again. "It's raining cats and dogs, Miss Victoria. My poor old bones hurt me terrible when it rain. Can't we stay here tonight and go home tomorrow?"

"We go to Fir Crest tonight!" I snapped. "As for your bones, they are cutting into my knees. Please arrange yourself so that I shall not be a cripple by the time we get home."

Suddenly Charlotte stifled a sob and began to giggle. I suppose that the situation did appear ridiculous. "Are you all right, dear?" I whispered. I felt her nod. "I feel like a fool," she said. "Like a perfect fool." Poor, lost child, I thought. It would be pleasant indeed to place her care in the hands of Lance Harcourt.

All the time, I was aware of Banneker's strong, silent presence in the carriage. I could also smell the wet slicker, and a kind of steamy male aroma, as though he himself were drying out in his flannel clothes. "Banneker, you were most brave tonight. Thank you very much."

"You welcome, Miss Victoria."

"I thank you, too, Banneker," Charlotte said softly. "I don't know what came over me."

"You welcome, Miss Charlotte."

Despite my warning, or perhaps because of it, Yetta's knees still tortured mine. Ignoring her as best I could, I told Banneker, "Please tell Amos to stop by the horse dealer's house on State Street, once we have rejoined the others. I would like to ask about the mare in Lance's stable."

"Yas'm," he said with the greatest enthusiasm. And even though the rain continued to pelt us, he swung lightly out the door of the moving carriage and up into the driver's seat with Amos. We stopped at Lance's long enough to hail the other men from the street. They came in a flash, as though they had been waiting sitting on their mounts. Then we clattered away again, certainly before Ambrose, that courtly near-corpse, had had time even to pull aside the draperies to see who we were. When the carriage pulled off with a smooth, though urgent energy, I knew that it was Banneker at the reins, and I sat more comfortably in my seat. Charlotte and I rode side by side, with Yetta across from us and her knees between the two of us, where the bones in them cut me laterally on the legs—certainly deliberately—rather than vertically as before. For the interview with the horse dealer, I decided that no shoes would be better than one. If he noticed at all, perhaps he would think I was absentminded.

The rain had almost stopped when we got to the home of Mr. Boswell, the horse dealer on State Street. His was a large, stately house, and Banneker drove confidently underneath the porte cochere, bounded down, and knocked at the lighted door. Almost at once it was opened by a liveried Negro. "What you want, nigger?" he said. Then he saw me and bowed most correctly. "Begging your pardon, ma'am. Can we help the ma'am in any way?"

Considering that I must have looked like a drowned duck, and barefoot in the bargain, I tried to compensate by sounding my most aristocratic. "I am Victoria Parkchester of Fir Crest. I should like to speak to your master at once."

"Yas'm." He bowed again and left, leaving the door ajar. What I could see of the foyer and sitting room was elegant indeed. At the same time, I pondered how the wealthy horse dealer would greet a motley crew such as we. Banneker was presentable enough in his long yellow slicker. He smiled at me reassuringly. And the carriage seemed worthy of the power and prestige of Fir Crest, if one ignored the newly instituted moans of Yetta, who was now mourning nearly at the top of her lungs. I wondered if the woman were mad, or had deliberately set out to make a nuisance of herself. Banneker went to the carriage. "Mama, shut your mouth! Don't you see where you at?" The groans subsided somewhat; if Yetta's bones were truly hurting, they were not completely impressed by opulence. Amos held himself erect, as though to offset Yetta's embarrassing performance. Charlotte, it appeared, was sleeping off her liquor. And the five riders were lined in a perfectly disciplined group on some of our finest horses. As for myself, I fluffed out my cloak, combed my fingers through my stringy hair, squeezed water from my hat, and tried not to look so much like a beggar woman when Mr. Boswell himself arrived at the door.

"Miss Parkchester!" He bowed over my hand. "We have not had the pleasure of meeting before, but your fame and that of Fir Crest have preceded you. Won't you please come in?"

I was most impressed by his graciousness. "Thank you, no. We have stopped only briefly. I would like to ask you a question in the strictest confidence. If it were revealed that I have come here, it could cause considerable embarrassment to persons of the highest importance."

Nodding, he pulled at his bottom lip. He was perhaps sixty, portly in build, broad of face, with spectacles perched on the tip of an extremely keen nose. His dress was impeccable. He was baldish, with a ring of white hair surrounding a finely shaped head. "I deal in confidentialities, Miss Parkchester. Feel free to ask whatever question. You will receive my honest answer." He seemed perfectly relaxed, although I was not unaware that an armed Negro stood some five feet to the rear and the left of him. To put me at my ease, he said somewhat apologetically, "These are difficult times. One cannot be too careful, what with all manner of riffraff descending on the South in droves."

"I understand perfectly, Mr. Boswell." I wondered if he had seen Banneker snake his arm underneath his slicker, certainly to hold the pistol there. One could not be too careful, indeed. "The question I have to ask you has to do with a mare with very distinctive markings. She herself is white. But she has a black mark on her left rump. My understanding is that the mark resembles a five-pointed star. Are you familiar with such an animal?"

"I remember it perfectly," he said. "I sold her to Mr. Lance Harcourt perhaps ten days ago. A fine gentleman, Mr. Harcourt is. I've known him and his father for years. The best, the very best."

"May I ask you, Mr. Boswell, where you got the mare?"

"Of course! Of course! I bought it from a gentleman some six months ago. I'm afraid that I remember little about him, for the transaction itself was a most favorable one." He laughed pleasantly. "Where there is an excellent profit, I forget the seller as quickly as possible, and concentrate on prospective buyers."

"Is there nothing you can tell me about the gentleman?"

He studied briefly. "He was blond, young, a patch over his eye. Obviously a gentleman of means. He said he had won the mare in a poker game and was not especially anxious to add her to his stock."

"Did he give his name?" I found that I was breathing very heavily, for the brief description of the mare's seller fitted that of the leader of the raiders.

"Of course. It is always necessary to give a name in these transactions."

Now he was obviously hedging. And it was Banneker who took up the questioning. "What name did he give, sir?"

Mr. Boswell studied him closely. It was only a brief perusal, but in that short while it was apparent that he, too, was aware that a new wind was sweeping the South, and that Negroes could now ask whereas before they had only been told.

"He said his name was Lincoln, sir. Abraham Lincoln. It is the name I have on the bill of sale. I shall show you a copy if you'd like." He reached into a vest pocket, came out with a gold watch, studied it, and put it away. "If not, I have an engagement at nine o'clock. It is now twenty minutes to nine." His manner had become brusque, almost unpleasant.

"We are quite finished, sir. Thank you for your time. And I trust that we shall see each other again under different circumstances."

"You are most gracious," he murmured, bending over my hand.

"And you have been most kind," I responded. And most stupid, I thought. Even the most crooked of dealers would think several times before buying a horse from a seller who concealed his own identity behind the name of the President of the United States.

"I trust that I have been helpful," he said. With a slight gesture of irritation, he waved the armed Negro away.

"You have been most helpful, indeed," I said as we walked toward the carriage.

Now he cocked an inquisitive ear. "Is someone in pain in your carriage?"

"It is one of my servants. Weather such as this affects her bones."

"Perhaps I could give you something for her?" He was clearly trying to make amends for revealing his outrageous stupidity.

Upon hearing his offer, Yetta increased the volume of her moaning tenfold. Until then I had had the distinct impression that she and Charlotte were whispering in the carriage. "Your offer is most generous. But she will survive until we reach Fir Crest."

He bowed uncertainly. "Your visit has been propitious in one respect. The rain has stopped. And it seems that the moon is coming out."

"Good night, sir. My thanks again."

"Your most humble servant," he murmured. Without turning, he stepped backward through the door, and it closed quietly and quickly after him.

So off we went to Fir Crest. The road that had been so crowded in the morning was now a sea of mud, and it was quite difficult to negotiate. But as we left Charlottesville farther behind us, and hit the gravel-covered highway, the wheels of the carriage sang on the pebbles, and the horses' hooves crunched in a marvelous rhythm. There were some forty miles between us and Fir Crest; the rain had indeed stopped; and the moon hung in the sky like a round and lovely yellow cheese mottled with age, certainly with more wisdom than I could come by at that moment. Yetta had resumed her moaning—indeed, she moaned for forty miles—and Charlotte was sleeping on my shoulder. From time to time, as though to keep me alert, Yetta stabbed me with her knees. The men had taken the formation of a single rider on each side of the carriage, and two in front and back. As before, Banneker rode at my side. After the rigors of the day, they seemed in a merry mood. Banneker began a lovely Negro chant, which the others picked up and tossed back and forth, like happy youngsters playing with a ball, until I found myself relaxing in spite of myself.

But it was difficult to lull my mind away from the problems that worried it. First of all, I found myself wondering if Lance Harcourt and Mr. Boswell might not have conspired in their story about the acquisition of the mare in order to throw off any questioner. Yet, each had seemed perfectly sincere in his account; and Mr. Boswell's description of the leader of the raiders was too precise to have been fabricated. More important, neither he nor Lance seemed the type to have truck with rapists and murderers. Until further evidence presented itself, if indeed it ever did, I had no choice but to accept their stories.

Next my mind turned to the matter of Lance and Charlotte. While I loved my sister dearly, it was impossible not to see that she was possessed of a wild streak which might eventually do irreparable harm to herself, and, worse, to Fir Crest. The order of my priorities was deliberate: Fir Crest was larger than us all. The sweat and blood of many generations of men and women, black and white, had consecrated it—to paraphrase Mr. Lincoln in his Gettysburg address—far above my poor power to add or to detract. All that I could do was to try to maintain the status quo. If my earlier imaginings were indeed fantasies, then there was neither danger to Fir Crest nor to any of its inhabitants. If my speculation had some basis in fact, then we could soon expect another tragedy to take place.

The full moon seemed to run along beside us, keeping pace with the carriage. Now we were halfway to Fir Crest, and the road was perfectly dry. No rain had fallen here today, and the carriage wheels seemed to hum with a sense of warm familiarity as they ran on friendly ground. There were great clusters of trees on either side of the road, like hulking black beasts. The sky was as lustrous as the inside of a moonstruck oyster shell. Even Yetta's moaning, blending with the rich voices of the singing men, became less an irritant. And I thought of Robert Gilliam, that he would be home in two days. Would he have changed much? Would he find me changed? If the blood of a New Orleans slut ran freely in Charlotte, it raced headlong in me at that moment, for I yearned for Robert Gilliam with every fiber of my being. My lips seemed to taste the sweet fire of his. My body warmed as I imagined his arms around me, the lean muscularity of his body pressed against mine, his deep blue eyes enveloping me like dark cobalt, his powerful manhood probing. . . .

And then, after a turn in the road, I saw the breathtaking beauty of Fir Crest, an alabaster monument ablaze with moonlight, a glittering white gem in the landscape around. The voices of the men fell silent, as though in awe. Even Yetta ceased her moaning. "We's home, Miss Victoria," she said somewhat happily.

"Yes, we're home," I said. I roused Charlotte, who remained in a drowsy state until the carriage had drawn up before the mansion. Then she seemed to come to full life.

"I've slept all the way," she said. "You must have been quite bored."

I assured her that I had not been. "Yetta was good enough to keep me company," I said, hoping that the old harridan could at least appreciate irony. Her only response was to grunt like a malcontented sow.

Benign appeared on the porch, holding a lantern, wearing her night clothes. "I heard the carriage coming," she said. "We was worried about you all."

"There was nothing to worry about, Benign. Please help Miss Charlotte to her room. I shall manage alone."

"Nothing to worry about?" she said, lowering the lantern. "Then what happened to your shoes? And how come you look like something the cat dragged in?"

I laughed. It was good being home again, to endure her gentle chastising. "There was a slight mishap," I said. And to Banneker and his men: "Good night to all of you. And thank you so very much." They muttered their thanks.

Banneker's teeth were stark white in the moonlight. "Anytime, Miss Victoria. Anytime at all." I waited on the porch until they clattered off with Yetta in the carriage. If luck were with me, they would leave her locked in the carriage house to moan the night away.

"It's after two o'clock, child," Benign said. "You go to bed right away."

"Yes, Benign." I followed her and Charlotte into the house. "Is Father all right?"

"He fine. He just grouchy, that's all. But he eat all right. And stay in his room just like he say."

"Very well, Benign. We shall talk in the morning."

I went to my room, undressed, and fell into bed stark naked. And dreamed that Robert Gilliam was naked with me. . . .

Having driven us all nearly mad for one reason or another, it appeared that the gods embarked on an appalling new strategy, and sent the raiders—led by the blond man with a black patch over his left eye, mounted on a magnificent chestnut stallion—to murder us in broad daylight. I heard the first gun shots at exactly ten-twenty the following morning when I was on my way downstairs to breakfast. I had thought of looking in on Charlotte and Father, but I was in no mood for Father's pessimism or Charlotte's tearful apologies. And the fact that I was ravenously hungry seemed ample reason to put off my visits to them at least until after breakfast.

The first shots exploded like firecrackers in the morning stillness; then there were screams, and the inevitable pounding of horses' hooves. As I rushed through the sitting room to the kitchen, I heard a sound that could only be metal on metal. Had the war—finally and ironically—reached us in full combat dress? For there were persons quite close to the house engaged in hand-to-hand fighting with sabers. It was as though the actual war, and its completion, had merely been a rehearsal and a postponement for this final battle here at Fir Crest.

I felt immensely calm, although my heart was racing. There was so much worth the fighting for that we could not possibly lose. The final irony seemed to be that whatever fighting had to be done would have to be waged by Negroes. With both Father and Charlotte wrestling their own private devils, I was the only white person at Fir Crest available for combat. But as I rushed into the kitchen, I was not concerned about the casual distinctions between black and white. Time and again the Negroes had proved their bravery and unyielding loyalty to me. Now it was time for me to prove mine to them, and I welcomed the opportunity to do so.

"The raiders done come back," Benign said. She was calmly spooning hotcakes onto a large black griddle. "Banneker already got the men out there fighting. There's about seventy-five of them raiders, led by the same man that killed your mammy. Looks like they made up their mind to take Fir Crest this time. Banneker's thrown a hundred of our men against them. You set down now, child, and eat your breakfast. You going to need all the strength you can get."

"Thank you, Benign."

She served my plate—fried ham, hotcakes with butter and honey—and poured a glass of milk. Under other circumstances, the idea of eating while bloodshed was going on right outside the door would have been unthinkable. But if Benign was made of the stuff that could throw together a good breakfast at a time like this, it was essential that I at least convince her that I was made of the stuff to down it. The hotcakes were thin, light, delicious. The ham came from our own smokehouse, and was of the finest quality.

"You have another glass of milk, child?"

"Please, Benign. Have you seen Charlotte or Father?"

She looked at me directly for the first time. If I felt that my home, my very existence, were threatened, Benign's sentiments were no less, to judge by her eyes. She was prepared to fight until the death, if things came to that. Fir Crest was her home, too.

"Charlotte and your father both sleeping. I give them something to make them sleep. Ain't no time for people to be running around getting in the way if they ain't willing to fight."

Had she found the laudanum and drugged Father and Charlotte secretly to get them out of the way? It was impossible to argue with her logic, but I was most pleased by the implication that she at least thought I was worthy of the battle. I drank the milk, dabbed my lips with the flowered napkin, and stood. "I'm ready," I said.

She took off her apron. "I'se ready, too." She reached to the side of the stove and came up with two rifles. Handing me one, she propped hers over her broad shoulder, stepped to the kitchen door, and cautiously opened it. The sound of war—shooting, shouting, screaming, horses neighing, sabers clashing—marched boldly into the kitchen and left me cold with fear. I wondered briefly if I were indeed mad. And Benign as well. Hotcakes, indeed! It would have been most comforting if I suddenly opened my eyes and found myself in bed, being awakened by her soothing hands from a terrible dream. But the April sun hung in the half-opened door like a pale yellow curtain. And the clamor of human beings struggling and possibly dying like animals was undeniably clear. I stepped in front of Benign. "Let's go," I said.

Benign grunted. "We ought to have on pants," she said. "Going out to kill somebody with dresses on—it just don't look right."

"This is hardly the time to be thinking of decorum," I said to Benign, although I knew she had been partly jesting.

"I still think we ought to be wearing pants," she said lightly. "Suppose we have to run?"

"I do not intend to run," I said evenly. "Nor do you." She nodded confidently. There was certainly madness in the air, like the contagion of spring fever. Crouching, we went down the kitchen steps into the yard. The rosebushes were filled with swollen buds, each with a drop of red, pink, or yellow at its tip. Banneker's office, where the candle house had stood, was our nearest shelter, and we made for it after giving a quick survey of the activity near us.

There were men on horses and afoot, fighting each other with sabers. Obviously, some of them were the raiders; and their opponents were from Fir Crest. Other raiders —white men as well as black—chased down Negroes with ropes, cutting vicious circles in the air, as cowboys chase down beasts. And even as I watched, I saw one of our men firmly lassoed and dragged along the road by a speeding horse. Benign and I practically crawled to the office building on our bellies, for there were bullets everywhere in the air, it seemed, like a nest of large hornets suddenly disturbed and gone berserk. Benign was close upon me, and we burst into the building and stood panting awhile.

It was my first time in Banneker's office, and I was impressed at its neatness. There were perhaps a dozen books dealing with law, thick and red-bound, lined on a desk made of simple pine. There were a quill, an inkwell, and some papers scattered on the desk. On one wall there was a portrait of the young Mr. Lincoln. There were several chairs, waiting patiently as though for guests who never came. Most of the building, however, was empty of furniture and other accommodations. Except for the driving energy of the man who studied here night after night, it might have been pitiful in its lack. But for the moment, I was concerned about matters far more important than Banneker's attempts to educate himself. From his office, I had a better view of what was happening at Fir Crest. Indeed, the first person I saw was Banneker himself, and he and his men seemed to be in deep trouble.

The distance from the crest of firs to the orchard nearest the house, and a bit beyond, is a little more than a mile. It slopes and curves simultaneously from the highest peak of the crest, where vicious bits of slate and other rock stand embedded in the ground like the edges of razors, on down through woods, open pasture, and then to the orchard. In terms of defense, if it is not carefully guarded beforehand, it is an open perimeter through which any enemy can pour and strike at the immediate heart of Fir Crest. With our men lined alone this arc, armed and disciplined as they were against any ordinary enemy, the raiders would have been helpless to get through. But it was obvious that the raiders had gained the initial advantage in a blistering surprise attack that had completely routed our forces.

Banneker was riding everywhere, at times sitting straight and firing, at others lying almost flat against his horse's neck, shouting to the fleeing Negroes to stand fast. Brave though they could be, they were farmers and field hands, not professional fighters. On the other hand, the raiders were brutal, terrifying, and well-organized, certainly worthy of being fled from. They seemed to be everywhere at once, white men and black in unkempt and mismatched uniforms of both North and South. They flew back and forth to prevent the establishment of a defense perimeter. And every time Banneker managed to cluster four or five of our men together, the raiders would swarm in and beat them apart, then withdraw to a distance, regroup, and mount the next attack. They worked with an almost uncanny awareness of how the land lay, of where the Negroes were grouped, and of which portion to harass in order to intimidate effective action from the rest. Had they learned so much from that single visit of several years ago? Or had they been fed intelligence by some person or persons at Fir Crest—so that they seemed to anticipate every gully, every rut and rabbit hole, even as they raced here and there striking terror in the hearts of everyone?

I saw no dead, and only a few wounded. So it appeared that terror was their main concern, for they could easily have killed us all, as disorganized as we were. Banneker made a valiant effort, but useless. I thought of having the great bell in the yard rung to summon help from the Gilliam place. But pride prevented me from doing so. We had not yet done our very best; failing that, I would then summon help from heaven or hell, if need be.

"It don't look like we doing so good, Miss Victoria."

"Indeed it doesn't, Benign." We had driven off other raiders, but these were better organized and far more determined. For another thing, they had been able to penetrate deeply into Fir Crest without being spotted. With Banneker resting from last night's ride, and others working in the fields, the raiders had struck secretly and found the defense line down. If there were a spy, or spies, at Fir Crest, they had done an excellent job of conveying their intelligence. The attack had certainly been a surprise one, which explained Benign's dilly-dallying in the kitchen. She wanted to give Banneker time to organize our forces. Failing that, she had wanted me captured unperturbed, with my mouth full of pancakes and sweet milk, as she obviously thought became a southern white lady about to lose every inch of her land.

Then I saw the blond man on the chestnut horse. He was tall, broad of shoulder, an expert horseman, sitting in his saddle as though he had been born there. And it occurred to me that our men were in such disarray because they, too, had recognized him; and his very presence had resurrected fear in their hearts. As I inspected him, it appeared that his entire army gathered around him for a moment's respite. They were well protected in the orchard, where apple and cherry blossoms over their heads only added to their grotesque appearance.

"They up to some devilment, sure enough," Benign said. We were crouched at a window facing the orchard now. To check on the defense, we gathered our skirts and ran the length of the building to the west window. Banneker had finally managed to place a line of men on their bellies at spaces across the length of the pasture. Between the last of them and the orchard, there was a no-man's-land, with the building where we were at the center of the gap. And from the south we could see Fir Crest, that magnificent mansion, serene, stately, and undisturbed in the sun, certainly the ultimate object of this vicious attack.

Then it was back to the window watching the orchard. While we had been making our rounds, the raiders had stripped a Negro naked and had strung him from the branch of an apple tree. He seemed to be perhaps in his early twenties, lean but well-muscled, eyes and nostrils wide with fear. His feet were a good six inches from the ground, and he rotated slowly at the end of the rope like a reluctant whirligig that had been insufficiently wound.

The blond man stood to his full height in his stirrups. Cupping his mouth, he said in a loud voice: "Now we're going to show you something. It will happen to all of you if you don't give up. We're through playing games." His voice was deep, cultured. Certainly he was no brigand of the ordinary kind. Had circumstances forced him into this unsavory business? Or was he thief, murderer, rapist, because he received some perverse pleasure from it? Watching the terrified Negro spinning slowly at the end of the rope, I was soon to know the answer to part of my question.

"Call Banneker," I whispered to Benign. "Tell him I need a horse." I had no definite plan in mind. But I was restless now, and felt almost cowardly, like a spectator at mayhem that concerned me more than most, and in which I had not yet played my part.

"What you want a horse for?" Benign said suspiciously.

"To ride," I said curtly. "Now, do as I say. Your voice carries better than mine, or I'd call him myself."

"No need to do that," she said dryly. "That's what I'se getting paid for." Before she went, she tapped my shoulder. "I think you ought to get out that window. What they going to do to that boy is going to be dirty."

I suspected as much, but I was too fascinated to move. The blond man was a born actor. To make sure that every eye was on the helpless Negro, he himself spurred his stallion into circles around the naked black. His intentions were not clear, but there was an awesome and expectant silence among his men, lined behind him, which indicated that they were familiar with whatever was about to happen, and relished it.

Benign had been at the west window, yelling for Banneker to bring horses. Did she plan on going with me, wherever it was I might go? It would be useless to try to stop her, under the circumstances, so I said nothing. When she returned, I said, "Did he hear you?" In truth, they had probably heard her all the way to the apple orchard, and to Richmond beyond.

"I hope he did, child. My lungs ain't like they used to be." Puffing, she glued her eye to the partly raised window, and watched with me.

After the leader gave up circling the Negro youth, he lifted his hand commandingly. Almost eagerly, another of that bunch bounded down from his horse. He was dressed in rags, as though they had recruited him a beggar from the street. As the leader's hair was brilliant yellow, his was equally red. It appeared that his face was blotched with freckles. Grinning, he swaggered over to the Negro and poked him in his flat belly, then turned him in the wind to inspect his tight buttocks. The youth began to scream then—he was calling pitifully for his mother—and his cries shattered the day's false harmony, certainly frightening all creatures large and small into desperate silence, even down to the garrulous crickets.

The blond man smiled up on his horse; the red-haired one slapped the hanging youth smartly on the thigh. Then he reached into the rear of his belt and brought out a long knife. The boy screamed incessantly: "Mammy . . . Mammy . . . Mammy . . . !"—and I found myself wondering who and where his mother might be. There were some two hundred men, women, and children who had been transferred to the barns in the low ground for safety, as was the custom when we came under attack. Perhaps his mother was there; perhaps she was wondering about her son.

The other raiders seemed eager with excitement. Most of them were grinning. Some spat tobacco juice. And others leaned forward on their mounts, so excited that it was almost possible to hear their hot breathing. Suddenly the red-haired man reached around and caught the boy's buttocks in an obscene embrace. At the same time, his right hand came up, working in a small rapid circle. The boy tried to jerk his body away, screaming hoarsely now. Blood spurted from him, spattering the white man. And then he stepped back quite proudly, holding up the Negro's genitals for all to see.

By some awful miracle, the youth was still conscious, still screaming; but his cries had taken on the sound of hollow wind that blows with neither force nor effect. Brutally now, as though he were slaughtering a hanging hog, the redhead rammed his knife into the youth's belly near the navel, cutting left and then right. Still the screams came, but softer now, almost surprised, gurgling with a kind of muted agony.

Undaunted, the redhead reached up, inserted the knife just beneath the breastbone, and ripped it down with both hands on the handle to the gaping wound in the boy's groin. Only then did the boy quieten, close to death if not dead. And the red-haired man reached into the cross-shaped openings he had made and ripped out the bloody guts there.

"Excellent!" It was the raider chief's voice, raised for all to hear. "Excellent, Mr. McKenzie! You are a showman indeed!" He spurred his horse lightly, blocking our view momentarily of the abused corpse. Now he took out his own knife, reached up disdainfully, and cut the rope. The poor youth's body fell limply to the ground.

"Now, why don't you give up?" the raider cried, this time cupping his mouth again. "There is no need for more bloodshed. But we'll do so if we have to!"

It occurred to me, in the most fleeting way, that he was bluffing. If he were so sure of himself, facing little or no resistance, why did he not move in and take Fir Crest, if that were his true intent? Horrified as I was, I managed to rise from my knees and run to the rear window. The Negroes were still lined along the pasture, but it was plain to see that they were in no mood to fight. Banneker, mounted on his horse, rode up and down among them, talking to each in what seemed a low, soothing voice. "Banneker!" I had to call several times before he acknowledged me. "Bring me a horse! At once!"

Still I did not know why I wanted a horse. Did I have some insane notion that I could negotiate with the bandit chief? Certainly not, for he had made it clearer than ever that his intent was to frighten away the Negroes and then to take control of Fir Crest. It seemed to me a strange strategy. I was more disgusted and confused than afraid. And there was no plan in my mind at all. Except that I needed a horse.

I stood in the doorway as Banneker approached, leading two mares by the reins. Even as he came toward me, the Negroes in the line broke. And four raiders suddenly appeared from nowhere, chasing behind them. They caught a black man and then a black woman. Laughing, they herded their captives back to the orchard. The man was silent, but the woman pierced the air with screams.

Banneker arrived at the door in a gallop and bounded down. His face was deeply troubled. "Them's some mean devils!" he cried. "What we going to do, Miss Victoria? They done scared them niggers to death."

"They have scared me to death, too!" I cried. I felt hot and wide-eyed. "But we have no choice but to fight! I shall fight! Will the Negroes let a woman—a white woman—best them?"

Even as I talked, I tried to mount the mare. There were four steps, which functioned nicely as a mounting post. But that damnable dress was in the way. I was so furious at the atrocity we had just witnessed that I tried to rip the skirt to free me to mount the horse. But Benign's hands caught me from behind. I had forgotten about her. "I told you we ought to wear pants," she said softly. But her voice was full of sorrow. She stooped in front of me and caught the voluminous skirts up, tying them in a knot so that they formed a kind of pantaloon that gave my legs free motion. I climbed from the steps into the saddle.

"Come here, girl." It was Benign, talking to the second mare. She caught the bridle and drew the horse to her. The mare's eyes seemed to survey Benign's bulk with the deepest possible suspicion. Nonplussed, Benign hitched her skirts up around her waist—it appeared that she was wearing a pair of men's red drawers—swung one leg over the animal, and plumped into the saddle. Despite the tragedy of the moment, Banneker was grinning. I myself felt somewhat light-headed and giddy, which helped ease my fear considerably. "Let us go and organize the men," I said. "They must stand and fight, or we lose everything."

"Yas'm!" he said smartly. He reached back and slapped the rump of his mount, and was gone in a flash.

But neither my mare nor Benign's, perhaps being female, was so swift or disciplined. Indeed, as though their business led them elsewhere, in spite of whatever we did or said, they carried us around the office building into plain view of the raiders in the orchard. For a second I felt close to hysterical laughter. Certainly we presented a ridiculous sight—a female Don Quixote and her black Sancho Panza. The two of us armed with rifles atop self-willed mares, going to what place, for what purpose?

"Get on up here, mare!" Benign said, and she kicked the horse hard in the side. By way of explanation to me, she said, "They smells that boy's blood, Miss Victoria. You got to be hard with them."

Fortunately for us, the raiders were occupied with other mischief and did not immediately see us. Some of them were raping the black woman down in the green grass. They clustered over and around her like buzzards over carrion. Some of them held their penises erect and exposed, waiting their turn. It was a vivid recreation of how my own mother had died. Another group had stripped the black male and had strung him by the wrists from the apple tree after the fashion of the one they had castrated and disemboweled. Over the whole grotesque scene, apple blossoms floated down with the delicacy of spring snow.

Even as I watched in horror, one of them stooped and lighted a pile of kindling under the Negro's feet. For the first time, he screamed. And the men, those who were not occupied with rape, laughed, and brought pieces of wood to make the fire larger. We were not within rifle shot of the orchard, but it was clear to me what I should do. Cursing under my breath, I dug my heels into the mare until she understood that I was in command. Then I readied my rifle. It would be a difficult feat, but the only merciful act that I could think of. There was nothing anyone could do now for the woman. But the man's screams rent the air as the flames reached greedy tongues higher up his writhing body.

Again I dug my heels into the mare. She responded immediately. And off we went, Benign somehow behind me, sitting as solidly as a rock. Soon we were within range of the orchard. I yanked the rein, and the mare came to a stop immediately. Rapidly, but most carefully, I aimed the rifle and fired. The Negro's body slammed back, but the rope held him and dragged his body forward again. A red stain appeared in the area of his heart, like the unfolding of a jungle flower. His head drooped to his chest. He would feel no fire now; he would feel nothing.

Right at my ear, another shot went off. I turned in amazement. "I tried to get that yaller-haired devil," Benign said. "But I missed. My eyes just ain't what they used to be."

Already we were on our way down to the pasture to join the Negroes. They were waving their hats as we sped through the dandelions, the clover and daisies, and the large-lipped lilies that seemed to give a sense of something almost sacred to the tall green grass. As we neared the Negroes, I heard some of them cheering. Others grinned. Some danced a jig.

Meanwhile, the raiders had collected themselves enough to realize what had happened, and a few bullets fell ineffectually behind us, for we were far beyond their range. Without having meant to, acting only from a sense of outrage and disgust, by saving the black man from being burned to death, I had rallied our Negroes at the same time.

The benefits were immediately seen, for the raiders were furious at having lost one of their victims. Certainly now the black woman had been raped to death. Without another available victim to spew their venom on, the raiders were now intent on total murder. Massed like the devil's own army, they came thundering down the pasture.

But our line held firm. Banneker gave the order to fire, and the air was rent with gunshot. Suddenly great gaps appeared in the ranks of the raiders. At least six of them hit the ground. Following Banneker's stern order, Benign and I lay flat in the tall grass. It seemed incredible that this could be happening in spring, that we were concerned about death when all around us seemed so intent on life. The delicate odors of spring were mixed with the vile and authoritative stench of gunpowder. There followed another great volley from our side, and more raiders hit the ground.

From the orchard, where he had remained in complete safety, the leader cried out angrily, "Retreat! Retreat!" And the raiders wheeled at once, returned to the orchard, and then thundered together up the road beyond the orchard. For the moment, Fir Crest had been saved; the defense perimeter had been restored; the Negroes had rallied; and the raiders had been routed, certainly not completely from Fir Crest, but far enough away so that we could repair our wounds, bury our dead, and then settle down to siege. For if nothing more was clear, this time the raiders had come to take Fir Crest, or to die in the trying.

FOUR

———◆———

Everything was very still, except for the liquid song of meadowlarks. I lay in the tall grass and watched Banneker smiling down at me. "That was mighty fine shooting, Miss Victoria." He towered over me like a colossus, proudly, and rightly so, for he had taught Charlotte, Robert Gilliam, and me how to handle a rifle when we were children. "Thank you, Banneker." He helped me to my feet, pulling so roughly, yet tenderly, that I almost fell into his arms. Desire was heavy in his eyes, but almost as soon extinguished. "You and Benign ought to go back to the house," he said, "before you get hurt. I'll send some men with you. Although I don't expect them raiders to attack again until after sundown, after the whipping they took."

I too was certain that the raiders would wait until dark before they came again. That they had been foolish enough to attack in broad daylight, as the first time, indicated that they were either arrogant fools—which I doubted most seriously—or that they had not anticipated active resistance. Theirs seemed more a war of nerves than of naked aggression, which puzzled me very much. Again I found myself wondering if their intention were really serious in terms of taking Fir Crest. Or were they merely concerned with giving the appearance of aggression, much as a dog growls to frighten away a potential enemy, until Fir Crest should fall into their hands like an overripe plum?

One thing, however, was most clear, although I had no hard evidence to back it up: Mr. Boswell, the horse dealer in Charlottesville, not only knew the true identity of the bandit chief, but had most probably contacted him after I had made my inquiries about the starred mare last night. So the bandits had come to take Fir Crest once and for all in this period of lawlessness. Or had they? Whatever their strategy, Mr. Boswell was unapproachable because of his position, even with proper authority to support my contention.

Mere coincidence could not account for the attack this morning. I could not fathom its true reason, for, given the initial confusion and disarray of our men, they could have marched all over Fir Crest. But they had not. Now there were some fifteen of them dead, while our only casualties were two men and a woman, victims of atrocity. We, of course, had casualties with minor wounds; but it was as though those brawny bullies were under strict orders only to inflict minor injuries rather than to kill. Even as they had galloped away—to the far woods in front of us, where it seemed they were leisurely setting up camp—they had seemed to do so with a sense of frustration and betrayal, as though the plum had resisted when they had been assured that it would fall. . . .

"Miss Victoria, you sleeping?"

"No, Benign. I was thinking."

She honored me with one of her eloquent grunts. "I didn't hear your brain making no noise," she said, giggling like a fat schoolgirl. "Well, we home. You getting down off that buckboard? Or you going to stay there all day?" I had killed a Negro for reasons of charity, and she was immensely proud of me. She herself helped me down from the buckboard, and sent its driver and the other men back to the meadow. I am certain that I was in a state of shock. I had never killed another human being before for any reason, however benevolent. Looking over my shoulder, I saw that the body hanging from the apple tree had disappeared. Before I could see more, Benign hustled me into the house. "It ain't never good to look back," she said. "You run along to your room. I'll send somebody to help you bathe and change clothes." She scratched most indecently in the general area of her thigh. "That grass got ticks and fleas. We both better get into something else."

I took her word about the parasites, although I felt no discomfort in that respect. "First, I'd like to check on Charlotte and Father," I said. "Haven't they been sleeping a very long time?"

She laughed roundly. Her gums were very red, her teeth sparkling white. "They still got some sleeping to do.

They'll wake up in three or four more hours, fit as a fiddle."

"What did you give them? Benign, I wish you wouldn't go around drugging my family. At least, not without telling me. It just doesn't look right."

She howled, as though discovering for the first time that white ladies, too, have a sense of humor. "I just give them some of my conjure, Miss Victoria. It's harmless. All it do is make you sleep. You wake up feeling fine." Her face became very sober. "Did you want your daddy and Miss Charlotte to see what them dogs did out there in the orchard? What you think it would done to them?"

My silence was all the answer she needed. However much she was being bitten by fleas—and it seemed that they were attacking her vigorously, from all her scratching—she insisted on seeing me upstairs, although I would have preferred to go alone, knowing the tremendous agility of fleas and the like. We stopped together at Charlotte's room, where Benign opened the door and peeped in. Then she closed it softly. "She sleeping just like I left her. The poor child was wore out."

"I'll see to Father," I said. It seemed that I had tempted her fleas long enough.

"If you say so, ma'am." She was certainly glad to go. Some turpentine in her bathwater would take care of the fleas. As I went down the hall to Father's room, I recalled the red underwear she had on. And I laughed aloud, easing some of the tension in myself. Who would have thought that Benign, that towering authority on all things feminine, would ever be caught in men's drawers?

The draperies in Father's room were closed, and the room was dark, but I could hear his regular breathing. The French windows were partly open, which permitted the entrance of a cool, comfortable breeze. I went to the bed and touched his forehead; he was perspiring slightly, so I pulled the sheet lower on his chest. Then I went to my room and bathed—first with a small amount of turpentine, in case Benign's fleas had decided to take up residence on my person, then in the fragrance of a perfume made from our own roses. After the servant had brushed my hair and pinned it in a rather severe bun at the back of my neck, I stepped into riding pants and boots, in case I were needed again in the field.

The balcony windows were open, and I stood there surveying the meadow where the Negroes seemed to be having lunch; the cabins, where some hundred blacks had elected to stay on, even in the face of the raiders' attack; Banneker's office building; and, finally, reluctantly, the orchard, which seemed, from my vantage point, to be a large bouquet of pink and white blossoms. Who would have thought they had showered their sweetness down on mayhem less than an hour ago?

From the balcony I had a clear view of the Negro cabins. Lined row on row, they seemed to be huddling against the possibility of violence in the afternoon sun. As I looked, I saw a person leave Yetta's cabin, which was the third building in the second row. It was a slight figure, wearing a gray cap, and the gray flannel pants and shirt favored by the Negroes. There was a furtive slant to the person's body—I did not know whether it was male or female—that seemed to imply that a theft had just been completed. It seemed impossible to me that a thief was at work at Fir Crest under the present circumstances, when we were in the midst of a battle for our very survival. I thought of calling out to the sneaking figure to stop; but whoever it was would not have heard me; and, in any case, if it were a thief, reason would dictate that he—or she?—ignore any alarm from me.

I dashed from my room, downstairs, and out through the west garden. It occurred to me that I ought to take a weapon only when I was nearing Yetta's cabin, half out of breath, feeling somewhat foolish—suppose that it had not been a thief, and I would have to face the malicious, mocking smile of Yetta herself?—but still determined to discover if a thief were at work at Fir Crest at such a crucial time.

The door to Yetta's cabin was open, which did not surprise me if indeed the person I saw had been a thief. In truth, as I had looked from the balcony, I had been reminded of the Negro youth we had seen skulking from Lance Harcourt's yesterday in Charlottesville. Was it possible that he had somehow managed to infiltrate the ranks of our Negroes at Fir Crest without my knowing it? Perhaps. But certainly not without Benign or Banneker knowing. Especially Banneker, who had looked at him in Charlottesville with such open disdain.

"Yetta?" There was a trilling in the air, as though swallows nesting nearby had answered me. But there was no response from Yetta's cabin at all. I had a dreadful sense of foreboding as I went up the steps. "Yetta?" Still no answer. I pushed the door slightly inward, and it gave on creaky hinges. Yetta was sitting in her chair with her back to the door. There was the obnoxious reek of jimsonweed still burning, probably from the pipe in her left hand. Her right was clamped around a mug of some sort that sat on a table beside the chair. In front of her was the other chair, probably the same one I had occupied on my visit here.

I called her name again, but she sat unmoving, without answering. For some reason, my eyes sought the Bible on which she had sworn never to tell Banneker the truth about my father—his father as well. The roots and herbs were still on the mantel, but their pungency was dominated by the nefarious smell of jimsonweed from Yetta's smoldering pipe.

Suddenly, fear hit me. It was almost impossible to move. But I forced myself toward her, taking a step at a time, as a child does when it is learning to walk. Some deep instinct told me not to touch the chair. Instead, I walked around beside it. And my stomach churned with revulsion and fear. Yetta's eyes were wide open, staring as though in pain and surprise. She sat as erect as any princess on a plain wooden throne. But a thin line of blood had drained from her mouth and dried at the corner of her lips. And her scrawny throat was cut from ear to ear, making what seemed a larger and more grotesque mouth. The bib of her apron was stained with blood; some had dripped to her lap and had formed a small puddle there. Holding my hand to my mouth, I turned and ran for the door in blind horror.

Suddenly, black arms enveloped me, as though I had run headlong into a Negro octopus. I screamed hysterically. Then the arms became strong hands, shaking me fiercely. When I was able to see, it was Banneker holding me. All my reserve left me, and I laid my head against his chest and cried. Awkwardly, he patted my hair, transferring my head to his shoulder so that he could move to where Yetta sat. I heard him suck in his breath, like wind pulled strongly into a tunnel. My head was near his heart, and I heard and felt it accelerate like a wild, frightened thing.

"Did you do this?" he whispered.

"No, Banneker. I swear I did not." As best I could, I told him what had brought me here. "The door was open. I found her like this."

When he eased his arm from around me, I felt naked and unprotected. The odor of jimsonweed had dissipated somewhat, leaving the malevolent smell of death. "She wasn't worth much," Banneker said softly. "But she was my mammy. I'm surprised she had that much blood in her."

"I'm sorry, Banneker. I'm terribly sorry."

His eyes seemed to turn maroon. "Why you sorry? You ought to be glad, after all she told you."

Now I sucked in my breath. "What do you mean?" I whispered.

"I mean that your daddy is my daddy. And when he dies, Fir Crest is mine, since I'm a man, and older than either you or your sister. Mama explained everything to me. She even told me how you made her swear on the Bible not to tell."

"She did swear," I said, still whispering, for it seemed as though my vocal cords were frozen with horror. "If she broke her vow, she will surely go to hell."

It was such a childish thing to say that even Banneker laughed. "She probably in hell right now. She was my mammy, but I didn't like her too much." He took the still-smoldering pipe of jimsonweed from her dead hand and sucked deeply. Yetta's eyes were yellow and bloodstained, staring.

"I'd like to leave," I said.

"Why?" He sucked again. "My mammy scare you?" Casually he leaned toward her and jammed her accusing eyes shut. "This is one of the nicest cabins in the quarter. She kept it real nice."

"Yes. I told her so."

If he had set a trap, I had stupidly fallen into it. "When? When you come and make her swear on the Bible?"

"She promised never to tell," I said.

"Well, she did. She told me everything. Swearing on that Bible don't mean a thing to niggers. It's for white folks. And people like Benign, as much as I like her. Mama kept that Bible here for decoration. She couldn't even read."

"I'd like to leave," I said; and I started for the door. But his hand snaked out and grabbed me.

"You leave when I tell you. How it feel being half-sister to a nigger like me? Don't look so scared. Niggers ain't all that bad . . . once you get to know us."

He was completely under the effect of the jimsonweed. His nostrils flared like a race horse's. His eyes seemed sleepy, sly, like the eyes of a serpent about to strike. His penis was plainly erect in the thin gray trousers, creating a small tent on his thigh. Guiding my hand to it, he said, "Feel. Feel it. You know you want to."

"How dare you!" I said. But my voice was weak and unconvincing.

He moved closer, curling my fingers around his organ. It throbbed, like a piece of hard wood with a life of its own. "Why are you doing this?" I said. Again my voice had dropped to a whisper, as though to speak louder might awaken his dead mother.

"Because I want to," he said. "I've wanted to for a long time." He let my hand go, and I jammed both in the pockets of my riding breeches. He laughed, and strolled around his mother. "If you didn't do this, who did?"

"I don't know. But it seemed to be a Negro running from the door."

He stood still and stretched, seeming to savor the pull of his pants against his erection. "Mammy said you was all ready to take us to the courthouse and say I tried to rape you. Did you say that?"

"I don't remember."

"I ain't never tried to rape you. When I set out to rape me a woman, she *raped*." He grabbed his erection in both hands and fondled it. "Let's get naked," he said. "Like we used to when we was children."

My throat felt as though it were being squeezed by a hot hand. He was reeling from the effects of the jimson-weed. To add to it, he took the mug from his mother's right hand and drank the concoction there. After swallowing, he shuddered, as though the drink tasted vile.

"I don't want to get naked," I said. "I want to go."

He ignored that. Untying the string around his waist, he

stepped out of his trousers and flung off his shirt. "Take off your clothes," he said. "Please, Miss Victoria. Unless you want me to tear them off."

His was the most perfect male body I had ever seen, as though Michelangelo had cast his most magnificent sculpture, oversized penis erect, in black marble. But even as I admired his physical beauty, I was at the same time trying to find a word, a phrase, anything, to stop him without offending, since the other Negroes would fight or not according to his will.

"Your mother is dead," I said. "We ought to respect that."

"Why? Mammy sent me to you that night I jumped off the balcony. Her being dead don't bother me at all. It bother you?" Generously, he snatched a patchwork quilt from the cot and draped it over Yetta's head and body, which made her presence all the more grotesque. "Now, take off your clothes. You don't have to worry about the raiders just yet. They won't come back until dark, if then. And every man in the meadow is armed. I come here to eat with Mama . . . and I find you. . . . Take off your clothes."

When I still hesitated, he reached out and unbuttoned my shirtwaist with surprisingly gentle fingers. My breasts seemed milk-white against the brownish-black of his hands as he caressed them, pinching the nipples almost cruelly. "Banneker . . . please don't . . . we'll both regret this later on. . . ."

"I ain't going to regret nothing. I got me five thousand acres of land I can't even claim because I'm a nigger. What I got to regret?"

Something clicked almost happily in my head then. "You mean you're not going to tell anybody what Yetta said about your being Father's son? I'm sure there's not a word of truth in it, but talk like that can hurt."

"It's true," he said, massaging more gently now. "The minute Mammy told me, I knew why I was different from every other nigger. I'm a Parkchester, just like you."

Gently I moved his hand away. "Then you should not be doing this," I said. I rebuttoned my blouse. "Now, what do you intend to do about your mother's lies?" Gradually I was regaining my confidence.

"What can I do? I'm a nigger. Who'd believe me?"

Now he had fallen into his own trap. "Then I shall be going," I said.

"Not yet you won't!" And he grabbed me so fiercely that all the world seemed to spin. I was limp in his arms, defenseless, for him to do as he pleased. His powerful organ struck at the leather of my riding pants. And again, and again, seeking entrance. Grabbing me roughly by the back of my neck, he yanked my head back and swallowed my mouth with his. In spite of myself, I felt a tremendous excitement. His free hand crushed first one breast, then the other. I had the insane sensation that he was going to eat me alive, like a cannibal, from the lips down.

Still, however, a portion of my mind was occupied elsewhere. *Whoever killed Yetta*, I thought, *was someone she knew and trusted. Someone who sat across from her while she drank home brew and smoked jimsonweed. Someone who was a Negro, or appeared to be. Someone who reached suddenly across the space between them, probably with a razor, and slashed her throat. But why? Why? Why?*

I took a deep breath as Banneker released me. His face was somber, almost petulant. "This ain't right," he said. "Not if we got the same daddy."

The day seemed filled with traps. If I acknowledged him as my half-brother, I would probably go free and without further molestation. At the same time, I would open the door for competition from his side for control of Fir Crest. If I did not admit that his father and mine were the same, I became a prime candidate for rape, or whatever other obscenity he might have in mind. I was grateful that he was still under the effect of the jimsonweed.

"Your father is mine," I said softly. "It is definitely not right that we should do this."

Reluctantly, but thoughtfully, he pulled on his trousers and shirt. "I'm real sorry, Miss Victoria," he said. "I guess it was the shock of seeing my mammy dead."

"What do you intend to do about Fir Crest?" I said.

He shrugged his magnificent shoulders. "What can I do?" Then he grinned. "You don't have to worry about me, Miss Victoria. I'm leaving here soon for Richmond. I'm going to be a politician. You and Miss Charlotte can have Fir Crest. It ain't big enough for me."

"You swear you won't tell?" I said.

He was very quiet.

"What is it you want?" I said, feeling my body flood with fear.

In answer, he stepped forth gently and took me in his arms. This time, his kiss was indescribably sweet. Then he laid his cheek against mine. "I won't say a word about your father or Fir Crest," he said, "if you won't say a word about me."

"I promise," I said. It seemed almost too good to be true.

"You swear?" he said.

"I swear."

He released me. Shaking his head, he seemed to rid himself of the jimsonweed's grotesque effects. He moved to the quilt covering Yetta and touched it. "Who you think did this?" he said.

"I wish I knew." Whatever excitement I felt was added to by the single, extraordinary fact that the murderer had finally come out into the open. All the other deaths—from Mother's until now—had either been too ambiguous or had presented the appearance of being accidents rather than unequivocal murders. This one was undeniably so. All that was lacking was motive, and Banneker put that in the form of a question: "Who would want to kill Mammy?" he said.

Given time, I was certain I could think of a thousand people, including myself. Certainly anyone who had ever endured her groaning had sufficient reason for murder. "I don't know, Banneker. Once we have driven off the raiders, we shall have to summon the sheriff."

He squinted through the window facing west. The sun hung there like a dark-red and malevolent eye. It would be night soon. "Yas'm," he said. "I'd better be getting back to the men."

"Thank you, Banneker. . . ."

"For what?" Now he smiled, showing his perfect teeth. "When I get to be a politician, that's when you have to worry about me." He winked somewhat daringly, walked to the door, leaped down the steps, and was gone.

My head was filled with disturbing sensations. I left the cabin, too, closing the door carefully behind me. Undeniably, a murderer was at work at Fir Crest. But who? I racked my brain as I walked back to the house. Whoever he was, I had seen him from the balcony. But again, the problem of motive presented itself. Who would want to kill Yetta, indeed? If anyone—including myself—wanted to keep her silent about Banneker's paternal origins, then why wasn't Banneker killed as well?

The answer came to me in the west garden. Because only Banneker and Yetta knew, and Banneker wanted the knowledge kept secret, possibly out of shame that he had been a slave to his own father. Yetta would want to keep quiet as well, for to reveal her dark secret would only serve to endanger her and Banneker, if Father's ire were sufficiently aroused.

Obviously, then, Yetta had told the secret of her affair to one other person, and had been killed for her efforts. Had the other person been the Negro I'd seen leaving her cabin? Was another mulatto son of Father's out there among the hundreds of Negroes, also with designs on Fir Crest? I shuddered at the thought. Still, it had been a Negro I'd seen leaving Yetta's cabin. However many people Yetta had told about Banneker being the true heir to Fir Crest under the law of primogeniture, she had told one person too many. Certainly with the South defeated, all manner of rights would come to Negroes that had formerly been denied them. Banneker's claim would be admitted to a court, and in the prevailing atmosphere where freed Negroes were thought to be better than their former owners, his claim might very well be upheld. I had only his word that he would not sue; but could I trust him? And, if the murderer was a Negro, how did one go about finding a single Negro among perhaps half a thousand? Finding a needle in a haystack would be far easier indeed. . . .

My breasts and lips seemed to burn with a slow, exciting fire where Banneker had touched and kissed me. I suppose that I should have felt unclean; on the contrary, I felt incredibly pure, as though I had been born into a world where evil had no dominion. Pausing in the garden, I watched the sun for a few minutes, how it seemed to sprawl over the crest of firs with almost arrogant beauty—heaven's peacock, spreading its beautiful feathers for all to see, touching the clouds with a faint pink like a lovely lady's blush. It seemed incredible, in all this tranquillity, that less than a mile north, a band of raiders was also watching the sun, and that when it went down, they would come with every intention now of destroying us.

I went inside the mansion and directly to Charlotte's room. She wore riding pants and a plaid shirtwaist. She was sitting before the vanity, tying her hair with a ribbon. "Benign has told me about the raiders," she said bitterly. "Is it true they are led by the same man who led the group that killed Mother?"

"It is true," I said. "I have seen him."

She seemed well-rested and relaxed; but her body appeared tense with carefully controlled excitement. "I shall kill him," she said softly.

"Banneker and his men will do the fighting," I said. "We shall fight only if it becomes necessary. For the time being, I think we would all be better off if we followed our usual routine."

She looked at me admiringly. "How can you be so calm?"

I dropped to my knees and hugged her tightly. "I am frightened to death," I whispered. "Someone has murdered Yetta in her cabin."

"Yetta! Who did it? Was it one of the raiders?"

I shook my head. "I don't think so. From my balcony I saw a Negro sneaking from her cabin. It appeared that he was one of our men, involved in petty theft. When I went to investigate, I found poor Yetta."

"How did she die?" Charlotte whispered. She had turned quite pale.

There was no need to spare her; eventually, she would find out anyway. "Her throat was cut. It seems that whoever killed her used a razor."

Suddenly Charlotte began trembling, and I wrapped my arms tighter around her. "What is happening to us, Victoria? I am so afraid that I feel like running away and hiding! And who are these raiders who come and plague us at their will? Benign has told me of the horrible things they did in the orchard. Who are they?" Her face had turned red and angry, and she had balled her hands into tiny fists.

"I do not know very much more than you, Charlotte. But there are things I have suspected for a long time."

"Things? What things?"

"That someone is trying to take over control of Fir Crest. That these raids, Mother's death, the fire in the candle house, even Emerald's death, and now Yetta's—that all are connected in some way. And that the person behind them is trying to bring us to our knees so that he can take over Fir Crest."

Charlotte stood, still trembling, her fists still clenched. "You are so much braver, so much more clever than I!" she cried. "I know that I am foolish and temperamental, too frequently so. But I promise—I *swear* to you, Victoria—that from this day forth, you can count on me as your staunchest ally."

"Dear Charlotte!" We embraced, two frightened children prepared to take on the world. "I have never doubted your good intentions. But how wonderful it is to hear you say those words! With your solid support, we shall fight for Fir Crest to the last piece of ammunition."

Almost as a warning, darkness fell. Charlotte went to light the lamps. "What about Father?" she said. "Have you seen him? Is he still annoyed with me?" Puckering her pretty lips, she blew out the sulfur stick. "I do hope these raiders have been defeated or driven off before Lance Harcourt comes with his father on the weekend."

I understood her anxiety to have the present conflict done with, although her comment did sound frivolous. "I am going to see Father now," I said. "I shall meet you shortly for supper. As I have said, we must follow the usual routine, before everything falls into chaos." We hugged each other.

"You are so strong, so brave," Charlotte said. "I wish that I could be like you."

"You are perfectly fine as you are," I said, smiling. Then she went downstairs to supper, and I to Father's room. I knocked once. "Come in," he said. His voice sounded full of strength. That, at least, was a good sign. I went into the room.

Surprisingly, Father was sitting at the escritoire in his cotton nightshirt, writing by candlelight. The shirt was open at the throat, and his neck was scrawny, almost raw in color, like that of a bruised chicken. It amazed me what ravages the war had done to him. His red hair was streaked with gray, and his eyes seemed watery, as though any moment he might break out in tears. Seeing me staring at him, he laid down his pen almost impatiently, but gently. "I was forty-nine when the war began," he said.

"Now I am fifty-four. Is it strange that I should look old and tired?"

"You look fine, Father." And I went around the desk to kiss him. He had been writing on a long sheet of paper, which I saw was his will. Immediately I felt a rush of panic. Had there not been a will before? He seemed to sense my dismay, for he said, "Because of the death of your mother, I am obliged to make a new will." Abruptly he stood. His feet were in slippers, but the lower portion of his legs and his ankles were naked, bony. Indeed, he had become a skeleton of a man, as though the devilish war had foreshortened his lease on life.

Suddenly he seemed to stagger, and put his hand to his head. "I feel almost as though I've been drugged," he said. Immediately I went to help him. "Perhaps you should lie down," I said. His skin felt almost clammy. "Perhaps," he said. He allowed me to lead him to the four-poster, where I plumped up his pillows and covered him with a sheet. "What is this I hear about raiders?" he said. As I told him about the attack, I lighted the lamps, which made his skin appear a sickly yellow. "This is the second time they have come," I said. "There is something about Fir Crest that seems to fascinate them, like bees around honey."

"And why not?" he said proudly. "It is a great and valuable estate. You have done a fine job of keeping it that way, against all odds." He coughed, as though to cover embarrassment. "And what has happened to the raiders? Have they been driven off?"

I shook my head. "Not yet. They appear to have massed in the woods to the north for a night attack."

"I doubt it," he said. "They are probably drifters, deserters, discharged soldiers still with an appetite for fighting. If they met sufficient resistance during the day, they will not return tonight."

I was out of agreement with him there, but it did not seem wise to push the issue. "Yetta is dead," I said gently.

He jerked up suddenly. "Yetta? Dead? When? How did it happen?"

His face had turned a ghastly white, and I found myself annoyed that he should be so stricken about the death of a black slut who had sired his illegitimate son. "Her throat was cut," I said harshly.

If it was possible, he turned even whiter. Yet, he remained silent, pulling at his bottom lip. I went to the windows facing north and looked out. Where the raiders had camped in the cluster of woods, several fires were burning. Other than that, what I could see of Fir Crest seemed peaceful with lights here and there in the Negro quarters. The full moon had not yet risen. If the raiders really were intent on taking Fir Crest, they would attack before the moon rose.

As I turned to go back to Father, he began to speak. "Yetta was the most exciting woman I have ever known," he said softly. "Even now, it seems incredible to me that a woman could have been so exciting. Yet, she had a quiet dignity completely unexpected in a Negress." He planted his somber eyes on mine. "She was the only woman I have ever truly loved. What a disgrace that I was not man enough to make her my wife! That I gave in to the abominations of racial superiority! As a woman, she was superior to any others I have known. As a human being, she was superior to us all."

How could he desecrate the memory of my mother by praising Yetta and her obscenities? What conjure had blinded him to the point that he would presume that any Negro woman was superior even to his own daughters? I do not know if he saw the shock and anger in my face, for we were both startled by the sound of gunfire nearby. I rushed to the window, but I saw nothing at first. Then there was another volley. I saw the small red spurts explode in the air over the meadow. Banneker and his men were firing, which meant that the raiders had resumed their attack.

Father was quite pale. He seemed ready to hide under the covers. "I have had enough of fighting!" he cried. "This is more than I can bear!"

I suppose I should have pitied him, but I did not. Poor quivering mass of a man! Even as I headed for the door, I wondered again if my real father had gone away to war and a weak impostor had come home in his stead. But I could not prevent myself from blurting out: "Then you would have Banneker and the other Negroes fight for you?"

He heaved a deep sigh. "Why not Banneker?" he said. "Go now. But first, blow out the lamps."

Angrily, I did as he instructed. Why not Banneker,

indeed? And why not Yetta, were she not now rigid in her chair with her black throat cut. At that moment, as I rushed down through the darkened house to the kitchen, I thoroughly hated my father. Not so much his cowardice, but his insistence that his evil spawn had worth beyond that of those who had loved him freely, legitimately, and respectfully.

Charlotte and Benign were already in the kitchen, sitting tensely at the table, where a shrouded candle burned. Charlotte seemed angry and impatient; Benign's face was set with stubborn determination. "Miss Victoria, this child here wants to go out there and fight like she a man. I done told her that there ain't no need for that right now. If it come to that, she'll have plenty of time for fighting."

"That's right, Charlotte," I said. I touched her shoulder gently, and it did seem that some of the tension left her. "Let us wait and see what happens." She nodded; I passed my hand over her hair, her cheek. Benign made three cups of tea. "It's all up to the Lord now," she said. Her face seemed golden in the candlelight. I wondered if she knew about Yetta; if not, now was certainly not the time to tell her.

And so we passed the night. At some point, the moon burst almost angrily upon the land. And we could see the fighting from the kitchen window. If the raiders had depended upon the cover of darkness to do their damage, they were thwarted at every turn. Incredibly, it was our Negroes who had the advantage on two scores. In their gray-colored garb, they blended perfectly inside the moon mist, moving steadily from bush to bush, and tree to tree, like gray ghosts. Once they were in the orchard, their black color also worked to their advantage, so that the raiders, who were primarily white-skinned, were at the mercy of the Negroes. Once, as I watched, a Negro leaped from behind a tree, dragged a raider from his horse, and nicely sliced his throat, then disappeared again inside the miasma.

Banneker, it seemed, was everywhere. While it was impossible to make out his features, it was easy to spot his broad shoulders, his height, and the bend and sway of his lean muscularity as he led group after group of Negroes against the raiders. Wisely, he had decided to fight on foot. With the moon cooperating and providing camouflage, with Banneker's sure knowledge of the environs of Fir Crest and, perhaps, excited as he might have been from his encounter with me in his mother's cabin, he commanded like a general.

The raiders were completely disrupted. Yet, they would not retreat. First they would withdraw, probably to lick their wounds and count their losses, which were considerable. Our own casualties were small. As of two o'clock the following morning, only three of our Negroes were dead, while the land was strewn with bodies of the raiders. The chief, he of the blond hair, might have done better to don a cap or to paint his face black, and those of all his men. But nonetheless, he moved back and forth in attack and withdrawal with what seemed an almost perfect harmony of presence. What manner of man was he to be so careless if the objective he sought were really worth the taking? Why had he not called retreat long ago? It was as though he were deliberately sending his men in to be slaughtered by our Negroes.

Charlotte, Benign, and I, along with some of the women house servants, cared for the wounded in the great sitting room at Fir Crest. But their wounds were slight; their mood was excellent; and their determination to prevent the taking of Fir Crest by anyone was beyond doubt. Once Banneker came with a slight injury on his left arm. I myself attended it. "Ain't nothing to it," he said, grinning. "But I don't want to get blood poisoning."

"You were perfectly right in coming," I said. I had already cleansed the wound, and was putting on a bandage. The contrast of the white cloth against his skin was startling. Small wonder that he could be ghost and defender at the same time. If, indeed, events were in the hand of God, He had done well by giving us Negroes in gray, moonlight, and, above all, Banneker himself.

Charlotte dozed from time to time on the sofa. But I was completely unable to sleep. I worked with Benign on the wounded, prepared coffee or tea for them, and then sent them back to battle. Whatever advantage we had during the night would be dissipated with the coming of dawn. At the same time, I wondered if there would be any raiders left, for they still came in great waves, fell dead under volleys from every hidden place, and then withdrew at a word from their leader.

The fighting was sufficiently distant from the mansion for me to go from the kitchen into the yard there. The moon was golden now, about to retire. In the east, there was a faint pink glow. My heart sank. Could we survive a daytime attack? In desperation, I looked up at Father's window. Why was he not here to advise us? Why had he left the defense of his land to his black bastard son? And even as I asked myself these questions, I saw the figure of Father briefly in the window. Then he disappeared. At least, I thought, he was man enough to view a battle from the security of his boudoir.

Then came the dreaded dawn, and the advantage our Negroes had enjoyed suddenly worked against them. Visible as they were in the first light of day, they were forced time and again to retreat, which they did in the greatest possible order. I could not help but admire their sturdy endurance and admirable discipline. And, at every turn, Banneker was there, shouting orders, urging the men this way and that. Surely they were exhausted. At the same time, the raiders must have been exhausted as well. It appeared that they had lost more than half their number. Even now, some twenty-five or thirty of them were massing beyond the orchard for what appeared to be a final onslaught. Now was time for all of us to fight. Resolutely I picked up my rifle. Charlotte and Benign already had theirs. On an impulse, I embraced them both. Who knew if we would ever see each other alive again? And what horrors awaited us if perchance we fell into the hands of the raiders?

"Let's go on and get it over with," Benign said. Like two children, Charlotte and I followed her out into the early-morning stench of spilled blood and gunpowder hanging over the surrounding freshness of spring.

Banneker had thrown a perimeter of men at a distance of some two hundred yards from the mansion, backed up by another line a hundred yards in between. It was this second line that we joined, a short distance from the east garden. And then there was no time to think, for the raiders bore down on the first line with a fury that was completely unsettling. The air was alive with bullets, shouts, the screams of the dead and the dying. Even as I watched, a gap appeared in the line, and perhaps five rampaging horses, eyes and nostrils flaring, slashed through. Immediately, our line fell into action. A tremendous volley went forth like the many fingers of an outraged God. The horses and riders fell in great pools of blood; like a well-oiled engine, the gap closed as the Negroes in the first line moved back into position.

I felt chills through my entire body. How proud I was! Behind me, although I dared not look, Fir Crest stood. For how much longer, no one could tell. Yet, it stood. In front of me, there were several of our men dead. Several wounded and dying were quickly taken to the first-aid area. Banneker, crouching low like a stalking panther, moved back and forth along the front line, smiling, encouraging; strong. Behind him, I saw the leader of the raiders alone in the orchard. He was grand on his stallion. But why, I wondered, did he not join his men in the charge? Surely his presence would have lent them strength.

But there he remained even as his men moved in for the second encounter. This time, they were met by barrages from both perimeters, for I gave the order to our men to fire, and Benign repeated it. We stood and fired over the heads of the reclining first line. When the guns sounded, I saw Banneker jerk his head around in surprise. Then, understanding, his eyes sought mine, and he smiled. As I watched, he screwed his body against the ground, leveled his rifle, sighted, and nicely shot a raider in the heart. This time, when the chief—still safe in the orchard—yelled the order to withdraw, only some dozen of his men were alive to follow it.

Suddenly there was a great commotion from the direction of the crest of firs. I looked, and my heart filled with excitement. Unmistakably, Robert Gilliam had come home, and was leading a troop of his men to help in the defense of Fir Crest. The Negroes cheered, and I cheered along with them. Charlotte and Benign locked arms and danced a jig. The raider chief saw the reinforcements at the same time. Abandoning his men, he took off in a frantic gallop, with some of Robert's riders separating to follow him in hot pursuit. Acting quickly, Banneker moved his men to surround those raiders who remained. And in a short while, even before Robert Gilliam had time to reach the mansion, the dozen raiders were dead. Some of them were castrated; some of them were pulled limb from limb; some of them were gutted—certainly out of revenge for what they had done to one of our own in the orchard. But all of them were dead.

Now the sky was so blue that it hurt the eyes to look at it. There were three buzzards flying lazily overhead, as though Mama and Papa had taken baby buzzard on an outing. All around Robert and me, there was the smell of freshness and greenness and growing things. The creek, where the last bottle of wine was chilling in the ice-cold water, ran at a rapid pace. The trees overhead were filled with lustrous green leaves ringing us in like a large wedding band. And above, the sky was blue, serene, massive.

Then, suddenly, Robert Gilliam was standing over me naked. He had his arms full of flowers. I was naked, too. Looking up at him. His skin was tanned to a rich olive color, almost as dark as Banneker's, as though he had gone without clothes on a long journey through wind and sun and rain. His parted legs, with a rich growth of curly hair around the organ and testicles, were muscular columns. The hair in his groin and armpits was slightly damp from being in the creek. "You're not dry yet," he said. Then, laughing, he showered the flowers all over me.

The Spanish blood in him seemed to surge in his veins, causing them to swell and then relax. His manhood had finally lost its tumescence, and seemed suspended inside of a peaceful satisfaction. Dropping to one knee, he kissed me blissfully. His deep blue eyes were gentle, yet thoughtful. Then he lay beside me, supporting his head with elbow and hand.

"I have been thinking," he said, "about all that you've told me. Indeed, it does appear that there is foul play at Fir Crest. Yetta's murder proves it."

"I had thought the same thing," I said. "But I am most intrigued by the raiders, especially their chief. It seemed to me that he was deliberately sending his men into battle for the purpose of destroying them."

Robert passed his arm over my breasts. "Again he has evaded capture. He seems clever and very assured. Why would he want to destroy his men?"

I shook my head. "There are so many unanswered questions. For example, who is he? And what is his true purpose in attacking Fir Crest? Even if you had not heard the fighting this morning, we would have driven them away. Now I fear he will come with an even larger army."

"But that is not logical," Robert Gilliam said. "If he wanted to destroy one, why would he bring another?"

That, too, had puzzled me. Yet I knew that the blond leader would return. Perhaps not soon, but in due season. However irrational his actions may have appeared to me, I was convinced that he was part of some larger and quite precise plan which involved Fir Crest and all within it.

Abruptly Robert Gilliam pulled me to him. "We can talk about these matters later," he murmured. "I have not had any woman since I left. I am hungry for you. . . . Hungry . . . hungry. . . ." His arms wrapped around me as he moved his warm body upon mine. His lips were wild and sweet to the taste, like some exotic red fruit. Raising slightly, he entered me. "I am hungry," he whispered. Then, his magnificent body began moving in slow, probing circles. The weight of him was almost unbearably sweet. The sunlight on his blue-black hair made it glisten like water in the bottom of a deep well, struck by the power of moonlight. My body responded to the thrusts of his with an almost maddening urgency. Now it was I who was whispering, "Hungry . . . hungry . . . hungry . . ." until he silenced me with his lips.

The trees around us seemed to listen to our moans, the hard slap of our bodies. And then, a slight wind rose. The birds seemed to gasp, as though they had been holding their breaths. Their twittering, and whistles, and warbling sounded full of the most exquisite joy. Even the creek seemed to join in the symphony. And as Robert thrust once—deeply, finally—his body quivering in and on mine, I saw three white doves overhead. The sky had changed from royal blue to an almost milky whiteness. I closed my eyes. Near fainting, I smelled the richness of many flowers crushed between his body and mine, and he pulled me almost cruelly to him—lips to lips, loins to loins—and we exchanged the sweet perfume of life. Yet, only two days later, all my dreams would come to a dreadful ending.

It was Friday, the following day, which also happened to be the first of May, when Yetta was put to rest in the Negro cemetery. Neither Charlotte nor I attended her funeral, as would have been customary. But I used for my excuse the fact that Fir Crest needed supervision in its restoration after the damage wrought by the raiders. Charlotte flatly refused to go. And Banneker—who had somehow managed to convince everyone that Yetta had died of natural causes, rather than as the victim of a crime—obviously went to the obsequies only out of a sense of obligation. He came to see me before the burial.

Now he was neatly dressed in a black silk suit that fit him like a glove. His boots were new as well, along with his white shirt and dark blue tie. He looked most elegant, and very serious. "Mammy left me a few pennies," he said. "I spent them on these." He indicated his attire with a downward sweep of his hand. "I'm going to Richmond as soon as the funeral's done. Now that Massa Parkchester's home, you all won't be needing me around any more."

"Banneker!" I felt unaccountably alarmed. It had been obvious for some time that he was preparing to leave. But I had not expected it to happen so soon. "Father is home, Banneker, that is true. But he is a different man. The war has done dreadful things to him. How will we ever manage without you?"

His broad chest seemed to swell with pride, and to deflate almost at once. "Mistuh Robert home now. He can help you."

Did I detect jealousy in his voice? "Mr. Robert has his own farm, Banneker, his own work to do."

"I got my work to do, too," he said. "My things already packed. I'm going to school in Richmond. You put Amos in charge the same way I was. Amos know how to handle things."

There was the sudden clanging of bells from the Negro church, where services would take place for Yetta's funeral. "I got to go now," Banneker said. "But I really come to give you this." He reached into his inner pocket and came out with a piece of folded paper. It was very old and in poor repair. But it made all the difference in the world:

I, Reginald Parkchester, do hereby affirm that I am the sire of the son born to the Negress Yetta on this 21st day of March in the year of Our Lord 1839.

/s/ Reginald Parkchester

Even as I rejoiced at Banneker's giving the paper up to me—did he really know its true value?—I cursed my father for a fool. What manner of man sired a bastard by a black slut, and then announced it to the world? Certainly an idealistic fool, and a weakling at the same time. Yet, it became apparent that for all the years I had known Father, and even before, he had been mouthing pieties even as he had succumbed to the most abominable passions. At that moment, I detested him.

I folded the paper and guarded it in my bosom. "Yetta told me there was no evidence," I said. It suddenly struck me that I was, indeed, talking to my black half-brother.

"She never told me nothing," Banneker said, "except a few weeks before she died. She told me then about Massa Parkchester, but she never mentioned this paper. I found it in her things."

The church bells seemed to be swirling now with almost giddy delight. "I think you should go before the funeral is over," I said. And I gave him my hand. Then, impulsively, I kissed him on the cheek. "Good-bye, Banneker. We shall miss you." There were tears in my eyes. Genuine tears.

He turned and left the sitting room, the mansion, without speaking, without looking back. He carried himself very well. He was handsome, intelligent, and outspoken. With more training—or perhaps with less—he would make a good legislator, even as he had been an excellent slave.

I was drying my eyes when I was interrupted in my thoughts by the simultaneous arrival of Charlotte and Benign. Benign was dressed for Yetta's funeral, and impatient to go, for they had been great friends. I wondered how much Yetta had told Benign of the business with Father and Banneker when she was in her cups. No matter now; she was dead, probably groaning and talking her head off in hell. I felt especially bitter about the piece of paper tucked in my bosom, which might easily have superseded any claims I had to being heiress of Fir Crest.

Charlotte was very upset. "Is it true that Banneker is leaving after Yetta's funeral?" she cried.

Benign grunted. "I wish you'd hurry up and tell this child, Miss Victoria, so I can go before they put Yetta in the ground. I'm sorry now I ever mentioned it."

Charlotte grabbed my arm. "Is it true, Victoria? What shall we do?"

I was disgusted, looking at the pain and passion in her face. As my father, in his youth, had loved a Negro woman, Charlotte, in hers, had loved—and still loved, if her face was any sign—a Negro man.

"Yes, it is true, Charlotte." Her nails were digging into my arms like claws, and I gently released them. "What we shall do is to continue as before."

The blood seemed to drain from her face. "Without Banneker? Whatever shall we do without Banneker?"

"Amos will be in charge," I said.

"Amos is a good man," Benign said. "Now, I got to go." She was grand in a black satin dress, black boots, and black bonnet with a silk band. "Poor Yetta," she said at the door. "She and me used to talk about which one of us might go first. And now I'm late for her funeral in the bargain." She lifted the side of her skirt and swept through the door with all the elegance of a black aristocrat.

I poured a sherry for myself and Charlotte, hoping to calm her. Did I dare tell her that the man she longed for, that the man she had given herself repeatedly to, was in fact her half-brother? And that his presence at Fir Crest, however much passion it might have evoked, was, at the same time, a menace to her inheritance and mine as well? Certainly Yetta had not told Banneker about his true status because she wanted to hold the knowledge as a trump card. To her own petty mind, lying to me about the paper Father had written had only strengthened her hand. Her lying and secrecy had also driven Charlotte and Banneker along the road to incest. Perhaps it had even caused the death of the woman Emerald. Certainly it had heated flames in Charlotte which still burned very brightly, although I doubted that she had resumed her illicit relationship with Banneker. Knowing her as I did, however, I felt it would have been only a matter of time before she picked up with him again, if he would have her. Now I had even more reason for rejoicing about his going. Now the church bells were tolling the low, solemn cadence of the dead. And I found myself thinking how glad I was that Yetta was dead—however much I deplored the way she died, and the mystery surrounding it—and that Banneker was leaving Fir Crest, however much I might miss him.

Charlotte gulped her wine and poured another. She was

indeed very distraught. "Have you forgotten about Lance Harcourt?" I cried. "He is coming tomorrow to ask for your hand in marriage! And here you are bemoaning the departure of a Negro field hand!"

She laughed shakily. "It is Lance Harcourt's coming that has me upset!" she said. "Oh, Victoria! I am so nervous! Of course the news of Banneker's leaving was a shock. But we all knew he would leave someday. I am surprised he has stayed this long." She rushed to me and crushed me in her arms. "Victoria, what will Father say when Lance Harcourt asks permission to marry me? Will he refuse?"

"No, no, Charlotte. He will say yes. You will see."

"I feel as though I am coming completely apart," she whispered. "How can you be so calm?"

Perhaps, I thought, because Robert Gilliam is coming with his father tomorrow as well. Perhaps, too, because I am not in love with Banneker while Lance Harcourt is coming to ask for my hand in marriage. I kissed her tenderly on the cheek. "Everything will turn out fine," I said. "You will see."

"Oh, Victoria! I hope you are right! I love Lance Harcourt so very much!"

I held her at arm's length and looked at her eyes. They were green and glistening. Perhaps she did love Lance Harcourt after all. But she was pining most grievously for Banneker, her half-brother.

When Lance Harcourt and his father arrived on Saturday morning, Fir Crest had been completely restored to its usual order. The elder Mr. Harcourt was stocky and paunchy, with the unmistakable air of wealth and good breeding about him, though perhaps gone somewhat to seed. Lance was splendidly attired in a suit of tan, with boots of the same color, but darker, and a pale yellow shirt with the usual ruffles; the senior Mr. Harcourt had squeezed himself into an outfit of drab gray, which made him appear especially funereal. But his face was jolly enough, with satisfied jowls and a rather pink cast. Like Lance's, his eyes were blue, but wiser and far more cynical, as though he had gazed upon the real world and found it not at all to his liking.

They came in a grand gilt coach attended by no less than six liveried footmen. Behind them rode a small army of Negroes in perfect formation, numbering close to twenty-five, some with rifles, others with pistols jammed into the sashes holding their gray pants. I met Mr. Harcourt on the front porch and apologized for Father's indisposition. He was most gracious, talking in a booming voice as though all within his distance were deaf. "Not too indisposed, I hope, to discuss the matter at hand?"

"Not at all, sir," I replied. Beside me, Charlotte was blushing, supremely calm, in complete contrast to her nervousness of just the day before. "This is my sister, Charlotte," I said. The old gentleman bent over her hand. "Most gracious," he murmured. "And most lovely indeed. Lance has made an excellent choice." Charlotte's color deepened, and she made a small curtsy. "You are most kind," she said. Her hair was fixed in small ringlets all over her head. She wore an empire gown of pale green, with a necklace and matching earrings of deep jade. Looking once in the direction of Lance Harcourt, she smiled, and then demurely lowered her eyes. Except for the obstinate absence of Father, it seemed a propitious beginning. The senior Mr. Harcourt was obviously disappointed that Father had not been present to see his ostentatious display. So it was left to me to comment upon it. "What an elegant carriage!" I said. "And so many men! You give the impression of being as rich as Croesus himself."

"Eh?" He aimed a quivering pink ear at me, as though he were perhaps deaf in the other. "Croesus, you say? Some neighbor of yours? No one I know by that name."

Smoothly Lance Harcourt interposed. "Croesus was a Greek king of great wealth," he said loudly, stepping around to the ear aimed at me. Charlotte would probably soon acquire herself a father-in-law, but he would be one who was half-deaf.

Apparently mollified by the comparison, Mr. Harcourt seemed to relax a bit. He slapped both hands on his belly, as though to be sure it was still there. "And where is this Parkchester fellow?" he said. "When will we see him to discuss business?"

"At once," I said. He was no more impatient than I, for Robert Gilliam had said Thursday that he would ride over today around noon. The clock in the sitting room had just struck eleven, as though I needed reminding. Today was an exact duplication of Thursday—the sky blue, cloudless, pure, serene. I felt untroubled, on the verge of happiness that Robert Gilliam would soon be here. And if all went well, that Charlotte would soon be lodged with her husband at Harcourt Manor. If Mr. Harcourt had come with his son to impress, I trusted that he was impressed in turn, for Fir Crest had never seemed more beautiful. As though reading my thoughts, Mr. Harcourt said, "You have a very lovely place here. I have heard about it, of course. But this is my first opportunity seeing it."

Now that we seemed to have reached an equal level, I decided to take him up to Father. "Please come this way, sir. Father is in his quarters. There is sherbet to refresh you. And wine, of course."

He laughed, showing teeth that were firm but quite yellow. "Wine, of course," he said. Linking his pudgy arm in Charlotte's, he followed Lance and me through the sitting room—where he commented on a few of the lesser pieces—and up the carpeted stairway and hall to Father's room.

For the occasion, Father had donned his major's uniform and seemed more vital than at any other time since he had come home. He was well-groomed and smiling as he extended his hand first to Mr. Harcourt, then to Lance. Above all else, he was a businessman. And today the discussion among men might center on marriage, but the representatives of each party would try to come out with the best possible advantage.

"My dear Mr. Harcourt!" Father said. "How good of you to come!" And to Lance, as though he had not publicly insulted him only a few days ago: "Lance, what a pleasure to see you again!" Charlotte had not been to see him since his insulting remark to her, and now he embraced her tenderly. "Forgive me, my child. All will turn out well. You will see." She flung her arms around him. "Oh, Father! It is so good to see you this way!"

Once we were settled, with Benign herself serving sherbet in crystal glasses with silver spoons, Mr. Harcourt clicked his yellow teeth, patted his swollen belly, and said, "I am most anxious to settle the matter under way. I have pressing business this afternoon back in Buckingham."

Politely Father demurred. "It is a matter of extreme complexity. May I suggest a glass of wine beforehand? It is from fox grapes, made here on the plantation. And the ladies should retire after that, as is customary." He waved a hand, and Benign came forth with the richly purple wine. Which delay appeared not at all to Mr. Harcourt's liking. But he had come seeking a bride for his son—an especially desirable bride, at that—and Father was obviously determined to press the advantage that anyone sought after retains over the seeker.

Charlotte and I finished our wine as rapidly as was decently possible. Then, excusing ourselves, with a kiss for Father to show our utter devotion to him, and our acquiescence in whatever decision he might make, we left the room and collapsed nervously in each other's arms outside the door.

"He is so *vulgar!*" Charlotte whispered. Her body was trembling. "And he also appears to be deaf."

"You are not marrying him," I whispered back. "And I believe his deafness is only in one ear. Come, now. Let us go downstairs and wait for Robert Gilliam. There is nothing more we can do here." Hand in hand, we went down to the east garden, which was already partly in shadows from the gentle sun.

Mr. Harcourt's coachmen and guards awaited in the front drive, as though to put the house under immediate siege unless their master's demands were met. For an instant I wondered about Banneker—how far he had traveled, how well he had fared—but the day itself seemed determined to keep my thoughts on an even keel. And those zephyrs of which the poets speak gathered great handfuls of May perfume and blew them our way in gentle puffs. It seemed a perfect day to discuss marriage arrangements. Robert Gilliam was coming with the Judge, possibly to do the same thing, for Robert could be quite unpredictable. My own nerves were better than Charlotte's—she fidgeted this way and that in her chair—for Robert and I were already married except in name only. The church ceremony would merely be a matter of formality.

"Charlotte, will you stop fidgeting so!" I said, but good-naturedly, for she seemed very close to the breaking point.

"I am sorry, Victoria. But what can they be doing up there so long?"

"It has been only a few minutes. Perhaps you would like to take a walk, or play some cards to keep you calm?"

"No, no." She shook her head vigorously. "That would never calm me. I feel like riding off now, wildly and rapidly, until the horse is unable to go on."

"Then do it," I urged. "No one will know the difference. They might be up there for hours. If they come out before you return, I shall make excuses."

She leaped up, looking quite wild herself. I wondered how Lance Harcourt had been able to arouse so much passion in a woman like Charlotte. But her agitation was certainly genuine. "I cannot go like this," she said.

"Then change into your riding clothes. I shall order the horse from the stable."

She turned to go, then turned back. "Tell Amos to bring me a stallion," she said. Holding her skirts high, she ran lightly from the garden and disappeared around the corner onto the porch. Smiling, I went to the kitchen and gave orders to Benign. "The child ought to be nervous," Benign grumbled. "It's the same way they done when there was slavery. Only, outdoors, without the wine and sherbet."

"Benign! What an awful thing to say!" But I, too, had noticed the similarity between the auction blocks of slavery and marriage. Indeed, the elder Mr. Harcourt had impressed me as having been a shrewd slave dealer, indeed. Would Father be a match for him? I felt a sudden urge to insert myself into their discussions and guarantee that Charlotte's dowry would be large enough to preserve her own self-esteem, but not so large as to appear that she had indeed been sold.

Benign was moving about the kitchen, making pastries and tarts, which would be served after the marriage arrangements had been agreed upon. She was so starched and pressed that she seemed to be a large stump gliding on hidden wheels. "Please tell Amos to saddle a stallion, Benign." I tasted a tart, which was quite delicious. "If I am needed, I shall be in either the orchard or the east garden."

"Yas'm." She seemed displeased; slavery was still very much in her mind. She herself had been bought and sold; how it must have rankled now to see her dear Charlotte being subjected to the civilized block.

When I got back to the east garden, Robert Gilliam and his father were riding side by side down past the orchard. My heart thrilled, and I nearly ran to meet them. But I restrained myself, for it would have been unseemly, especially if Robert had indeed come to ask for my hand.

He was smiling as they pulled up in the yard. Judge Gilliam was his usual glum self, which was quite deceptive, since he could sometimes be very amusing. He, too, had been ravaged by the war. But, possibly believing less in the goodness of man, he had been less disillusioned than Father. He was wearing black boots, a white suit and shirt with shoestring tie, and a white palmetto hat. "Good day, Victoria," he said from atop his horse. "It is a pleasure to see you again." Then he climbed down, and we embraced.

"I am so pleased to see you again, Judge Gilliam."

Robert was standing behind us now, and when the Judge released me and I turned, his arms and lips were waiting hungrily for me. The Judge made a sound halfway between a grunt and a snarl—which meant that he was withholding judgment for the moment—and went into the mansion.

"It is only two days since I saw you," Robert said. "Yet, I've missed you every minute."

"I've missed you, too," I said. We were holding hands, standing some distance from Mr. Harcourt's retinue, who kept their eyes straight ahead.

Robert laughed when I told him who they were. "They seem to be a king's army," he said. "How long will these discussions take place? Father is going to speak to your father about us."

He was so casual, but I knew that was his way. He would not stand still longer than five minutes in any talk about dowries and properties when it came to the woman he loved. "It might take a long time," I said. "Mr. Harcourt seems in fine mettle. He intends to bargain down to the last stalk of corn for his dear son."

Robert's lips curled. "I think it's obscene. I have instructed Father to ask for nothing but your hand." His eyes twinkled. "Only your hand. The rest of you can stay here at Fir Crest."

"And what good is a hand without a heart?" I said lightly. I did not know whether I approved or not of his evading the ritual or of trying to alter it. Certainly it had been established to place some kind of value on the bride. But as I looked into Robert's eyes, I knew that the ritual going on upstairs now would be of more value to the bargainers than to the bride and the prospective groom. Could they bargain away life? I saw Robert's very life in his eyes, given to me, holding me, like a distant and unyielding light. Could they put a price upon the way my heart beat and my skin tingled as he touched me, kissing me tenderly? If hearts could speak where there is love, a tremendous silence would abound.

But we were interrupted by the stormy exit from the mansion of Judge Gilliam, who obviously had not been admitted, and justly so, to the discussions. "I have been told to wait in the garden," he said sourly. "Benign, that black beast, plans to stuff me with sherbet." Although he sounded gruff, his mood was pleasant enough, and Robert and I both laughed. "I shall tell her to bring you bourbon," I said. He nodded and smiled. He seemed quite pleasant when he smiled. "That's a good girl," he said. "You'll make a fine daughter-in-law, if you keep me filled with bourbon."

We were joined by Charlotte in her riding outfit. She seemed to have lost some of her agitation, but she was still quite nervous as she greeted Robert and Judge Gilliam.

"So, the little girl is going to become a bride," Robert said as they embraced.

Unaccountably, Charlotte began to cry. "Oh, Robert, I am so afraid!"

"Of marriage?" Judge Gilliam interjected with perfect disdain. "An institution made in heaven for fools on earth." Benign had come up with the bourbon and glasses during this exchange, and she slammed them on the table to show her clear disapproval of the Judge's remarks. Then she glided away like a graceful mastodon.

"We've been feuding like this for nearly thirty years," Judge Gilliam said of Benign. "If she weren't such a black beast, I'd long ago have taken her to wife."

Which mention of marriage made Charlotte positively wail. Robert and I were both very concerned, but the Judge sprawled in the wrought-iron chair, occupied with his bourbon. Certainly his inopportune vulgarisms had killed off Robert's mother before her time—a sensitive, delicate Spanish woman of the highest breeding. But none of this latter seemed to be troubling Robert as he led Charlotte to the roses with her head on his shoulder.

"I was going to take a ride," she said between sobs. "But now I'm so upset, I'm afraid I cannot."

Even then, Amos was leading a magnificent stallion down from the stable. Poor Charlotte, I thought. Wanting to ride her troubles away in the wind. "I still think a ride would calm your nerves," I said. "But certainly not as you intend. Robert, will you take her to our place in the woods?"

He seemed very reluctant. But Charlotte clapped her hands with delight. The place where Robert and I now made love had been "our place" when he, Charlotte, Banneker, and I had been children. When any one of us was troubled—including Banneker—the others knew where to look. "Please, Robert," I said.

"Certainly, Victoria. Will you ride over once the decision has been made?"

"I shall, Robert. Meanwhile, you and Charlotte can get to know each other better." Charlotte was a distance away from us, being helped into her saddle by Amos. "Especially now since she will be your sister-in-law."

He kissed me quickly, swung into his saddle, and went up the road with Charlotte at a comfortable pace. I went to the table and sat with Judge Gilliam where he was drinking bourbon. He was also in a pensive mood. "I am an old man," he said. "I have been a lawyer for some forty years, a judge for half that time. Would you believe, dear Victoria, that I have never betrayed the confidence of a client?"

"I am sure you have not, Judge Gilliam." He had drunk more than half of the bourbon, and it was obviously affecting him. His eyes seemed watery, almost as though tears were waiting not far beneath the surface to show themselves. And his color had turned quite red.

"I am not drunk, my dear," he said, laying his hand on mine. "On the contrary, I am quite sober. For the first time in my career, I find that I am the hub around which the destinies of many men and women revolve."

"Is that not consistent with being a judge?" I asked. I felt a great unease. For as long as I had known him, I had never seen him in such a mood.

"No man can play God," he muttered. Quickly he poured himself a drink and gulped it down. "You'd better have one, too, my dear. I think you're going to need it."

Now I grabbed his hand. "What is it, Judge? Have you talked with Father? Is he refusing to sanction the marriage between Charlotte and Lance Harcourt?"

He shook his head. "He did not mention that. Last night, quite late, he sent Amos to ask me to come over to-day to discuss a matter of the greatest urgency. A short while ago when I went upstairs, he came from his quarters long enough to tell me what the business would be." Again he poured bourbon, drank, and filled his glass again, now toying with it. "Your Father wants to change his will. He wants to leave Fir Crest to Banneker. It is disgraceful that he would disinherit his own daughters for a nigger."

There are times when I find that it is best to be silent, in spite of all. It was Benign who cautioned me when I was a girl either to bite my tongue or to count to ten or twenty—one hundred, if need be—before answering hastily under extreme provocation. So, as Judge Gilliam looked at me, waiting for my reaction to his first betrayal ever of a client's confidence, I deliberately sent my mind wandering along other paths.

Banneker was of course waiting there, when we were children. It seemed the appropriate day for such memories—Banneker the oldest, then Robert, myself, and Charlotte—naked in childhood, unknowingly in love, too young to even know that love is the most deceptive of all human emotions. . . . It was a day much like any other. As usual, Banneker led us from the immedate area of the mansion, strutting with his tight butt and long legs, his superior knowledge of and about everything, not only because he was the oldest, but because he was a slave, and black, both of which made him unique in our children's minds.

It was a day of huckleberries and chinquapins, of squirrels almost maimed or killed by quickly flung rocks, of cold creek water freezing the throat and then melting in the stomach as it curled around itself like a benign snake. Charlotte was sleeping underneath an elm tree—dear, fat-cheeked, chubby Charlotte—and I was restless and curious about a sudden silence that had descended on the woods whereas before there had been the laughter and shouting of Robert and Banneker. Walking softly, I came across them hugging each other in the green, green woods. They were both naked, the black boy and the white. From the position in which they were standing side by side, I could see that both their organs were equal in size, both quite erect. Then they faced each other, rubbing their bellies and organs against each other's. But what impressed me most was the way they held to each other, as though without each other they would most certainly disappear from the face of the earth. It was almost a sacred scene, certainly something too beautiful and too private to ever mention to anyone. Nor had I ever done so. Benign's advice, then, about biting one's tongue or counting even to a million before speaking about certain things, had already been a part of me before she'd even mentioned it. . . .

"Child, are you daft?" It was poor Judge Gilliam, shaking me most rudely by the shoulder. "I tell you that your land is going to be left to a nigger, and you sit there daydreaming."

"Banneker is not a nigger," I said, which sounded surprising even to myself, considering that matters of such moment were being discussed. He was my half-brother, and if he was my father's choice to be heir of Fir Crest, he was my enemy as well. Yet, I felt the need to defend him. "Nigger" was a hateful, contemptuous word. I could never hate Banneker, nor feel contempt for him. Before he left Fir Crest, had he not given me the only legal evidence in his possession of his right to Fir Crest? If Father had suddenly gone daft, then it seemed that Father was the one who needed considering. And Judge Gilliam as well. If he had betrayed Father's confidence, why? The explanation was simple enough. He knew that Robert wanted to marry me, and I would be far more to the Judge's liking as mistress of Fir Crest, wealthy and independent in my own right, than as a near-pauper subject to the whims of my black half-brother. First, however, before I reacted to the Judge's announcement, I wanted to see how much information he really was privy to.

"You know, of course, that Banneker is Father's son, sired by him and Yetta?"

The judge spat contemptuously. "I've known it for years. That does not change matters one bit. My dear child, I am only concerned for your welfare, and that of your lovely sister. Even now, they are debating her dowry. But what can she bring to a marriage without an estate?" Anxiously he slid forth in his chair and grabbed both my hands with his. "You must talk to your father. As you know, we fought most of the war together. Sometimes I felt that he was . . . ah . . . slipping over the edge, if you know what I mean. . . ."

"I am not certain that I do, Judge. Are you suggesting that Father is legally incompetent, and therefore unable to make a new will?"

He drew back in a fine display of dreadful surprise. "My dear child! What a terrible thing to suggest! Why, your father is as sound as a gold piece! If I am suggesting anything, it is that you go immediately and talk him out of his absurd ideas. You are the one to do it, and to do it now. To be arranging a marriage with the Harcourts, while he fully intends to leave Charlotte with little or no property or wealth upon his death, is absolutely unthinkable! If I did not know your father well, if I did not care for him as I do, I would say that he is indeed mad to even think of leaving something as valuable as Fir Crest to an uneducated Negro."

"Perhaps he will leave Charlotte and me what he considers our rightful share," I said.

Now the Judge squinted. "Would you be content with that?"

"No."

"Then I suggest you talk to him at once."

Politely I demurred. If I saw Father now, I would certainly strike him, which would be a most unsuitable thing to do in front of the Harcourts. At the same time, I was not so alarmed as Judge Gilliam about Father's plans, since neither he nor Father apparently knew that Banneker had already left Fir Crest. Also, a will was not legal until it was probated upon the death of its maker. Any such will made by Father would have to be probated in Judge Gilliam's court. What the sly old Judge was really suggesting was a deal of some sort. Certainly any will not to his liking that involved me as either future or prospective daughter-in-law would never see the light of day in his courtroom.

I felt surprisingly calm. Aside from Banneker's absence, and the completely impossibility of knowing his whereabouts, I still had the paper that he'd given me, thereby abrogating his rights to wage a legal battle for Fir Crest upon Father's death. A will leaving everything to him was an entirely different matter. While Judge Gilliam was apparently crooked enough to make it disappear, Banneker was clever enough—if he ever knew of its existence, upon the death of Father—to have such a will probated in another court. Sitting in the shadow of Fir Crest, I felt a sudden chill pass over my shoulders. Among the Negroes, it is said that someone is walking across your grave when that happens. As long as Father was alive, he could be the author of the most harmful mischief. However depleted he appeared to be, there was no hope that he would die soon. "Perhaps I shall go talk to Father," I said to Judge Gilliam. "I do think the matter warrants immediate attention, if only for Charlotte's sake."

"You are perfectly right," Judge Gilliam said. He even stood, and pulled my chair back for me. "Be firm with him, but not overly so, for you know how your father can be. As your legal adviser, as well as his, I must point out that he should be made aware that certain . . . ah . . . restraints can be placed upon him until his competency is determined."

"I understand, Judge." In other words, he could have Father declared legally insane at the drop of a hat. I did not know which scandal would be worse—to have Banneker named heir to Fir Crest or to have my father declared mad. I felt slightly mad myself as I went into the mansion and upstairs to where the discussion was taking place. I felt like a pawn in a bitter and crushing game of chess, where each time my safety was assured, a greater threat appeared from another quarter. I banged on the door louder than I intended to, and the resonant male voices all ceased talking at once.

"Who is it?" Father answered.

I opened the door and walked in. "Forgive me, Father. But I must talk with you at once about a most urgent matter."

"But we are at a crucial point in this discussion!" Father cried. His sallow face seemed damp; his hair was undone, as though he had been clawing in it; and in every respect, it appeared that he was getting the worst of the discussion. As for Lance Harcourt and his father, they appeared quite serene. Indeed, the elder Mr. Harcourt felt confident enough to suggest that a break at this point might not be ill-advised. "These matters are sometimes quite tiring," he said. "Furthermore, my son and I have some private points to be clarified."

Father seemed very reluctant to leave with me, but I was determined that he should not stay. He apparently saw the resolution on my face, for he shrugged, mumbled a few words of apology to his guests, and went with me into the hallway. I carried him farther away from his own door, near that of Grandmother Parkchester's room, so that our discussion could not be overheard.

"What is so urgent that you have dragged me away from the Harcourts?" he said rudely. "Things were going quite well."

"Indeed? From your aspect, they were going quite well for the Harcourts. And what have you promised them? And have you told them that you plan to leave everything, whatever you have promised to give them, to Banneker on your death?"

His face turned even paler, if that were possible. He reached out and held to the wall for support. "You have been talking to Judge Gilliam," he said accusingly. "I thought he was my friend."

"Father!" To that point, I had been extremely cool, although the ingredients for fury were cooking inside me. Now they came spilling out, like a pot that boils over. "You are concerned about your friend even as you are preparing to disinherit both your daughters for a nigger!" The word was still distasteful to me, but it felt good in the saying. For it indicated the utter disdain in which my father held me and Charlotte—that he should make us the laughingstock of the entire South, that he should make us subject to a nigger who had once been our slave.

"Judge Gilliam has violated my confidence," Father said. "I think there are boards, commissions, which frown upon that sort of thing."

Was it possible that he was indeed mad? For the first time in my life, I touched him in anger. I caught him by his scrawny shoulders and shook him soundly, until his face was quite red. When I released him, he was breathing heavily. "You are to listen to me carefully," I said softly but intensely, "for I shall not repeat myself. Judge Gilliam has told me how you often acted irrationally in the war. I myself am prepared to swear in a court of law that you have acted irrationally here as well. . . ."

His eyes grew wide and frightened. "You would have me declared mad?"

"Yes! Unless you stop this ridiculous plan of making Banneker your heir! He is not to receive even one weed, not one grain of corn, in your will! There is to be no mention of him anywhere! If, from this day forth, you even speak his name, I myself shall have the papers drawn up to have you committed."

He was trembling like a whipped cur, but I felt no sympathy for him. I myself was trembling with passion I had never felt before. That he should lie with a Negress was vile enough; but that he should drag out his bastard these many years later and hold it up for all the world to see— that was insupportable.

"Banneker is my son," he said stubbornly. "He is brave and resourceful. I watched him from my window as he drove the raiders off. Don't you understand how proud I felt?"

"And what of me?" I cried. "And Charlotte? Did we not also fight? Have we not worked like slaves—worse than slaves—to preserve Fir Crest so that you could come home and go straight to bed? What manner of man are you, that you are so blind to what is fair and proper?"

"I am your father," he whispered pitifully. "You have no right to speak to me thus."

"I am your daughter, and I have every right! You will do as I have instructed, or I swear by all things holy that I shall see you rot in a madhouse!"

It seemed as though his knees would give way. I propped him against the wall, holding him there by sheer force. "As for your discussion with the Harcourts, you are dragging things out far too long. Whatever their demands, accede to them. You are not bartering over a slave; you are discussing your daughter's dowry."

For a moment I thought that he would faint. Instead, he pushed me away, turned, and started up the hall. But I was not finished with him. Moving quickly, I stepped in front of him, barring his way. "The paper you gave to Yetta, giving legitimacy to Banneker, is in my possession," I said.

"Did you kill her?" he whispered. "I have wondered since you told me. You are quite capable of murder, you know. You have just murdered me."

Indeed, he was quite mad. "I, murder Yetta? For what reason?"

He shrugged. "Does passion need a reason? I have always admired your strength, Victoria. I did not think I would live to see it turned against me. I shall do exactly as you say."

I felt giddy with triumph. "Then there will be no further problems between us, Father. Once you have made your new will, I shall discuss it with Judge Gilliam. But for now, you are to return to the Harcourts and finish matters at once. Charlotte is with Robert Gilliam down at the creek. I shall ride to tell them that all has been agreed upon . . . including my marriage to him."

"Very well," Father said. Shoulders sagging, he went back into his room. I had deliberately withheld from him one important piece of information—that Banneker had left Fir Crest—for I feared that it would make him more determined to have his way, and quite unmanageable.

My legs were weak, and it took every effort to make it to my room, where I lay on the bed until I felt calmer. Then I changed into riding clothes, went downstairs, and ordered my horse from the stable.

Judge Gilliam was still in the garden drinking bourbon. "You have seen your father?" he asked eagerly.

"I have seen him. All is well. He will do the right thing. When the new will is drawn up, you and I together will make certain that it is proper."

The Judge nodded graciously. "You are indeed a remarkable woman. I shall keep you informed."

We said good-bye, and I mounted Sally. In a short while, I was ascending the crest of firs, on my way to meet Charlotte and Robert with the good news that our marriages had been approved. But the best of it—that I had bent Father to my will—I would keep to myself for the time being. Perhaps I would keep it to myself forever.

While I did not feel a saint, neither did I feel a sinner. I certainly was not proud of myself; but we at Fir Crest had been raised to believe in a 250-year-old tradition of excellence and perpetuation. That Father had come from the war sufficiently unbalanced to think of giving away all that generations of Parkchesters had worked and fought to preserve meant that someone had to step in and stop him by whatever means. He himself would probably be grate-

ful for what I was doing, once he returned to his proper
senses. *You have just murdered me.* What an odd and
forceful thing for him to say, particularly when I had surprised him in the process of murdering me.

Although the day was delightfully warm, I felt wrapped
in a sudden chill. I spurred Sally on, for we had been riding slowly up the crest of firs and down to Robert Gilliam's. And as the mare speeded up, I felt an incredible
sense of liberation. Love was also very much in the fore-
front of my mind, and I thought how incredible it is that
flesh—Robert's and mine—blended together, seems to
speak with liquid voices and tongues of fire. Certainly love
is more than physical, but the body is a door through
which the soul enters its proper dwelling place, and there
embraces its flaming mate. Today he had worn a faded
blue shirt, blue pants, and black boots. But as he had embraced me in the garden, I had felt as though he and I
were both naked. Certainly to my eyes he had come to ask
for my hand naked, assured and pleased with his manhood, proud and excited because I was woman—his
woman. And Sally beneath me seemed struck by my excitement, as though it filtered down to her from me. And
her hooves bit into the dirt with an almost happy sound as
we rode past the fields and up into our place—Robert's
and mine. And there in the center of the ring of old trees,
certainly in the very spot where Robert had possessed my
nakedness on two occasions, he was now struggling with
my sister Charlotte in amorous embrace.

He was barefoot, shirtless. The muscles in his back
bunched in fine ridges as he fought to contain Charlotte.
Her shirtwaist was torn, and her lovely breasts were fully
exposed. Even from where I watched in utter dismay, still
mounted on Sally, I could see that my sister's breasts were
bruised, excited, bleeding in spots. Her hair was undone,
and her lips were pulled back in a leonine snarl, the teeth
white and dangerous. Valiantly she struggled against the
man I loved, the man who claimed to love me—half-
naked, his eyes wild and body rigid as he tried to possess
my sister.

"Victoria, help me!" she cried.

I dared not dismount, for I was certain that my legs
would not hold me. Blind with anger, I reached for the
pistol in my saddle pack. Even as my fingers touched it,

my entire body seemed to turn icy cold with anger. Was there no honor among men? Was not one of them to be trusted? I withdrew the pistol from its holster, cocked the trigger, and fired into the air. The explosion resounded in the stillness like the sudden dropping of a lethal cannonball. At once Robert unhanded Charlotte and whirled. His eyes were wild, impassioned, his lips twisted. "Victoria!" It was all I permitted him to say. He was standing with his legs apart, that arrogant stance of all men who view women as mere creatures of pleasure. It was an incredible scene, all the more so because I was almost breathless with love and excitement for him even as I hated him. I aimed the pistol at his head, then his heart, his genitals. Father had said I was capable of committing murder, and I was on the verge of doing so. Now it was Charlotte who called my name. Hiding her breasts under her hands, she ran to me and half-swooned against the mare. "Kill him!" she cried. "He claims to love you, but he has tried to violate me! Kill him!"

I squeezed the trigger, and dirt leaped up between Robert's legs. "Victoria!" he cried. I gave him time for nothing else. Again I placed a shot in the ground between those parted legs. "Leave here!" I cried. "Leave before I kill you!"

"I would remind you," he said quite calmly, planting hands on his lean hips, "that this is my land. If anyone should leave it is you and your sister." But I was not so easily dissuaded, for the place had been "ours" since childhood. Now Robert had violated it even as he had tried to violate my sister. "Leave!" I cried. This time I aimed for his heart, that false repository of all his lying declarations. We glared at each other across the distance of universes. Then he went to his horse, swung into the saddle, and rode off. He had left his boots and shirt in a pile on the ground. Later on, I thought, he would send for them.

Some perverse notion caused me to dismount. I collected his boots and shirt and flung them into the creek. By the time he sent for them, they would be on their way to Richmond, for the current in the creek was strong; farther along, it joined the James River, which flowed past Richmond into Chesapeake Bay and the Atlantic beyond.

Now Charlotte was beside me, then sobbing in my arms. She had covered her nakedness with her riding jacket. I hated the touch of her, but I put my arms around her and said soothing things until she was able to talk. "What happened?" I finally said. Yet a little while longer, and she would be Lance Harcourt's wife, with him to account to even as he protected her.

"It all happened so quickly," she said, "that I am not quite sure. One minute, Robert and I were chatting amiably. The next, he had grabbed me passionately and tried to make love to me. I fought him as best I could, for he is very strong. Thank God you rode up when you did."

There were bruises on her face as well as on her arms and breasts. I disliked the way she clung and trembled, the whine in her voice, the very smell of her, which was not unpleasant, but nonetheless distasteful. All her life I had been as much mother and father to her as sister—lying for her, overlooking her shortcomings, forgiving her peccadilloes, soothing her when she awakened from nightmares, even surviving nightmares that she had created for me by her own blundering stubbornness and stupidity. I could rest comfortably now, for all that soon would end. I would not be marrying Robert Gilliam, but she would marry Lance Harcourt if I myself had to perform the ceremony.

"Let us go," I said. "The marriage between you and Lance has been arranged."

She was still trembling, holding to me for dear life. "Not yet, Victoria. Please. Let us wait awhile. I do believe you are angry with me. I swear to you that I did not provoke Robert Gilliam at all. I have always cherished him as a brother, never as a lover. Are you angry, Victoria?"

"Yes." It seemed no time to lie.

"Are you angry with me? Please tell me, Victoria, for I could not bear to live if you are angry with me about what has happened."

I was amazed at the extent of loathing and disgust I felt for her. Might not all of us be better off if she were dead? I felt guilty no sooner than the thought formed in my mind. Like all women, she was a victim of men. Lovelier than most, she aroused the basest instincts in the loftiest men. Was I right in condemning her?

I tightened my arms around her. "Forgive me, dear Charlotte. I know that you did nothing to provoke Robert. Like all men, he sometimes lets his passion rule his reason."

"Will you ever forgive him?" she asked, snuggling closer. There was a nasty bruise on her left shoulder, almost the exact imprint of Robert's hand.

"I shall never forgive him. But that is not important now. We must return to the house and make plans for your wedding."

She said nothing, but it seemed that her belly, where it touched mine, seemed first to recoil, then to churn with the unmistakable movement of life. Alarmed, I pushed her away.

"You are pregnant!" I cried.

She dropped to the ground in a near-faint. I felt like kicking her. "Stand up!" I cried. But she bent closer to the ground, holding her belly with both hands, crying again. Angrily I caught her by the chin and forced her to look at me.

"Whose child is it? How long have you been pregnant?"

Again, as when I was locked in love with Robert, the wise and weary old trees seemed to be listening with bated breath.

"It is Banneker's," she said. "And I am well into my fourth month. I did not know for certain until the day he left. Then it was too late to do anything."

"And what would you have done?" I said bitterly. "I asked you—I *ordered* you—to leave Banneker alone." My voice was sharp, the muscles in my face tight with horror. "You fool! You fool! Do you not know that Banneker is your half-brother?"

She looked so shocked that I could only pity her, and my anger dissolved into compassion.

"How could that be?" she whispered.

"Father had an affair with Yetta before either you or I was born. Charlotte, dear Charlotte . . . why did you continue with Banneker? I told you to stop. I pleaded with you. Now look what has happened."

She seemed to be deep inside her own thoughts. "Yetta always gave me something to drink before. Now Yetta is dead." Desperately she grabbed my hands. "I shall kill myself, Victoria! I could not bear the disgrace!"

"Hush! You are talking foolishness! Are you certain that it was Banneker? Might it not have been Lance Harcourt?"

She shook her head firmly. "It was Banneker. I saw him

only once after you told me not to. I had never seen him like that before. He was cruel, bitter. He wanted to hurt me . . . and he did . . . dreadfully. . . . At the last moment, he whispered, 'I'm going to give you something to remember me by.' " Ruefully she patted her stomach. "I suppose this is what he meant. I had never felt him in me so deeply before. I think I knew then that he had planted his child in me."

"Damn Banneker!" Would we never be free of his name, his deeds, the consequences of his deeds? "First he has an affair with you. Then Father wants to make him sole heir to Fir Crest."

"Sole heir?" She stood then, strong, defiant, unafraid. "Father must be mad! And what is to become of us?"

"Do not worry about that. I have already talked him out of it. Judge Gilliam is backing us up. Father is not well. It will take time to undo the war's damage. Our main concern now is what to do about you. I shall speak to Benign. Surely she will have some ideas."

"Dear Victoria! I am so relieved that you know now. I should have told you as soon as I suspected. But I was afraid." She seemed considerably better; and with my help, she was able to mount the stallion. "But what will become of you and Robert Gilliam?" she said. "Will you ever see him again?"

"Never." I climbed atop Sally.

"What a pity," Charlotte said sadly.

"A pity indeed!" I snapped. If it were possible, my heart was dissolving in bitter tears.

We rode back to Fir Crest in a chaos of silence, until I finally blurted out: "You say that Yetta used to give you something to prevent pregnancy. Did she also give you the laudanum?"

Charlotte moved her mount closer to mine, as though we would be overheard by malicious tongues. "No, it was not Yetta. It was Grandmother Parkchester. She used it herself. I was young then, and I did not know it was wrong. When I did find out, it was too late." Now our legs in our stirrups were touching, we were that close. "You made me see the light, Victoria. I thank you very much for that."

"You're very welcome," I said dryly. But at the same time, my head was reeling. Grandmother Parkchester!

What an extraordinarily evil thing to have done! I pitied Charlotte even more as we approached Fir Crest, and I was more determined than ever to protect her from the irresponsibility of others. Grandmother Parkchester had made her a drug addict and a bawd; Father had spoiled her and diluted her discipline. I had always loved her, but had my love been sufficient? Whatever had sent her to the slave cabins to seek out Banneker had, hopefully, been corrected. Now it was necessary to eliminate all evidence of those trips.

When we got to the mansion, Father, Lance Harcourt and his father, and Judge Gilliam were smoking, drinking, and chatting on the porch. They seemed peaceful enough, even Father; and they greeted us cordially. "This is an especially important day," Father said. Except for a slight wildness in his eye, he appeared quite normal. "I am happy and sad at the same time, for I have agreed to give both my daughters in marriage."

Lance and Charlotte embraced; Father and the senior Mr. Harcourt shook hands. "Hear, hear!" Judge Gilliam cried, applauding lightly. Only then did he seem to notice the absence of his own son. "And where is Robert, Victoria? This is a most auspicious day. He should not be absent."

"He said there was pressing business at the farm," I said. "Perhaps he will be along later."

The Judge pulled out a gold watch and consulted it. "I cannot wait; I have business of importance myself." He said good-bye to everyone. When it was my turn, he hooked his arm in mine, and I walked with him to his horse. "The discussion went extremely well with your father," he said. "Banneker's name was never mentioned—I think perhaps he was making a bad joke earlier—and he indicated that you are indeed heiress of Fir Crest, under the existing will, as well as in the new one he intends to draw up. He is to ride to my place in one or two weeks with the new will. Of course, I shall keep you fully informed."

"Of course, Judge." He kissed me on the cheek. I wondered what he would say when he found out that Robert and I would never be married. Would he still have such an interest in our internal affairs at Fir Crest? He mounted his horse with help from Amos, and rode off waving.

Then it was time for the Harcourts to depart. Lance had been especially silent, almost sullen. But the senior Mr. Harcourt was well into his cups. He climbed into his carriage with surprising agility for his size and weight. Lance slid in after him. "Lance," I said, "I would like to welcome you to our family." His voice was quite glum as he thanked me. He hardly seemed the picture of a happy prospective bridegroom, and I wondered what had happened to suddenly throw him into such bad humor. The driver and footmen had taken their positions, and the entire retinue circled the mansion and then thundered away. As for Charlotte and Father, they had gone upstairs together. So I was left alone on the porch. Alone, it seemed, in the entire world, which appeared to have capriciously and dramatically aligned itself against me.

FIVE

A week later we attempted to bring about an abortion in Charlotte. For some inexplicable reason, Charlotte wanted the thing done in Mother's room, in Mother's own bed, which struck me as being grotesque and altogether uncalled for. But Charlotte insisted until I finally gave in. I hardly cared at that point whether or not she abort. I myself was filled with such pain that I would have agreed to anything that did not add to my own devastation, for Robert Gilliam had made no effort of which I was aware to get in touch with me. Nor I with him. Even Benign took an entire week to decide to take charge of the operation. She was opposed to it for Christian reasons, which impressed me as being ironic and unbecoming, that a converted black savage could presume to be more Christian than decent white folk.

Nonetheless, on the following Saturday morning the three of us gathered like thieves in Mother's room with all manner of bottles, jugs, herbs, lotions, roots, towels, pots, pans, talismans, and even a Bible—which seemed to belong to Benign—for the purpose of killing Banneker's baby, which was clinging to the walls of Charlotte's womb. Curiosity had compelled me to ask Charlotte that morning about Lance Harcourt's bad humor of a week before. "He wanted me to go with him to spend the weekend in Buckingham," she explained. "When I refused, he became annoyed." So there was love after all, which seemed to justify the thing we had gathered in Mother's quarters to do. Father's room was across the hall, but he had been in complete seclusion since giving his consent to the marriage agreements. Neither Charlotte nor I knew what dowry he had decided upon for us; in due season, he would have to tell us. Until then, we would have to be content—I more so than Charlotte, for I was most anxious to see what value he had placed upon me. Benign continued in service to him, and kept us informed of his welfare. But he had let it be known that he did not want to be disturbed by anyone. I, for one, was willing to leave him in seclusion. Charlotte was unaware of all others but herself all week. She was a bundle of nerves waiting for Benign to give in. And when Benign finally gave her consent, we went to Mother's room, tucking Charlotte into bed with a plain white shift, and began the abortion. I was not unaware of a further irony: if Father had wanted Banneker to be his heir, then Banneker's heir was about to be murdered in the womb, only a few paces away from Father's room.

Benign had raised the sheet and was busily working between Charlotte's legs. Perhaps to put Charlotte more at ease, she said, "I hopes you know you might die from this. If you don't, I hopes you learn to keep these here legs closed." Normally, Charlotte would have had some kind of retort, but she seemed terrified and in great pain as Benign knelt closer and closer, working assiduously with what seemed to be a kind of bellows that she had inserted inside of Charlotte.

"I feel as though I am going to burst!" Charlotte cried. "What is it that you're doing?"

Benign raised her head long enough to say, "I killing Banneker's child, that's what I doing. What you think I doing?"

Except for the circumstances, I might have smiled. I watched Benign until she finished under the sheets. Then she tucked them in nicely around Charlotte's feet and gave her something to drink. "This is for the pain. In a little while, you going to feel terrible pain."

"I already feel terrible pain," Charlotte said.

"You should've kept your legs closed," Benign said. "Now, drink this. I got other work to do, in case you didn't know."

Charlotte drank the concoction and then lay back while Benign arranged her pillows. "Why do you dislike me so, Benign? You never have a kind word for me."

Benign seemed surprised. "You think I dislike you, child? Would I be doing this if I didn't love you? You just talking foolishness."

Charlotte touched her large black arm. "You're right, Benign. I am talking foolishness. And I love you, too, even though I do cause you trouble."

Benign grunted. "Ain't no trouble at all. It just mean I going to roast in hell. When the baby come, it'll pop out like a grape seed." She turned, took several steps, and then said, "It's going to be dead, in case you didn't know. Now, I got to go fix dinner. We having roast lamb. I don't suppose you'll be wanting any."

Charlotte made a face and turned her head. To keep from smiling—at least, to keep Charlotte from seeing me smiling—I picked up the Charlottesville *Gazette*, which I had brought along, and which had only recently resumed publication. Benign left the room, closing and locking the French doors. Charlotte was staring at the canopy, and seemed to be in deep thought. I began to read the lead story in the paper:

BANDITS KILLED BY U.S. TROOPS

Charlottesville—While bands of terrorists continue to operate in and around our fair city, one of the most nefarious of them was given the death blow last week when soldiers of the United States Army entrapped a group of some two dozen brigands and killed them in close and bloody combat. Later, as a warning to other looters, sackers, and raiders, the body of the leader and six of his men were placed on display before the Jefferson Museum in downtown Charlottesville. This correspondent saw seven of the most ungodly men who ever lived. But it was the aspect of the leader that caused the most comment. For he was obviously of good family, quite blond, certainly very attractive when alive, with a black patch of leather over one eye, which had been lost, according to rumor, in a duel about a lady of questionable virtue. Many people came to see the corpses, and expressed satisfaction that the federal soldiers had acted so decisively. Their presence here is welcomed more each day, as unscrupulous persons converge upon our fair city from all over the globe, a phenomenon that is said to be occurring all over the South. . . .

I folded the paper and laid it aside. So, at last, the bandit chief was dead, for the description fitted him to perfection. I wanted to show the story to Charlotte, but she had fallen asleep. So I was left to my own thoughts, which centered around the newspaper's rather lurid descriptions of what was then taking place in the South, and of what was happening in the North, especially in Washington.

Upon the South's defeat, the area had quickly been divided into five military districts administered by a high-ranking army officer. We in Charlottesville were in the district commanded by Brigadier General Eustace Witherspoon, a humane and proper gentleman from Boston who was, at the same time, quite blind to the realities that surrounded him.

When a civilization such as ours collapses in ruins and dust, and the land is occupied by the conqueror, he is faced with several pernicious problems, the attempted solution of which became known as the Reconstruction, and which involved not only the South, but the North as well.

In the North, in Washington, D.C., there was political turmoil. While President Lincoln had been committed to a policy of benevolence toward the South, other factions in Congress were equally determined not to show even an ounce of mercy. This latter group appeared to be backed by President Andrew Johnson, who went to war with Congress from the minute he assumed the presidency.

Johnson was a Tennessean, from a dirt-poor family, and his early politics—for he had been in office only a few weeks—soon smacked of contradiction. On the one hand, it was said he limped slightly as a result of ill-treatment as a child, and one would have expected his own misfortune to have made him amenable to the aims of the Negroes. Yet, by breeding and inclination, Johnson was a southern white man who, like any southerner, must have been appalled by the prospect of some three million freed blacks roaming the South, free to do as they pleased, yet ill-prepared to do more than cause trouble, which was generally settled by the army to the disadvantage of whites. Johnson certainly was aware of this, and presented legislation designed to bring about the slow integration of Negroes into the larger population. Confronting him was a Congress that was almost hysterically pro-Negro, egged on by abolitionists and other do-gooders, who invoked the ghost of

Lincoln to add greater fuel to the fires of emotionalism. Indeed, had not sounder minds prevailed, it is possible that the entire country would have been given to Negroes as a kind of *mea culpa* for the fact that slavery had existed at all. Later events would enforce the present reality—that ruins and eventually settle, and must be restructured for the betterment of the general society. At the moment, however, even the smallest explosion in Washington sent shock waves through the entire South. . . .

Charlotte moaned, and I left my thoughts to attend to her. She was breathing heavily, and seemed somewhat feverish, but Benign had warned that that might happen. I dabbed her forehead with a towel, and held her hand for a while until she appeared to go back into untroubled sleep. It struck me as grossly unreal that Mother was dead, that we were here in her bedroom for the purpose of aborting Banneker's baby from Charlotte's body—indeed, that most of us had survived, while Mother had been our first casualty, and that the war had come to its conclusion without her being here to welcome it. All her books and newspapers were as she had left them. Her silver thimble was on the dresser, and I handled it lovingly. If indeed she had been a New Orleans prostitute before marrying Father, I had known her only as kind, genteel, remarkable in every way. And I would remember her thus, regardless of what Father might say. . . .

There is a kind of spider that rides a thread of its own web as it seeks a proper home even as it is blown this way and that by the spring wind. Riding the shock waves emanating from the War Between the States, and taking advantage of the concussion and dislocation following that explosion, came an army of drifters, grafters, and ne-'er-do-wells who found the South defeated and bleeding, and proceeded to bleed her even more. Those individuals, men as well as women, had already established firm bases in the ruins, breathing the dust of destruction, worming their way into the political, social, and economic life of an injured society.

As for the Negroes, they were, in those early days of freedom, leaning more heavily than ever on their former owners. Whereas one may have anticipated desertions in droves, the exact opposite was true; and, in the prevailing disorder, it became clear that if the main purpose of the war had been to free the slaves—and not even the silliest abolitionist could have believed that—then what had come from such a costly and bloody encounter was that blacks and whites alike had both become subservient to the North, to its mores, its moods, its morals, and especially to its bloated sense of superiority. . . .

I heard a key turn in the door, and Benign came into the room. "Is she all right?" she said, feeling Charlotte's forehead.

"She seems to be," I said. "Will it take long, Benign?"

"As long as it takes, missy. That ain't no white child up there. That's Banneker's child, and he going to hang on for dear life. It's going to take some time."

She sounded proud and yet complacent; and I found myself wondering if perchance she might not be enjoying the spectacle of seeing Charlotte and me in these most dismal of circumstances. If a mulatto child was about to be aborted, the lofty ideals of both North and South had long since gone down the drain, perhaps even before the first shots had been fired at Fort Sumter. Benign herself had asked me if I'd thought that Negroes were worth fighting a war over. Watching her as she fussed over Charlotte, I was, as usual, impressed by the way she incorporated gentleness and delicacy into her every movement, despite her massiveness. If Charlotte was a symbol of the South bloated with the seed of its slaves, then Benign was a pawn in a contest that had little to do with her or her kind—Mrs. Beecher Stowe to the contrary—but was designed to impose the authority of the federal government upon the individual states. Well, the authority had been imposed; now it was up to the federal government to enforce it.

Charlotte groaned and opened her eyes. "I feel sick, Benign. I feel as though I'm going to vomit."

In a flash Benign had an enameled basin on the bed. "You just go ahead and throw up, honey. But try to hold it if you can. It'll just make things worse."

"Yes, Benign." She closed her eyes, apparently to sleep again—trusting, content even in pain, almost gullible in her blind faith that things would turn out as Benign said they would.

It was an incredible sensation that caused me to cry out

audibly. Benign turned at once. Her great dark eyes raked me up and down. "What's the matter with you, child?"

"Nothing, Benign. Nothing at all."

She grunted, and went on fussing over Charlotte. Then, leaving more instructions—"If she wake up again, give her some of that stuff in the green bottle, about a teaspoonful. If she start going into labor, you call me right away, you hear?"—she again went out, probably to attend to the roasting of the lamb, locking the door again behind her.

I had been thinking earlier along the line of symbols. Certainly I myself epitomized the plight of thousands, perhaps millions of white men and women throughout the South, who were prepared for a new beginning, provided that the new South rested firmly upon the foundations of the old. Clearly there had been imperfections in slavery, and Charlotte, as well as Father, was an example of authority gone wild, wherein slaves were used for the basest purposes simply because they were there, owned as surely as though they had been a favorite jacket or a comfortable pair of boots. A tremendous moral strength was needed in humans to keep one from abusing the other, especially when the other group—those millions of pliant, grinning, groveling blacks—seemed to take great pleasure in being used.

It was this thought that had caused me to cry out. "What is the matter with you, child?" And I had said that nothing was the matter. But it seemed to me then that everything was wrong. And I settled down in Mother's favorite chair and tried to apply myself to a consideration of that black beast—to use Judge Gilliam's expression—known simply as Benign. Was it possible, for example, that she was, in some way, responsible for all the death and destruction that had taken place at Fir Crest since shortly after the war's beginning?"

There were stories that reached us of large and aggressive black women who performed miracles in terms of freeing their people, getting them passage on the so-called underground railroad, sending them to contacts in the northern United States, and even farther into Canada, where they would forever be free of one kind of bondage, but certainly subject to another. To my awareness, Benign was not involved in this kind of thing. But . . . was she involved in the taking over of Fir Crest? No other human was better equipped, by virtue of her position, and the trust and confidence we placed in her, to function as a viper in the very breast of Fir Crest.

That the evidence against her was almost nonexistent could have been a greater indication of her cleverness and guilt. That she had suffered the most terrible loss—husband, sons, and other relations—in the candle-house fire, and her subsequent serenity, might easily have been a sign of her madness. For surely whoever it was that worried Fir Crest almost unto death, who assaulted and withdrew, then assaulted again—whatever mind was behind such strategy certainly belonged to a madman. Or a madwoman. Looked at that way, Benign seemed the most probable suspect, precisely because she seemed the most unlikely. Could she, from the kitchen at Fir Crest, command an army of brigands? Could she ruthlessly snuff out the lives of her entire family in order to gain Fir Crest? Could she, in friendly conversation with Yetta, suddenly reach over with a straight razor and cut the other woman's throat?

She could. She was the strongest woman I had ever known, capable of the most amazing feats. With the bandit chief dead, as reported by the Charlottesville *Gazette*, with the South in an uproar, suddenly conscious of the minds of millions of blacks who heretofore had been merely bodies—and, even then, practically invisible—anything was possible in these days of atonement and revenge. And Benign had taught me long ago that she, more than any other human, could do the impossible without batting an eye. . . .

"Victoria?"

"Yes, dear?"

Charlotte was smiling, and her face was radiant, like in paintings by the old masters of saints just as they have looked into heaven. It seemed incongruous that she was so complacent in the very bed where Mother had been raped to death.

"What is it, dear?" I thought perhaps she might have wanted a drink of water, she sounded that calm.

"I think the baby has come out," she said quietly.

I rushed to the bed and inspected. There, in a pile of blood and slime, was Banneker's perfectly formed child. It was unmistakably his, and it was quite dead.

I was seized with the deepest possible horror. As for Charlotte, she was smiling, as though the act of abortion had made her quite mad. Frantically I rang for Benign. She came huffing into the room in seconds. I was too horrified to speak, so I only pointed. Efficiently Benign folded the sodden sheets carefully around the dead child, wrapping them into a perfect bundle. Then she enclosed it in yet another sheet. "I'll get rid of this," she said. "You rest, child," she said to Charlotte. And to me: "You'd better have some brandy. You look like you need it."

Indeed I did. But what did she need? Dead babies to get rid of? Five thousand acres of choice land, with her at its helm? Two white women and a half-mad white man under her absolute control? As I drank first one brandy, then another, I became determined to watch her ever more carefully. And, if need be, to fight her with all the resources at my command. Which were not many. I had a rifle, a long-barreled pistol, and a derringer under my personal control. Now, lined against me—if Benign indeed was the secret enemy—were herself and some five hundred Negroes backing her. Plus a federal army that would give her the right in any dispute. Looked at that way, any encounter between Benign and me would not merely be a conflict, it would be a massacre of incredible proportions. . . .

On Benign's advice, Charlotte agreed to spend the next several days in bed. "I got to do more things to you now that we done sinned. A few more won't matter." With the ordeal over, Charlotte seemed in extremely high spirits, and restless to return to her own room. This was done with Benign and me supporting her between us. Actually, Benign could have picked her up and carried her alone. And my mind returned to undefined suspicions that taunted my very reason.

Was my imagination playing tricks on me again? I had imagined that Robert Gilliam loved me, and that had proved false. I had seen—or thought I'd seen—the lock on the candle house snapped shut during the fire. Later on, Banneker had brought it to me opened. But could he not have been acting in concert with Benign? And what of the only real evidence that did exist: *someone* had cut Yetta's throat. An agent of Benign's? As she supported Charlotte's weight against hers, all my reasoning seemed utterly without basis. If her intention was to get rid of us all, why not simply drop poison in our food? Still, I felt a sense of great unease. Was it possible that I was losing my mind?

After we had put Charlotte to bed, Benign went to check on Father. I wanted to tell Charlotte of my suspicions about Benign—if they could be called that, rather than mere wool-gathering—when Benign herself burst back into the room, beaming from ear to ear. "Lawd!" She clapped both hands together. "Massa Parkchester say he feel fine. He say he want a dinner party one week from today. He seem his old self again, except he say he don't want Judge Gilliam to come."

Charlotte sat up in bed, with tears streaming down her cheeks. "Oh, I'm so glad!" she cried. And suddenly Benign and I had hooked hands and were dancing in a joyous circle around an imaginary maypole. If Father was coming from his room, it meant that he had, finally, come home again. But even as Benign and I laughed and danced, I felt a deep suspicion moving underneath the outer layer of joy. Who was this woman that she could perform an abortion, roast a lamb, put Father back on his feet, and dance a jig with me all in the same day, all within a few hours of each other? Certainly her talents were so varied that murder and sedition must be numbered among them. I felt dizzy, almost panic-stricken, as though I were locked with some huge beast in a *danse macabre*. But as we whirled, her eyes were full of gladness; her smile appeared quite genuine; and, but for my own nagging suspicions, I would have felt that today was the happiest at Fir Crest for a long time. Charlotte must have thought so, for she bounced on the bed and clapped her hands in time to our grotesque whirling. "We shall have . . . only Lance Harcourt . . ." I managed to say between huffing and puffing, "since he and . . . Charlotte are engaged. . . . I do not want . . . to overburden Father . . . on the first occasion. . . ." It seemed an extraordinary thing to say, under the circumstances. Benign danced and danced, carrying me with incredible speed. Before I collapsed breathless on the bed, where she eventually flung me, laughing happily, I wondered if she had wanted to see whether she could make my heart burst by dancing. . . . But my heart was still intact, insofar as its structure was concerned; and it cried out woefully: *Oh, Robert Gilliam, why did you betray me?*

None of us, except Benign, saw Father for the entire week that followed. He did, however, let us know by way of Benign that he wanted Dr. Seymour, the elder Mr. Harcourt, and Mrs. Pennington, the lady from Charlottesville, to be included among the guests. Also, he outlined a most elegant menu—cream of asparagus soup, stuffed breast of partridge, French-style string beans, parsley potatoes, glazed beets, assorted fruits and pastries, three kinds of wine, plus liqueurs before and after dinner. Thankfully, Dr. Seymour sent his immediate regrets, apparently since there would neither be sickness nor death that he knew of. Father and Mrs. Pennington were very old friends, and it was another encouraging sign that he wanted her among the guests. Judge Gilliam's name was conspicuous by its absence, which meant that Father was still smarting under the fact that the Judge had spoken to me about the will. No one mentioned Robert Gilliam, but he was very much in my mind. There was a continuous conflict between the part of me that wanted and needed him and that part that could not bear to see him after his attempt to make love to Charlotte. Indeed, I awakened most mornings with a sense of the greatest apprehension, as though I might look in the mirror and see that madness had crept upon me while I slept fitfully, or that I might find that the rafters of Fir Crest had collapsed around me in the night.

One morning I was breakfasting in the east garden when it seemed to me that the house had assumed gigantic proportions. There were Negroes everywhere upon it, like large black ants, washing windows, touching up the whitewash where it had been eaten away by the elements. But for some reason the mansion seemed almost double its size. I blinked my eyes and rubbed them, and when I looked again, it held its usual serene aspect. But I was most troubled—there was a frightening turmoil inside me, and I had been aware for several days of a sense of the greatest uncertainty. Of course, it had to do with Robert Gilliam, his dreadful betrayal of me; the lies he had told even as he had possessed me; and the plans we had made about the future, certainly filled with the usual blend of foolishness and fantasy, but nonetheless true to my mind.

Obviously, to his, they had been merely a way of toying with me without any consideration at all for my own feelings. It was during this week preceding the dinner party that I found myself drinking more and more heavily—secretly, of course, in my room—but it gave me little solace. Finally, in desperation, I went into Father's study on the first floor and opened the top drawer in the desk there. The laudanum I had taken from Charlotte was where I had left it. Like the lowest kind of thief, I dropped it into the pocket of my dress and sneaked to my room. I remember praying before I drank it—that it would kill me . . . and that it would not kill me. Either way, I would find peace from the anxiety that seemed to squeeze my brain in an ever-tightening fist. I turned the bottle to my lips and drank. Then I lay on the bed, waiting for the event to happen.

But what came to pass frightened me even more, although it took place inside a kind of haze, as though all reality had been covered over with gauze. Quite plainly, I saw Father, the figure of him looming like a colossus over Fir Crest. There was no sign of Charlotte, but I was a small ant trying to climb his boots. He laughed, looking down at me. With a large finger, he brushed me to the ground. And then his boot rose above me like a darkening of clouds, and came down, and crushed me. . . .

I leaped up. Certainly I was drugged, for a part of me felt completely at ease, almost somnolent. But then there was the devilish other part that whispered desperate and evil thoughts to the portion of my brain that was alert. Father was taking over control of Fir Crest. He preferred to deal with Benign rather than with me. He had taken charge of the dinner party. Somehow—perhaps with the help of Benign—he had not only regained his strength, but was determined to flex his muscles in a fine show of force. Perhaps the most insulting part of all was that he—with the help of Benign—had planned the menu. Well, as long as he stayed in his room, I could perhaps do something about that.

Despite the small clamoring of tiny warning bells, I went to the kitchen. Benign was working over the stove. "I have decided to change Saturday's menu," I said. Even to my own ears, my voice sounded thick.

Benign turned, completely unruffled. "Your daddy made

up this menu. If you want it changed, you ought to talk to him."

"I am talking to you!" I cried. "What is this coalition that suddenly exists between you and my father? Are you attempting to take Yetta's place? Or mine? Do you intend to have me run off the land, along with Charlotte, while you become mistress of Fir Crest?"

Whatever she was stirring in, Benign dropped the spoon and was on me in a flash. "Now, you listen to me, child." Her voice was low and deadly. "I know what you been thinking in that mind of yours. I know you been in your room drinking, just like your mammy and your grand-mammy did. I know right now you got that opium stuff in you, which is the only reason I don't wring your neck like a chicken. But you understand one thing, missy. If I'd ever wanted you dead, you'd been dead long ago. Now, get away from me until you come to your senses. And when that happen, I want you to come and apologize to Benign just like you used to make Benign come and apologize to you." Without further ceremony, she spun me around and shoved me from the kitchen. Filled with confusion, I went to my room and sprawled on the bed. The nerve of her! I thought. Yet, my head was filled with hysterical laughter. I slept. When I woke up, my head was filled with pain.

But I did not apologize to Benign. She reacted, in turn, by building a large barrier between us. She went about her duties as before, but I could sense her absolute distaste for me. I wanted to apologize to her, to seek comfort in those familiar arms. But I had suddenly become obdurate—certainly due to the liquor, and the laudanum, which I continued to take in smaller doses. And to a tremendous yearning for Robert Gilliam, which sometimes made me want to crawl on my knees to him, all the way from Fir Crest to the Gilliam place. While I was in one of these moods, I happened across Amos and asked him where he was going. "To Judge Gilliam's," he said. "Massa Parkchester sending him a message."

"May I see it?" I said.

He was in every way the same trustworthy, respectful Amos. He shook his head respectfully. "Massa Parkchester say only Judge Gilliam supposed to see this." Before I could say another word, he spurred his mount and fled.

Thus the Reconstruction was upon us with all the fury

of a raging storm. My authority at Fir Crest had been completely undermined. I was without fiancé, without lover, without power, without even the respect of niggers. Father, in his room, exercising complete control over the affairs of Fir Crest, was worse than any carpetbagger. What could I do? There was nothing to do. I flopped in the dirt beside the road and wept bitterly. Beyond me, the fields, the mansion, even the very sky itself, seemed disdainful and indescribably distant. I was, indeed, without consequence in the scheme of things.

Then, suddenly, the day of the dinner party was upon us. The morning dawned rainy and overcast, but by noon it had cleared, and the sky and Fir Crest itself seemed as though they had been scrubbed blue, white, green, and a host of other colors by a gigantic brush. When I arose late in the morning, I was almost afraid to look at myself in the mirror. But, attended by two servants—Benign had completely deserted me—I managed to make myself presentable for the arrival of the first guests at four o'clock.

Before I went into the sitting room to greet Lance Harcourt and his father, I went into the kitchen. It was rich with the odor of spices and food, combined in a way that only Benign knew how. I was dressed in an empire gown of powder blue. My hair was arranged almost severely, with curls at the side, but a most unseemly and unsightly bun at the back. I had allowed one of the women to put a multiple strand of pearls around my neck, even though I knew that they did not fit the dress. My earrings were also pearl, also out of place. I stood in the kitchen doorway until Benign turned from the stove and acknowledged my presence.

"What you want, child?"

Her face was twisted like a thundercloud. She herself was starched and clean in a blue dress with white apron. For the first time that I could remember, she had taken off her head rag, and her hair was gray-white, parted in the middle, gathered in a bun at her neck. I had never seen her so angry before. Rather, the anger seemed to pour from her and ooze around me, like a dreadful poison.

"What you want, I said. Can't you see I'm busy?"

I drew a deep breath. Certainly I had not become completely different from the way I had been. "I have come to tell you that I am never going to apologize to you. I have come to tell you that I love you, I miss you, and I respect you. But I shall never apologize. To do so would weaken me, and I am weak enough already. I have been having problems, that is true. Robert Gilliam swore that he loved me. I allowed him to make love to me, once that you know of, once that you do not. Recently, the day the marriage agreements were made, I surprised him trying to make love to Charlotte. I have been distraught ever since. If you love me, as you say you do, you will bear with me during this time of turmoil." I had said perhaps too much, but I could not stop myself. I had taken several sherries and a draft of laudanum before coming downstairs. But it seemed to me that I was handling myself very well. "If you require that I kneel to you, that I beg your forgiveness, then you are dreadfully mistaken. I am free to think as I wish, as you are free also. I am free to do as I wish. In this respect, we are different. You work for me—for my father, if you wish—but I promise you that I shall never apologize. You have erected a wall of silence between us. I find it most painful. If it is your desire that the silence continue, then so be it. That is what I have come to say."

Her lips broke in a slight smile. "You look a mess," she said. "Who dressed you up like that? You go right on back to your room, and Benign'll be there in a minute to make you look pretty. Run along, now."

But I did not run along. I could not have moved away from her if my life depended upon it. All at once, I began crying. Again she moved with surprising speed and grace. And her large arms were around me, comforting me, her deep voice saying soothing things. "All you need is a man," she said. "Why don't you forget your pride and send for Robert Gilliam? If he was trying to do something to Charlotte, you can bet your life that Charlotte was trying to do something to him, too."

It was a thought that had crossed my mind a thousand times. But I could not deny the evidence of my eyes. "Charlotte was trying to defend herself," I said.

Benign grunted. "Like she did with Banneker? You run along to your room. I'll be up in a minute."

At the door, I turned. "Benign, I do indeed apologize for treating you the way I did. Will you forgive me?"

"Ain't nothing to forgive," she said amiably. "We all get

our asses up once in a while." She reached out and slapped me on the rear, as though to put it back in its proper place. "Now, you leave liquor and that other stuff alone, you hear me? If you don't, Benign going to take a plank to your behind."

"I hear you, Benign." I left the kitchen smiling. As I mounted the stairs, I heard the loud voice of Mrs. Pennington as she arrived. She was the last guest. By the time Benign made me presentable, they would have had their before-dinner drinks and would be on their way to the dining room. I was most anxious to see Father, to study his demeanor, to see whether the strength he had been exercising by fiat were a real or an imaginary thing. Whether, in truth, it was an offshoot of Benign's own strength, or an actual recuperation of his powers.

I went to my room and undid my hair, took off the pearls, and waited for Benign. She came almost immediately. And in less time than it takes to tell, she had made me most presentable. There was no time for curls, so she parted my hair in the middle and brushed it down to my shoulders until it shone. I still wore the same dress, which showed my breasts almost indecently. But she looped a strand of fine turquoise around my neck, and clamped matching earrings in place. "Now you look fine," she said. I twirled in the full-length mirror. "Thank you, Benign," I said. "Shall we promise now never to argue again? I don't know what I'd do without you."

She laughed heartily. "A little argument's good for the soul," she said. "But if you can't bear a little argument, then Benign's going to do her best not to argue with you. Just stop taking them things you taking. And stop thinking I ain't telling you the truth. I never harmed nobody or no thing at Fir Crest. This is my home. Why would I want to harm you or anybody else here?" Now her tone softened, and struck me dead center in the heart. "We colored folk, we pretty decent, once you really get to know us." She left without another word. I wept quietly for a while, making certain that I did not disturb my makeup. Then I went downstairs to the guests.

Father was seated at the head of the table, which was most magnificently laid with our finest linen, crystal, and silverware. At the opposite end of the table was the elder Mr. Harcourt, who was so decorated by ruffles at the collar and sleeves that he resembled a shorter and fatter version of his son, who sat to Charlotte's left. My seat was to Father's right, directly across the table from Charlotte, and next to Mrs. Pennington.

"My dear, how lovely you look!" she exclaimed. Father and the other two men rose as I took my place. Charlotte, whom I had not seen much of these days, smiled at me warmly. She was dazzling in pale green, with the jade necklace and pendant earrings that were her favorites. Mrs. Pennington, as usual, resembled a rather stout rainbow. And Lance was handsome and elegant in sedate gray, replete with ruffles.

But it was Father's aspect which impressed me most. He appeared as though five years had not been cut from his life. His color was good, his deep blue suit was impeccable, his eyes were lively and somewhat amused, and his hair seemed to sparkle in the lights from the chandelier. "I am twice blessed with two such lovely daughters," he said. Gallantly he bowed over my hand. Then one of the servants moved in to seat me, and the dinner party was under way.

It was clear at once that we had been summoned by Father first of all as a demonstration of his ability to do so. At the same time, he sounded the theme for the rest of the evening by commenting, "I have been thinking about women, the female of the species, for several weeks. And I have arrived at some conclusions which I would like to share with you."

Slurping soup, the elder Mr. Harcourt hastily wiped his mouth and said, "By all means, old fellow. A most enjoyable subject, women. Have you discovered what it is that makes them tick?"

"I thought," Mrs. Pennington said rather icily, "that it was the heart, the same organ that makes gentlemen tick, as you put it."

Father held up an admonishing hand. "Not necessarily the heart," he said. "Unlike men, who are motivated by a sense of honor, it seems to me that women are motivated by a sense of greed. . . ."

"What a horrible thing to say!" Charlotte said. And she shoved her soup away. Benign, who always served at such occasions, snaked in her arm and gently pushed the shallow bowl back into place. Lance had finished his soup—

indeed, he had shoveled it in as though he were starved to death. There was a lavish centerpiece of spring fruit, and he took an apple and bit into it with his strong teeth. "It has been my observation," he said, "that men use honor to mask their greed. Women are more honest. As gentlemen, we might be wiser to use the word 'necessity' rather than 'greed,' as a concession to the ladies present." He inclined his head slightly toward Charlotte, who beamed, and resumed with her soup.

Mrs. Pennington, who could be led to hell and back by anyone under the age of thirty, tapped the table appreciatively with a small purple fan that she wore tied to her wrist. " 'Necessity' is precisely the word," she said. " 'Greed' sounds so commonplace, so *vulgar*. We are in an age of greed now in the South, and it is not a pleasant place to be. I have decided to go to Holland until all this turmoil is over."

Father smiled. "One does not escape greed—necessity, if you will—by taking a voyage, Olivia. First, however, let me tell you what my observations have been about the female of the species."

I began busily spooning my soup, for I knew that he was preparing himself to mount an attack on me. Strangely enough, I felt quite calm. All his talk of greed obviously was for my benefit. If he thought that my desire to preserve Fir Crest smacked of greed, then so be it. While he appeared eminently sane for the moment, there were other means to neutralize him if insanity were inadmissible.

"If we are to be precise," Father said, "there is a necessity in the female to dominate the male of the species. Oh, I know it will be said that men have held the upper hand over women for hundreds of years. But the careful observer of history and politics understands that, in truth, the hand that rocks the cradle does rule the world."

"And what does this have to do with greed?" Mr. Harcourt said. He seemed almost red-faced with excitement, although I could not understand the reason why.

Again Father held up a hand. "In a minute, my dear friend. In a minute. It is honor which concerns me now. When I was younger, I had a son by a Negress. His name was Banneker. I understand that he has recently left Fir Crest to study in Richmond. One of my most trusted servants knows where he is. Even now, there is a rider on the way to Richmond to find him and tell him that honor has triumphed over greed. I have decided, in spite of all, to name my son as heir to Fir Crest upon my death. If I were a greedy man, or were I to give in to the greed of others, I would have decided differently. Not that I am any less greedy—needful, would you say?—than the next man; but hopefully I am more honorable than most."

There was an extraordinary silence that seemed to last for several moments. My own heart was beating so loudly that I felt sure it could be heard completely around the table. Glancing at Charlotte, I saw that her color had turned extremely pale. Lance Harcourt seemed a study in consternation. As for Mrs. Pennington, she seemed slightly amused and somewhat bewildered, as though not completely sure of what was going on.

It was the elder Mr. Harcourt who broke the silence. "My dear fellow!" he cried. "And what of the arrangements we have made in the matter of my son marrying your daughter?"

"They will be honored to the fullest," Father said. He seemed to hide a sly smile behind his napkin. "Indeed, I am riding over to Judge Gilliam's tonight to have the will drawn up, and to sign it. So you see," he said to Mrs. Pennington, "Holland is not quite far enough away when one is faced with the terrible threat of greed. To have a son is an honor; a man honors his son, however unseemly the circumstances of his birth might have been, whatever color that son might be."

"I am not certain," Mr. Harcourt said, "that I would be pleased with the idea of my son having a mulatto for a half brother-in-law."

"My dear Mr. Harcourt," Father said firmly. "it does not matter in the least what the pleasure of you or your son might be. Perhaps it would be helpful," he said to the table in general, "if it were known that the Harcourts are absolutely bankrupt. Your dowry, my dear Charlotte, is in the amount of one hundred thousand dollars so that the Harcourts may continue with their pretense of wealth and importance. If the amount seems excessive to you, Charlotte, you have your dear sister, Victoria, to thank. She instructed me to accede to the demands of the Harcourts, although they could have been had for a fourth of that amount."

"I am most insulted!" the elder Mr. Harcourt cried. But he held his chair. Benign stepped behind him and refilled his wineglass, which he emptied at once. Lance had turned quite red, and bit most viciously into his apple. Surprisingly, Charlotte seemed not at all disturbed. She tapped her wineglass with a lacquered nail, and Benign filled it. After taking a small sip, Charlotte said, "If you have gathered us here, Father, to make public everyone's business, perhaps you would like to tell us what happened to you in the war that has driven you mad?" The comment was all the more devastating because she kept her eyes lowered, reaching for Lance Harcourt's hand at the same time, to show where her solid support lay.

"Is anybody going to have any partridge?" Benign almost bellowed.

And Mrs. Pennington rejoined: "Partridge! What a delight! I am absolutely mad about partridge!"

With which Benign dropped a huge stuffed breast in the lady's plate, and looked around for more takers. Father signaled to her, and she went to serve him. Then he reached over and tweaked Charlotte's cheek gently. "Necessity dictates that you tolerate madness in me, my dear child. But I shall not tolerate impertinence in you. A hundred thousand dollars is small enough to pay for the Harcourt name, although most of that, I understand, will go for accumulated debts." Now he turned to me, and I found myself growing warm, for I had been waiting for just this moment. "And why are you so quiet, my dear Victoria? Are you afraid that I shall reveal how you threatened to have me put in a madhouse if I made Banneker my heir?"

Now I accepted a stuffed breast from Benign, who seemed to lay it in my plate with a warning. "Afraid, Father? Certainly not. As you have been speculating about women, I have been doing the same about men. Robert Gilliam and I have broken off our engagement because I caught him in the midst of the most abominable infidelity. Therefore, I am not subject to your whims as regards my dowry. As for Banneker being heir to Fir Crest, I pledge you before all gathered here that if such a thing is done, I shall fight him to the highest courts, if necessary. Fortunately, it is my understanding that Banneker does not wish to be heir to Fir Crest. He has his sights on more splendid goals."

Now Father seemed less assured. "You lie!" he cried, flinging down his napkin.

"Are you so certain?" I said coolly. "Let your rider find Banneker in Richmond. And let him return with Banneker's answer, if you are so certain. You speak of honor so glibly, yet you have dishonored our mother, Banneker, and even Banneker's mother by speaking of them so publicly. I warn you, Father, that I am not speaking lightly. Now, I suggest you eat your partridge before it gets cold."

He went at the fowl in a sort of bewilderment, like a child just learning to use knife and fork. And with that act, the tension seemed to ease visibly at the table. Mr. Harcourt moved his chair in closer, the better to rest his elbows upon the lace. When Benign gave him one breast, he demanded another, which she dropped onto his plate as though it were a cold, dead rat. Lance and Charlotte, basking in the sunshine of each other, seemed to have forgotten the unpleasantries of a few moments ago. And Mrs. Pennington was completely occupied with food and wine, casting appreciative glances at Charlotte and Lance, as though she would like to have them permanently encased in a museum dedicated to the beautiful young.

With Father's tirade over, but hardly forgotten, the dinner proceeded smoothly enough. He himself seemed to go through several moods before he became jovial again. But the earlier bitterness had been replaced by the old charm for which he had been famous before the war. While I did not trust it, he was in top form, and flattered poor Mrs. Pennington until she dropped a cream pastry in her lap. He apologized to all for his insulting remarks, including myself. And by the time we had arrived at the liqueurs, at what appeared to be a relieved gallop, everyone seemed to be in a relaxed mood.

Suddenly Lance's and Charlotte's faces turned a brilliant hue, as though they had just experienced a golden-colored orgasm; but it was merely the sun going down in the west windows facing them and behind me. I could feel the sun's gentle warmth on my back. Mrs. Pennington, beside me, shivered with delight, and let her brightly colored shawl fall from her shoulders. And I decided then that I would

ride over to see Robert Gilliam tomorrow. Certainly he
deserved a chance to state his side of the story. At the
same time, I would have an opportunity to discuss Father's
secret message and to discuss with Judge Gilliam the matter of the will.

"Tell Amos to tie my horse out front," Father instructed
Benign. "Then he may go about his business. I shall call
him when I am ready to go to Judge Gilliam's."

There is a sense of ease and rest at the end of each day,
and it seemed to descend over us at the dinner table. Normally, coffee would have been served in the sitting room,
but Father had ordered it at the table. Despite whatever
forbidden revelations we now knew about one another,
there was a sense of peace in the dining room. I could not
help but marvel at the manner in which all of us, including Father, had comported ourselves. Surely the old South
had died and a new one was upon us. Father's insults
would have had no place in polite company before the
war; and had he been bold enough to do so, he would
have immediately become a social outcast. More important, however, had been our reaction to his remarks. Normally he would have finished his dinner alone, subject not
only to the indignant departure of family and guests, but
to the disapproving silence of servants as well. Perhaps we
had carried a sense of good manners to an extreme before
the war. If so, Father seemed determined to reconstruct
them in obverse proportion to his own need.

He had been steadily drinking, as we all had, and
seemed quite drunk, although still capable of lucidity. I
remember the circumstances most clearly, because I had
foolishly allowed myself to be lulled into a false sense of
security. Amos had brought the horse, and I could hear it
grazing noisily in the front yard, which meant that it had
broken its tether, and was probably gorging itself on
Benign's prized wisteria. Lance Harcourt had excused himself—to wash his hands, he said—although soon thereafter, I spotted him on the front porch smoking a cheroot.
Some few minutes later Charlotte excused herself and
joined him there. They were standing quite close together
along the line of my vision. Darkness was fast falling, and
bats were shrieking around the house as they embraced
and kissed quickly, almost secretly. Then they moved from
my sight.

The elder Mr. Harcourt was saying pretty things to Mrs. Pennington, who obviously was annoyed by his age. He, too, was quite full of wine. Mrs. Pennington, after repairing herself from the accident with the first cream puff, had apparently decided to make up for the loss by consuming three more. With her brightly dyed hair, and in her multiple colors, she seemed as though she had absorbed energy and extracted the most marvelous hues from the setting sun, and now was doling them out almost stingily as she ate, saving most of it for her young people in Charlottesville, recoiling at the same time from Mr. Harcourt's boorish nonsense.

With Father and me seated in such close proximity, we made an attempt at small talk, which soon died. My impression was that his mind was beclouded with wine. For my part, I felt a keen sense of strangeness and isolation as he made feeble efforts to revive the conversation.

"Do not judge me too harshly, Victoria," he said. "Perhaps I was not born to remain rational beyond the age of fifty. Certainly the war has left unpleasant marks upon my personality. Do you find me so impossible to bear?"

"Indeed not, Father. It will take time for you to heal."

He seemed to find that most amusing. And he threw back his head and laughed. "Olivia!" he cried to Mrs. Pennington, his eyes quite wild again. "Did you hear what my daughter said? She is twenty-three, yet she speaks of time as though she were an expert on the subject."

For some reason, Mrs. Pennington seemed to tense, as though bracing herself against an imminent blow. "How interesting," she said; but she shoved away her cream puff, laid down her fork, and took a rather large drink of wine.

Father touched my arm. "Olivia and I were engaged for a brief time some twenty-five years ago. Did you know that? She, too, was concerned with time. I needed to sow my wild oats, but she wanted to marry me at once. For security, Olivia? As I remember, you were as poor as a church mouse. Was it accidental that you had poor Mr. Pennington and all his money waiting in the wings?"

Mrs. Pennington stood so quickly that her chair overturned. "I refuse to be insulted by your remarks," she said evenly to Father. "I have known you too long, and cherished our friendship too deeply, to allow you to insult me. I am simply going back to Charlottesville. It is getting late,

I have had a magnificent dinner, and there are some young people awaiting me at home. Please excuse me." Over all her colors, her shawl had even more. Wrapping it around her shoulders with the greatest dignity, she said her good-byes—refusing my offer and Mr. Harcourt's to accompany her to her waiting carriage—and left.

Father toyed with the stem of his glass. "She always was overly sensitive," he said softly. But his eyes looked hurt and bewildered.

"I think I shall get some air," Mr. Harcourt said. "Then I must be going, too. Pressing business, you know."

"Of course," Father said. The wine was in front of him, and he refilled my glass as well as his own. As the elder Mr. Harcourt went outdoors, Charlotte and Lance came in, holding hands, and resumed their places at the table.

"What a glorious sunset!" Charlotte cried. Her eyes were bright and full of love for Lance Harcourt. "It was indeed beautiful," he said. At the same moment, there was a growling of thunder, and Father got up from his chair. "Then I should be riding to Judge Gilliam's," he said, "before the rain sets in." He rang for Benign, and when she came, sent for Amos.

Meanwhile, the elder Mr. Harcourt was saying good-bye. He was quite drunk, and slobbered somewhat over my hand. But he was decent enough, even if he were bankrupt, being dragged off happily to Buckingham in his gilt carriage, with the liveried coachmen and the armed Negroes, waving backward in the twilight as though he had not a care in the world. Lance announced that he was going to Charlottesville from Fir Crest; and a horse, along with a dressing kit, was left behind for him to use.

I felt a great sense of relief that the mad dinner party was over—there was no other way to describe it. At the same time, I felt a sense of apprehension about Father's trip to Judge Gilliam's. To calm myself, I went into the yard where the horse was grazing at random. He had indeed eaten Benign's wisteria, and had wandered around to the east garden, where he had begun with the young roses. I led him back to the front of the house, just in time to hand the reins to Amos as he rode up.

Charlotte, Lance, and I were together in the yard to bid Father good-bye. Except for the presence of Lance Harcourt, it seemed an eerie repetition of the scene five years ago when Father had ridden off to war. The sun had completely disappeared now behind the crest of firs, making it stand out like the dark, angry hump of a bull's back. And I found myself wondering if Father really was serious about leaving all of Fir Crest to Banneker. And was he in any condition to ride, much less to transact business? Even as he sat astride his stallion, he sent for another glass of wine, which he downed with absolute gusto, then handed the glass back to Benign. "If it were not so expensive," he said sardonically, "I would break it." Then, saying good-bye to all, he rode off with Amos in the gathering darkness.

Less than forty-five minutes later—a light, misting rain had begun to fall intermittently soon after their departure—Amos was back in tears to say that Father had fallen from his mount on the slippery ascent to the crest of firs, had smashed his head against the sharp slate rocks there, and was quite dead.

His body was sprawled grotesquely on the rocks, and there was blood under his head, and around it, where his skull had been crushed in the fall. The buckboard with Amos and the other Negroes had arrived at the crest of firs before us. Now the Negroes were standing around with lanterns, to hold back the darkness, and a single gray blanket to wrap Father's body in.

Charlotte was weeping in Lance Harcourt's arms, but I was quite dry-eyed as I stared down at Father. His eyes were wide open, staring at me almost accusingly. There was a piece of paper in the pocket of his shirt. I stooped quickly and took it out. A glance told me that it was indeed his will, and that he had named Banneker his heir, before I quickly folded it again and concealed it in the bosom of my dress.

The light rain had stopped falling sometime halfway between our journey from Fir Crest to its now gruesome namesake. I knelt again over Father, this time closing his eyes and his mouth, the latter from which a thin stream of blood was draining. "You may cover him, Amos, and take him away," I said. The hill smelled oversweet, almost funereally, of the perfume of firs. The lanterns glowed like angry red eyes; there was an evil chill in the air; and farther beyond, the aroused rumbling of thunder belched like

several hounds about to break their bonds. The carriage
we had come in, along with the buckboard, was at the
foot of the hill. I did not feel especially inclined to return
to Fir Crest in it, so I told Amos to unhitch the horses
from the carriage, and that one of us—probably Lance—
would ride the horse that had thrown Father.

"That horse, he didn't throw Massa Parkchester," Amos
said. "Miss Victoria, that stallion is a very manageable
horse. I looked everything over carefully after the accident,
and it appear to me that Massa Parkchester's saddle give
way."

"Saddles don't just give way, Amos!" I said sharply, for
I was suddenly filled with fear. "Now, do as I say, and
we'll have no more talk of this!"

"Yas'm," he said. Already the other men had covered
Father and had laid him out on the buckboard. But I was
thinking of what Amos had said. Saddles *don't* just give
way. Unless they are tampered with. Was I again falling
headlong into a quagmire filled with tantalizing and dangerous questions for which there were no answers? Every
so often, lightning flashed in lascivious winks, reminding
me that I might be either mad or a fool.

Just then, Charlotte said most clearly, "Amos, I want
that stallion shot as soon as you get back to the stable."
She had left Lance's side and seemed like one of the
Furies herself as she stood on the windswept peak.

"That's a good horse, Miss Charlotte," Amos dared to
say. "If anybody's at fault for Massa Parkchester being
dead, it's me. The stallion didn't throw him. After I saw
he was dead, I looked at the saddle. The girth was loose."
He hung his head, a perfect picture of abjection. "If anybody's at fault, it's me, Miss Charlotte."

"That does not bring Father back," Charlotte said angrily. She whirled and snatched a rifle from the saddle of
one of the riders, whether to shoot Amos or the stallion—
or both of them—I did not know. For Lance grabbed the
rifle from her even as I moved to do the same. "Calm
yourself, Charlotte," Lance said.

But she fought to get away from him. "The stallion
must be shot!" she cried.

She was giving way to hysteria, and I slapped her soundly. "The stallion shall not be shot," I said. "Now, it is

time for all of us to go. No need at all will be served if we lose control of ourselves."

"Yes, Victoria." She sounded as docile as a child. Lance released her and went down the hill. Then, only Charlotte and I remained, with me holding a lantern from one of the Negroes. I heard the buckboard clatter off, and then we were quite alone, except for Lance at the foot of the hill, apparently with the horses and the offending stallion.

"I am sorry that I struck you, Charlotte," I said. I wrapped my arms around her, and she hugged me back.

"It is all right, Victoria. It was needed. Now, I think we should pray, just the two of us together. This is now a sacred place, made so by Father's death."

It seemed a strange request, and I had never known her to be exactly religious. But it was obvious that Father's death was affecting her more stringently than it was me.

So I set the lantern on the ground, trying to ignore the massive red stain where Father's blood had spilled. I clasped my hands in front of me, feeling a perfect hypocrite, if not a fool. For however much I might miss Father, it was clear now that the original will obtained—Grandmother Parkchester, to Father, to Mother, to me, and then to Charlotte—and that I was, indeed, mistress of Fir Crest.

Waiting for Charlotte to kneel with me, I heard a sudden movement behind me. And I turned. And remained frozen with horror.

My sister Charlotte was holding a large rock in her upraised hands, preparing to knock my brains out. There was no mistake about her intentions, for they showed most clearly on her face. Not only was there a fine madness there, but it was full of hatred and revenge. With her long, red hair streaming, her eyes flaring wide—as though propped open by the intensity of her emotion—she seemed to growl like some wild animal as the rock came down toward me.

I moved perhaps quicker than I had ever done in my life. Throwing my body to one side, I smashed against her legs, unbalancing her. She tumbled backward, but I heard her fingers as they clawed into dirt and rock, and she came back for me. It was now clear to me—and this was only the most fleeting of thoughts—it was now clear to me who had been causing murder and mischief at Fir Crest, although then I did not know how.

She came across the rocks with her arms outstretched, apparently determined to push me from the peak. But again I eluded her. Despite the weak light from the lantern, I was still able to make out the large, staring eyes that seemed filled with a kind of insane humor, the twist to the mouth that curved in a sneer. And when she spoke, her voice was certainly that of madness, for it made my blood turn to ice.

"I've hated you for years!" she cried, certainly in a voice stolen from the grave. "I was Father's favorite until you turned him against me. You and Mother both were always so very proper, yet so very stupid. How I used to laugh at you and her behind your backs!"

Her words were coming out in a rush. Suddenly she clutched her head and heart, as though she had been struck by invisible blows. "I am not well," she said shakily. And then her voice seemed to drop one full register, full of confidence and loathing. "Perhaps that is why I am going to kill you, as I killed Mother, and Grandmother Parkchester. . . ."

"You killed them?" I cried.

She laughed like a pure bawd. "Didn't you know? Didn't you even suspect? That's how stupid and arrogant you are. Not only them, but the negress Emerald as well."

"But you were in Charlottesville then!" Surely this was a nightmare—full of wintergreen, and the roaming wind, rain that came and went in whispers, and a moon that played hide-and-seek with a sky scowling with clouds.

"Oh, I was in Charlottesville when you found Emerald," Charlotte said. She seemed to be breathing with difficulty, as though the excitement of remembering threatened to choke her. "I shot her the day before. I went to look for her after you said I could go see Lance. I found her near the creek. There were gunshots all around us—they were hunting game for Thanksgiving, you remember? I made her kneel. She cried and begged. She apologized for attacking me, and called me mistress. But then it was too late. I made her turn around. One more shot didn't make any difference at all. And that was that. Then I went to Charlottesville and had a most marvelous time. . . ."

"Why? Why?" Something told me that as long as I

could keep her talking, I was safe. Where was Lance Harcourt? Had he gone to sleep in the carriage?

Charlotte drew herself up haughtily. "Why, you say? Because I hated her, too. Possibly because of Banneker, I am not sure." Now she hugged herself, as though to contain giggles. "I killed Yetta, too," she said. "If anyone is responsible for poor Yetta's death, the fault lies with Benign for being so talkative, and with you, Victoria, for being so unspeakably arrogant. Benign herself was arrogant. 'I'm going to give you a little something to make you rest,' she said. Some of her witch's potions, as though I were too weak to fight for Fir Crest like everybody else. When she wasn't looking, I poured it on the carpet. After she left, I piled blankets underneath the sheets to make it look as though I was sleeping. Then I dressed up like a Negro and went to Yetta's cabin. No one noticed me, for there was intense fighting going on. Yetta had told me before about Banneker being Father's son. That was the night you came galloping to my rescue in Charlottesville. Yetta said she had the proof in her cabin—that was when you were talking to the horse dealer. So I went to her cabin while the raiders were attacking, but she had no proof. I had carried with me a straight razor, one of Father's. As she was talking, smoking her awful jimsonweed, telling her lies, I reached over . . . and that was that. . . ."

"She had proof," I said very quietly, as though to speak loudly might cause her to explode. "It was a paper signed by Father. Banneker found it among her things."

Charlotte shrugged. "No matter. She lied to me. She paid for it, like Mother did." In the lantern light, her face turned obscenely ugly. And when she spoke again, she spat out the words as though she had tasted dirt. "Mother was evil. *She* was a slut. I was hiding under the bed when the raiders came, as I said. I watched their boots as one after another they possessed Mother. And she *loved* it! She was laughing and drinking with them, encouraging them, saying the bawdiest things. I was horrified! When it was over, when it was all done, she was very drunk. She told me that I was too proper. . . . Then she said she was tired. She lay down and fell asleep immediately. She was completely naked, horrible-looking. . . . I held a pillow over her face. She struggled awhile . . . and that was that. . . ."

Again I asked a single, horrified question: "Why?"

But she was wrapped up in gloating, and either did not hear me or ignored me. "I loved Grandmother Parkchester," she said wistfully. "I really didn't want to kill her. But she stood between me and the land. As you do. . . . Benign did check in on me after your self-righteous scene about the laudanum. And she told me about the guards, and her being a watchdog, starting the next day. What an insult to be kept like a common prisoner! And on orders from my own sister! If anyone is responsible for all these deaths, it is you!" She paused, breathing heavily, holding first her heart, then her head. When she resumed, she sounded calmer, but her voice was full of delight. "If I was going to be guarded, then I had to act at once. I stole from the mansion to the candle house. First I locked the door. Then I set it afire on the far corner. I slipped back to my room only seconds before Benign came to get me. That's how I was in the kitchen with you and Benign when the candle house exploded. Aren't I clever?" She smiled, those marvelous dimples falling into place on either side of her mouth.

"Then it is Fir Crest you want?" I said. The wind rose, whipping her cloak around her.

"Perhaps," she said. "Perhaps not. It is you I really want. I want you dead." And she rushed at me. But again I sidestepped, and again she went to the ground.

That gave me the opportunity I'd been waiting for. "Lance!" I cried. "Lance, help me!" Almost at once I saw his figure coming up the hill, carrying a lantern by his side. *Thank God!* I thought. I started for him. "Help me, Lance! It is Charlotte! She is mad!"

And he *laughed.* Coming toward me, holding the lantern high now so that I could see his face—the leather patch over one eye, the bright blond hair, obviously some kind of makeup on to change his features. His teeth seemed white and evil as he laughed. However impossible it seemed, Lance Harcourt was the bandit chief!

I was caught between the two of them, and I felt paralyzed with fear.

"Do not be afraid, my dear," he said, setting his lantern down. "It's all really very simple once you understand it.

As for the newspaper story, I wrote it myself and paid to have it published in the *Gazette*. The editor is a friend of mine, with secrets that best remain unsaid." He was speaking in that deep, resonant drawl that I had come to recognize from the bandit chief as he had ordered his men about. "Don't look so surprised, for heaven's sake!" he said, laughing again. "Did I not tell you that I had studied acting under John Wilkes Booth? Some months after that, I was riding the highway past Fir Crest when I saw Charlotte in the woods. I had never seen such a beautiful creature before. I was completely smitten, as they say. We made love on the spot—this was shortly after the war began, shortly after your father went away on his fool's mission. I was penniless, desperate; and I told Charlotte so, in perhaps the wisest moment of my life. She told me about you, and the old lady, and Fir Crest. We decided, between the two of us, to take it over by eliminating all obstacles. As you know, Charlotte is very headstrong and temperamental. Sometimes she went too far, as with the Negress, and all those poor people in the candle house. But she was always clever, so there was really no problem."

Now I knew that I was finished. I was caught between two mad people practically in the middle of nowhere. Even now, Lance Harcourt was taking his pistol from its holster. "Harcourt Manor is indeed bankrupt," he said, "and has been so for a long time. So I turned to raiding plantations, looting, robbing . . . until I met your dear sister. . . . With you out of the way now, I shall marry her, and we shall live happily ever after."

"Then it was you who loosened the girth on Father's saddle?"

He shook his head unhappily, even as there was a tremendous roll of thunder, as though another presence had come upon us. "No, it was dear Charlotte, her idea. My plans are less haphazard, more precise, although hers did work. In the last attack on Fir Crest, for example, I sent my men against your handsome Banneker in order to get rid of them. They were excited at the idea of murder and robbery. But it upsets me. Every time I mentioned disbanding, they acted as though they might cut my throat. So I used the raid as an excuse to get rid of them. Banneker did me a favor by killing off the rest. I want Fir

Crest in one piece. But I indeed do want it . . . and for that to happen, my dear, you must be eliminated."

He raised the pistol and aimed. I was aware that Charlotte was somewhere on the ground behind me. And that Lance Harcourt, as mad as she, was aiming his pistol at my heart.

"You will be caught," I said weakly. "Someone will find out."

"Who?" he said, laughing. "In the existing disorder, you'll barely be missed. Charlotte and I will be married as planned. There will be no problem."

He aimed carefully, and a shot rang out. I was amazed to see him spin backward and tumble head over heels down the hill. The lantern stuck to his hand as though welded there, even as he sprawled, quite dead, at the bottom of the crest of firs.

Then everything seemed to happen in a flash. Above and beyond me, Robert Gilliam was balanced on a high rock, holding a smoking rifle. At the same moment as I noticed him, Charlotte rose from the ground, growling deep in her throat, and came for me again. And again I sidestepped. But she tripped on a rock and went plunging over the cliff. She fell silently, not one scream; and the only indication that she had hit the bottom was a dull thud that came to my ears, brought by the soft wind.

Then I was crying in Robert's arms. "Thank God," he said. "I saw the lights here. They lingered too long, so I decided to ride over and inspect. Thank God I did."

I was too overwrought to say anything. He patted my shoulder, my hair. "Don't try to talk," he said. "I heard Charlotte's full confession. What she didn't tell you was that she tore her clothes at the creek and flung herself into my arms when she heard you riding up. Obviously she wanted to cause trouble between us. I was trying to keep her off me, Victoria. It is you I love. Do you believe me?"

"I believe you, Robert."

It was perhaps an awkward time to kiss, but I would have been unable to move without the transfer of some of his energy to me. And as his sweet lips touched mine, I knew that the nightmare, finally, had come to an end. "Let us go home to Fir Crest," I said. He nodded, And, hand in hand, we went down the hill to the waiting horses.

Bestsellers from SIGNET You'll Want to Read

Other SIGNET Bestsellers You'll Enjoy